TOO LONG AT THE DANCE

By Mike Blakely from Tom Doherty Associates

The Last Chance
Shortgrass Song
Too Long at the Dance

MIKE BLAKELY

TOO LONG AT THE DANCE

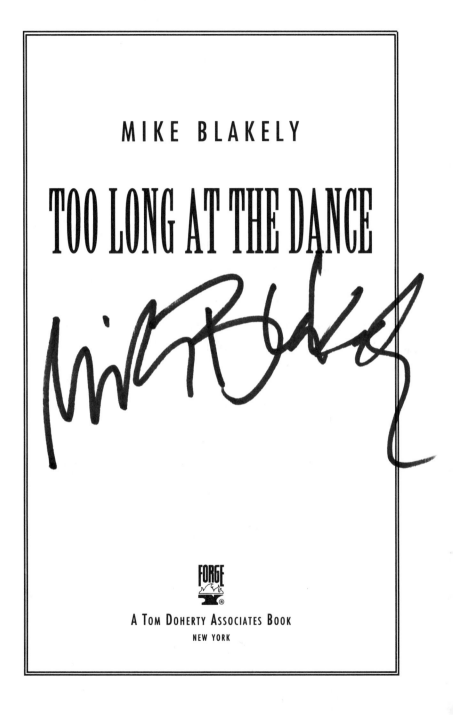

FORGE

A TOM DOHERTY ASSOCIATES BOOK

NEW YORK

TOO LONG AT THE DANCE

Copyright © 1996 by Mike Blakely

A Forge Book
Published by Tom Doherty Associates, Inc.
175 Fifth Avenue
New York, N.Y. 10010

Forge® is a registered trademark of Tom Doherty Associates, Inc.

Library of Congress Cataloging-in-Publication Data

Blakely, Mike.
    Too long at the dance / Mike Blakely.—1st ed.
        p.   cm.
    "A Tom Doherty Associates book."
    ISBN 0-312-86093-5 (acid-free paper)
    I. Title
PS3552.L3533T66   1996
813'.54—dc20   95-33673
                                                         CIP

First Edition: February 1996

Printed in the United States of America

0 9 8 7 6 5 4 3 2 1

To Jim B. Blakely, *my grandfather*

ACKNOWLEDGMENTS

Bob Gleason—novelist, editor, and friend—inspired the title for *Too Long at the Dance* at the Teddy Roosevelt Rough Rider Saloon, in the Menger Hotel, next door to the Alamo in San Antonio, Texas. There, Bob and I, along with our mutual friend and fellow novelist, R. J. Pineiro, were celebrating the end of a Texas book tour over a few cold Shiner Bocks. Bob told a story (as Bob will) about some armed robbers who lingered at the scene of their crime long enough to get caught—shot to death by cops, I believe he said. In Bob's story, one of the participating officers remarked that the crooks had ''stayed too long at the dance.''

I was almost finished with this novel at the time, and still did not have a workable title. For his timing and his conversation, his guidance and his hard work, I thank Bob Gleason.

As for that mutual friend of ours, novelist R. J. Pineiro, I am indebted for his expert advice on purchasing a new computer system, upon which I now render these acknowledgments.

For sharing his understanding of Indian spirituality, I thank Dr. Carl A. Hammerschlag.

For help on the subculture of the fiddler, I thank Doc Blakely and Champ Hood.

For assistance on other musical matters—Larry Nye, Donnie Price, Scott Boland, Debbi Walton, Dorinda Barrett, Champ Hood, Craig Toungate, Fletcher Clark, Eric Blakely, John Arthur Martinez, Stephen Fromholz, Larry Boyd, Mike Siler, Jerry Harkins, J. D. Rose, and KFAN.

For my hat, and the story behind it—Manny Gammage, the Texas Hatter.

For assistance and inspiration—Martha Mondragón-Guerin, Norman Zollinger and Ginna Zollinger, Bob Nelson and family, Candy Moulton and Steve Moulton, Sierra Adare, Michael Gear and Kathleen Gear, Page Lambert, Elmer Kelton, Mary Elizabeth Goldman, C. F. Eckhardt. And most especially Rebecca Blakely and Eric Blakely, Doc Blakely, Pat Blakely, and Kim Blakely.

I

Colorado

1884

ONE

C ALEB RUBBED HIS trigger finger smoothly around the inside of the glass lantern chimney, a black smudge of soot collecting on his callused digit. Peering wide-eyed into the tarnished mirror held to the wall with horseshoe nails, he rubbed his blackened finger under one eye, smearing the soot across the curve of his cheekbone.

He lifted the chimney from the coal-oil lantern and swabbed another lode of blackness from the bottom, painting it under his other eye. He probed deeper into the lantern globe, leaving a translucent band around the top and bottom of the glass, long overdue for a cleaning. He smeared the soot on his eyelids, across the bridge of his nose, and over the squint-creases reaching for his temples.

A gust whistled through cracks in the board and batten wall, and Caleb Holcomb heard ice crystals pitting against the lone window. He grinned at the raccoon mask he had darkened on his face, admiring it from sundry angles, like a painted lady checking her rouge.

The warmth of the potbellied stove and the smell of fried bacon from the lean-to kitchen made him dread the first step outside. But he had stayed here long enough. His belly was full of breakfast and his pockets jingled with silver. The weather would be warming down in Texas, and if he intended to get in on a roundup, he would have to start this week, if it wasn't already too late. No sense putting it off any longer.

Milt Starling limped through the open door clenching an iron coffeepot by the handle with an old rag. ''It's plain you ain't buyin' supplies around here!'' he blurted. ''The coffee you boil would bog a Missouri mule.'' He stopped short, for Caleb had turned to face him. ''What in the name of hell have you done to yourself now? Is that war paint? You look plumb crazy!''

Caleb lifted the makeshift latch and let the door blow open. White morning sunshine burst across virgin snow like the tail of a comet sweeping the High Plains. ''I'd rather go coon-eyed than snow-blind.''

The saloon keeper squinted at the harsh glare and scowled. ''All right, close the damn door! Where do you think you're goin', anyhow?''

Caleb kicked the door shut. He shrugged as he slipped a feedsack over his rugged old Mexican guitar, the catgut strings stretched against a neck as thick as a wagon tongue. ''Ridin' grub line.'' He checked the latches on his fiddle case and picked it up.

''You might just as well wait till the snow melts. Man's a lunatic to ride out in weather like this.''

''The Stanley Ranch is just eight miles south on Rush Creek. I'll hole up there overnight and be that much closer to Texas. Probably see you come summertime with a herd headin' north.''

Milt hissed. ''Why you'd punch cows when you could just as easy lay up here and fiddle of an evenin' is a mystery to me. You've got cow fever, boy! It's like gold fever. It'll ruin you yet!'' The old forty-niner dismissed Caleb with a curt wave and turned back into his saloon, never one for lengthy farewells.

In spite of Milt's arguments that he should stay, Caleb could tell the old man was tired of having him around. After thirteen winters adrift, he had come to know when his welcome was worn out.

His first step into the cold wind braced him for the ride ahead, but the soot shadowing his eyes enabled him to take in the vast frosted beauty of the Colorado plains without squinting much. Milt's advice wasn't all nonsense. Another blizzard this late in the season was unlikely, and the snow would surely melt in a day or two. He might have ridden more comfortably tomorrow or the next day.

But Caleb had awoken this morning with a familiar lust to wander that he had never been able to curb. After a week of entertaining the hard cases and rakehells at Starling's Road Ranch—drunks crowding him as he tried to fiddle; glad-handing him with glazed eyes; snoring off hangovers on the cots Milt rented—after such a week he looked forward to riding alone. He would smell the snow instead of the tobacco smoke. Hear the music of wind through his spurs.

The animals waiting for him at the hitching rail were different as ice and lightning, but they seemed to complement each other. Whiplash wore the swell-fork saddle, for he sometimes gave a pitch or two on cold mornings. He stood at the rail already head-high and anxious. The ash-gray mule, Harriet, stood beside him sleepy-eyed, her nose actually resting on the rail as if she were too disinterested to hold her own head up.

Caleb looped the handle of his fiddle case to the old mule's pack saddle, lashed the guitar down opposite, and covered both with the tarpaulin. Whiplash pranced a circle as he mounted, but Caleb kept the stallion's head too high to buck. A week of free oats had varnished a gloss on his spotted rump and rounded his belly.

"Come on, girl," the drifter said to the mule, clucking his tongue at her, and she ambled stoically into the trail of hoofprints the stallion had punched in the foot of new snow. Harriet was obedient to the point that she didn't even require a lead rope.

A lyric he had been trying to conjure for some time crossed his lips, the melody yet cumbersome but the meter well defined:

We have known our finer hours,
And you can see it in our faces
And we've all earned our places
In the blizzard and stampede
And we've tried to mend our ways
But we're all too damned bull-headed
Yet, there's common ground we've treaded
And on one thing we're agreed:

This thing agreed upon had not yet occurred to Caleb. Whatever it turned out to be would have to serve as a framework for the rest of the lyric. It would probably give name to the song. Not that he was going to think about it too hard. It would come to him somewhere, sometime—probably when he expected it least. No sense rushing a thing like a song lyric. It wasn't as if anyone was anxious to hear it.

Starling's Road Ranch—a paint-shy collection of shacks and sheds—stood on the stage route one team west of Kit Carson, Colorado. Caleb gave it a parting glance over his shoulder, noting that the snow on the rooftops lent something picturesque to the place. It would be well to remember it that way. He didn't know when he might drift back to these climes.

Heading south at a long walk, he thought about his animals. It felt good to have rested them this week, and to have fed them well alongside the stagecoach teams. The mule was a loan from Buster, and it was a luxury to have her along. He could still hear Buster's advice:

"You gonna ride that ol' Whiplash, you don't want that fiddle on him. Time's gonna come he'll pitch you and everything you own off his ol' wild-ass back. Take ol' Harriet to pack your poke on. You don't never have to buy no feed no-ways.''

She had Buster's disposition in many respects. She didn't look for trouble; she never avoided work; she kept her head on straight and made herself appreciated.

Whiplash was another brand of animal. The stallion had belonged to Caleb's brother, Pete. Some said Whiplash had killed Pete, but Caleb judged that kind of talk wilder than the horse. It was probably true that Whiplash had shied and thrown Pete Holcomb into that canyon, but the horse didn't deserve all the blame. Certainly he wasn't a man-killer, as Piggin' String McCoy had once claimed.

The white blanket with coin-sized black spots on Whiplash's rump betrayed the Nez Percé bloodlines. Folks were calling them Appaloosas these days, as they had come from Nez Percé country along the Palouse River in Washington State. They were scarce since the army had destroyed the Nez Percé's herds in 'seventy-seven.

Caleb valued every spotted horse he had ridden since the age of six. It was then that the old Holcomb Ranch—long since fragmented by homesteaders—had gotten the brood stock for their line of Appaloosas from a mountain man called Cheyenne Dutch. That was the only good Caleb ever heard of Cheyenne Dutch coming to, for the old son-of-a-bitch had ended up killing Caleb's brother, Matthew, in a sawmill that was being used as a dance hall at the time. Whether Cheyenne Dutch was a lunatic or just a mean bastard was something Caleb had never figured out. The old Holcomb Ranch manager, Javier Maldonado, had killed Cheyenne Dutch in the same shoot-out, and Caleb guessed he appreciated that. Javier had once been one of his finest friends, but that had come to pass, too.

Oh, well, all that was done. He had lost two brothers, his mama, and a lot of friends along the way—killed and scattered and gone the way of renegade Indians. He was just a drifter, anyway, and nobody cried much over his hard luck, so it was his own burden to pack here alone in a snowed-over wasteland.

Ah, but certain things made it go easier. A good horse. A pack mule he didn't have to lead. A saddle that fit well between his legs. And the things that fit well in his hands: the Winchester model '77; the walnut grip of the Colt .44; the stout slick neck of the Mexican guitar; and the fiddle, more delicate in his hand than a lady's wrist, and more faithful to his caresses.

Whiplash plodded willingly through the snow, casting showers of frozen white powder ahead of his hooves with every step, almost as if he had sense enough to create them on purpose. Caleb rode light in the saddle today. It felt good to be moving, and his spirits wouldn't be mired. He was remembering something. A wonderful thing had occurred when last he left Holcomb Ranch, and he could not shake the glow of it from his thoughts, nor did he want to.

This thing of wonder involved his father, Colonel Absalom Holcomb—one-legged Ab Holcomb, who had fought on the winning side of the Mexican War and the War of the Rebellion, and on the losing side of the fence wars that had decimated his once-borderless ranch.

Thirteen years ago this spring, Caleb had left his home on Holcomb Ranch to spend his first year adrift. He had left cussing his father with words so vile that he now regretted them as deeply as any he had ever uttered. He had said, among other things, that as far as he was concerned, old Ab Holcomb could shove his peg leg right up his ass.

He had since returned every spring to Holcomb Ranch—to visit with Pete before Whiplash threw Pete into Cedar Root Canyon; to work the roundup back when the ranch was big enough to warrant one; to sing and play with Buster Thompson, the former slave who had taught him more than music—and never once during those annual visits had his father spoken a single word to him. Rarely had they even looked at each other in thirteen long years.

But this past winter Caleb and Buster had strung a telephone system to a barbed-wire fence, and one day he had unexpectedly placed the earpiece against his head to hear the voice of his father, and his father had said something civil to him.

And this spring, Ab had taken to using a walking stick, his good leg having taken on a touch of rheumatism. And three weeks ago—the day Caleb had left to ride grub line—his father had used that walking stick in a momentous way. They had all come out to see him off—Piggin' String McCoy and his bride-to-be Tess Wiley; Buster and his little boy, Frederick; Pete's widow, Amelia, whose beauty drifted in and out of Caleb's dreams and idle thoughts like a painted tanager; Dan Brooks; and Ab Holcomb.

Yes, Ab Holcomb for the first time ever had come to see his son off as he rode Whiplash up the Arapaho Trail and vanished into the Rampart Range. Ab Holcomb had waited to catch Caleb's eye, and he had raised that walking stick, thrusting it once at the sky as a farewell gesture.

And Caleb had answered. Thank God he had found a way to respond. He had touched the trigger finger of his right hand to the brim of his hat, and brushed it forward with a nod. With those parting gestures, the father and son had communicated more than they had in the past thirteen years.

And now he was riding light in the saddle, for he had pulled an idea down from the crisp prairie air. He was going to do something he had never done before. He was going to write a letter to his father. It would read swift and shallow; some cryptic reference to business. Maybe a telegram would be better. One the old man would not even have to answer.

Papa . . . Mules selling cheap in Dallas. Expect a carload in two days.

Of course, Amelia, too, had smiled and bid him farewell that day, but her eyes had revealed her disappointment. She had wanted Caleb to stay to help raise Caleb's nephew, Little Pete. Was that all she wanted? Caleb couldn't tell. Was it right to be thinking of her like this now, his stomach all full of fluttering aspen leaves? His brother's widow? Was it wrong to have always thought of her just so? She only became more beautiful as the years passed. He could see her now. My God, was he going snow-blind?

By late afternoon, the limitless field of snow had made a mockery of the raccoon mask, and Caleb was squinting. As Whiplash plodded steadily up Rush Creek, the rider took his bandanna off, stood in the stirrups, and fished in his pocket for his old bone-handled knife. Measuring the kerchief carefully against his face, he cut two tiny slits in the faded red cloth.

He took his hat off, clenched the brim in his teeth, felt the cool air on his head for the first time since leaving Starling's Road Ranch. He tied the bandanna around his forehead, adjusting it until he could look through the slits his knife had made. He couldn't see much, but the glare diminished. Anyway, it wasn't as if he was going to run into a tree or fall off a cliff out here. All he had to do was ride up Rush Creek till Whiplash found the Stanley place.

The sod and scrap-lumber ranch rose from the drifts before sundown, a thin smear of smoke in the sky first giving it away. Snowfall had caught on the edges of sods used to make walls, lending an appearance of lace.

When Caleb reined his mount in, old Harriet continued to plod so methodically along that she butted Whiplash's rear, giving him cause to lurch.

"Howdy in there!" Caleb shouted, waiting a respectable distance from the sod house. He rubbed the stallion's withers to settle him and pulled the bandanna from his face so he wouldn't look like some sort of outlaw.

The door cracked. "Howdy, yourself." A shotgun barrel followed the words out into the evening, all plum-tinted by the new snow and the sinking sun. "You want somethin'?"

"Just a place to light for the evenin'. Name's Caleb Holcomb."
A silence ensued, and the shotgun barrel dipped out of sight. "Put your stock in the shed. Bring some firewood in, if you don't mind."
"I don't mind," Caleb said, spurring his horse forward.

TWO

ROSE STANLEY HAD done about all a woman could do for a sod house. She had found some way to fix wallpaper to the sods—a fine flowered print, weather-stained near the ceiling in places. Rugs covered every square inch of the dirt floor. Good furniture stood neatly arranged, including a rocking chair, an armoire, and a large bookshelf well provisioned with leather-bound tomes. A large framed portrait of some faraway patriarch hung over a writing desk.

A Singer sewing machine stood against one wall, with a decorative covering of some kind hanging out of it where Rose had been stitching upon Caleb's arrival. Evidence of the seamstress's work hung from the curtain rods, the chair backs, and the two children.

At first, they had cowered behind their mother when Caleb stepped in with the load of wood, the fiddle case, and the sack-covered guitar. They had clutched nervously at her skirts, each risking only one eye to peer at the man with the strange black eye-mask painted on his face. Caleb had forgotten he was wearing it. But now the children were warming up to him, and sat near him, staring with open mouths at the way he sawed on the fiddle. The little boy put his hands over his ears on "Boil That Cabbage Down," but he did so grinning.

Caleb had washed his face, and the outdoor glare had become a purple glow through the lace curtain. The drifter was earning his supper, absorbing the charms of a real family home, sloughing off the hard veneer of Starling's Road Ranch.

"Say, Caleb," Joe Stanley said, out of breath from dancing hook-in-wing with his wife. "Did you know that Rose has the prettiest singing voice in Colorado?"

"Then she's got to sing something."

Rose halfheartedly tried to dissuade the men, claiming that she had a stew on the stove to tend. Soon, however, she was requesting a guitar accompaniment to "Cowboy Jack" in the key of E. Rose Stanley did sing

well, and could almost bring a tear to the eye as she sang the saddest part
of the song:

> *But when he reached the prairie*
> *He found a new made mound*
> *And his friends they sadly told him*
> *They'd laid his sweetheart down*
>
> *Your sweetheart waits for you, Jack;*
> *Your sweetheart waits for you*
> *Out on the lonely prairie*
> *Where the skies are always blue*

The family joined Caleb in applauding Rose as she blushed and turned to
tend the stew. Then, as Joe Stanley was trying to bring to mind the title of
a song he had known as a boy, a voice called from the cold:

"Hallow the house! Hallow the sod shanty!"

Joe Stanley had his shotgun down from the rack in two seconds and
was straining to see something in the twilight through a crack in the door.
"What do you want?" he demanded.

"We come to see the fiddler."

Caleb put his guitar aside and felt for the grip of his Colt. "How many
are they?"

"Can't tell," Stanley said. Then he shouted, "Ain't you never seen a
fiddler before?"

There was a pause, then the rough voice chuckled from outside.
"Friend, I don't like augurin' down the muzzle of a twice't barrel. S'pose
I git down and come in there?"

"You know 'em?" Stanley asked.

Caleb shook his head.

"You on the run for anything?"

Caleb shrugged. "Nothin' I did on purpose."

Stanley let the barrel of his shotgun down. "Bring yourself on in," he
shouted. "Alone!"

Caleb shooed the children over to their mother and took a position behind Joe Stanley's right shoulder. He heard the spurs jingling outside as
the boots stomped slush away on the sandstone step. The door swung
open, and every last recklessness known to humankind came into the
house at once.

It started with a hat, trail-stained and curled, ducking low to get under
the transom. The dark eyes under the brim quickly checked the attitude of

Stanley's shotgun, and the fiddler's revolver, then glanced around the rest of the house. When those eyes saw the woman, a large gloved hand rose to take the hat away from the head, unveiling a pressed mass of dull brown hair, not shorn since winter set in.

"Ma'am, I beg your pardon for callin' your house a shanty."

The smile made mounds of the sun-cured cheeks, bunched flesh into wrinkles, spread a bottle-brush mustache wide over a set of large straight teeth. The jaw was like an ox's, bristling with several missed shaves over a bright red silk scarf tied tight around the neck.

A long oiled duster lay open, hooked around a holster on the right hip, the pistol grip jutting forward for a cross-draw, giving the impression of left-handedness. The shirt and pants were drab, heavy, worn, filled with limbs that sprouted like old oak branches from the ample trunk. The trouser legs disappeared into the tops of boots that wore a set of large-roweled spurs.

"You the fiddler?" he said.

"Name's Caleb Holcomb."

"Walker C. Kincheloe." He reached his glove beyond Joe Stanley to shake with the fiddler, then offered the same glove to Joe. "You must be Mr. Stanley."

Joe put the shotgun back on its rack. "I am. This is my ranch, and Caleb's a guest here."

"Not for long." The big smile flashed again, and Kincheloe winked at the little girl peeking out from behind Rose Stanley's skirts.

"What do you mean by that?" Caleb said, stepping up to Joe's side.

"You've got to come back to Starling's Road Ranch."

"What for?"

"We need a fiddler."

Caleb smirked. This character seemed to have made up his mind for him already. "I'm headin' south first thing in the mornin'."

"I'll pay you," Kincheloe said. "But we'd best ride now if we're gonna get the dance started before midnight."

Caleb snorted in consternation. "I don't need your pay, and I make up my own mind when I ride."

"No guest at my house gets run out of here by anybody but me," Joe Stanley said. "Now you'd better get back on your high horse and ride out of here, Mr. Kincheloe, before your welcome gets worn thin."

Walker C. Kincheloe flexed his stubbled jaw and sighed. "All right, just listen. I got this outfit of knock-kneed cow waddies so green they wouldn't burn if you set 'em afire with coal oil. We're three days out of Kansas with a string of horses for the roundup in Powder River country—

three- and four-year-olds mostly, and some of 'em no more broke to the saddle than a bull elk.

"Well, one of my boys—a good boy, even if he was green—got on one of our broncs this mornin', and the bronc like to have jumped a-straddle of his own head. The boy had a sawed-off shotgun tied to his saddle horn that took to swingin' and I guess something hooked a hammer, 'cause it went off and blew a hole in that poor boy you could reach through. He had about five minutes to live, and he spent 'em beggin' me not to leave him buried out there on the plains.

"Now, I ain't no equal of a dyin' boy in a augurin' match, so I not only promised him we'd bury him at the first habitation we come to, but that we'd hold a big wake in his honor, git drunk, throw a dance, and draw for his possessions. I honestly believe he died happy.

"That's why I've got to have you come back with me to keep my promise to that boy, and the sooner we git in the middle of our horses, the better."

Caleb came close to giving in, but a gust from outside drove smoke down the stove chimney and reminded him how cold it was out there. Besides, he didn't know for sure whether anybody had really been killed or not. "I'm sorry about the boy," he said, "but I've got my own promises to keep. There's some Arapahos in the Territory expectin' me to help get 'em started farmin' this spring, and that's after I get in on a Texas roundup. I don't have a day to spare. Milt's got a washboard. You can keep time on that, and the boys can dance all they want."

Walker C. Kincheloe's hands rose to grasp the lapels of his duster in an attitude of defiance. A glare grew in his eyes like the sun rising on snow-covered plains. "You'd put a damn Indian ahead of a dead cowboy?"

"That's enough!" Stanley said, and reached for the shotgun, which he now regretted having put away prematurely. "You don't cuss like that in my home!"

Kincheloe's hand moved from his right lapel, reaching inside the duster to the left shoulder. A Colt revolver matching the exposed one in the cross-draw holster flashed into view, sounding its warning as it cocked.

Caleb had not even thought about reaching for his pistol until he was already staring at the muzzle of Kincheloe's. He put his hand on Joe Stanley's shoulder. "Easy, Joe. Leave that shotgun be."

"That's good advice, fiddler. Now git your things and git ready to ride."

Caleb grimaced with anger. He had seen gall like Kincheloe's before, mostly from rakeshells without too much in the way of smarts to boast of. But this character was crafty, having exposed the gun on his hip and reached for the hidden one in his shoulder holster. He was not all mean, either. He had a sense of humor and a gifted jawbone. He looked to be pushing fifty and had vague reflections of the things he had seen looming like fog in his dark eyes. Some men were talk. Walker C. Kincheloe was business.

"Mister, if it wasn't for Mrs. Stanley and her younguns, I'd just as soon let you shoot me as shanghai me."

"If it wasn't for them, I'd have already shot you. Not hard enough to keep you from fiddlin', of course." The glare was gone, and Walker C. Kincheloe was flashing his big smile again.

The musician turned to put on his coat and pick up his instruments. "So long, Joe. Mrs. Stanley. You kids mind your mama, now, hear?"

"And you mind me, Kincheloe," Joe Stanley blurted. "If you ever come back around here, I'll shoot you without speakin' a word."

Kincheloe laughed as if he both admired and considered harmless Stanley's threat. "I'd better take this twice't barrel with me, then. I'll put it someplace you'll find it in a couple of days, if you look hard enough." He took the shotgun from the rack and took Caleb's Colt from its holster as he passed, then he backed out of the door behind the fiddler.

The musician found Whiplash waiting for him, saddled, the rifle boot empty. Harriet stood behind with the pack. Three mounted men, or maybe boys—it was hard to tell in the dying light—waited with the animals.

"You got a lead rope for your pack mule?" a thin voice said.

"Turn her loose. She'll follow." Caleb tied his instruments down and mounted. It was colder now that the sun had gone down, and he was giving up a warm bed to back-track and wear Whiplash down. It was like losing two days. The more he thought about it, the more he fumed. "I owe you for this, Kincheloe."

The big man just laughed. "You can make it up to me at Starling's."

THREE

WALKER C. KINCHELOE handed a whiskey bottle to the drifter and sat down beside him at the table. His ears were still ringing with good fiddle music, and his head was humming with drink. "How'd you come to be a Indian lover?" he asked.

By this time, even Caleb was in higher spirits. The swallow he took now was not his first of the long night. The young drovers working for

Kincheloe had turned out to be a comical bunch of roughs, green as the trail boss had claimed. The dead boy was laid out in an open box made of boards pulled from one of Milt Starling's wagon beds, and his live comrades were gathered around him, as if to include him in their ribald conversation. It was about three in the morning, Caleb guessed, and the musical wake seemed to have come to a merciful end.

"What do you mean?" Caleb asked, still a little rankled to be missing a quiet night in the Stanley home.

"You said back at Stanley's place you had to teach some Arapahos how to farm."

"That don't make me an Indian lover. I've rode with some Indians. Rode after others. Fought with some, killed a couple. Old Chief Long Fingers gave me my own Indian name: White Wolf. Gave it to me the day he died. I camped with Comanches one winter when I was a kid, but it wasn't by choice." He turned the bottle up again.

Walker studied the musician with a touch of new respect. "Comanches are the worst of a damn bad lot, although the Sioux and Cheyenne ain't no more of a betterment to make you take note." He spit, the glare returning to his eyes.

"You sound like you're an Indian *hater.*"

"You're goddamn right I am."

Caleb waited to hear why, but Kincheloe wasn't telling. It wasn't the kind of thing you asked about.

After a few seconds, the big man slapped his thighs and brightened. "About that trouble back at Stanley's—like I said, I promised the boy." He wasn't apologizing, nor even explaining; he was just stating the facts according to Walker C. Kincheloe.

Milt Starling limped by, grinning. "I tolt you this mornin'," he said. "I tolt you what a damn fool idear it was to ride out." His laughter crackled like scared chickens.

"Mind your own business, old man," Caleb said.

"Maybe I can turn you back on yourself," Kincheloe offered. "Can you catch a horse out of the remuda without whirlin' your rope over your head?"

Caleb drew his eyebrows together. "As long as you don't mean right now."

"You know the difference between a swaller fork and a chinga'o flickerbob?"

"Hell, they're well nigh opposite!"

"You a dally man, or hard-and-fast?"

"Hard-and-fast, except when I'm throwin' a brush loop, or heel-ropin' calves."

Walker C. Kincheloe nodded in approval, crossing his big arms on his chest. "I know you can ride green stuff, judgin' from that spotted stallion you got out there. All right, I'll do it!"

"You'll do what?" Caleb said, drawing back apprehensively.

"I'll let you work the roundup with our wagon this spring. Hell, we're a hand short now, anyway." He gestured toward the makeshift coffin. "Might as well have a fiddle player in the outfit. Ever seen Powder River?"

"Nope," Caleb admitted. He was trying to look uninterested, but he was intrigued. He had owned a horse named Powder River for many a year—a good Appaloosa horse that had pulled him out of some rough places. He was probably going to arrive late for all the Texas cow work, anyway.

"That country is God's cow pasture." Kincheloe turned to the cowboys gathered around the corpse. "Say, boys! Fiddler's goin' with us to Powder River!"

The bend of the Big Sandy came into view below, hazed in a pall of ruddy twilight from the far-off west. Caleb drew rein at the divide and looked down on the timbered tributary, letting the herd of trail-broken horses file past him. He rode a small sorrel mare, followed by Whiplash on the lead rope. The stallion tended to fight when driven with the rest of the herd, so Caleb kept him on a short line. Harriet trailed faithfully along behind the Appaloosa.

The horses were thirsty, and there was no holding them back any longer. The swing riders had moved around to point, but now the herd tested every gap in the line of mounted cowboys, and Walker C. Kincheloe finally bellowed, "Let 'em go," for they were bunching up and beginning to bite and kick. Once released, they galloped to the creek bank to plunge their muzzles into the cold water until the cowboys could push them across to the flats where they would spend the night.

Caleb watched the dust cloud rise as young N. C. Kincheloe rode up to his side and stopped. "I reckon we're gonna camp here tonight," the musician said, hungry for conversation after the long day on the left flank.

"I reckon we ain't. These Arbuckles can camp. You and me get a roof over our head."

"How you figure?"

N.C. stood in the stirrups, the leather of his new saddle squeaking like the chirping brags of a young buckaroo, full of himself and his cowboy swagger. And N. C. Kincheloe was that young buckaroo, from the points of his spur rowels to the crow feather sticking out of his hatband. He was eighteen, carefree, and as glad to be alive as any hawk who ever called down to the trodden earth.

"See that ranch up the creek aways? That's Mrs. Llewellyn's place. She's an old friend of Daddy's, and I figure he'll want you to play some fiddle music for her tonight."

"Can she cook?" Caleb asked. They had made the last three days on hardtack and jerked beef, driving the remuda from Starling's Road Ranch without a chuck wagon.

"Caleb," young N.C. returned, "time you leave Mrs. Llewellyn's house, you'll have to stand on your head to buckle your gun belt."

Caleb grinned and spurred the sorrel. He reached Big Sandy at a trot, whistled at a few horses lingering in the muddied water. By the time the herd had begun to mill, Walker C. Kincheloe and his son, N.C., were loping to Caleb's position.

"Come on, fiddler! You can put your damn fightin' stallion in Kate's corral!"

Kate Llewellyn was around forty, as tough of muscle as any cowhand and possessed of a certain hard beauty. Her hair flowed back like a casual stream over a rounded stone, streaked with as much white as auburn. Her skin was weathered, but not yet seamed deep; her hands were talons ready to seize any task.

She had been expecting Walker C. Kincheloe's outfit. After hugging Walker and N.C., and shaking hands suspiciously with Caleb, she began stoking the stove, heating pots with beans and ground coffee, filling pans with cornmeal, and opening can after can of sliced peaches.

"You are a sight for sore eyes," she would say to Walker every time she looked at him, and her smile would gleam as her eyes misted.

The bell of a grandfather clock in the parlor chimed seven times, and Caleb began to play, hoping Kate would find herself more agreeable to having him in her house. She didn't seem to take much to strangers.

He started with the harmonica, thumping his heel to "Little Brown Jug" on the hollow plank floor. Another tune or two and he reached for the mandolin he had taken down from the pack saddle. "Bear Creek Hop" got Kate Llewellyn's hips swaying.

"Fiddler," Walker C. Kincheloe said, getting in Kate's way to lift a lid and smell, "play 'The Old Chisholm Trail' for Kate. She's partial to that one, best I recollect."

"You just get away from my stove," she warned.

Caleb reached for his guitar and made his fingers pluck a lively rhythm. He started with the verses he had heard most often, adding obscure ones he had heard once or twice—verses made up on various cattle drives and set only in the memories of a few musically inclined punchers like himself. He threw in some nonsensical rhymes, and even a couple he had made up on his own, singing ". . . ti-yi yippi yippi-yay yippi-yay . . ." between each one:

> On a ten-dollar horse and a forty-dollar saddle
> I started up the trail just to punch Texas cattle
>
> Come a ti-yi yippi yippi-yay, yippi-yay,
> Come a ti-yi yippi yippi-yay . . .
>
> It's cloudy in the West and it looks like rain
> My darned ol' slicker's in the wagon again . . .
>
> I woke up one mornin' on the Old Chisholm Trail
> Rope in my hand and a cow by the tail . . .
>
> Stray in the herd and the boss said to kill it
> So I hit him in the rump with the handle of a
> skillet . . .

"Come a ti-yi yippi yippi-yay yippie-yay," he sang, hearing Kate Llewellyn now singing with him. "Come a ti-yi yippi yippi-yay!" N.C. was just sitting and grinning, admiring the musician's gait on the guitar. Big Walker was still making a nuisance of himself around the stove.

> . . . Well there's more verses, but I can't sing
> 'Cause my mouth is full of piggin' string

"Come a ti-yi yippi, yippi-yay, yippi-yay; come a ti-yi yippi yippi-yay!" He raked a final flurry across the strings and relished the way Kate threw her head back to laugh, a ladle in one hand, the tail of her apron in the other.

"Walker Colt Kincheloe!" she exploded suddenly, catching him with his fingers in the hot cornbread. She thumped the ladle ineffectually down on the felt crown of the big man's hat.

Caleb laughed, then isolated the new piece of Kincheloe's name. "So that's what the 'C' stands for,'' he said. "Walker Colt! You're named after a pistol!''

"Well, I'll be a son-of-a-gun,'' N.C. said, with well-rehearsed timing. "You know what mine stands for, don't you? Navy Colt. That's my name. Navy Colt Kincheloe.''

Walker was scowling at Caleb. "Not many fellers your age have heard tell of a Walker Colt.''

"My papa's got one,'' Caleb said proudly. It reminded him. He needed to write old Ab that letter soon.

"Where'd he come by a Walker?'' the big man asked.

"Kept it since the Mexican War. He rode with Walker.''

Kincheloe's mouth dropped open for a second in rare surprise, then he scoffed, "Your daddy rode with Sam Walker in the Mexican War?''

"Yes, sir,'' Caleb said, thinking how strange it felt to now brag on the father he had scarcely mentioned to anybody during the past thirteen years. "He was there the day Captain Walker died.''

Saying it, Caleb almost choked. He had never really given old Ab credit for much in the past, but now the thought of his father riding with Sam Walker impressed him as much as it did Walker C. Kincheloe. When they were talking again—his father and him—he would ask him about the old days, the Mexican War, the Civil War, the charge down Apache Canyon where the Rebels had shot his leg off . . .

"Well, I'll be a son-of-a—''

"Mind your tongue,'' Kate warned, smiling at him out of one side of her mouth.

"Where'd you say your daddy lives?'' Walker asked.

"Just up the tracks from Colorado Springs. He's got his own town there, where his ranch used to spread before the nesters got the better part of it. Holcomb, Colorado, is the name of it.''

"I'll have to stop there and swap windies with him sometime. I'd like to see his old Colt. Is it converted?''

Caleb shook his head. "He hasn't used it since he fought for the Union, so it still shoots cap-and-ball.''

"That's good. Those old guns ought to be left alone. If a man wants a cartridge gun, he can buy it new.''

Kate banged a wooden spoon against the rim of a pot. "That's enough gun talk. Now, belly up here, and feed yourselves so those other poor boys can come in and eat, too.'' Her eyes landed on Walker and twinkled. "Walker Colt Kincheloe, you are a sight for sore eyes!''

* * *

Caleb didn't try standing on his head that night, for he was pretty sure even that wouldn't have enabled him to get his gun belt buckled around his bulging gut. The hour of fiddling after supper did little to reduce his girth. He went to bed warm, tired, and happy.

When the grandfather clock struck four times, he rose from his pallet on the floor, figuring he might endear himself to Kate Llewellyn by bringing in some wood for the stove. He was an old hand on the grub line, having often borrowed a bed and a meal in exchange for some music and talk. But to earn his welcome was Caleb's mission, and he was willing to do more with his hands than coax music from stringed instruments.

To his surprise, he found Kate already outside, splitting billets with an ax. "Mornin'," he said, nodding as he began to stack split wood on his arm.

He had carried three loads into the big lean-to kitchen when Kate straightened and leaned the ax against the stack of cottonwood logs. It wasn't the best to cook or heat with, but it was about all that was available on these streams out here on the plains. "That'll do for breakfast," she said.

"Yes, ma'am." Caleb reached for the ax. "I'll take and split you some for later." As Kate went inside, he began the methodical exercise, swinging the steel wedge easily overhead, letting the tool do most of the work. He would pause now and then to look at the moon, down to its last quarter among millions of stars in the west. He would listen for sounds of trouble with the remuda, but didn't really expect to hear any. The weather was good, and the horses were trail-broken by now. Then he would set another log on end and swing the ax, feeling fully satisfied only when the piece would split clean through with a single stroke.

"You're name's biblical, ain't it?"

Caleb turned. "Yes, ma'am."

"You know what it means?"

He shook his head, ashamed. Pete would have known. Pete used to teach a Sunday school on the ranch, back when Holcomb Ranch had had enough cowboys to make up a Sunday school. He wondered why Pete had never told him, but then Pete was a good brother and a good Christian, never preachy.

"It means 'dog.' You know who Caleb was?"

"Can't say that I do, ma'am."

"He was the one that Moses sent to spy out the promised land. He liked what he saw there. I guess Caleb wandered for forty years with Moses. I'm not sure. I'll have to look it up. I don't guess you'd know, would you?"

"No, ma'am." He rested the ax on his shoulder, looked at the ground in front of her, too embarrassed even to meet her gaze.

"Wouldn't hurt you to pick up the Good Book every now and then."

"I guess not."

"Where did Walker find you, anyhow?"

"Wanderin' in the wilderness." He smiled, showing his teeth under his mustache, and looked her in the eyes, noticing how they shone with an honest reflection of moonlight.

"How long you been wanderin'?" she said.

"A fair piece."

"Where does your mother wait to hear from you?"

"In heaven."

She paused. "Since when?"

"Since I was six."

Kate softened a little. "You've split enough wood. I'm obliged not to have to do it for a spell."

He leaned the ax handle against the pile.

"You do right by Walker out there. He's rough as a cob, but he's good as any man that e'er drew wind."

"I wouldn't mean to cross him," Caleb said. "I'd hate to see him riled."

"You sure would. I've seen him riled, and he'd as soon kill you as cuss you when he's riled. He's had a hard life, that's why. Like me. Walker found me out in the wilderness, too. The Cheyenne killed my folks and took me captive when I was eighteen. I had to look up at my own mother's hair hangin' from that lodgepole while they raped me, one by one—over and over. Walker shot every one of them devils. No man has touched me since, and none e'er shall."

Caleb felt as if he had fallen from his horse and had all the wind knocked out of him. Never had he heard such a thing spoken of by a woman—especially the woman herself.

"That was in sixty-eight," she continued, "the same year they got Paterson."

"Who's Paterson?" he asked.

Kate's eye caught a spark of starlight. "Walker hasn't told you about Paterson?"

"No, ma'am."

"Well, don't ask him. He'll tell you when he wants you to know. Now, saddle you up a horse and bring the graveyard shift in for breakfast."

Caleb nodded. "Yes, ma'am."

FOUR

Ab strapped the leather rigging of the wooden leg on around his thigh and rose, habitually testing his balance before he took his first step of the day on the peg. He took up the walking stick leaning against his bedstead and hobbled into the main room of the cabin.

Ordinarily, he would have roused Lee Fong and demanded that the cook fix his breakfast: three eggs, a slab of ham, biscuits, preserves, and coffee. But he was up a good two hours earlier than usual, and the fewer people who knew what was going on this morning, the better. Someone would ask a lot of questions later, and though Lee Fong was just a Chinese cook with a wild imagination, the railroad would use every bit of testimony they could get from anybody.

The end of the wooden leg tapped on the old puncheon floor as Ab made his way through the main room and to the front door. The rusty hinges of the old board door creaked as he eased it shut, and the cool spring darkness soaked through his jacket as he set the latch.

Ab was pleased to see the lantern light in Buster's house a quarter mile away. He had often wondered just how early that black man rose. Did he even sleep? He had known Buster Thompson twenty-four years now—since the day he came to this ranch, a fugitive slave—and he had never seen Buster so much as take a nap. Come to think of it, he had never seen Buster in a bed, sick or sleeping or otherwise horizontal. Well, he had a kid: a little pickaninny boy. He had to have been in a bed at least once!

Colonel Absalom Holcomb felt the rare grin as he stepped down from the porch of his log cabin. The smile almost hurt, so foreign was it to his countenance. He buttoned the jacket and took cautious strides toward Buster's Cincinnati House—so called because its pieces had been constructed in a Cincinnati factory and hauled west on the railroad for assembly here. Caleb had given it to Buster, having won it in a poker game in Texas.

The old man sighed and stopped to look up at the stars. Where was Caleb now? For a while this past winter, he had thought Caleb was going to stay on. They had come to some sort of silent understanding—Ab and his drifting son. They had spoken one day on the bobwire telephone: the first words they had exchanged in a dozen years or more. And they had gestured vaguely to each other early this spring when Caleb had ridden away: Caleb with his hat, Ab with his walking stick. It was something to build on.

He looked back at his cabin, finding the stob end of that cursed ridge log in the moonlight. He should have burned that cabin down the day the ridge log rolled off and killed Ella. At least he should have burned the ridge log. But it was already notched to fit into place, and it wasn't as if the log had a mind of its own. God, what a horrible day. And poor Caleb thought it was his fault.

He shook his head suddenly and started walking toward Buster's place again. This was no time to start brooding about all that again. There was work to be done today. Holcomb, Colorado, was in trouble. The railroad was trying to kill it. Well, the Denver and Rio Grande hadn't reckoned with the wrath of Colonel Absalom Holcomb.

He stepped up to the kitchen door and peered through the glass. Buster was there by the stove, fully dressed, pouring a cup of steaming drink. Ab tapped on the glass as quietly as he could, fearful of waking Gloria. That wench's temper could make even a white man cringe.

Buster opened the door. "Colonel, what in the world are you doin' out there this time of the mornin'? Come in here and warm yourself."

Ab stepped in. "I need your help this morning."

Buster smirked. "I know that. This here's a day like any other day, ain't it?" He chuckled to make it sound less offensive. "That don't make you come around this early."

"I've got something I need done in town before sunrise."

"What you gotta do so bad you can't wait for daylight?"

The colonel grimaced. "Don't ask so many questions, Buster. Just get over to the barn and hitch a buggy."

Buster pointed to the stove. "Can't I have my coffee first?"

Ab opened his jacket and pulled his watch from his vest. "Oh, all right. I guess we've got the time." The truth was, the smell of the coffee had made him want a cup for himself.

Buster grabbed another cup for the old man. As Ab sat down, Buster looked again to make sure his eyes hadn't deceived him. But there it was, strapped around the colonel's waist as big as creation. "You ain't gonna rob your own bank, are you?"

"What in Hades is that supposed to mean?"

"You're wearin' that ol' Walker Colt. I ain't seen you strap that on since the Indian trouble in sixty-eight. Ain't you got a law in that town of yours against side arms?"

"I founded that town. I can wear a weapon there if I want to. There could be trouble where we're going this morning."

Buster snorted. The colonel often got a little full of himself where the town was concerned. "You want me to bring my gun, too?"

"If you shot anybody, they'd lynch you from the nearest telegraph pole."

"I guess so. You ain't got a tree in that town big enough for a dog to piss on."

Ab took the coffee, blew across the open mouth of the cup, and finally took a slurp. "Buster, do you ever sleep?"

The homesteader shrugged. "I turn in late, roll out early."

"Probably sleep standin' up, like a horse."

When they finished their coffee, they went to the barn to hitch a horse. "What kind of tools we need for this dangerous job we gotta do this mornin'?" Buster asked, hooking the traces to the buggy.

"We'll need some grease. A whole five-gallon tin of it. And something to smear it on with." Ab Holcomb was standing in the open doorway, watching his hired man work, offering nothing in the way of assistance.

"Smear it onto what?" Buster asked.

"A trowel or something like that will do."

Buster sighed and got the trowel. He loaded the heavy tin of grease and climbed up to the seat, waiting for Colonel Ab to join him, carefully placing the peg leg on the running board. The old man lay his walking stick down on the floorboard, and they drove toward town in the dark, each enjoying fifteen minutes of the ride in silence, until Buster asked exactly where they might be going.

"Take the turn to the depot," the old man ordered.

When they arrived, Ab stood in the open buggy, hooked the tail of his jacket behind the old Walker Colt, and looked around. "I don't see anybody about. Go ahead and get started."

"Get started doin' what?" Buster said. He gestured so suddenly that he shook the reins, and the horse stepped forward, bringing Ab down onto the seat.

"Grease the tracks."

"What do you want the tracks greased for? Don't you want the train to leave out of here on time this mornin'?"

"I want it to stop!"

"Don't it always stop?"

"Not anymore. The railroad sent notice a while back. As of today, Holcomb will no longer have rail service. The train's just going to pass through without stopping."

Buster squinted. "Why didn't you tell nobody?"

"Because it would cause a panic, that's why. Anyway, I don't intend to let it happen. When we grease these tracks, it'll stop, all right."

The hired man shook his head. "I don't know, Colonel. I ain't so sure I want no part of greasin' no tracks."

The old man grunted and hopped down from the seat, feeling the rheumatism flare in his good leg as he landed. "I'll do it myself, then!" He threw the trowel out onto the graded bed of the railroad and started struggling with the large tin of grease. It was pitiable to watch him hobble inch by inch, trying to feel for footing with a stick of dead wood strapped to his knee.

Buster rolled his eyes to the heavens. He set the brake on the buggy, climbed down, and took the tin of grease from the old man, lugging it to the nearest rail of smooth steel. "Give me that, and git back in the buggy. They see the tracks of that peg leg here and they'll know sure 'nough who done this. Why you got to do it this way, Colonel? Why didn't you hire a lawyer or somethin'?"

"They didn't give me time." He panted. "You know how the Denver and Rio Grande operates. You can't trust 'em. Not since the day General Palmer sold it."

Buster eased the tin of grease down on a railroad tie. "You're just askin' for trouble, Colonel."

"They're trying to kill this town, Buster!" The old man choked back the emotion in his throat. "If they kill my town, they'll kill me. It's all I got left."

Buster stared for a time, thinking. It had always been like this. He was the only man in the world Ab trusted. This was just like old times, in a way. Buster had hatched many a scam like this with Colonel Ab. They had manipulated homestead laws to gain sole possession of Monument Creek, illegally fenced section upon section of public range for Ab's personal use, established a bank to mortgage the farms of the nesters who had taken Ab's ranch from him. Now the railroad was the enemy. He had to grin. The old man thought the whole world was against him. Always had.

"How thick you want it?" he said.

"Thick as Pennsylvania mud."

FIVE

THE LOCOMOTIVE WHEELS spun wild and ineffectually, like whirligigs on edge, getting nowhere. The conductor stomped down from the lead passenger car and shouted at the engineer.

"The wheels ain't catchin'!" the engineer shouted back over the chug of the steam engine. "There's somethin' on them tracks!"

With long angry strides, the conductor marched down the tracks, stopping to poke his finger into a glob of something clinging to the side of a rail. "Goddamn it!" he blurted.

From his seat on the depot platform, Buster held the laughter down in his chest.

"This is a God-fearing community," Ab said sternly. "Save your blasphemies for Denver."

"Who did this?" the conductor demanded. "Now we'll be behind schedule getting to Colorado Springs!"

Ab grunted. "Well, you wouldn't want to startle anybody—showin' up on time, I mean."

Buster laughed out loud. He hadn't heard the colonel exercise his sense of humor so much in twenty years.

"I want to know who greased these tracks."

Ab turned to his hired man. "You remember back in seventy-four, don't you, Buster?"

"You mean the grasshoppers?"

"That's right. Came down on us in a cloud that shut out the sun. So many of them lit on the tracks that the train couldn't run for the grasshopper grease."

"That must be what happened last night, Colonel."

"Bullshit," the conductor said.

The door to the mail car slid open and a postal bag flew out, the air settling from it as it lay on the platform.

The conductor stomped up the steps to the platform and faced Ab. "You could grease the tracks every day, Colonel. It wouldn't do you any good. The company has decided to abandon the narrow gauge tracks through Holcomb and build a standard road from Denver to Colorado Springs."

The surprise showed on Ab's face. "So what? Grease'll stop a big engine same as a narrow gauge."

The conductor smiled. "The new tracks won't be passing through Holcomb. They've found a better route out on the plains. Not so many grades out there. Come fall, Holcomb won't have service anymore. Grease won't stop a train that don't come."

The laughter died in Buster's chest and he stood up beside the colonel.

"How do you know all this?" Ab demanded. "You're just a conductor."

"The notices came out this morning. Yours is probably in the mailbag there." He pointed to the flat canvas bag on the platform.

Ab hobbled to the mailbag, using the crooked handle of his walking stick to snag the canvas and lift it.

"Here, now!" the conductor said. "You can't open that. That's for the postmaster."

"I *am* the postmaster in this town," Ab said, stirring the envelopes in the bag.

"Then why haven't you ever picked up the mail before?"

The colonel paused to glare at the conductor. "I've got a town to run here. I've got a bank, a general store, a boardinghouse, and a café to look after, not to mention four miles of irrigated farms along the creek and what's left of my ranch. I don't have time to sort mail!"

The conductor waved a disdainful hand at the colonel and stomped back onboard his train.

There were only a handful of dispatches for Holcomb, and Ab quickly recognized the official envelope of the Denver and Rio Grande. He handed the mailbag to Buster, tore the end of the envelope off, and began to sort through the leaves of the letter. It included a map of the proposed new route several miles east, across the plains.

"Colonel Ab," Buster said taking another envelope from the bag. "Look at this."

"I don't have my eyeglasses, and I can't make any sense of this at all. I'm going to my office."

"Colonel. There's another letter for you here."

"Well, bring it along, Buster. I can't very well read it without my eyeglasses."

"It's from Caleb."

The walking stick and peg leg punctuated the statement as the old man turned back toward Buster. He thought about the five-minute walk to the bank and his office. He couldn't wait that long. Buster was like another father to Caleb anyway, having just about raised the boy himself. "Read it."

Buster tore the envelope open and unfolded the single leaf. "Says,

'Colonel . . .' How 'bout that. He calls you 'Colonel,' just like me.''

"Read it, read it!''

"Says, 'I have drifted up to Powder River country, east of the Big-horns. I am hired on for the roundup with a ranch manager name of Walker Colt Kincheloe. Walker has taken a yearn for a string of Nez Percé horses after watching Ol' Whiplash work. If you will tell Amelia to hold some good stock till spring, I believe Walker will pay top dollar. Your son, Caleb.' How 'bout that, Colonel. He signed it 'Your son,' just as big as a killin' hog!''

"So he did,'' Ab said, squinting at the signature. That smile was hurting his face again.

SIX

A B WAS STILL reading and rereading the letter from Caleb when the head cashier rapped sharply on the door and stuck his head in.

"There's been an inquiry on the Ingram estate, Colonel.''

Ab folded the letter and looked over the tops of his lenses. "From who?''

"The Mayhall brothers. What shall I tell them?''

Ab drummed his fingers on his desk for a moment. "Tell them to come in, of course.''

When the cashier withdrew, Ab rose quickly and posed over his map of Monument Park. He heard the door open, but did not look up. The door closed loudly, but still Ab pretended to study his map, rubbing his chin as if in deep thought.

"Colonel Holcomb,'' Terrence Mayhall said.

Ab pointed a long, stiff finger at the pressed-tin ceiling and made a meaningless mark on the map with his pencil. Then he looked up at the four brothers: Terrence, Frank, Edgar, and young Joe. "Sit down,'' he said, gesturing impatiently at some chairs scattered across the room.

Terrence Mayhall stalked across the office in rolling, muscular strides and plopped down in a chair facing Ab's desk. The eldest of the brothers, he was shorter than the other three, yet he still outweighed Joe, the youngest, and equaled Frank and Edgar in bulk, his muscles gathering thicker on his shorter frame. He was the leader of the clan, the planner, the speaker, and the longtime rival of Ab Holcomb in Monument Park's land trade. It was Terrence who had brought his three younger brothers here from

Georgia to file on public land that Ab Holcomb claimed as his own. More than any other one man, Terrence Mayhall had brought about the downfall of the old Holcomb Ranch, and reduced Colonel Ab to a town father whose town was now in peril.

Frank, Edgar, and Joe pulled chairs up to the desk and sat, arms and legs sprawling wide.

"We want to buy the Ingram place," Terrence announced.

Ab sank slowly into his stuffed cowhide chair. "You do, do you?"

"Yes, we do. You might just as well sell it to me as anybody else. My money brings what any other man's does. The Ingram place borders mine and I already put a good amount of sweat in it just tryin' to help Ingram before the fever killed him."

Ab propped his elbows on his armrests, laced his fingers together, and stared at the homesteaders.

"We have as much right as any man to make a fair offer on it," Mayhall continued. "Don't try to keep us out of the bidding, Holcomb. I'll find out what it sells for if you don't let me have it, and it had better not be lower than my offer. I won't stand for being treated unfair. I've got a lot of friends in this valley, and I'll organize a boycott of everything you own if you take a lower offer than mine."

Ab clapped his palms against his armrests and leaned across the desk, glowering at the burly little Georgian. "Mr. Mayhall, I have no intention of treating you or any other customer of this bank unfairly. This is business. Your offer will get fair consideration. But do not suppose to make rash threats against me."

Mayhall's jaw muscles bulged. "I've never made a rash threat in my life. If you'd ever played poker with me, Colonel, you'd know that I don't bluff."

"I don't play poker," Ab said, missing the point entirely. He settled back in his chair again. "I guess the land office told you what the asking price is."

"I won't go *that* high," Mayhall said. "You're asking too much for the so-called improvements on the place. They're not good for anything but tearin' down. That house is a shack, and the shed is made of rotten boards."

"Well, you're more familiar with the place than I am," Ab admitted. "What's your offer?"

"Knock twenty percent off your askin' price."

Ab made some calculations on a scrap of paper. He shook his head. "You're forgetting the fences and the well. The windmill's not worth much, but the well is a good one. I'll meet you in the middle. Ten percent.''

Mayhall shifted in his chair, and his three brothers moved to either side of him, like ripples from a stone cast in the water. ''All right,'' he said. ''We have a deal.'' He held his hand over the desk.

''We don't have a deal just yet,'' Ab said, regarding the thick hand with indifference. ''I would like to know how you intend to pay for this land.''

Mayhall doubled his hand into a fist and shrank back into his chair. ''We'll need a loan, of course. All of us together don't have that much cash.''

''You know what our interest rates are?''

''Your teller already figured the payments for me.''

''What are you going to put up for security?''

''Why do I have to put up security? If I can't make the mortgage payments, you can just take the Ingram place back.''

''This bank doesn't own the Ingram place, Mr. Mayhall. The Holcomb Land Office does.''

Mayhall's fists seized the chair arms. ''But you own both businesses, damn it! We've been sittin' here talkin' land office business, ain't we?''

''And now we are talking bank business. I don't own this bank, Mr. Mayhall. I am merely an officer and a stockholder here, same as with the land office. They are two separate entities. Now, what do you have to offer for security?''

''If I don't come through with the mortgage payments, your damned bank can have the Ingram place!''

''What if land values drop? The bank will have lost money. You don't realize how much I have to think about here, Mayhall. No, I've got to have more security to make this kind of loan.''

''In the off chance that I quit makin' my payments *and* land values dropped, you could just have your damned land office give the loan back to your damned bank.''

''It doesn't work that way.'' Ab leaned back in his chair, looked down his nose at the Mayhall brothers, and gloated. Moments like this made life worth enduring. This town was power. He could not let the railroad destroy it. ''And don't swear again in my office. You can save your profanities for those ramshackle houses your wives keep for you on that so-called farm of yours.''

Edgar Mayhall flinched as if snake-bit and came out of his chair. ''Now it ain't business anymore, Holcomb!''

"Sit down, Edgar!" Frank Mayhall ordered.

"Like hell! You heard what he said about our wives!"

"You're not even married, Edgar. Now, sit down!" Frank said.

Ab remembered the old Walker Colt belted around his waist. He rose slowly, feeling for firm footing with his peg leg. He hitched his jacket behind the butt of the antique revolver and glared back at Edgar Mayhall's scowl.

There was tense silence in the office for several seconds, then Frank Mayhall began to chuckle. Quickly, he threw his head back and laughed outright.

"What do you find so funny?" Ab demanded.

Frank grabbed Edgar by the arm and pulled him down into his chair. "That old cap-and-ball gun there," Frank said. "That thing must've been forged when granddaddy was a pup."

"It served me well enough with Walker in Mexico, not to mention in the Battle of Glorietta Pass where those Texan Rebels shot my leg off."

Frank Mayhall laughed again. "Battle? Holcomb, Glorietta Pass was naught but a skirmish aside what we seen in the war. I seen piles of dead men that would outnumber both sides at Glorietta Pass. Edgar was just a whelp, so he didn't join, but even he taken some shots at Yankees when Sherman come burnin' Georgia. Joe was still in foldin' britches when the war ended, but me and Terrence, hell, we wore out a dozen cap-and-ball guns like that the four years we served."

Ab had never been much for arguing off the cuff, so he just covered his offended Colt with his jacket and sat back down. "I don't care," he said.

"We didn't come here to brag about the war," Terrence reminded his brothers. "We come here to buy the Ingram place, so let's get it done and get back to work."

"You still haven't said what you intend to put up for security on the loan," the colonel said.

Terrence wheezed against the inevitable. He had known it would come to this. "A quarter section of my ranch."

"Which quarter section?"

"What difference does it make?"

"It makes a great deal of difference. The security has to equal the loan in value."

Mayhall sighed and rubbed his jaw. "I'll put up my southeast quarter section."

Ab looked through his eyeglasses at his map and put his finger on the appropriate square. "That's nothing but a cow pasture. It doesn't even have a well. It's not even on the road."

"You're not going to take it from me anyhow. I pay my debts, Holcomb."

Ab frowned and looked at the map again. "I'll take this quarter section right here," he said, thumping the map with his long old finger. Mayhall got up to look. "That's right in front of my house. Hell, that's my front yard!"

"It's got everything the Ingram place has," Ab explained. "About the same amount of acreage has been broken, it's fenced, it's on the road, and it has a well."

"My younguns keep their old saddle horse in that pasture!" Mayhall complained.

"Like you said, Mr. Mayhall, I'm not going to take it from you as long as you make your payments, so what difference does it make?"

They glared across the desk at each other. Terrence pushed himself back on his tree-branch arms and looked alternately at the map, then at Ab. "All right, have it your way. Do we have a deal, now?"

"We do," Ab said, sticking his hand out over the desk. "Come back in the morning. I'll have the papers drawn up."

Mayhall shook the colonel's hand briefly, then turned for the office door. Chair legs yelped across the floor and the other Mayhalls rose, young Joe looking somewhat confused by the entire meeting.

Before he left, Terrence paused to look back at the old man. "I can't figure you, Colonel. I didn't think you'd sell me the land or loan me the money. I guess you've changed your mind about havin' neighbors in your park."

"Not at all," Ab said. "I've changed my methods to suit the new times. I just got back one of my quarter sections from you. On paper, it's as good as mine until you pay off your loan. If you have a hard year or two and can't make your payments, well, it's mine in fact, not just on paper. Even if you do pay off the loan, the first thing you'll do is mortgage more to borrow more to buy more. That's the way people are. They can never own enough. So, I've got you pinned down right where I want you. If you want to own any more of my park, you have to pay me for the privilege."

Terrence Mayhall propped his hands on his hips and shook his head. "You're a caution, Colonel." He chuckled as he left the office. "You and that pistol."

SEVEN

CALEB, SINCE THE days of his boyhood, had loved mountains in all their wrinkled and timbered mystery. Now he rode up a sloping grade of Powder River range, reaching ahead with his eyes, leaning just far enough forward in the saddle to make Whiplash angle his ears alertly forward. Beyond the ears of the stallion, the Bighorns loomed.

But in his thoughts, Caleb might just as well have been riding back to the Front Range of his memory—the Colorado wilderness he had grown up with. Holcomb Ranch had looked something like this in those days before the railroads and the settlers and the towns.

This was like going home. Better, in a way. There was no ridge log here to fall on his mother. No Cheyenne dog soldiers to haunt the dark draws of the foothills. No plow to push while his brothers chased cattle. Too bad his brothers were both dead now. They had never really ridden together—all three of them. It would be well to bring them here.

He coughed the thought away and determined to enjoy this place for himself alone. "This is good country," he said to Walker C. Kincheloe, who rode beside him on the left flank of the remuda.

Walker shrugged. "Gittin' crowded. The big outfits are stockin' too many cows. It was better country when I come here in sixty-six."

Caleb squinted. He remembered the year of '66. His twelfth year. "Those were hard old days."

"I cut my teeth on hard ol' days." He rode several steps in silence. "I'd left Texas with the heel flies after me and drifted up here to freight for Uncle Sam. I was about your age, I guess. This was virgin country, and them Sioux Bad Faces wanted to keep it that way. That was the year Fetterman led eighty men to slaughter."

"Were you here for that?"

"I was haulin' timber that day, but made it into Fort Phil Kearny without gittin' scalped. Next day, we went out to load the carcasses of all them paper-collared soldiers. Captain Fetterman and Captain Brown had blowed each other's brains out before the Indians could git 'em, and I can't say that I blame 'em. That was a sight to twist a buzzard's paunch. Them red devils had butchered men, and cut 'em every which way, and strung guts out. It was so bad we didn't know which insides went with which carcass, so some of them horse soldiers got buried with foot soldiers' guts, and some infantry got buried with cavalry guts. I reckon they got it all sorted out at the Pearly Gates.''

Caleb glanced at Walker for some sign of jocularity, but found none. It wasn't a laughing matter in his view anyway, having once seen a butchered man himself—a friend of his on the buffalo range whom the Comanche had caught alone. That was old Elam Joiner, a ghost who haunted Caleb the same way Walker C. Kincheloe was haunted. Some way. Some how. Something was always galling Walker.

The big man spat for the first time in a mile, shifting his quid of rough-cut tobacco to the other cheek. ''That was the year they got Paterson.''

Paterson! Kate Llewellyn had spoken that name, warned Caleb against asking too many questions. He was about to ignore her warning and ask anyway when a shout came from a high roll ahead. It was N.C., waving his hat over his head.

''What the hell has that boy found now?'' Walker said. ''Come on, fiddler.''

They spurred their horses to a lope, and Whiplash increased to a gallop, possessing an instinct for running in the lead.

N.C. was standing on the ground, having dismounted to give his lathered horse some breathing room in the cinch. His mouth could barely hold back the grin. He had ridden ahead of the remuda to scout for any kind of trouble along this last leg of the trail to the TW Ranch, where his father was manager. Something had brought him back to the remuda in a hurry.

''What's wrong?'' Walker asked.

''Nothin'. I just seen a buffalo, that's all.''

''Don't feed me a mess of bull corn, boy. Where did you see a buffler?''

N.C. pointed quickly and began tightening the saddle cinch. ''Over that high roll, yonder. Down in that coulee. He ain't movin', he ain't grazin', he ain't even chewin' his cud. He's just standin' there broadsides.'' The boy jammed his boot into the stirrup and swung upward to the seat.

''Show me to him, son. You come on, too, fiddler. I want your witness in case it turns out to be a wild hog or somethin'.''

''Daddy, can I shoot him when we get there? I didn't have nothin' but this carbine, or I'd have shot him already.''

''You found him, son. You can shoot him. I'll leave you use my elk gun. Unless he's one of them Indian spirit bufflers and has run off underground like a badger.'' He pulled a face at the musician and shook his reins.

Caleb felt his nerves begin to writhe as they covered the two miles of ground in a long lope. It had been a while since he had seen a buffalo, though he had seen more than his share in seventy-four, as a skinner, and then a hunter of bison on the Texas plains. A wild buffalo bull, standing witless against a field of grass, was a sight to stir the blood of even a man who had seen and killed a thousand just like him.

N.C. slowed to a walk as they neared the crest of the high roll, then all three men dismounted, Walker pulling his long-barreled Ballard hunting rifle from the saddle scabbard and handing it to his son. They left their horses standing and snuck to the crest in a crouch, finally dropping to a crawl as the view began to appear over the hill.

"There he stands," N.C. whispered, jutting the barrel of the Ballard through the grass.

Caleb felt his heartbeat in his throat. He wished suddenly that he were alone here and could just look at the old bull for a while, but N.C. was already flipping up the adjustable rear sight.

"How far you reckon, fiddler?"

"About three-seventy-five."

Walker grunted. "I figured more like three-ninety."

"He's downhill, though. Set the sight where you'd usually set it for three-seventy-five."

N.C. looked at his father for approval.

"You heard the man," Walker said. "And don't jerk the trigger. It's fine as frog's hair."

N.C. pressed his elbows into the sod and thumbed the hammer back ceremoniously.

"Don't shoot through the grass," Caleb advised. "At this range, even a stalk of grass might throw your shot off."

N.C. swallowed hard, the suspense thinning his patience. He let the rifle hammer down and used the barrel to push aside the grass in front of the muzzle. Having cleared a path for the bullet, he cocked the rifle again and settled in for the shot. He held his breath as long as he could, but the bead would not rest on the bull's shoulder. Finally he exhaled and rested his face on his sleeve.

"Oh, hell, son, what's the worst that could happen? You could miss and have to shoot again. Now, hurry up and get the job done, or I'll let the fiddler do it."

N.C. lifted his head and set his jaw. He drew in a breath and held it several seconds. The big gun hurled an eruption of noise behind the bullet and clouded the air with smoke. Looking over the sights, N.C. saw the bull rock backward and fall, rolling to one side as his heavy head slammed to the ground.

Caleb pulled his fingers from his ears. "Good shot, N.C.!"

"I'll get the horses," the boy said, springing from the ground.

Walker gloated as if he had made the shot himself, until his son arrived on horseback, trailing the two other mounts. They raced to the kill, N.C. gasping at the size of the animal.

"He's a big one," Walker said. "Wonder what the hell brung him here."

"Maybe he's been holed up in the foothills," Caleb offered. "Or just drifted in from the range. Could have come here to die."

"Could have, hell—he's dead, ain't he?" Walker laughed and clapped his hand down on N.C.'s shoulder. "Son, I'll wager you just kilt the last wild buffler ever to tread Powder River range!"

Father and son beamed down at the dead brute, ran their hands through its shedding mats of winter fur, grasped the stout curved horns to gauge the heft of the woolly head. But Caleb only gaped in dread. He had helped clear another range of buffalo. Now the fences would come; and the railroads; the homesteads; the windmills; the roads. West would fly the eagles, leaving Caleb to watch another wilderness waste away to the drone of fiddle and guitar.

> *We kilt off all the buffalo*
> *And elk, and deer, and pronghorns*
> *And we stocked so many longhorns*
> *Now the tall grass no more stirs*

Like the hips of a walking fat woman, the rolled buffalo hide wagged on the back of Caleb's pack mule. Harriet had taken to plodding along on the left flank of the remuda, as if she had some interest in herding the horses north. Watching from behind the mule, Caleb had become mesmerized by the rhythm of the green hide shifting left and right to the tempo of that nameless tune he had been crafting in his head. The tune pranced through his thoughts, and he moved his fingers on the reins as if they possessed frets.

The trail from Cheyenne, where the nearest railroad passed, had taken several days to cover, and every now and then a breath of wind bearing Caleb's own bodily odor would remind him of how long he had gone without a bath. He could feel grime in his clothes and on his skin. His hair was pressed like duck feathers to his head, and dirt from half a dozen counties mingled under his fingernails. He was thinking of a long soak in warm water, a cooked meal on a table, a cot, and whiskey in a clean tin cup.

"Did you see that log mansion back on North Crazy Woman Creek?" Walker C. Kincheloe said, snapping the musician's trance. "That was the headquarters of the CU Ranch. I used to work there. A bunch of fer'ners own that spread, and one day a new dude in the syndicate shows up, fresh from skippin' across the dew, and the first face he come acrost was mine, so he says, 'You there!' ''—Walker snapped a ramrod's posture into his spine to mock the Britisher—"says, 'Is your master at home?' '' I says, 'Mister, the son-of-a-bitch ain't been born yet.' And that's why I used to work there.''

Caleb chuckled. "I used to work a lot of places, too. Now I mostly ride grub line.''

"Where'd you lose those chow hooks?'' Walker asked.

The musician spread the fingers of his left hand. "Once was the day I played right-handed, like most strummers. Back in seventy-two I got caught in a blizzard chousin' outlaws into No Man's Land, and frostbite killed my fingertips. Some of my pals clipped 'em off with a dehorner. Couldn't press down on the strings, so I had to learn to play everything left-handed.'' He gritted his teeth, shook his head. "That was a hard winter.''

"Well, brace yourself, Hard Winter. You ain't seen the comin' of a Bighorn blizzard yet. Anyway, right now it ain't but spring, and time to tune up and yodel. That's the chimney smoke of the TW headquarters over that high roll.''

Caleb felt his spine tingle like a dog with hackles on end. He spurred Whiplash to keep abreast of Walker. The young drovers began to hoot far across the remuda, and even the trail-weary horses lifted their heads in the herd. The air was brisk, and the sun sterling.

And then there was the nickname. Caleb had been called the Colorado Kid, and Crazy Cal, and even Catgut Caleb Holcomb that time he joined the wild west show. He had never liked any of those monikers. But Walker had just pinned upon him an appellation so unexpected and appealing that it slipped about him like a pair of long handles fresh off the clothesline. He had always wanted a good nickname, but it wasn't a thing you could give to yourself with any kind of integrity attached to it.

As he tried it on in a whisper—"Hard Winter Holcomb''—and hoped it would stick, the ranch headquarters played out below. Surmounting high ground, the drifter saw for the first time what was to be his home for a while. A stone mansion stunned him at first glance, like the one his late brother Pete had built for Amelia back on the Holcomb Ranch. To find such an edifice here, so far from polite society, was like drinking rich brandy from dirty cupped hands.

Behind the mansion loomed a huge log barn just made for dances, with an adjoining corral of aspen rails large enough for the whole remuda of two hundred horses, the gates flung wide and waiting. There were two bunkhouses built along the lines of shotgun barrels, several sheds, a large smokehouse, and a distant privy.

In the yard of a small whitewashed house whose stovepipe issued smoke, a chuck wagon stood, the wagon bows exposed like the ribs of a carcass, canvas spare. The chuck box was open, the single leg propping up the work surface, and around it stalked a burly man by whose manner and stance Hard Winter Holcomb could tell even from this distance was the outfit's cook.

Within a minute, the whole complex came alive like an ant bed some-one had stepped on. Horses swarmed, leery of the gateway but anxious to get closer to the smell of hay. Cowboys whistled and hollered, waved their coiled ropes or their hats. Vested men came out of the mansion, puffing smoke from pipes clenched tight between their teeth. And then, like the signal flag of a sentry, the skirt caught Caleb's eye.

It wasn't much of a skirt, barely over knee length above the riding boots; hardly billowing, and not at all ostentatious. But a skirt out here lured like a dry fly on still waters. The young woman stood with her hands on her hips, a tight-fitting white blouse pressing adequate curves against the wasp-waisted jacket. She stood like an empress or an overseer, taking command of everything within her realm. Caleb couldn't see her face be-neath the brim of the black velvet hat, but when she turned her head to watch the broncs bunch at the gate, a regular plume of silk-straight hair rolled over one shoulder, flashing like lightning in a night sky.

"Walker, did you kill me back in Colorado? I think I see an angel." The musician careened comically in the saddle.

"That's the boss man's baby sister," Walker said. "You just go ahead and pitch forkloads of love songs at her, if you want. Boss man will make some big talk about havin' me drag you by the heels behind a wall-eyed horse, but I'm a friend of yours, so don't worry yourself. He'll have to get somebody else to do it. Then again, that little gal is liable to drag you herself."

"Why didn't you tell me there was womenfolk about?" Caleb com-plained. His shirttail was flapping and it was too late to do anything about it.

"Didn't want to scare you off the place, knowin' how shy you are." The big man laughed and loped forward to cut Harriet away from the remuda and into the barn.

Caleb followed, feeling the roof come over him like a protector he hadn't known since the railroad depot in Cheyenne. He got his boot soles on the dirt floor and twisted the kinks out of his legs and spine before stripping Whiplash of saddle and bridle. He was helping Walker with the heavy buffalo hide when the presence of some misplaced splendor filled the barn.

"Walker, you scoundrel!" she said. "You've gone hunting without me again. What have you killed?"

Walker swept the hat from his head and smiled. "It wasn't me, Savannah, it was N.C. He's gone and killed the last buffler on Powder River."

Savannah glanced casually at the stranger. "I wonder if he would let me have the robe?"

Walker laughed. "He'd chew it squawlike for you if you tolt him to!"

There was a black leather tie under her chin holding the velvet hat on. She loosened it and pushed the hat back off her head, letting the leather tie hold it against her throat. "Where's Little Dan?" she asked, flipping her hair over the hat and shaking it across both shoulders. "I didn't see him ride in with the others."

Walker rubbed his jaw. "He ain't comin' back. He's finished his brandin'."

"What do you mean?"

The big man swooped a toughened hand upward at a slant. "Crossed the divide. Gone to the last roundup."

"He's dead?" Savannah asked, the news knocking a chink in her poise.

"Deader than rusty horseshoe nails."

"How long?"

"Long enough to quit grievin' over."

Savannah stared at a dark corner of the barn for a moment, then her mouth closed and she shrugged. "Does his family know?"

"They was all waitin' on him, far as I know."

She nodded. "Who's this?" she asked, pointing at Caleb as if he were a new horse or something.

"That there's a drifter I shanghaied down in Colorado. Everybody calls him Hard Winter Holcomb."

Caleb had been standing hat in hand since Savannah entered the barn, trying not to squirm under her occasional indifferent glance. Now he saw her take a few sashaying strides toward him, the riding skirt swinging seductively around her knees. He stood his ground, but it wasn't easy, for he hardly felt presentable. She put out her hand and he took it, encased as it was in a small, soft deerskin glove.

"It's been a long winter as well as a hard one, hasn't it?" she said, wrinkling her nose and sniffing. "A long winter without a bath."

Caleb thanked every angel in heaven for the dim light of the barn, for he knew his untanned forehead must have been glowing with embarrassment. He let her hand slide out of his, aware of how firmly she had shook—like a man. This was her spread, all right, and she wanted him to know it.

As she turned aside—her dark lips smirking—she caught sight of the instruments on the pack mule. "Are you a violinist, Mr. Hard Winter?" she said, making considerable light of Caleb's new nickname.

"No, ma'am," he announced, slapping his dusty hat back on his head. "Violin players smell like toilette water. I'm just a left-handed fiddler."

She whirled on him, struck by the insolence hidden among his words. The nostrils of her tiny nose flared. Her eyes glared, and Savannah was seeing him as a man for the first time now, taking note of his features. The mustache was unkempt, but flamboyant; the face aged early, thoughtful; the shoulders broad, if a little too angular; the stance proud, but not overbearing. She flipped the silken mane at him and stalked out of the barn.

Walker C. Kincheloe laughed at them both. "Watch yourself, Hard Winter. That little gal is mean as eight acres of snakes when somebody sasses her."

Caleb shrugged. "Who knows what sass talk is to a woman? I never had much luck with 'em, not countin' the painted variety."

"Whores don't take luck, they just take money. That little lady there, on the other hand, will take a lot more out of you than money."

"Oh, she don't look so awful dangerous."

"That's just it. She's like a three-year-old. Just when you think you've got her broke and trained to the saddle, she'll cut out from under you so quick you'll be kissin' your own shadow. You'd better stay shy of her if you know what's good for you."

Caleb grinned as he began untying the green buffalo hide from his pack saddle. "I've never been known for doin' what's good for me."

EIGHT

WALKER ENTERED THE barn about two hours after dark, his eyes pulling instantly toward the wail of the fiddle. "By golly, ol' Hard Winter cleans up pretty good," he mumbled to himself. The way the fiddler made his spurs ring in time to the instrument he galled with the bow was a thing to behold with the eyes as well as the ears.

A flash of something like sunlight on a white bird's wing drew his eyes to Savannah, who was whirling with N.C. on the wooden floor. The saddle racks and wheelbarrows and sacks of feed had been stacked to one side to make room for the dancers. There were other female dancers besides Savannah—wives and sisters of cattle investors, several house servants from various ranches, and even an English girl visiting the CU—But little Savannah was the one who made the boys gawk. Every couple of turns, she would toss her head back to make the light of lanterns gloss her hair. N.C. looked awkward and nervous trying not to step on her little feet, but Savannah danced as an eagle courting gracefully in the air. And there was something else Walker could not help noticing. Her gaze kept returning to the fiddler, even to the point that she would snap her pretty face around like a spinning ballerina to keep an eye trained on him.

The jig ended and Caleb poked the guitar player, Woody Fletcher, approvingly with the end of his bow. Savannah said something curt and polite to N.C. and left him standing. She flitted then to the musicians—Caleb, Woody Fletcher, and Joe Frank Abbot, who could play a little harmonica—and clapped her hands, discussing possibilities for the next number.

''Walker!''

The big Texan looked casually to one side to find his boss, Hiram Baber, beckoning respectfully with a couple of fingers. He had a bottle neck in the other hand, and Hiram drank only the finest. Walker C. Kincheloe smiled and pushed his hat back.

Hiram was a young cuss about Caleb's age, and used to being pampered all his life back in New York State, but he was all right. Hiram had come west more for a taste of fleeting adventure than for business reasons. He could have remained on the East Coast and taken over any number of the Baber family mercantile or shipping interests, but Hiram wanted to start something rather than take something over, and Walker respected that, even if it had been handed to him.

The thing about Hiram was that he had a respect for geography, climate, and tradition. He had built the big mansion and brought servants with him, but beyond that the young man tended to hold to the ways of the West—the ways that had kept men and dreams alive while others withered and wasted away. Hiram would not ask a cowboy in his employ to do anything he was not willing to at least try himself. He had been flung from the bowed backs of green-broke horses, lashed by gale-driven snows, parched on long summer trails.

Unlike most of the Scottish, English, and East Coast owners of the herds that had come to multiply along Powder River, Hiram lived here year-round. He had immersed himself in the cow culture, and was doing well, making huge profits his first few years. Yet he left plenty of time for recreation, and had stomped like an envious child just this afternoon upon hearing that N. C. Kincheloe had shot what was surely to be the last buffalo on these ranges. Hiram's office walls were replete with fowling pieces, hunting rifles, and bamboo fly-fishing rods. He was doing more than just chewing up the country and spitting it out. He was feasting upon it, digesting it, fleshing himself out on it like a four-year-old beef. You had to like Hiram Baber.

"Welcome back, Walker," he said, pouring a glass for his manager. "I've looked over the horses. They seem to have come through in fine shape."

"They'll do," Walker said, shaking hands as he took the brandy. "They've all been rode once't or twice't. The boys can handle 'em."

"Who's that violinist Savannah's talking to? I don't know that I like the way they're acting in public."

"Name's Caleb 'Hard Winter' Holcomb. Good Colorado boy."

"Boy?" Hiram said. "He's full grown if he's a day."

"And so's little sister, if you haven't noticed lately. Don't worry about ol' Hard Winter. He's cut from good cloth. Good hand, too, and with the roundup comin' around, I'll need him."

Hiram sighed and took a deep draw from the brandy glass. "Yes, the roundup. I've been meaning to talk to you about that." He gestured toward a couple of nail kegs, and he and Walker sat on them, resting their elbows and their drinks on a barrel of smoked pork packed in lard. "There have been some changes while you were gone. You won't be able to run the roundup this year."

Walker stiffened. "The hell I won't. I've never been abler in my life."

"I know," Hiram said. "It has nothing to do with your capabilities." He paused to choose his words more carefully. Walker C. Kincheloe was a proud man. "There's a new law. An appointed foreman will regulate the roundup this year."

"Appointed? By who?" the big man demanded.

"The Wyoming Stock Growers Association."

"That's a rich man's social club. What in the hell makes 'em think they can regulate squat?"

"It's more than just a private association now, Walker. It's an official arm of the territorial government. The legislature met while you were in Kansas, and passed some bills designed to regulate the range cattle industry. They put the Wyoming Stock Growers Association in complete control."

Walker snorted. "How many members are in that rich man's club?"

Hiram shrugged. "Four or five hundred, I guess."

"And how many cattle owners operate on the government range?"

"Who knows? Perhaps a couple of thousand, counting the owners of small herds."

"Then how come a few hundred—not even elected—get to regulate for everybody?" He brushed his hand across the top of the barrel as if to wipe the silly law off the books.

"Because they own the vast majority of cattle in the territory. Probably ninety percent or better."

Walker laughed. "Did the legislature give cows the vote?"

"This is serious, Walker. It's not a joking matter."

"Hell, I ain't jokin'. Government is supposed to represent the majority of people, not the majority of cows. That's a law that don't make no damn sense. Just because the Stock Growers Association is a bunch of rich bastards don't mean they get to regulate everybody. Hell, nobody elected 'em, Hi. It's just a damn rich man's social club."

"You're right, and everybody knows it, Walker. I spoke against this bill myself, and I'm a member in good standing of the association. The newspapers were against it, the people were against it. But the legislature snuck it through on the last day of the session, so the newspapers wouldn't have time to whip up sentiment against it. It's dirty politics and everybody knows it. I'm sure it's unconstitutional, and time will bear that out, but for now it's the law of the land."

"It's the law of the damned. Hell with it. They send a foreman to regulate my roundup, and I'll send him back to Cheyenne branded and earmarked. Why the hell does a roundup need to be regulated, anyway?"

"It's the maverick question," Hiram replied, unconsciously keeping a watchful eye on his sister.

"What question? A maverick is an unbranded beef. That's plain as ears on a mule."

"But who does it belong to? That's the question."

"Where I come from, it belongs to the man with the longest rope and the fastest runnin' iron."

Hiram shook his head. "The Texas system won't work here. In Texas, the longhorns had been wild for generations. They belonged to no one. Here, the herds were brought in at great expense by men like me, and Chauncey Shanahan over there." He tipped his head toward a wiry Scot who stood glaring at them through the danced-up dust, his arms crossed over his chest.

"That don't mean you and Shanahan get to lord it over the rest of us little men. This ain't Scotland. You won't find no serfs and peasants punchin' cows. The little outfits have got a right to a maverick just as sure as you.''

"I agree, Walker. And that's why I've given you the choice up until now of branding mavericks for your own herd or branding them for me at five dollars a head. If the rest of these operators would follow our policy, there wouldn't be a maverick question.''

"The bastards just can't stand the thought of another man gettin' ahead, can they?'' Walker emptied his glass and suggested to Hiram that a refill might be appreciated.

"They don't understand cowboys. I would just as soon that every hand who works for me own a few head of beeves. They'll look after the range better if they have a stake in it. But Shanahan over there, and too many others like him, are afraid that you native boys are going to brand every last maverick for yourselves and crowd them out of the industry.''

Walker rolled his eyes. ''I wish you'd quit callin' the cow business the 'industry.' Cows don't build nothin'. Anyway, if a maverick don't belong to whoever catches it first, who the hell does it belong to?''

Hiram drummed his fingers, stalling. ''You have to admit, Walker, there have been some abuses. The independent operators start their round-ups a little earlier every year, and some of them are pulling calves off their mothers—making mavericks—even shooting another man's cow to brand her calf. You remember the day we found that cow of mine shot through the head away out on the range, and a little bawling calf standing over her with a fresh brand?''

"And you remember what happened to the man that brand belonged to. He got his ass back to Nebraska, and only hit the high places on the way. He's lucky me and the boys didn't leave him lay like he left your cow. That's the way to handle abuses.''

Hiram restrained a smile, for he really didn't like to encourage Walker's fighting temper. ''There has to be some sort of regulation, Walker. The country is growing up. The new law has a name—coined by the newspapers. They call it Bill Maverick. And according to Bill Maverick, all mavericks now belong to the Stock Growers Association.''

Walker pondered the ramifications for a moment. ''The rich men get all the mavericks? What if I wanted a damn maverick, by God? What does Bill Maverick say about that?''

"The mavericks are to be rounded up, under supervision of the appointed roundup foreman, and branded with the letter M. Then they are to be auctioned off to the highest bidder. So you can bid on mavericks, like anybody else, Walker.''

"Don't try to whitewash it, Hi, I can see through it. Once was the day I could rope and brand a maverick and it was mine. Now I still have to rope and brand it for the damn roundup foreman, but then I have to turn around and buy it!"

"It could have been worse, Walker. The first version of the bill said that anybody who wanted to bid on mavericks had to put up a bond of three thousand dollars. Well, that was such a blatant attempt to keep out the small operators that I raised hell about it, and so did a lot of other people, and we got that provision stricken from the bill."

"Congratulations," the big man said sarcastically. "What I want to know is, who gets the money when the mavericks are auctioned off? The government?"

"The Stock Growers Association," Hiram said, sheepishly.

"Goddamn, Hi! Has the country gone to hell? How come the association gets the money?"

"Bill Maverick says it'll be used for the payment of cattle inspectors, and other like purposes, although it doesn't say what 'other like purposes' means."

"I'll tell you what it means!" Walker blurted over the fiddle music. "It means buyin' drinks and whores at that fancy rich man's social club in Cheyenne! It means if I buy a maverick, I never see the money again. If you or Chauncey Shanahan buy one, you get the money right back through your blasted association."

"I know it's not fair, Walker, and that's why I don't intend to let it stand. But for now, Bill Maverick is the law of the land, and if you openly disobey it you'll land in jail, and I'll be kicked out of the association. In Wyoming, that's the same thing as getting kicked out of the beef industry."

Walker glared suddenly.

"I mean, the cow business. It might get worse before it gets better. There's a measure up for consideration before the Stock Growers Association that requires members to fire any cowhand who owns cattle. I won't do that, of course; I wouldn't ask you to choose between your job and your property. But I'm just warning you. We might have to make some temporary concessions until we can send Bill Maverick packing back to England, or Scotland, or wherever these elitist ideas come from."

"New York?" Walker suggested.

"Just give me a year, Walker. Play along with the new system until I have a chance to expose the corruption of it from the inside. I'll go to the newspapers before next winter's session of the legislature, and we'll get Bill Maverick stricken from the books. But if I get kicked out of the association, I won't have any way to gather evidence." He noticed that Walker's glass was empty again and tilted the bottle over it. "Just one year. Can we drink on it?"

Walker smirked at the bottle of fine brandy. He didn't know many Texans he would make concessions for, much less rich New Yorkers. Why in the devil did he like Hiram Baber so much? "Never let nobody say that Walker C. Kincheloe don't give a man a chance, Hiram. All right, I'll give you one year to do it your way, then I'm goin' back to the Texas system. If Bill Maverick gets to be a yearlin', and he's still rangin' Powder River country, I'm gonna hog-tie and castrate him." He raised the glass and clinked it against Hiram's, then turned to watch Savannah steal the show right out from under Caleb Holcomb's heels.

NINE

CALEB SAT ON the back of a hardheaded Kansas cob, trying to feel horse trouble through the saddle and accomplish mathematical computations at the same time. There were twenty-six chuck wagons evenly spaced along two miles of Powder River; each chuck wagon fed ten or twelve cowboys, and each cowboy needed ten mounts to finish the roundup. The question was this: How many horses grazed the valley of Powder River here, how many head of cattle would they collectively herd onto this range, and how long would the grass hold out?

Old Snuffy made an almost imperceptible hump rise in his back, and Caleb noticed it too late, his mind being more occupied with numbers than with horsemanship. Suddenly every remuda, every chuck wagon, and every cowhand in sight became part of the same blur. He tried to draw his knees up under the forks of his saddle, but his rear was already a foot above the cantle. He pulled leather, but that only brought his chest down harder on the saddle horn. He felt the wind explode up his throat, and came to dazed and gasping on the ground.

He knew he must not have landed too hard because he heard his friends laughing, the laughter growing nearer and louder, the ringing of spurs harmonizing with the ringing in his ears.

"Get up, Caleb." It was N.C. pulling at his arm. "What were you thinkin'? I could see from over yonder at the chuck wagon that ol' Snuff was fixin' to break half in two."

"I was just calculatin'," the fiddler wheezed.

"Calculatin' what?"

"Must be dern near three thousand head of horses in this roundup." He prodded the tender middle of his chest, thankful that he hadn't busted a finger, which would have relegated him to harmonica playing. "And I had to saddle that one."

The horse was brought back around at the end of a rope, blindfolded with a bandanna, and held by the ears so Caleb could get back on. He spent the rest of the daylight hours taking some bronc out of Snuffy, avoiding anything that resembled arithmetic.

When dusk came, the drifter rode to a high point and swept his eyes across the valley. The smoke trails of twenty-six campfires slanted northward on a day-old chinook. Remudas moved like snails up the slopes, and with them, the nighthawks drifted—boys, mostly, fresh from the towns, given the greenhorn job of night-herding horses. Caleb heard the nearest nighthawk singing a tune in a boyish tenor voice.

There was a good sound in the air: the nighthawk's vague tune; the horse noises; the clack of wooden spoons against metal pots; the laughter of young men; and, above all, hooves—thousands of them—grinding and thumping ceaselessly against the ground like the long muffled roll of thunder one hundred miles away. The absent strain was that of bawling cattle. But tomorrow it would begin, and Caleb knew he would hear his share of it.

He smiled, and urged Snuffy cautiously toward the TW remuda.

There was a meeting shaping up at the TW wagon, it being more or less centrally located among the camps. Managers from the twenty-some-odd big spreads streamed in, some bringing a few hands with them, most tying their mounts to stakes driven into the ground, except for those who rode favorite pet horses. The captains of the few wagons funded by small outfits arrived, as well as some representatives from distant roundups—the Sweetwater, the Platte, and Laramie River ranges—who had come to claim any cattle that might have strayed. Few of the owners were present, but Hiram Baber and Chauncey Shanahan were among them.

Just after Caleb arrived and stood downwind of the wagon for a minute or two to smell the grub, a new face appeared in the crowd. It became quickly obvious that the face belonged to the roundup foreman appointed by the Wyoming Stock Growers Association.

"You know him?" Caleb asked N.C. when the boy arrived at the circle that had formed upwind of the fire.

"Name's Dave Donaldson," N.C. said. "Used to manage a big ranch down in Chugwater country."

"Does he know this country?"

N.C. shrugged. "He came up last year as a rep for the Chugwater roundup. I guess he knows which way the river runs. Nobody knows this range like Daddy, except maybe some old Indian somewhere."

Dave Donaldson tossed his hat onto the brake handle of the chuck wagon and stepped up on the wheel hub to rise above the crowd. "Everybody here?" he said.

"Everybody who gives a damn," Walker shouted, a smile on his face. "And some of us that don't."

A stilted chuckle rippled halfheartedly through the crowded punchers. Dave Donaldson didn't so much as smirk.

"Winter's been mild," the official foreman began. "This chinook has got 'em driftin' north, so that's where we'll work hardest. I want a dozen outfits to start at the mouth of Clear Creek, fan out against the mountains, and work south across all the Crazy Woman forks. Then I want three outfits each on North, Middle, and South Powder River forks. Two outfits can work Salt Creek, and the other three outfits can spread out east and pick up strays. Any questions?"

Hiram Baber took a step toward the foreman. "Dave, I just came down from Clear Creek country hunting lions. I saw only a few head of cattle, and scarcely any sign."

Donaldson took his hat from the brake lever and slapped it on his head. "With all due respect, Mr. Baber, if you knew huntin' beef like you know huntin' lions, maybe you'd have seen more. Don't worry. These boys know how to roust 'em out of the coulees. There's cows up there. You just have to know where to look."

Hiram's face darkened at the insubordination, but he heard Walker clear his throat and glanced to see his manager calming him with a disinterested smirk and a slight shake of his head.

"Y'all elect a captain among yourselves to make the assignments of which outfits will carry out my orders," Donaldson said.

"I elect Walker C. Kincheloe!" shouted Woody Fletcher.

"Me too!" yelled another TW man.

A shout of approval went up and someone slapped Walker on the back.

Donaldson frowned and stepped down from the wheel hub. "I'll be camped with the CU wagon, in case anybody needs anything." He strolled to his horse, mounted, and waited.

Chauncey Shanahan had caught Hiram by the arm and pulled him aside. "What about your man?" the Scot said, proudly thickening his brogue.

"What do you mean?" Hiram said.

"Has he sold his herd? I have it he owns almost a hundred head. That cannot be overlooked. If he will not sell his herd, you must find yourself another manager.''

Hiram crossed his arms over his chest. ''Neighbor, Walker C. Kincheloe is the best cow man between Powder River and the Gulf of Mexico. I'd be a fool to fire him. If he wants to own a hundred head of cattle, I don't see that they'll crowd my thousands, or yours, either.''

''It's the principle. We've got to protect our range.''

''Our range? It's open range, Chauncey.''

Shanahan drew himself up and grabbed his lapels. ''You know the rules of the association. You've got to fire a man who owns his own brand.''

''I'll hire and fire whomever I please.''

The Scot turned on his spurred heel, strutted to his horse, and rode away with Dave Donaldson.

''Hiram!'' Walker shouted. The big man had gathered the bosses of every wagon in the valley and wanted Hiram in with the crowd.

''Hi's right,'' he said, when his employer joined the group. ''There ain't no cows up on Clear Creek. Dave Donaldson don't know horse shit from wild honey. Winter here ain't been as easy as it has in Chugwater country where he's from. It'll take more than a two-day chinook to drive the herds that far north.''

''What can we do about it?'' one of the wagon bosses said. ''Donaldson is the roundup foreman.''

''Y'all elected me captain, didn't you? Now, first thing to do is forget every damn word Donaldson said. I've seen doves flyin' east three days now. You know what that means. The buffler wallers is brimmin' out there, and that means rain. Rain means grass, and I guess cows still eat grass, unless the goddamn Stock Growers Association has banned it.''

A genuine laugh went up around the Texan.

''They'll be driftin' east, not north. I seen a tetch of that red Salt Creek clay in Powder River, too. You seen it? Above the camps? That means good rain in the south. Ed, looks like you got a good remuda.''

''Good enough,'' Ed replied.

''Why don't you take the furthest loop. Go plumb to the head of Belle Fourche and Little Powder.''

''All right,'' Ed said.

''Doc, Kid, M.T., Buddy, Henry, and Sonny—why don't y'all take your outfits to the divide, east and north of here. Figure out among yourselfs what order you fan out in. You fellers with the three cooperative wagons, why don't y'all work east and south, down to the head of Salt Creek, and hell, you might as well swing around to South Fork. The rest of us will work our home ranges. CU on Crazy Woman Creek, TW on Clear Creek—like that. Everybody savvy?''

The hats nodded, and men began to turn for their horses in groups as Walker had assigned them.

''Y'all come back around after supper,'' Walker shouted. ''Ol' Hard Winter'll have y'all stompin' dust two miles high, and I'll contest any man in the valley to tell a bigger lie than Walker C. Kincheloe!''

TEN

THE BAWLING OF cattle had become Caleb's substitute for silence. When all other strains dwindled, it remained. He had just fifty-two head of cattle in front of him, trotting for Powder River, five miles west, but the drifter could hear the collective moan of thousands. For two days he had looked at the sun through a haze of prairie dust. It coated everything with a fine grit, and Caleb cursed it for making the moving parts of his weapons grind like millstones.

Across the rolls of the great plains he saw herds of near-wild longhorns converging toward the west, like bunches of buffalo in the old days. The real work had not even begun yet. These three days had been spent riding, scouting, hunting, pushing cows. Now they would be bunched, held, sorted, roped, branded, tallied. And yet it was this work that he yearned for. He hadn't thrown a rope in a while, and he was feeling rusty. It would be well to get that first catch made, to hear the saddle creak under the strain.

Half a dozen head of beeves split from the herd of fifty-two running ahead of him and disappeared from sight as if the plains had swallowed them up. The drifter leaned west and stroked the tired mount with his spurs.

He found the cattle doubling back up a washed-out draw. He rode above them, hollering, but they only ran faster up the washout until Caleb forced the green mount down the steep bank, into the draw, ahead of the escaping beeves. Cattle scattered, trying the dirt banks without success, finally turning back toward Powder River.

Caleb kept behind them at a lope, the horse finding his footing in ir-regular leaps. The draw came to a fork that turned back in a dogleg to the right, and half the cattle in the draw tried it as a last route of escape. The horse seemed to have caught the spirit of the roundup by now, and turned after them even before Caleb could pull the rein.

"Git up!" he hollered, urging the mount. His herd was breaking up, and it would take hard riding to bunch it again. God only knew where the main body of the herd had gotten off to. He passed the first cow, then a yearling heifer, and finally the four-year-old steer who had begun all the trouble in the first place.

The drifter was mad now, and he let the steer know it, cutting hard in front of him, whipping him with the knotted end of his rope. They were near the head of the draw—near escape—when the steer doubled back, defeated. The rider set his jaw and turned, then almost pulled the mount back on himself, thunderstruck. He whirled full circle, searching, until his eyes found what had startled him. A rib cage protruded from the wall of the cutbank, half covered. Above it, one shadowy eye of a human skull stared into oblivion.

Caleb had all fifty-two of his beeves moving in a tight bunch when he came over the rim of Powder River's broad bank. His horse was frosted with sweat, its tongue lolling past the bit. A huge dark mass, new to the valley, stretched around bends in the river both upstream and down. It was volatile—like quicksilver in the palm of one's hand—constantly changing shape, seeking escape, breaking apart.

After watching his handful of cattle merge with the thousands, he rode to the TW chuck wagon for a drink of water from the barrel. Caleb had seen and worked many a roundup, but never anything like this. He had seen buffalo in numbers like this, down on the Southern Plains, but never thought he would see so many cattle in one place. The incessant bawling was like the humming of bees in a huge swarm.

He took his saddle from the jaded horse he had been riding and turned the animal back into the remuda. He had been keeping Whiplash staked away from the remuda to keep him from fighting. The cook, who happened to like fiddle music, had been looking after the Appaloosa—taking him to water, moving him to fresh grass.

Now Caleb saddled Whiplash and rode toward the nearest branding fire, passing back by the remuda. He saw Walker and N.C. afoot among the horses and decided to wait for them to get saddled up.

"Watch 'em!" Walker warned. "They'll wheel on you, son."

Caleb helped the wrangler hold the remuda as the father and son worked through them, looking for chosen mounts they knew they could rope from.

"I said watch 'em, N.C.! You're gittin' too close. That ol' hoss could wheel and kick your head in before you could read his brand! Now, back off!''

A walleyed dun tried to break from the remuda then, and Walker leapt in front of him, hissing and waving both arms. The dun planted both front feet, ducked his head, whirled like a roper's loop, and caught Walker hard in the chest with both hind feet, one sharp hoof slipping over his shoulder and raking the side of his head. The big man's boots left the ground and he landed square on his shoulder blades in a pile of dung.

N.C. was already there when Caleb dropped from Whiplash, the son trying to help, but afraid to touch his father. ''Daddy? You all right?''

Walker's eyes were blinking, his chest heaving for air. An ugly scrape extended from his cheek to his ear, the flesh peeled away, but not deep enough to bleed badly.

''Daddy? Say somethin'.''

Walker filled his lungs with dusty air. ''Now, you see what I mean? I tolt you, boy!''

''Yessir,'' N.C. said. ''I'll back off.''

''Help me up.''

Caleb and N.C. grabbed the big man's arms and lifted him, the musician unable to hold back the laughter.

''What're you laughin' at, fiddler?''

''You've got horse shit all over your back.''

''Damn good thing, too. Broke my fall.''

Caleb helped them catch their roping horses from the remuda, and the three men rode into the main herd of cattle. The fiddler let the loop of his rope swing in his right hand as he eased through the herd, looking for unbranded stock. A calf came around the hind end of a cow branded Cross T, and before the fiddler could think, he whirled his loop twice and threw almost straight down at the hind legs of the calf. The calf all but stepped into the loop. The roper jerked up the slack, taking two turns around his saddle horn, and reined quickly toward the branding fire.

''Cross T,'' Caleb said, dragging the calf backward to the men afoot at the fires. Woody Fletcher knocked the calf over, doubled a front leg, and sat on the bleating calf's shoulder, while Joe Frank Abbot applied a smoking Cross T iron to the little brute's hip. Caleb let the rope go slack and the calf trotted back to the herd, bawling for its mother.

Walker had a big heifer roped by the head, pulling it hard toward the fires. When within easy reach of the men afoot, N.C. made a graceful throw at the heels, pointing his trigger finger at his target as his father had taught him. He jerked the slack as the hind hooves were caught, took a couple of dallies around the horn, and stretched the heifer out with Walker. Woody grabbed the heifer by the tail and pulled her over, as Joe Frank Abbott applied the *M* brand that meant maverick.

"Whose brand is that?" Caleb asked, coiling his rope for another throw.

"Bill Maverick's," the big man replied.

With the ropes off the heifer, N.C. ran her toward the herd of mavericks one of the boys was holding to one side.

"Who's Bill Maverick?"

"He's an illegitimate little bastard sired down in Cheyenne. His daddy's a territorial senator, and his mama's a greedy old whore who'd do anything for money. I won't speak her name, but her initials are WSGA. Bill Maverick ain't never throwed a loop or tended a brandin' fire, but he thinks he owns every damn head of unbranded stock in the territory."

Walker galloped away and left Caleb to unravel what he had said. The drifter decided he needed to spend a little less time fiddling and a little more time listening to campfire talk.

Toward sundown, every man who owned a brand or represented an owner came to the herd of mavericks to bid on the unclaimed animals. Dave Donaldson, as official foreman of the roundup, conducted the sale. Caleb came along with Walker and N.C. to see how the new system of mavericking would work.

"Cut that brindle out," Donaldson shouted to one of the boys. "Who'll start biddin'?"

"One dollar!" Walker shouted.

Chauncey Shanahan straightened in the saddle of the tall dapple-gray horse he rode. "Five."

"Six," Walker countered.

"Ten."

"Eleven."

"Fifteen!" the Scotsman barked.

"Fifteen dollars?" Walker said. "That beef wouldn't bring that much barbecued in hell!"

The owners of the small outfits burst into laughter.

"Sold at fifteen dollars to Chauncey Shanahan of the CU," Donaldson said, making a mark in his tally book.

The next several head of stock brought ten dollars each, and each was brought by a member of the Wyoming Stock Growers Association. Directly, a white-faced heifer was cut from the herd.

"Nine dollars!" Walker shouted.

"Ten!" said another small-time operator named Jack Flagg, who worked for the Bar C. Flagg was a sober man, educated and serious about making his own start in the cow business. It was said that he had once taught school somewhere. He dressed well, and was particularly fond of black hats.

"Fifteen!" Shanahan blurted.

"Anybody else?" Donaldson asked. "Going once . . . Going twice . . ."

"Wait just a damn minute," Walker said. "Jack, I'll buy a half interest at ten dollars, if you'll buy the other half."

Flagg smiled, for the heifer was young enough to someday pay off even at that price. "All right, partner," he said, tugging the brim of his black hat.

"Twenty dollars from Kincheloe and Flagg," Donaldson said. "Anybody else?"

"Twenty-five!" Shanahan said.

Walker looked at Flagg, who nodded. "Thirty dollars."

"Fifty dollars!" Shanahan roared. "You've no business owning cattle if you work for a member of the association!"

Walker scowled, the long scrape on the side of his face hurting. "This is a damn racket if ever I did see one. Hi, are you gonna go along with this?"

Hiram shrugged. "It's the law, Walker."

"A law made by rich men *for* rich men. Hell with it. There's other ways to get mavericks, law or no law. Come on, boys."

Caleb and N.C. spurred their mounts to catch up; Hiram Baber overtook them shortly.

"Walker, don't fly off the handle. You told me you'd give me a year."

"So I did."

"What does that mean? Are you going to give me a chance to work this out?"

Walker reined his horse back. "I said I would, didn't I?"

"Good," Hi replied. "But don't go talking about mavericking like that in front of Shanahan and Donaldson. They'll use that kind of talk against you."

"All right, I'll mind my tongue, Hi."

Hiram nodded and turned back toward the maverick herd, leaving Walker, Caleb, and N.C. to speak alone.

"You didn't happen to leave us some mavericks holed up out there somewhere, did you, Hard Winter?"

Caleb smiled with one side of his mouth. Maybe what Walker needed was a change of subject. "No, but I'll tell you what I did leave out there. Bones."

"What kind of bones?"

"Human. A whole skeleton."

The Texan jerked his horse to a standstill and looked at N.C. with his mouth open. "How old?"

"Hard to say," Caleb replied, suddenly nervous at Walker's strange reaction. "Old enough that I didn't see any clothes or other things around. Didn't look long, though. I was pushin' cows."

"Can we git there before dark?"

Caleb glanced at the sun, nodded.

"Let's go."

ELEVEN

They left their horses near the head of the draw and walked to the edge.

"There it is," Caleb said, pointing down.

The two Kincheloes stared down for several seconds.

"Stay here," Walker said. He slid down the steep dirt bank, the slick soles of his boots slipping under him. He approached the skeleton from below, searching the ground. He stooped to pick something up.

Caleb looked west to see the sun shrink behind trees on the Bighorns. As he watched, the pall of dust over Powder River turned from orange to gray.

"It's just some squaw," the big man said from below. "Probably Crow."

"How can you tell?" N.C. asked.

"There's elk teeth all over the place, with holes drilled through 'em. She was wearin' one of them Crow squaw dresses decorated with 'em."

"Wonder what killed her," Caleb said.

"Who gives a shit." The big man picked around the skeleton for more evidence. He looked up at N.C. "It can't be him, son. I'm sure of it." He smiled, but his eyes were sad.

"That's good," N.C. said.

Caleb felt like an outsider at some intimate family affair. He had about made up his mind to turn around and wait with Whiplash when he saw

Walker swat at the skeleton. A dismembered hand flew across the draw. The big man grabbed an arm bone and started beating the skull with it. He let the bone fly and kicked the ribs in, grunting and growling like a madman. He went crazy down in the wash, his fists pounding on the side of the dirt bank, bones cracking and flying around him.

"Come on," N.C. said, grabbing the fiddler by the arm.

"But . . ." He pointed back at the draw as the boy pulled him to the horses. He could still hear Walker's maniacal wail. "What about Walker?"

"Leave him be. Get on your horse."

"But . . ."

"Just do what I tell you, Caleb. You don't know him."

They climbed into their saddles and started out at a lope, slowing to a walk when beyond earshot of Walker. N.C. stared blankly ahead, his carefree recklessness invisible now.

"N.C.," the drifter said.

"Yeah?"

"Was there ever a Colt pistol called the Paterson?"

"Yeah," N.C. said. "The Colt pistol factory was in Paterson, New Jersey, for a while, so they named one of the early models the Paterson."

"Paterson Colt Kincheloe was your brother?" the drifter asked.

"Or *is* my brother."

"You don't know whether or not he's alive?"

"Nope," N.C. said.

"When was the last time you seen him?"

"I never saw him. Daddy says I favor him."

Caleb rode beside the young cowboy in silence for a while, remembering Walker's crazed frenzy down in the draw. "If you expect me to leave your daddy like that back in that draw, I think I got a right to know what happened."

N.C. looked at him and nodded. "I was born the year of the Fetterman massacre. Paterson was already eight that year. After the massacre, Daddy got nervous about keepin' Mama and Paterson at Fort Phil Kearny—scared the Sioux would overrun the place. Mama was carryin' me at the time. Daddy was a civilian freighter at the fort, and Mama took in laundry." N.C. pointed to the dark silhouette of the mountains against the gray sky. "Fort Phil Kearny was along the Bighorns over there."

Caleb looked, thought about the skeleton back in the draw.

"Anyway, first chance Daddy had to send Mama and Paterson south, he took it. The army scouts said the Sioux had moved on up into the mountains, so Daddy put Mama and Paterson in with a train of freight wagons headin' south. He stayed at the fort to keep workin'. The train was guarded with soldiers, and Daddy figured it was safer than the fort.

"When they got out of Sioux country, the soldiers thought they was safe, and they got careless. The train would stop every day at noon so's folks could have dinner and rest, and one day Cheyenne attacked the train to get the mules and horses. There was maybe a hundred or two hundred warriors.

"Anyway, they stampeded the mules, and Paterson happened to be helpin' the herders. They tried to get the herd back to the wagons, but the Cheyenne cut about half of 'em off, killed one of the soldiers drivin' 'em in, and taken Paterson captive. Three cavalry boys volunteered to go after him while the rest guarded the train. All three of 'em was shot down and scalped in sight of the train, and the Cheyenne rode off with most of the mules . . . and Paterson.

"They said Mama went into labor right then and there, and it lasted two days. I was born in the back of a wagon about five miles north of Denver. Mama died when we got to town. They said she could have lived, but she just wouldn't. Somebody took care of me till Daddy came after me."

Caleb couldn't think of anything to say, so he kept his mouth shut. The stars were out before N.C. spoke again.

"What's the first thing you remember?" the young cowboy said.

Caleb brushed one branch of his mustache aside. "I never thought about it."

"My first memory was the day I met my daddy. I was about two years old, and everybody kept tellin' me my daddy was comin' to get me that day. I still remember it. I'd never seen a man in buckskins before, bein' brought up in Denver, and sheltered pretty much. He sure put a shock on me. I cried."

Caleb chuckled. "Where'd he been the first two years of your life?"

"Huntin' Paterson. He got on the trail of those Cheyenne dog soldiers and just wouldn't let up. The Cheyenne taken a bunch of captives in sixty-eight, and Daddy run across several of 'em. Traded horses and things for some of 'em, when the Indians would trade. If they wouldn't trade, he'd take 'em back by force. You remember Kate Llewellyn? Daddy rescued her from a Cheyenne camp."

Caleb nodded. "No sign of Paterson?"

N.C. shook his head. "The only thing Daddy found out was that the Cheyenne had traded him to some other tribe. All the time I was growin' up, Daddy would take off every now and then to go hunt for him. Every time there was Indian trouble, he'd go join the army scouts, hopin' to find Paterson alive after some skirmish, I guess. But, bein' a scout, he got on the wrong side of the Indians, and they must have taken Paterson somewhere out of the way where Daddy couldn't find him. I'm afraid we may never see him again, but I wouldn't say so to Daddy. He's got to have some hope, or he'll go plumb crazy.''

That wasn't difficult for Caleb to believe. From what he had seen, Walker was near to lunacy at this moment, back in that draw, beating hell out of a skeleton.

''Don't never tell nobody I said this, Caleb, but I almost wish them *was* Paterson's bones back there in that draw. At least that would put an end to it.''

They rode over the rim of the Powder River breaks, saw the campfires dotting the valley. They should have felt hungry, but neither did.

''It's a good thing, you tellin' me,'' the fiddler said. ''I wish I could do somethin'.''

''You can.''

''What?''

''Daddy's gonna be hell to live with for a few days. He's liable to get hisself into trouble. I can't handle him alone.''

Caleb swallowed. He hadn't bargained on tangling with Walker. ''Just tell me what to do when the time comes.'' He was hoping the time wouldn't come. Kate Llewellyn had warned him about getting on the wrong side of Walker C. Kincheloe.

They got to camp, said nothing, forced themselves to eat. Someone asked Caleb to get his guitar out of the bed wagon, and he obliged, urging the boys to sing what words they knew to ''When the Work's All Done This Fall.''

> *Charlie was buried at sunrise, no tombstone at his head*
> *Nothing but a little board, and this is what it said:*
> *Charlie died at daybreak, he died from a fall*
> *And he'll not see his mother when the work's all done this fall*

Caleb had given the guitar to Woody Fletcher and was playing discreetly in the background with his mandolin—his thumb just fluttering across the strings in a muted tremolo—when Walker rode back to camp. The big man had his hat pulled low over his eyes. He left his roping horse to stand, and walked to the chuck box on the back of the wagon. No one took much notice of him, as a nighthawk called Little Ben was singing a ballad in a good tenor voice.

Caleb caught N.C.'s eye, and they both saw Walker take the jug of whiskey from the cook's box and retreat into the darkness on foot.

The singers were still taking turns an hour later, but most of the boys had rolled in their blankets, and one was already snoring. Two riders trotted almost into the firelight and jumped down with their spurs jingling.

Dave Donaldson stepped into the light first, his eyes angrily sweeping across the men. Chauncey Shanahan was close behind.

"Where's Walker?" Donaldson said.

There was a silence, then N.C. said, "He ain't here."

"That's his ropin' horse standin' right there."

"Do you see him?" N.C. said. "I told you he ain't here."

Caleb slid the mandolin under the forks of his saddle.

Hiram Baber stood up. "Something wrong, Dave?"

Donaldson cut his angry squint from N.C. to Hi. "Walker sent the outfits out different from what I said. He changed my orders."

"You're goddamn right I did!" Walker emerged from the darkness and slammed the whiskey jug down on the chuck box so hard that a tin cup bounced off. "Why do you think the work's goin' so fast?"

"Roll your cotton and git at daybreak," Donaldson ordered. "I'm foreman of this roundup."

"The boys elected me captain," Walker said, wading clumsily through the men around the fire. "Nobody elected you shit. Hell, you couldn't get elected if nobody'd run against you. You don't know the country, and you don't know cows. Hell, you don't know your ass from a badger's den."

N.C. squatted beside Caleb. "Take your rope off your saddle," he said, rising to stroll toward his father's horse.

"You're damn near fallin'-down drunk," Donaldson blurted. "Leave this roundup now, or I'll bring you up on charges."

"This ain't the goddamn army! Get the hell out of my camp!"

As he passed by the cook's fire, he grabbed an empty pothook made of curved iron about two feet long, warm from hanging near the flames. He stepped over the snoring cowboy on the ground to get at Donaldson, but the foreman retreated, pulling his pistol from the holster as he walked backward.

"Wait!" Hiram Baber shouted, but no one listened.

Caleb was rising with his rope when Walker used the pothook like a club to hit the revolver in Donaldson's hand. The gun fired, the sleeping cowboy shot upright with a snort, and men scattered.

Donaldson was spun sideways by the ferocity of the big Texan's blow, and used his left fist to backhand the place where the horse had raked Walker across the face that day. The big man scarcely even winced, catching the pistol now in his left hand and knocking Donaldson's wind from his chest with the curved black end of the iron hook.

Now the pothook struck the side of Donaldson's head as the foreman doubled over. Walker struck again with the weapon, and again, drawing a stream of blood at Donaldson's ear.

"That's enough, Walker!" Hiram Baber shouted.

Holding his coiled rope in his right hand, Caleb rushed forward and grabbed the iron hook, but the big man wrenched it free as if from the grasp of a child. The fiddler could not say how the elbow came around so quickly, but it snapped his head back and staggered him. His left eye throbbed with pain, but his right glimpsed N.C. leaping the cook fire on Walker's horse, the rope whirling above his head.

The wide noose caught under Walker's right arm, burned the left side of his neck as it tightened. N.C. turned the horse, pulling his father away through the coals of the fire. "Heel him, Caleb!"

Walker hurled the pothook at Dave Donaldson's head, just missing him. He roared like a bear, drew his Colt from the cross-draw holster, and fired, the shot kicking up dust near Donaldson's bleeding head. Caleb whipped his noose around twice and flipped it into the path of Walker's spurs as the big man backpedaled. The spurs hooked the noose, and Caleb took up the slack hand over hand. As Walker fell backward, the pistol fired again. The first shot went up into the air, the next toward the wagon, shattering the whiskey jug Walker had set there not long before.

The bear's roar changed to a panther's scream, then to the howl of creatures yet to be created.

Caleb looped the rope around his hips to better hold the tension around Walker's legs. The Colt fired three more times, and Caleb prayed he would not be hit. N.C. dragged his father away from camp; dragged him over his own hat, which had only now come off his head.

"Hold him!" the boy shouted, jumping down from the mount. The horse pranced backward, keeping the rope taut. The revolver was waving in the air, clicking against spent shells, its owner squalling a hellish yodel. N.C. snared the fist with the loop of his pigging string, jerked it tight, rolled his father with his boot. With both hands on the pigging string, he muscled the big arm behind Walker's back, looped the line around the other wrist, and pulled them together. He put a knee on Walker, as if holding down a big calf, and tied the hands behind his father's back. Only now did he reach into his father's jacket to remove the Colt in the shoulder holster.

"Turn loose," he said to Caleb. He took the fiddler's rope, wound it around Walker's neck, and cinched the legs up behind his back, trussing the big man up on the prairie ground. He walked back to the horse, rode the mount a few steps forward, and took his rope from the saddle horn.

"Leave him," the boy said.

Walker was only grunting now.

"You'll cut his blood off like that," said Hard Winter Holcomb.

"I'll loosen him in a little while. Now, git. Don't look at him like that."

Caleb felt sick with worry. How had any of this become his business? What would Walker do when N.C. turned him loose? He probably wouldn't kill his own son. But a drifting no-'count fiddler?

Dave Donaldson was conscious and sitting up when Caleb got back to the campfire.

Chauncey Shanahan was railing at Hiram Baber. "He should be banished from the territory!"

"Nobody here has the authority to kick anybody out of the territory," Hi replied. "And nobody gave Donaldson the authority to use his gun. He shouldn't have pulled it out in another man's camp."

"Your man attacked him!" Shanahan said. "It was attempted murder!"

Hi smirked and held his palms up. "If Walker had wanted to kill him, Dave would be dead right now. This isn't the first fight to break out at a roundup, Chauncey. Let's not make more of it than that."

Shanahan fumed, then marched to Dave Donaldson and pulled him to his feet. "We'll settle this in Cheyenne, Hiram Baber." He guided Donaldson, staggering, to the horses, and they rode away.

TWELVE

THE RIDER CAME at a long lope through a swirl of fog—a time-haze in the mind of the tortured dreamer. Once, when the memory was fresh and the fog yet formed, the dreamer had seen through the eyes of this boy rider, for it was he who had made the ride. Now he saw the boy from odd perspectives, distant and detached:

From above, the shadow of the felt brim gliding uncurbed across the rough ground.

From behind, the dust raised by the hooves of the fleet mare mingling with time's fog.

From ahead, the tears of ire and horror streaking the rider's dirty cheeks, trailing away into his thick shocks of unshorn hair.

The boy loped long through this fog, frothing his mount with lines of sweat like waves breaking on a barren shore. The mare ran head high, the bridle reins held short in her mane, tight in the boy's left fist.

The right hand gripped the butt of the big Colt revolver, and this the dreamer could still feel—smooth warm walnut steel-pinned to the heavy frame. He wore the long barrel under his belt, but held the arch of the pistol grip in his hand for the false comfort the weapon lent.

It was horrible, knowing where the ride would end, and whence it had begun. Yet there was beauty in the way the boy flowed with the smooth lope of the mare; glory in his victory over a fear so immense that it made the dreamer tremble even now.

The dreamer had been here before, but it was the way with this dream to make it the first time for the boy. Always the first time. It was the way with this dream to take the dreamer's voice, lest he should warn the boy about things to come, about consequences, about a long life worse than slow death.

The fog lifted at times to reveal the landmarks still plain in the mind of the dreamer: The lone live oak at the head of the draw, the bluff overlooking the pecan grove, the falls where the creek joined the river.

It was here that the boy leaned back on the reins, slowing the mare to a walk. The noise from the falls would cover any sound the horse might make. And just downstream was that rocky ford on the river, running swift with last night's rain. There grew timber where he would wait in hiding. But he must hurry.

The fog was clearing, and everything the dreamer possessed was streaming back into the boy of long ago. They were coming. He must hurry. He drew the revolver from his belt and dropped from the saddle. His heart beat as if it would burst, for he knew they must be near. Then the four riders rounded the bend above the pecan grove, and the boy, in his terror, could not even breathe.

THIRTEEN

CALEB THREW THE ropes aside as Walker's eyes fluttered open and darted.

"Oh," the big man said. "I'm here." He saw his saddled horse standing nearby. His son's and the fiddler's were there, too, and the fiddler's pack mule. "Where we goin'?"

"Mr. Baber's sendin' us back to the TW."

Walker found his revolver in his hand. He put it in the holster, and rubbed his wrists as he nodded. He saw a plate of food and a tin cup. He pointed at the coffee, too stiff to reach for it himself just yet.

There was light in the sky, and work had commenced. As he ate, he noticed Caleb's eye, dark and puffy. "Did I do that, fiddler?" he asked.

Caleb felt the eye, not realizing until now that it showed. "I guess."

Walker shrugged. He wolfed down a mouthful of bacon and potatoes. "You probably had it comin' for somethin'."

Hiram Baber waited until Walker was on his feet and presentable before he rode from the herd. "Mornin', Walker," he said, getting down from his mount.

"Boss." The big man nodded as if nothing had happened. "How come you want to send me and these boys back home?"

"You know why, Walker. You almost split Dave Donaldson's head open last night."

"I believe I remember him pullin' a gun on me. I don't think he was gonna give it to me as a gift."

Hiram sighed. "I had some of the boys cut your stock out of the herd. That's them across the river. If we find any others, we'll bring them back to the TW with us."

The big Texan raised a menacing eyebrow. "How come you cut 'em out?"

"After that row last night, the association has me over a barrel. They've been pressuring me for a long time to fire you for running your own spread, and now they're talking about prosecuting you for disrupting the roundup. I suggest you take your herd and hole up on that homestead of yours in the foothills. Put the summer in building your own outfit."

"I'm fired?"

"Of course not. You'll stay on the payroll at top wage. I'll quit the range industry before they make me fire you, Walker. But for now it would look better if you'd headquarter on your own spread and clear out of the TW for a while."

Walker raked a spur across the ground. "Makes it look like I'm fired, don't it?"

Hiram didn't answer.

"Hell with it. I quit." He pointed his finger at the Easterner. "You make it known that I quit, *Mr. Baber*."

"Now, Walker, you don't have reason to call me *mister* in that tone of voice!"

Walker had his foot in a stirrup, but paused to look over his shoulder before mounting. Hiram was bowed up like a bulldog. You had to like Hiram Baber, even if he did hail from New York State and belong to that rich man's social club. "I'll tell you what, Hi. If you'll make a determined effort to say 'cow business' instead of 'range beef industry,' I'll fight any snot-nosed bastard that has the gall to name you *mister*."

Hiram watched the Texan mount. "Now, that's a deal. Holcomb," he added, reaching into his coat pocket.

Caleb turned Whiplash, surprised to hear his name spoken by Baber. "Yeah?"

"Carry this letter to my sister, if you will. You're welcome to stay around the TW. I'll have work for you into the fall."

Caleb got down from his horse as Baber approached and took the letter from him at ground level. "I'll be glad to take the letter, but I'll have to drift south after we get back. Thanks for the offer, anyway." He mounted, slipping the letter carefully inside his vest.

As they rode away at a walk, N.C. cut between his father and Caleb. "How come you got to carry the letter?" he said, rather bitterly.

Caleb shrugged.

Several hundred cattle milled between the three riders and Powder River, so they pushed slowly through the melee of rattling horns and moaning voices, N.C. continuing to grumble about Caleb getting privileges he hadn't earned.

"You may be older than me, but I've got time on you in this outfit."

"Hell, don't get riled at me," Caleb said. "It wasn't my damned idea."

"Then let me carry the letter."

"Do I look like that big a fool?"

Walker chuckled, but he hadn't paid heed to a word of the conversation. His loop made two backward revolutions—vertically at his right side—building with each turn. It made two quick rounds over his head and lashed out like a lizard's tongue, snaring a pair of horns among the hundreds.

Caleb judged the beef as Walker pulled it toward the nearest branding fire. It was a yearling bull, well formed, unbranded.

"Heel him, son!" the big man shouted as they came close to the fire. "Y'all got Bill Maverick's iron hot?"

"You bet," said one of the hands.

N.C. made a cold throw and caught one hind leg.

Walker had turned his mount to face the roped bull, and the horse was leaning back to keep the rope taut. "Tail him down for me, Hard Winter!"

The drifter rode up to the bull, grabbed the tail, and pulled hard, slamming the brute to the ground. He reined aside and saw Walker stalking toward the fire to take the iron from the cowboy who had picked it from the coals. They were near the CU wagon, and Caleb happened to see Dave Donaldson's head rise above the side boards, wrapped in a blood-stained bandage.

"Funny thing about Bill Maverick's brand," Walker said in his loudest speaking voice. "You turn it over, and it makes a *W*. That's my brand, duly registered. Now, if a feller was to get in a hurry, and not look at which side a maverick fell down on when his partner tailed him, why, he could accidentally make ol' Walker Colt Kincheloe possessor of said maverick."

The big man carried the glowing iron to the bawling young bull, and put his boot against the backbone of the brute. He held the smoking metal just off the hair, prepared to burn the M on the bull's hide. He looked up, grinning at the CU wagon.

"Mornin', Dave!" he called out, and when the cowboys turned their heads, he inverted the iron handle in his grasp and made the brand sizzle on the brute's hip. "Come up, Ol' Shine!" he bellowed, and his horse obeyed, slacking the rope.

Deftly, Walker loosed the head rope, and N.C. dragged the bull backward to keep it from getting up and butting his father. When Walker was mounted, N.C. slacked his rope. The bull got up and trotted back toward the main herd.

"*Adios,* boys!" The big man waved his hat, and rode west behind the bull.

Caleb swallowed and fell in behind Walker and N.C., well aware that Walker had just made him an accomplice to cattle rustling, albeit by the twisted Bill Maverick laws of Wyoming Territory. As they cut through the main herd again, Walker stayed on the tail of the fresh-branded bull, pushing it all the way through the main herd and to the other side, across Powder River, and into his own small bunch of beeves.

They said nothing. The smell of burned hair and flesh lingered a while. The upside-down *M* on the mavericked bull oozed and bled a little, until the dust caked on it and made it stop.

FOURTEEN

A B STOOD ON the depot platform, his arms crossed over his chest. Steam and cinders drifted by the authoritative expression he purposefully held rigid on his face. His eyes drilled the conductor, who was just stepping off the train. The conductor looked up, saw the old man, and Ab released an insolent snort that made his shoulders lurch.

Greasing the tracks had paid off. The railroad was grudgingly continuing to serve Holcomb rather than bother with cleaning the tracks daily, or sending an investigator to catch the culprits. Even so, Ab knew it was a temporary victory. He had driven a one-horse gig out onto the prairie yesterday and had found survey stakes driven along the new railroad route.

He had pulled several of them out and thrown them aside, but it was tedious getting in and out of the gig with the wooden leg, and he couldn't reach the short stakes from his seat. He had tried running over the stakes for some time, finally realizing that nothing he could do to the stakes would stop the new road from bypassing his town.

The word would be out now. Questions would be asked. Panic would begin. He had to hold this town together somehow. It was all he had left worth anything to him, what with a wife and two sons in the ground, and a third off gallivanting around somewhere.

He slipped a finger inside his jacket and touched the folded letter in his breast pocket—the letter from Caleb. There was no way around it. He had to save this town. He had to leave something for Caleb. Maybe Caleb would come home to stay before Ab went to join Ella. Ab could not for the life of him see why not. Everything Caleb needed was here. The wild mountains to the west. The open plains to the east. The town where he could play his fiddle at dances or picnics. No saloons, of course, but did that boy have to get drunk to play? Not much ranch left, either, but there were horses to train and ride. What was that boy doing out there?

"Mornin', Colonel."

Ab's glare angled down the depot platform, then softened. "Mrs. McCoy."

Tess giggled. "I still ain't used to that."

"What do you mean?"

" 'Mrs. McCoy.' When folks call me that, I always want to look over my shoulder to see who they're talkin' to." She slapped her thigh and laughed. "I was just plain ol' Tess Wiley for so long. Now to be 'Mrs. McCoy'—I declare."

Ab grunted. He didn't quite see the high significance of being a cowboy's wife. Tess's husband had worked for him long enough that Ab knew Piggin' String McCoy didn't own any pedigrees. Well, the honeymoon was hardly over, and Tess would surely soon enough see the ere of her ways. "Full up?"

Tess knew the routine. Colonel Holcomb asked the same question of her every time she crossed his path. She ran the boardinghouse Ab owned in town, and about all he ever wanted to know of her was how many rooms were vacant and why.

"One vacant."

"Why?"

"Mr. Taylor left town."

"Who's that?"

"You know, the little bald-headed man who sold machines to all them farmers. He said there wasn't much point in him stayin' around here if he couldn't get his orders in on the railroad. Don't know what he meant by that, do you?"

"I'm sure I don't. What brings you to the depot?"

Tess unrolled a sheet of paper in her hand. "I'm gonna pin notice of the vacancy up on the wall in case anybody should get off the train and need a room."

"Fine," Ab said, nodding his approval. "Good day, Mrs. McCoy." He strode down the landing, the end of his peg leg thudding against the thick planks.

When he arrived at the bank, Terrence and Frank Mayhall were waiting outside his office door.

"What's the meaning of this?" Terrence said, shaking a newspaper in Ab's face.

Ab took the paper and read the one-column headline on the front page: NEW ROUTE STAKED FOR DENVER AND RIO GRANDE. "Step into my office," he said, not wanting to cause a stir in the bank lobby. He slammed the door behind the Mayhall brothers, rattling the glazed glass.

"How long have you known about this?" Terrence demanded.

"Known about what?" Ab said, sitting behind his desk. He wished the Mayhalls weren't here. He wanted to take the peg off and rub the stub of his knee.

"The railroad," Terrence said.

"There's nothing to know. The railroad changes its mind every other week about some schedule or some route. I never credit anything they say.''

''When they drive stakes, it's time to credit what they say,'' Frank said calmly, pulling a chair up to the front of the desk.

Terrence picked the paper up from the desk where Ab had dropped it. ''It says here that Holcomb will lose rail service. How long have you known about that?''

''What business is it of yours how long I've known anything?''

''Did you know before we bought the Ingram place?''

''What if I did?''

''Then you sold us the place under false pretenses,'' Frank said, his arms draped casually on the armrests of the chair.

Ab's eyebrows rose at Frank's choice of terminology. ''What would you know about such things as pretenses? You are a dirt farmer from Georgia.'' Quickly, he raised his palm. ''Nothing wrong with that, of course. I was a dirt farmer from Pennsylvania when I came here, but I didn't claim to be an expert on law.''

''We want out of the Ingram deal,'' Terrence blurted. He sat on the edge of his chair, reached out, and put a fist on the desk. ''The railroad pullin' out changes everything. We can't get supplies anymore without going to Colorado Springs. We ordered a new drill, and nobody will ship it here because the D.R.G. says we don't even have rail service now. We barely had enough to make mortgage payments on the Ingram place as it was, and now we're not gonna make it, because you didn't tell us about the new route.''

''This bank is not responsible for predicting the whims of the railroad,'' Ab said. ''Besides, you're getting worked up over nothing. I just came from the depot, and the train stopped this morning, just like always.''

''Listen, Colonel,'' Frank said. ''They've driven stakes. They're gonna build a new road and bypass this whistle-stop town of yours. It's already putting a squeeze on us we hadn't counted on. We can't pay wagon freight back and forth to Colorado Springs and still make our mortgage payments on the Ingram place.''

''That's not my problem,'' Ab said. ''Can't you see I've got my own worries? There's the land office, the boardinghouse, my truck farms, this bank . . . I don't have time to keep your books for you. I can't help it if you've overextended yourselves.''

Terrence pounded his fist on the desk. ''Goddamn it, Holcomb! You knew about the railroad, didn't you? You wanted us to buy the Ingram place!''

"Easy, Terrence," said Frank, pulling his brother back. "And watch your tongue. You know how the colonel hates cussin'.''

"One more outburst," Ab warned, glaring at Terrence. He pointed a long old finger at the ceiling, then at the door.

"Here's the problem, Colonel. Costs have gone too high for us. We can't meet the mortgage on the Ingram place, and if we don't, you'll take it and that other quarter section we put up for security. Now that just don't seem fair, seein' as how things have changed. So, what we want is for you to let us out of the deal. We've already made two mortgage payments. We don't expect to ever see that again. You can keep that for your trouble. Then, just take the Ingram place back, and go on to sell it again. Won't cost you nothin'.''

Ab sighed and intertwined his fingers across his chest. "You men just don't understand, do you? This is not the Kingdom of Absalom. I can't do just whatever I please. I have to show a profit for the investors who built this town, this bank, the land office. You took your chances when you signed that mortgage, and if you can't meet the payments, you'll have to pay the consequences.''

The Mayhall brothers sat in silence: Terrence fuming, Frank refusing to show any hint of consternation.

"You've still got land to spare," Ab offered. "You didn't mortgage your whole spread, did you? You'll get down to a leaner weight now. Probably just what you boys needed.''

Terrence sprang to his feet, his burly frame quivering with rage. "Let's go, Frank, before I kill this old bastard.''

Frank smiled and rose slowly. "Easy, Terrence.'' He put his hand on the muscular shoulder and looked at Ab. "I couldn't hold him back if I tried, you know, Colonel. Never have been able to whip him. Hell, me and Edgar together can't whip Terrence when he's riled like this. 'Course, if Edgar was here, we'd be holdin' him back. He was so mad I wouldn't even let him come down here with us. He said a bullet's too good for you, Colonel. Wanted to gut you with his frog sticker.''

Ab thought about the Walker Colt in the desk drawer where he had left it, but he didn't reach for the drawer. Terrence Mayhall could come over the top of the desk in half a second if he wanted to. "Threats won't get you out of the Ingram deal.''

"Maybe not," Frank said, pulling Terrence toward the door. "But that Ingram deal's gonna get you into more hell than you ever bargained for. You just remember that we offered you a way out, and you wouldn't take it.'' He put his hat on. ''You just picked a bad fight, Colonel. There's four of us Mayhalls, and only one of you. Who do you think's gonna fight us with you? That no-'count fiddlin' son of yours?''

Ab moved with such a flinch that his peg leg rapped the bottom of his desk. He reached for the drawer, his vision blurring with rage. He put his palm on the butt of the Colt, but Frank Mayhall's hand gripped his wrist like the talon of an eagle.

''Easy, Colonel. You don't want to give us a reason to kill you. That would take all the fun out of stompin' your world into dust. I don't aim to take you down with a bullet. I aim to use the law.'' He wrenched the ancient weapon away from the tired old man. Strolling across the office, he dropped it disrespectfully on a chair by the door. ''We'll see you in the courthouse, Colonel.'' He smiled and tipped his hat.

After they left, Ab rubbed his wrist where Frank had gripped it. They were four strong young men, full of themselves. Ab was old, tired. They hated him, and he had given them good reason, beginning years ago when he had refused to help Terrence Mayhall prove up in Monument Park, just so he could take over Terrence's claim.

He reached a trembling hand into his jacket and touched the letter. Where was Caleb?

FIFTEEN

CALEB STOOD ALONE at the open door of the big house. He pulled his hands out of his pockets, tried hitching his thumbs over his gun belt instead. The house maid had been gone a full five minutes. Savannah should have come down by now. Maybe it would serve better to turn his back to the door. He faced about, walked to the steps of the wide veranda, leaned against a column.

The Bighorns were beckoning to the west, holding thin clouds like tufts of white hair snagged on the barbs of a wire fence. It was time to move on. Red Hawk was trying to learn farming down in Indian Territory. Caleb should have been there to help by now. He had promised old Chief Long Fingers. He could not go, of course, without spending a day or two in the Bighorns. Hell, Red Hawk was probably not in that big of a hurry to become a farmer, anyway.

He felt something like a scorpion crawling down his back, and turned to see the cool blue eyes staring.

"Mornin'," the drifter said, taking his hat from his head. He willed his eyes to remain above her buttoned collar, though he noticed she looked him over quite casually from spurs to bandanna.

Her right shoulder was against the door facing, her arms crossed, gathering her breasts beneath the smooth folds of the white silk blouse. "Did you want something?" she asked.

He reached into his vest pocket for the envelope. "I have a letter for you from your brother." He approached her, his heels and spurs making lazy music on the porch floor.

Savannah straightened to take the letter. She glanced at it and tossed it onto something inside the house. "Thanks," she said, leaning casually against the door frame again.

"Aren't you gonna read it?"

"Maybe later, if I want to."

He caught himself staring at the curve of her cheek, wishing he could caress the back of her neck with his fingers and stroke that smooth round cheek with his thumb. "Well," he said putting his hat back on, like throwing a saddle blanket on a horse, "that was all."

"What are you doing today?" she asked, smiling as if to make fun of whatever he might have planned.

He scratched the back of his head, tilting the hat over his brow. "Gittin' my outfit ready to leave tomorrow."

She scoffed. "That should take all of fifteen minutes. Want to take a ride with me?"

Caleb caught his answer in his throat, determined to pace himself. "Where to?"

"Where would you like to ride?"

"High country," he said, jutting his thumb.

"Can I ride your stallion?"

"Whiplash? No, ma'am."

"Don't call me ma'am," she scolded. "I'm younger than you are. If I can't ride your stallion, I don't want to go. I can handle any horse you can ride, Caleb Holcomb. That spotted stallion doesn't scare me."

"That spotted stallion killed my brother. Threw him into a canyon while he was shootin' at a deer. But that ain't the reason I can't let you ride him. He just needs the rest, that's all. You can ride him some other time, just as far as you please."

She stepped out onto the porch. "You mean it?"

"Sure."

Her eyes narrowed, and she put her hands on her hips. "What 'some other time' did you have in mind, if you're leaving tomorrow?"

"I reckon I'll drift back this way soon enough. Maybe help Walker with the work this fall."

She tilted her head forward and smiled. "I'll hold you to it, you know. If I have to come and find you in Colorado, I will ride that stallion."

"Like I said, you're welcome to ride him some other time. Don't put yourself to any trouble. Now, do you want me to saddle us a couple of horses out of the stable, so we can ride into the mountains, or not?"

"Yes," she said, turning back into the house. "Just give me a few minutes."

Caleb strolled to the stables and chose a pair of pet horses to saddle. He fitted them with good saddles and waited. He led the horses out to the rail and waited some more. He loosened the cinches, and the minutes turned to an hour. Finally, Savannah arrived, having changed into her boots and riding skirt, carrying sandwiches wrapped in cloth napkins.

As they rode out, they passed by the corrals where N.C. was working with a two-year-old bronc.

"Sorry you couldn't come with us," Savannah cried, almost laughingly. Then she tossed her pale blond hair at him and spurred to a trot.

"You've got a mean streak in you," Caleb said.

"Don't you?"

He thought for a few seconds. "I've done some mean things, I guess. Mostly out of ignorance."

"That's a convenient excuse."

She rode to his right, and as they talked, Caleb noticed that she glanced often at the Colt revolver in his holster. After an hour, the open plains gave way to slopes of evergreens and aspens. Savannah chose a place in the sun, where the wind barely made the new aspen leaves flutter. Spring grass was bright green here, and a diamond-clear stream of fresh melted snow shushed them nearby where it fell over black rocks.

They ate the sandwiches and gave equally cryptic answers to questions about each other's lives. Savannah got some cold water in a tin cup and offered Caleb a drink, and they drank it all.

"Teach me to shoot that pistol," she said.

The drifter drew the weapon. "You don't know how?"

Even her sneer was pretty as she looked down on the plains, for she could see the TW mansion from here. "Hiram taught me to use a rifle, but he won't let me have pistols. He's afraid I'll shoot myself in the leg." The tin cup was hanging by the handle from her finger.

Caleb's smile lifted his mustache as his gaze fell to her skirt. "That would be a shame."

She looked at him without turning her head, and smiled bashfully, though she didn't blush. "I'm not afraid of getting shot. Are you afraid to teach me?"

He put the revolver back in the holster. "That cup will be your target." Taking it from her, he put it on a rotting log some twenty paces away. He drew the Colt again, stood beside her, and faced the target. "First you cock it," he said, showing her how to pull the hammer back, "then you aim it, and pull the trigger." He eased the hammer back down and handed the weapon to her.

Savannah took the gun, smiling. "It's heavier than I thought," she said. She wouldn't let Caleb know how nervous she was. The hammer was harder to pull back than she had imagined, and she had to use both thumbs.

"Watch it," Caleb warned. "Like your brother says, the barrel's short. It's easy to shoot yourself."

She scoffed and lifted the weapon to aim.

"Not like that." He took her arm in his hands and straightened it, locking her elbow. She had surprisingly sinewy limbs, he thought, for a spoiled rich girl. "It'll kick. Keep your arm straight."

She held the gun at arm's length as long as she could, but it wavered impossibly in the air. "It's heavy," she complained, letting it drop.

"Use both hands," he suggested. He reached around her shoulders to put her left palm on the gun grip. "Don't aim all day. Go ahead and shoot."

She lifted the weapon again, and Caleb slid his hands back to her shoulders, holding her steady. The pistol fired, rearing high in her grasp, and she fell back against him.

"How did I do?" she asked. The ringing in her ears made her feel out of control.

"Well, you hit the mountain. Try again."

Savannah's second and third shots kicked up dirt. Her fourth and fifth shots blew chunks out of the rotten log.

"You're shootin' low. Don't bury the bead so deep this time."

She cocked the pistol, feeling more at ease with it now. She held her breath as she aimed, and pulled the trigger with both sights aligned on the target.

The tin cup rang and tumbled to one side.

Through the whining in her ears, Savannah could hear Caleb laughing, and she felt his strong hands on her shoulders. She let the gun drop to her side in her left hand, knowing it was spent now, and harmless. With her right arm she reached above her, taking in the back of the drifter's neck, warm under his shaggy brown hair. She looked up, smiling, her eyes dancing, and pulled his face down on hers.

She felt his hand slip around her waist, his fingers spreading out on her stomach. She broke away from his lips and turned to face him, finding his shirt buttons in her face. "You're tall," she said. "I should stand uphill."

Cautiously, Caleb stepped around her, feeling off balance as he moved to stand below her on the slope. She put her arms over his shoulders, and raked his hair with the fingers of her right hand. Her left hand still held the Colt. She kissed him again, and leaned against him so hard that he thought they would both fall down the mountain.

"Caleb Holcomb," she said, breaking away from him. "Would you like to roll with me in this fresh spring grass?"

Caleb forgot about pacing himself. "I would," he admitted.

Her arms dropped from his shoulders, and she slipped the revolver into his holster before backing away. "Not until you let me ride that stallion." Her smile was wicked, and beautiful. Her eyes glinted.

He watched her walk toward the horses, yearning now for a cold handful of mountain spring water to splash in his face. She looked back at him once, and laughed. Little Savannah Baber had a reckless mean streak.

SIXTEEN

N.C. SHUDDERED AND let his weight settle on the damp flesh of the whore. He caught his breath, lifted his head, and took his first close look at her through the rouge and eye shadow. He suddenly wished it was later— darker.

"Somethin' wrong?" she asked, her voice strained under his weight.

He shook his head quickly, pushed his knees deep into the goose-feather mattress, and floundered off of her. He banged his shin on her bony knee and rolled heavily to one side, making the bedsprings squeak like a fence tangled with cattle. "Mind if I lay here a minute or two?"

She rolled toward him and patted his hairless chest. "Quick as you got done, I guess we can both take a rest. Nothin' but a bunch of stinkin' cowboys down there, anyway." She billowed the linen covering them with a blast of cool air. "You smell cowboys on me?"

N.C. drew a whiff. He smelled some rank things here, but didn't know for sure that they originated with cowboys. "You smell plumb sweet to me," he said.

He closed his eyes and put his hand over the whore's hand on his chest. She dug her nails playfully into his flesh, and he smiled. Right now, he appreciated few people more than this whore, whatever her name was. Not that it mattered. You could tell they didn't use their real names, anyway. This one was called Lacy, or something like that. He only wished Savannah Baber could see him right now. That would sure knock her down a peg or two.

It was still on his mind the way Savannah had snubbed him the day he left the TW. Caleb Holcomb was getting his outfit together to leave, Savannah watching from the stables, when Walker marched up and said, "Hard Winter, I decided N.C.'s gonna go with you."

He had forgotten exactly what Caleb had said, but it had been something to the effect that he didn't need a kid tagging along behind him like his pack mule, Harriet.

"I got no choice, Hard Winter. I shouldn't have got you and the boy tangled up in that trouble on Powder River, but I did, and now both of you'd best stay out of the territory till this Bill Maverick bullshit floats on downstream."

It had taken some convincing, but Walker C. Kincheloe did not take no for an answer when he wanted something. N.C. threw a bedroll together and saddled up with Caleb. That was when Savannah came loping out of the stable on her best thoroughbred to ride with them a mile or so south.

She engaged in some shameful flirtations with Caleb, behaving as if N.C. wasn't even there. The fiddler, oddly enough, just seemed put out with her. Savannah kept asking when he was going to let her ride that stallion, Whiplash, and Caleb kept saying that it was pretty much up to her, as he would just as soon she ride him the next time she had the chance.

"I will ride that stallion, Caleb Holcomb. If you think I'm just teasing, you're in for a surprise. I'm not some ignorant little farm girl, you know."

N.C. still hadn't figured out what she meant by that, and Caleb's response had made no more sense:

"I've known some farm girls could show you a thing or two."

Savannah had turned back about then, without so much as saying so long to N.C. That had irritated N.C. to no end, and he was about as cordial to Hard Winter Holcomb as the fiddler was to him the first few days they rode together. Then they got to Cheyenne, and things began to look up.

Caleb got them cots and meals in the back room of a parlor house in exchange for playing the fiddle, and N.C. ended up getting free use of a whore by virtue of the fact that he was a friend of Caleb's and the girls liked the way Caleb sang. And, also, it was N.C.'s first time with a whore—or any woman, for that matter—and these soiled doves believed in making customers out of boys. They had laughed a great deal about that prospect, and had given him his choice among them.

After that, he was proud to ride with Caleb Holcomb. They boarded the stock cars to ride to Denver, then to Dodge City. Caleb made train fare by playing in various dives and disorderly houses, and N.C. went broke paying prostitutes. Caleb had loaned him the three dollars to pay Lacy, or whatever her handle was. For the life of him, N.C. could not see why every man in town with a livelihood did not visit the whorehouse at least once a day.

The bed moved, his eyes opened, and he heard the fiddle wailing "Fire on the Mountain" downstairs. Squeaking springs drowned out the music and Lacy rolled out.

"You'd better git," she said, "or Maude will want you to pay double fare. It is just so damn busy here lately with leather-legged cowboys."

They rode south from Dodge, for there were no rails into the Cheyenne and Arapaho reservation. Caleb pushed hard. Green grass was high, and it was well past time for plowing and planting.

"You didn't get you a whore back there, did you?" N.C. asked.

Caleb sighed. He was sick and tired of hearing N.C. describe the details of his encounters with damsels of spotted virtue. The boy had talked about almost nothing else since Cheyenne. At first, it had been amusing, but now it was getting tiresome. He wondered if he had ever gone on like that about whoring. "No, I didn't get no whore there. Or Denver, or Cheyenne."

"How come not?"

"I don't take that trail no more."

N.C. walked his horse beside Whiplash for two silent miles. "Why the hell not?" He turned a worried stare upon Caleb. "You didn't use yourself up, did you?"

The drifter chuckled. This boy knew cows, but he was sure ignorant on life. "What is your opinion of whores?"

"Hell, I like 'em!"

"That's plain. But would you marry one?"

"Lord, no!"

"Why not?"

"Hell, every man in the country'd have beat me to my honeymoon!"

"So you're sayin' a whore ain't good enough to marry."

"They don't want to marry. They ain't the marryin' kind."

"But if you found one that wanted to get married—a real pretty one at that—would you marry her?"

N.C. thought so hard that his eyes squinted. "I don't think I could, Caleb. They ain't got no . . . What do you call 'em? Manners?"

"Morals?"

"Yeah. I like 'em and all, but hell, they'll do anything."

They came to a creek and took a few minutes getting up and down the slick muddy banks.

When they were across, Caleb said, "You know what makes it possible for a whore to earn her keep?"

The boy grinned so wide that his ears touched the brim of his hat. "Yeah, that thing between her legs!"

"That's only half of it. The other half is that thing between your legs. Whorin' is a two-part proposition. If a whore is no-'count, then the man who whores with her ain't no better. That's why I swore off of 'em."

N.C. snorted. "I don't see how a man could swear off of 'em, once he'd sampled 'em. I guess I'll just be no 'count."

"I reckon folks'll think that's what N.C. stands for." The fiddler sneered at a new drift fence he saw about a half mile ahead, the fresh wire still glinting in the sunshine. When they reached it, they had to pull staples from posts, let the barbed strands down, cross their stock, then replace the wires.

"It ain't possible, is it?" N.C. asked, a worried look on his face.

"What?"

"That a man could use hisself up whorin'?"

The drifter smiled as he mounted the Appaloosa stallion. "If it was possible, I guess I'd have done it."

They reached the Cimarron on the second evening, and camped on the south bank. N.C. was making himself handy around camp and Caleb was playing "Fisher's Hornpipe" on the mandolin, his fingers going up and down like the parts of some machine.

"Are we in the Indian Territory yet?" N.C. asked.

"Generally."

"How come you're goin' to help this bunch of Indians, anyway?"

Caleb took his time finishing the tune, then looked at the boy. "When I was a little kid in overalls there was still Indians around our place on Monument Creek. Arapaho, mostly. My mother made friends with 'em, givin' 'em beef and stuff, seein' as how it was their land we were squattin' on. There was this chief named Long Fingers that got to be good friends with our neighbor, Buster.

"Well, the government took their reservation, and after Sand Creek, moved 'em to Indian Territory on the Washita. Years later, Buster got me to track ol' Long Fingers down for him. I was driftin' then anyway, so I would stop and see old Long Fingers every year or two, carry letters back and forth between him and Buster. I got to be good friends with him, myself.

"This past spring, the Indian agent gave him a pass to visit his old range on the Monument. That's when he asked me if I'd help Red Hawk learn farmin'. Long Fingers figured it wouldn't take long before they open up the Oklahoma country, and take the tribal lands from the Indians. They're gonna have to know how to farm if they want to survive. You can't get enough to ranch on with a homestead.

"Anyway, I told Long Fingers I'd help 'em, and he give me an Indian name. Called me 'White Wolf.' Said that's the way I sing—like an old white wolf. He rode up the Arapaho Trail and crossed the divide that day."

N.C. stood on his blanket and let his knees buckle. He lay back on his saddle by the fire. "I never knew no Indians before. They ain't still scalpin' and killin', are they?"

Caleb targeted a bright orange ember, and spat, satisfied with the sizzle that erupted. "I wouldn't test 'em on it by foolin' with any young squaws."

Two days later, they reached the Canadian, which was running high and muddy. They dismounted and disrobed, wrapping their clothes in their slickers, tying them into bundles and slinging them across their shoulders to keep them dry. Caleb tied his instruments high on Harriet's pack saddle, and they waded in.

The water was cold, and N.C. hooted as his grip tightened on the saddle horn. He grinned through his fear of the swirling torrent, and heard Caleb boldly singing some lines from "Three Thousand Texas Steers," which gave N.C. some comfort until the fiddler got to the part about the cowboy who drowned crossing the Concho.

"Two of us in the whirlpool," Caleb sang loudly through one side of his mustache, "and one must there go under . . ."

They clung to their saddles, swam around some driftwood, and felt their horses take footing on the far bank. They were naked and shivering, the horses well winded when they finally stopped at the top of the south bank.

"I guess you know a song for everything," the boy remarked, anxious to get his dry clothes back on.

The next day turned out so sunny and windy that by noon the ground had dried and dust began to blow. They came to a fence, and Caleb cussed every strand of it.

"Do Indians run cattle?" N.C. asked.

"Some, but mostly they lease to Texans. Somebody needs to tell Red Hawk these Texans are overstockin' his range. There's hardly grass enough to feed your horse of a evenin'."

As they neared the crest of a high roll, Caleb pulled rein and pointed at the sky. "You see dust hangin'?"

N.C. squinted. "I thought I noticed it. You don't reckon it's Indians, do you?"

"Well, it's their land, ain't it? Let's ease over the top by them trees and scout the country."

They angled toward a clump of twisted oaks on the crest and walked their mounts slowly, looking for riders beyond.

"Column of fours," Caleb said, pointing toward a timbered creek bed. "That's the army."

"Thank God. Let's go down there and ride with 'em."

"You crazy? They'll think we're boomers and take us back across the line."

"What the hell's a boomer?"

Caleb sighed. Had he ever been this ignorant? "Settlers squattin' on Indian lands. They claim the Indians ain't got no right to it, and it's public domain. They organize in Kansas, and send parties down here all the time to stake claims. The army keeps runnin' 'em out, but they keep comin' back."

"Hell, let's just tell 'em you come to help Red Hawk."

"I don't have the right papers. You're supposed to get a pass or somethin' from the Indian agent."

They watched through the twisted oaks as the column rode on up the distant creek.

"If I wanted to get arrested, I could've stayed in Wyoming," N.C. moaned.

Caleb scoffed. "Yeah, kid, you're gittin' to be a regular outlaw everywhere you go."

SEVENTEEN

R ED HAWK TURNED his eyes away from the three Texans sitting across from him on his porch, and looked out at the rain. He rocked his chair a few times, then stopped. "That's not enough, gentlemen," he said. "The range is getting used too hard, and I want you to cut your herd back. Of course, I don't want to lose any revenue, therefore I'm going to ask for a dollar and a quarter a head this season. I know another party who is willing to pay it."

"Goddamn, Red Hawk," said Ball Grimes, oldest of the three men. "Maybe somebody'll pay that, but will they help you keep them boomers out?"

"The army is keeping the boomers out." Chief Red Hawk looked out over the muddy lane in front of the frame house he had built. A young hound trotted in from the rain, leapt onto the porch, and shook. The pup turned a couple of circles, then collapsed on the porch floor, sounding like an armload of stove wood someone had dropped.

It was hard for a soul raised against the solid earth to ever get used to these hollow-sounding houses. At night, Red Hawk would prowl through the rooms in his moccasins, and the lumber would creak, and loose windowpanes would rattle. It was spooky. He understood why the old ones clung to their tattered tepees.

Ball Grimes recrossed his legs. "You don't understand the government, Red Hawk. When I say keep the boomers out, I mean you gotta have a lobby in Congress standin' up for the right of the Indians to keep this reservation."

"You are a lobbyist as well as a cattleman?"

"No, but the cattleman's association pays a lobbyist."

"So do the confederated tribes. You don't have to educate me about the way your government works. I saw Congress in session when I went to Washington as part of a delegation a couple of years ago. Anyway, the party that is willing to pay a dollar and a quarter a head also belongs to a cattleman's association, and I'm sure they'll do their earnest best to keep the boomers out."

The rancher spit a long brown stream into the rain. "You're a horse-trader, Chief. All right, we'll up the ante." He nudged the men on either side of him. "Let's go thin that herd out like the chief said, boys."

Grimes and his partners stood, shook Chief Red Hawk's hand. The chief was smiling when they left. Not because he had negotiated successfully. Red Hawk suspected the Texans would not thin their herd at all. They would continue to pay the same amount in lease fees, and probably add to the herd. He was smiling because the talk of boomers had reminded him of old Chief Long Fingers.

"Boomers," Long Fingers had once told him, "is a funny name. The whites have many strange tribes."

Long Fingers was the wisest man Red Hawk had ever known, but there were things about Americans that the old chief had never been able to grasp. The boomers were not a tribe. There were no tribes among the whites, no warrior societies. White men were pitiable in the aloneness and the individuality they so foolishly cherished. They were souls adrift like feathers caught up in a whirlwind. As individuals, they could trust only themselves, and therefore could not be trusted. Their volumes and volumes of laws proved how untrustworthy they were. In the old days, the Arapaho had lived by the laws of common sense intended to benefit the tribe: the People. White men had no tribes.

Against this evil tribelessness, Red Hawk must preserve the integrity of the Arapaho Nation. He must not fail. The spirit of Long Fingers hovered everywhere around him, reminding him, speaking to him in dreams. For now, there was the reservation—such that it was—to give the People some sense of their humanity above all humanity. But the boomers would have their way eventually. The reservation would be allotted to the Arapaho in severalty, and each individual would possess his own little piece, as if that were the way the Great Spirit had intended it. Then there would be nothing tangible left to show the People their allotted place in the world. Then, only the Mystic could keep them one. This was something else the white man could never comprehend.

"When they all speak the English," Long Fingers had warned, "still, do not let the People forget what the name means. We are *Inuna-ina:* the Mother of All People. When the Arapaho are gone from the world, evil will destroy everything good. What hope remains for a people who have no mother?"

Red Hawk looked after the three Texans, and saw them in the mist with two other white men who had ridden down from the north. They spoke some, then parted ways, the two new riders coming up the lane, passing shacks and ragged tepees, square fields wounded by the plow and made ugly with mud. A pack mule followed the two riders, and upon the pack Red Hawk noticed the bulge of a guitar under the tarp.

He stood when they arrived, and bid them come onto his dry porch. "I have been expecting you, White Wolf."

This was welcome information to the musician. He had wondered if Red Hawk would believe him when he explained that old Long Fingers had given him the Indian name. "He told you before he left, did he?"

Red Hawk shook his head. "The spirit of Long Fingers came to me in a dream the night he died. Then he told me you are named White Wolf. He told me many other things, too. Do you ever dream of a white wolf?"

Caleb sniffed. "I don't put much stock in dreams."

"Sometime when you get exhausted—maybe even drunk—and then go to sleep—a hard sleep, and long—you will dream of a white wolf, and it will mean something."

"Yeah? What?"

Red Hawk shrugged. "Only you can say." He looked at N.C. "Who is this colt?"

"This here's N. C. Kincheloe. He's ridin' with me for a piece."

Wide-eyed, N.C. shook the chief's hand.

"Hell of a house you built here, Red Hawk."

"The roof leaks inside. I had no previous experience with shingles."

"I'll help you fix it when the weather clears up," Caleb said.

"I will be grateful for that. Want some coffee?"

"Sure."

"Bring any?"

Caleb smiled. "I'll get it."

"I'll chunk up the stove. You can put your horses in the shed around back."

Red Hawk went inside, and N.C. followed Caleb to the pack mule.

"How did he know my middle name?" the young cowboy said.

Caleb squinted at him. "Oh hell, boy, he just called you a colt, like anybody else'd call you a pup or a cub. Don't get spooked."

"He knew me," N.C. declared. "He knew your Indian name, too."

Feeling under the tarp covering the pack saddle, Caleb located the cloth sack he had filled with ground coffee back at Dodge City. "Red Hawk will fill your head with all sorts of bunkum to get what he wants out of you. Don't pay no mind to that dream talk."

"Daddy says Indians know things they won't tell white men, even if you was to torture 'em with hot coals. He says they can disappear into the ground, and make other people disappear, too."

"I guess if they could do that, they'd make every white man in the world disappear, wouldn't they? Now, take the horses around to the shed, and dry 'em off best you can."

N.C. took the reins, keeping a cautious eye on the windows of Red Hawk's house. It was dark inside, and he couldn't see anything, so he just kept on. Rounding the back corner of the house, he looked for the way to the shed, but some ghostly movement from the corner of his eye made his neck twist back like a spring.

She wore a yellow dress, with a bright red blanket covering both shoulders and enfolding both wrists. Her hair was loose, black, and gleaming, hanging full across one side of her bodice, revealing half the necklace of grizzly claws. Her face was turned to one side—for she was near enough to fog the glass with her breath—and her bare throat looked soft where it curved to meet her jaw. She was pulling up on the window sash, trying in vain to lift it. She pulled so hard that a long tendon appeared aside her throat, and her breast pushed the shining black hair flat against the pane.

N.C. stumbled over a bucket left out of place and attracted her attention. Their eyes met for a moment, startling them both, then the girl in the window sank into the darkness of the room and disappeared.

Once under the shed roof, N.C. unsaddled the horses and forked some hay to them. He found an empty burlap sack to rub them down with, then trotted back through the rain to the front door, daring to glance at the window on the way. He stepped over the hound dog pup, shivering on the porch floor. When he knocked, he heard Caleb holler for him to enter. He wondered if he would meet the girl inside. He hoped she would not be offended that he had looked in at her.

He took his slicker off and left it in a heap on the front porch, finding nothing to hang it on. He passed first through a parlor with no furniture, only buffalo robes and blankets on the floor, and a bucket catching drops of rainwater. A woman sat in the corner, stripping bark from willow switches with her teeth—not the pretty young thing he had seen in the window; maybe her mother. The woman didn't look up as he passed through the room. N.C. came next to a kitchen, where Red Hawk and Caleb sat at a table.

"I can handle a team," Red Hawk was saying. "I have no trouble plowing, planting, or cultivating. But it gets dry sometimes, and last year grasshoppers ate about half of everything."

"Did they come in a cloud?"

The chief shook his head, and made his hands crawl across the table.

"We can put up grasshopper fences and stop some of them."

"Grasshopper fences!" N.C. blurted, taking his hat off and sitting at the table.

"A strip of tin so high ought to do it." Caleb measured the height by holding his hand vertically on the tabletop.

"They'd jump over it," N.C. insisted.

"They ain't smart enough to know they can. They'll pile up against it like range cattle do when a norther drives 'em south against a drift fence.''

"What about drought?'' the chief asked.

"It helps if you plow in early winter. That way the soil is loose enough to soak up spring rains. But when it gets really dry, you need to irrigate some of the river bottom. You'll get flooded out there in wet years, but it'll pull you through in a drought. We'll take a ride when it dries out and see if we can't find a place to ditch some water out of the river.''

N.C. forced a blast of air between his lips. "I'd hate to be a farmer. Grubbin' in the dirt, and fencin' out grasshoppers.''

The rain on the roof and the drops falling musically into the parlor bucket made the only sounds in the house until a peal of thunder shook the lumber frame. Red Hawk stared through the rain-streaked window with no expression in his eyes.

Caleb gritted his teeth and glared at N.C. "Listen, boy. Red Hawk's killed buffalo a-horseback with arrows and lances. He's counted coup and taken scalps in battle with Utes before he was your age. I was there when he killed the comanchero, Angus Mackland, and if ever a man needed killin', he was the one. On his poorest horse he could outride you if I was to mount you astraddle of Whiplash, and he could beat you shootin' any gun you own at any distance. As long as you're under his roof, you'll mind your tone of voice.''

N.C. shrank back in his chair and considered crawling under the table. "What did I say?''

"It's all right,'' Red Hawk said. "He didn't mean anything. He's just a colt; he doesn't understand.''

N.C. looked hard at the profile of the chief, the straight nose dominating his features, the lips pulled tight and thin like a line. "How'd you know my middle name was Colt?''

Caleb rolled his eyes. He could smell the coffee now, so he rose to fill the cups.

Red Hawk guarded his expression, thought back to everything he had said to the green cowboy. Slowly he swept his eyes across the kitchen, until they found and held young N.C. Kincheloe. "I didn't know for sure. When the ghost of Long Fingers came in my dream, he told me White Wolf would be coming with a colt. I thought he meant a horse. But, thinking back on it, Long Fingers smiled at me when he said it in the dream. He makes jokes like that sometimes. When you and White Wolf arrived today, I judged your stock, and thought maybe the colt was you. So I called you a colt to see.''

Caleb grinned as he handed a cup of coffee to Red Hawk. "His front name's Navy. His daddy named him after a pistol.''

Red Hawk drilled the young man with a stare. "Then he's not to blame if he shoots his mouth off."

Caleb started laughing, his laughter sure and strong.

But N.C. felt the Kincheloe pride bow his back, and he pushed himself up higher on the arms of the chair. "Is that your daughter in the back room?" he asked, his voice straightforward.

The chief looked suddenly at him, a bit surprised. "What do you mean? There is no one in this house but the three of us, and my wife in the parlor."

N.C. shook his head and pointed toward the corner room, whose closed door he could see across a gloomy hallway. "I saw a girl tryin' to open the window in there when I took the horses around. A real pretty Indian girl, wearin' a bear claw necklace, a red blanket, and a yellow dress."

Red Hawk felt a wave of dread consume him. "That is my daughter's room, but she is away at the Carlisle School in Pennsylvania."

"I know a pretty girl when I see one," N.C. insisted. "There was a girl in that room."

Red Hawk rose, his knees scarcely able to hold him up. "I dreamed last night. A colt came to me on the plains. It was like long ago, when the plains were open, and no houses were there. This colt spoke to me."

N.C. looked uncertainly at the chief standing tall above him. "What did he say?"

"He said, 'Your daughter, the one they call Susan Red Hawk, loves you. And she is going home.' "

The chief turned, for the hallway was behind him. N.C. watched him walk to the bedroom door, and open it, bathing the hallway with the foggy light of a rainy day. The chief stood at the door for a moment, looking inside. He turned to young Navy Colt Kincheloe.

"You see," the chief said. "There is no one here." His eyes were sad, his mouth turned down. He looked toward the front door, though he could not see it, for the hallway opened sidewise into the parlor. But he stared that way—northward—until the pup on the porch howled, his young voice squeaking. The howl of a hound was a poor strain on a day such as this.

"That pup never makes a sound," the chief said, and his eyes were wild, as if with fear, glistening even in the dark hallway. Lightning flashed miles away. "The thunderbird is blinking his eyes."

Footsteps, like those of heavy boots, stomped upon the porch, and spurs rang; the ringing was slight, as if from tiny rowels. There was silence for a few seconds, then a fist rapped three times on the door, accompanied by another peal of rattling fury.

"I must see who has come," Red Hawk said, and he vanished up the hallway to answer the door.

Caleb put his cup of coffee on the table and strained to hear as the door squeaked open. The voices only mumbled: Red Hawk's low and reverent; the other halting and rough. All fell quiet for a long time, and thunder shook the earth again.

Low over the drops of rain and the echoes of the thunderbird—eerily, like a cross-tuned fiddle playing down some lonely draw—Caleb heard Red Hawk's song of mourning rise. He ignored N.C. as he walked past him and burst out onto the porch.

The chief stood in the rain, his palms catching drops, his eyes searching the gray. His wife stood beside him, weeping, looking confused.

N.C. came out behind Caleb, and the two of them acknowledged the soldier standing on the porch, his hat brim and slicker still dripping.

"This came," the soldier said, holding a limp leaf of paper in his hand. Neither Caleb nor N.C. reached for it.

The Arapaho were coming out of their shacks and tepees, some of them already trotting down the lane to Chief Red Hawk.

"Leave him," Caleb said to the soldier. "You'd better come in and have some coffee."

EIGHTEEN

THE WINCHESTER LOOKED odd and felt unbalanced with the carpenter's level clamped to the side of the barrel, but it was the only way Caleb knew to shoot the path of the irrigation ditch without fancy surveying tools. When he was a boy on Monument Creek, Buster Thompson had surveyed the irrigation ditches like this on the Holcomb homestead. It was funny what a person's brain could remember.

Placing the rifle on top of a five-foot tripod made of straight willow poles, the fiddler looked down the sights at Tommy White Fox, a promising young member of Red Hawk's band. Fifty yards away, Tommy held a single pole, five feet high. Caleb aimed his Winchester at the top of the pole that Tommy held, just as if he intended to blast it to splinters.

"All right," he said, once he had the sights trained on the target.

N.C. looked at the level. "You're high." N.C. judged the ground between himself and Tommy White Fox, waved the young Arapaho to the east.

Tommy moved ten paces and stood his pole on the ground again. Caleb aimed at the top of it, and N.C. watched the bubble in the level. "All right," Caleb repeated, holding the rifle steady. N.C. waited for the bubble to settle. "Mark it!" he shouted, loud enough for Tommy to hear him, and he watched as Tommy drove a stake where his pole had stood.

All day it had gone like this, and N.C. was worried fretful that some white man would happen along and see him working afoot. As he had suspected, farming did not at all suit him. Hitching the mules and cultivating was bad, but making the grasshopper fences had been plain demoralizing. Caleb had started him out cutting and spreading tin cans, and riveting them together into six-foot strips. He had been promoted to clipping discarded ceiling tin after that, and finally put in charge of erecting the fence.

"Don't tell Daddy," he had said. "Please, don't tell Daddy you ever made me build fences for bugs."

This surveying for ditches was more interesting, but it was still done afoot, and N.C. knew it would only lead to digging. And digging, and digging, and digging. Caleb claimed they could dig the ditch with a one-mule walking plow, but N.C. knew much of the dirt would have to be moved by grubbing hoe and shovel, and few of the Indians were interested in doing anything but watching.

He glanced up at the riverbank above him and saw the usual gathering of blanket Indians lined up on the brink.

"They sure do love work," Caleb said, reading N.C.'s eyes. "They could sit there and watch it all day."

N.C. managed a smirk. "Lazy as hell, most of 'em."

"When those old boys were bucks your age, hell, work was for squaws. All they wanted was to hunt, fight, and raise horses, and they didn't go at it lazy, either."

N.C. grabbed the tripod of willow poles and walked toward the stake Tommy White Fox had just driven. "I'm about through listenin' to what every man born was doin' when they was my age."

"Hey," Caleb said. He pointed at the riverbank.

N.C. looked. "Well, I'll be damned. Thought he'd never come around."

Red Hawk was coming down the riverbank, driving two mules before a dilapidated buckboard. The rusty walking plow rocked in the wagon bed as the buckboard trundled down to bottom land.

For two weeks Red Hawk had fasted on and off, singing monotonously at all hours, roasting in his sweat lodge, railing in his native tongue, wandering aimlessly about, praying. The death of his daughter, it seemed to the white men, would bring the death of Red Hawk himself. They had gone ahead with the farm improvements without him. In fact, N.C. had begun to think that the prolonged mourning was nothing but a put-on, and that the chief was just taking advantage of the circumstance to have white men do his farm work for him. He remembered burying his friend back at Milt Starling's Road Ranch, where he had first met fiddlin' Caleb Holcomb. The cowboys had mourned maybe two or three minutes over the mound of fresh dirt all mixed in with dirty snow. Red Hawk was taking it all just a little too hard.

He still hadn't quite figured out what had happened the day the soldier came to tell Red Hawk his daughter had died of typhoid fever in Pennsylvania. He had been over and over it, and knew damn good and well he hadn't seen a ghost. That girl was real. But Red Hawk was milking the mystery of it for all it was worth, and N.C. was weary of hearing about dreams and spirits and talking colts. Still, it improved his outlook somewhat to see the chief coming to help now, with the digging about to commence.

"What should I grow here?" the chief asked as he drew in the reins. He swung down from the seat and gestured toward a bucket of well water he had brought along, most of it having splashed out coming down the riverbank.

"Ordinarily, you'd grow some vegetables you can eat at home and sell at the fort," Caleb answered. "But it's too late for that this year. Maybe you can get in a crop of alfalfa hay if you can keep the horses out."

Red Hawk nodded. "Maybe next year we can plant some squash or melons. I like potatoes."

N.C. took the gourd dipper and drank deeply, letting the water run down his chin and the front of his shirt. He caught his breath and mopped a sleeve across his mouth. "You gonna dig with that plow?"

"Sure," Red Hawk answered. "I assume you boys will be ready to ride tomorrow, so I'll take over from here, now that you're almost finished marking the ditch."

N.C.'s heart raced.

"Ditch?" Caleb said, smiling. "That's no ditch, that's the Arapaho Canal."

Red Hawk grunted.

"Yeah, we'll need to be workin' our way toward the Sacramentos. I figure I better stop in and visit with my younguns."

"We're leavin' tomorrow?" N.C. asked for reassurance.

Caleb looked at him with his face all twisted with wrinkles. "You didn't think we'd stay here and watch the alfalfa grow, did you?"

N.C. grinned and slung the water from the gourd. "I knew *I* wasn't goin' to."

Red Hawk put his hand on the young cowboy's shoulder. "You were brought here for a reason. It was you who was to tell me of my daughter's death. It would have been no good to hear from that soldier."

"I didn't tell you. I didn't know a thing about it."

"You told me in the dream. And you saw my daughter's spirit in the house."

"Oh, that," he said, leaving it lie.

"I am going to give you a name now. I have been thinking on it for several days. Yesterday in the sweat lodge, I saw you in a vision. Only, you were not in the shape of a colt. You were in the shape of an eagle."

"If I was in the shape of an eagle, how did you know it was me?"

"It was you," the chief said, "and you were diving down to catch a rabbit on the ground. But when you sank your talons into the rabbit, a hand reached out of a pit and captured you by the leg. The rabbit was tied there, and you were fooled." The chief turned to speak to Caleb. "I captured eagles that way in the old days, to get feathers to make my headdress."

"So, what's my name?" N.C. asked.

"Your name is Eagle-on-the-Ground."

Caleb was taking a drink from the gourd when he heard the faint call of the eagle. Looking up, he saw it banking, a mile high, the sun glinting on the white flag of tail feathers. He sighed so heavily that droplets of water arched from his mustache. This was a hell of a time to see an eagle flying north. He shifted his eyes to take in the young cowboy. N.C. was staring upward, his mouth open. The boy looked about as dizzy as a one-eyed dog in a slaughterhouse.

"Well, Eagle-on-the-Ground," Caleb groaned. "You might as well take yourself on up to the shed and start gettin' our outfit together." It had taken him years to earn his name, White Wolf, from Chief Long Fingers, and it irked him considerably that N.C. could drift in here, moan about working afoot for a couple of weeks, and get an Arapaho handle hung on him on account of some dream. He couldn't help but think Red Hawk was awful liberal about doling out monikers. On top of that, the fiddler scarcely cared much for listening to a bunch of mystical hullabaloo from N.C. all the way to New Mexico. "Go on. Me and Red Hawk will finish markin' this Arapaho Canal."

Already the eagle had vanished in its vast realm, and N.C. only nodded. His horse was tied in the shade of a willow at the river's edge, and he walked there with his own visions of eagles occupying his thoughts.

Cinching his saddle down tight, he mounted and rode at a walk up the riverbank. He ignored the blanketed old ones sitting near the road. He felt the name, Eagle-on-the-Ground, taking shape in his mouth, but for some reason he couldn't bring himself to speak it.

Then he remembered his father. What would Walker C. Kincheloe say about his taking an Arapaho name? He didn't think the Arapaho had ever crossed his father, but Walker tended to lump red men together.

He was approaching Red Hawk's shed when he saw her. It was the girl he had seen in the window, only now stepping out of Red Hawk's back door, and closing it carefully behind her. She wore a different dress, but it was her, and she was real as a thousand head of cattle. He jerked at his reins, and the bridle jingled, catching her attention. She looked at N.C., gasped, and bolted.

"Hey!" he shouted. "You hold up, there!" He spurred his mount, overtaking her easily as she ran 'round the house and into the lane. "What were you doin' in there?" he demanded, cutting his horse in front of her.

She dodged once or twice, but realized she was caught. She fell back against the trunk of a large cottonwood and looked up at the cowboy, gasping for breath. "Let me go," she pleaded. Her eyes darted with fear, but the rest of her face gave away nothing.

"Why do you keep snoopin' around Red Hawk's house?"

"I only wanted to get something that was mine."

N.C. noticed that she was holding a necklace of bear claws and elk teeth, and she lifted it now in her grasp to back up her story. Gradually, he became aware of an uneasy thought: too bad he was leaving tomorrow— leaving this pretty Indian girl behind. He sensed his father's presence across the miles and felt ashamed. "If that's yours," he said, "why'd you have to go sneakin' into Red Hawk's house to get it?"

"My father doesn't let me go into the houses your people live in. He says they are haunted with evil spirits. Now, please let me go, before someone sees me talking to you and tells my father."

"What was that thing doin' in Red Hawk's house, if it belonged to you?"

"Susan was my friend, and I traded necklaces with her before she went away. I only wanted to trade back. I was looking for the necklace the last time you saw me in her room, and I almost got caught when Red Hawk came back into the house. I had to crawl out of the window!"

"Why didn't you just ask Red Hawk for the necklace?"

The desperation showed in her face now, and her eyes darted, hoping no one would catch her here talking to this white boy. "I am only a girl!"

she blurted. ''I don't bother a chief with things like a necklace! Anyway, I am Cheyenne, not Arapaho, and he isn't even my chief. I don't even speak his language.''

''You both speak English.''

''It's not the same thing. You white people don't understand how a chief must be treated. Will you let me pass now? Please, I'm begging you. I don't want to get caught.''

His heartbeat had slowed since catching her, but still it beat so strong that it almost made him dizzy. ''What's your name?'' he asked.

''I won't tell you.''

''If you don't, I'll tell Red Hawk I caught you in his house.''

''All right,'' she said, shaking the necklace. ''But, don't laugh at me. It's a good name in the Cheyenne language. In your tongue, it means 'She-Rabbit.' ''

N.C. did not laugh. ''My name,'' he said, trying it on for the first time, ''is Eagle-on-the-Ground.''

NINETEEN

THE TWO SETS of spurs rang at each other like noisy mockingbirds arguing sharply across a treetop. Red Hawk—padding silently toward the tepee on the south bank of the Washita—grimaced at the senseless noise white men had brought to his world. The young cowpuncher whom he had named Eagle-on-the-Ground actually had two jinglebobs on each spur, the sole purpose of which was to make more noise ring from the steel.

''I didn't do nothin','' N.C. suddenly blurted, adding his nervous voice to the rowel music.

Caleb glared back over his shoulder, for he was stalking ahead irritably, his arms and legs swinging in long pendulum motions. ''I warned you about foolin' with Indian gals, didn't I?''

Red Hawk veiled his amusement.

''I don't see why we don't just ride like hell and forget the whole thing,'' the boy said.

''You may not have to come back this way, but I do,'' Caleb snapped. ''It's time you learned to face up to your own trouble.''

''What trouble? I'm tellin' you, I didn't do nothin' but talk to her. What would happen if we just rode out?''

''Tell him, Red Hawk,'' Caleb said, for he didn't really know himself what might happen.

"One of two things," the chief said. "Lizard would ride after you; maybe kill you or something. Or he would report you to the Indian police, and the army would throw you in jail at the fort."

"For what?"

"Whatever he told them you did to his daughter."

"But I didn't do nothin'!" he shouted.

Red Hawk stopped fifty paces from the tepee. "Let me tell you about Lizard," he said, glancing around, as if about to share some secret. "He has 'heap medicine,' as the soldiers like to say. To the Indians, yes, but also to white men who have known him. There are soldiers alive today who will swear that Lizard can vanish right into the ground like a fog."

N.C. swallowed hard, panting.

"I used to ride with Lizard," Red Hawk continued. "In seventy-four, we were stealing horses beyond the reservation, harassing wagon trains and cattle drives. The army knew about us, and they put Lizard and me and seventy others in chains and took us east to imprison us in Florida.

"We woke up in a camp in Mississippi one morning, and found Lizard's handcuffs and leg irons on the ground, still locked. No one had even heard his chains jingle in the night. The soldiers went searching for him, but they never found a trace of him, even though the ground was muddy all around. He turned up in the Spanish Peaks in Colorado about a year later, but no one could bring him in.

"I spent three years a prisoner in the old Castillo de San Marcos in St. Augustine, Florida. I learned to speak English there—to read and write—and when I was released, I went on to two more years of learning at the Carlisle School in Pennsylvania. When I got back to the reservation, I became a follower of Long Fingers, because Long Fingers understood the white man's power. I joined the Indian police and tried to make a way in the future for the Indian, and especially the Arapaho.

"But Lizard was still a fugitive, and sometimes bounty hunters would go looking for him. Some of them came back and said Lizard would show himself just so he could disappear, and they would never see him again. A couple of those bounty hunters did not come back at all.

"So, I got permission to offer Lizard amnesty if he would return to the reservation. I rode to the Spanish Peaks to find him. I just camped, and waited for him to come to me, and he did. I brought him back to the reservation, and he hasn't caused any trouble since then.

"But Lizard has scars left by white men. And Lizard has visions, and his visions say the Indians will one day rise above the power of white men, and crush them into the soil. Lizard does not see any future in his daughter messing around with any white cowboy."

N.C. shot a worried look at Caleb. "I didn't do nothin' wrong." He pleaded with his hands, and glanced uncertainly at the tepee. "Hell, what kind of place is it you can't talk to a pretty girl out in broad daylight?"

"Indian Territory," Caleb said. "Come on, we might as well get this over with. Hope he doesn't want your scalp or somethin.' " He winked secretly at Red Hawk.

They started walking again, then stopped. Lizard had appeared before his lodge, and was standing there, glaring at them. The sun had risen over the timber of the Washita's bank, now illuminating the old warrior. He wore a trade blanket over one shoulder and under the opposite arm, revealing the shoulder of an old deerskin shirt. The blanket covered the rest of his getup, hanging to his feet. He gathered its ends in front of his chest with his fist.

As they approached, N.C. studied Lizard closely. The old warrior's hair was parted neatly in the middle. On the right side of his face, a thin braid hung. On the left side, his hair was pulled back behind the ear. The thick welt of a straight scar started on the warrior's left cheek and extended to the ear, which was split deep like that of a steer ear-marked with a swallow fork. The eyes looked bottomless, the mouth frowned.

When they reached the lodge, Lizard said nothing. He only turned and stepped gracefully through the oval entrance hole. Red Hawk went next, followed by Caleb, then N.C.

Sights and smells accosted N.C.'s senses, for he had never stepped inside a tepee before. A fire was burning low, but the smell of smoke could not cover the odors of old skins, tallow, gun grease, and roasted meat. N.C.'s eyes adjusted to the gloom, and he saw hides with Indian paintings lining the inside of the lodge poles. Most depicted battles or hunts: Indians on horseback shooting arrows and guns. Red paint showed plenty of blood flowing from wounded animals, enemy warriors, and soldiers.

Searching the floor of the tepee, N.C. saw hides spread underfoot. Through the thin smoke of the fire, something moved, and he caught sight of two bright eyes. They met his for just a moment, then returned to the ground. It was the girl—She-Rabbit. She was on her knees, wrapped in a drab blanket, her long hair hanging along the sides of her face as she cowered.

Lizard jutted his trigger finger at the ground below N.C.'s boots.

"He wants you to sit," Red Hawk explained.

But N.C. thought of his father, and Kincheloe pride stiffened him. "I sure ain't gonna sit down just because he tells me to."

"Maybe we ought to all just sit down about the same time," Caleb offered.

Red Hawk gestured to Lizard in sign. The men exchanged glares, and Red Hawk began slowly sinking, bending his knees. The white men, and Lizard, followed the chief's example, until all of them were nearly seated. Suddenly, Lizard sprang upward, and for a mere second glowered down at N.C.. Then he dropped to a sitting position on a couch made of rolled hides. As the white men crossed their legs, making room for their spurs, Lizard pinched some shavings of cedarwood from a pile and dropped them on the fire. They crackled as the flames licked them, and the old Cheyenne dog soldier signed at Red Hawk.

"He wants to know what you were doing with his daughter yesterday," Red Hawk said.

"Just talkin'," N.C. insisted.

Red Hawk made the translation: his right palm, upturned, jutting forward from his mouth.

Lizard returned the same sign as a question.

"About what?" Red Hawk said.

N.C. rolled his eyes, and swept them past She-Rabbit. He caught a glimpse of her expression, pleading with him without even looking at him. "I asked her about a necklace she had."

She-Rabbit closed her eyes, hoping the white boy who called himself Eagle-on-the-Ground wouldn't tell her father that she had snuck into Red Hawk's house. That would dishonor her father to the point that she didn't know what he might do. He might marry her to the first ugly brute to ask for her, just to be rid of her.

"He wants to know why a man would be interested in the necklace of a girl," Red Hawk said, making and reading sign as quickly as one could speak.

N.C. paused. "I wanted to buy it from her."

She-Rabbit's eyes flew open. He was lying to protect her. That was good. But how could Eagle-on-the-Ground know that her father, Lizard, could smell lies like a buzzard smelling death.

"What for?" Red Hawk asked.

N.C. shrugged. "A souvenir. Thought I might give it to my gal."

"What gal?" Caleb blurted.

"Savannah," N.C. said.

Caleb laughed.

"Lizard says you were seen chasing his daughter on your horse."

"Couldn't get her to stop and talk," N.C. said. "I guess she didn't want to have nothin' to do with me."

Silence and stillness filled the lodge, until Lizard spoke, looking at the ground between himself and She-Rabbit. Immediately, she lifted the necklace over her head, drawing her long hair through its loop. She handed it to her father without looking at him.

"He says since you want to buy it, you will pay twenty dollars for the necklace," Red Hawk said, taking the string of bear claws and elk teeth from Lizard.

"Like hell I will!" N.C. blurted. "I don't even . . ."

Caleb interrupted him, grabbing him by the shirt collar and pulling him to his feet. "Tell Lizard we'll need to discuss this." Stepping in front of the cowboy, Caleb took a twenty-dollar gold piece from his vest pocket and slipped it into N.C.'s hand. "If you tell him you ain't got no money," he whispered, "he'll know you're lyin' about the whole thing. Just give him the twenty, take the damned necklace, and let's get the hell out of here."

Caleb stepped away, and N.C. handed the gold piece to Red Hawk. The exchange was made, and N.C. found himself holding the necklace over which She-Rabbit had risked getting caught in Red Hawk's house. He looked at her, and found her staring pitifully at the ground.

"All right, let's go," Caleb said.

"Wait," N.C. replied. He thought for a moment, considered giving the necklace back to She-Rabbit, but knew that wouldn't suit old Lizard. He could think of only one way to smooth the whole matter over with her. Right now, he really didn't care what Lizard would do.

"Red Hawk," he said, "tell Lizard I'm givin' him this as a gift. I guess he'll do with it as he pleases, but I've decided I can't see as how it could favor anybody more than it does his daughter." He let Red Hawk sign the translation, then handed the necklace to the battle-scarred warrior.

Lizard glared momentarily, then snatched the gift from N.C.'s hand, only to toss it on the ground in front of She-Rabbit. He grumbled something to her, and she put the necklace back on, thankful to have it. She only wished she could thank Eagle-on-the-Ground before he left forever.

"I don't guess he's gonna gift you with my gold piece in return," Caleb grumbled, and watched as Lizard tucked the coin away in his shirt, as if in reply. "Let's go."

The white men turned for the entrance when Lizard spoke again, standing as his voice filled the tepee. His words took the time of cedar smoke rising to the vent hole above.

"What did he say?" N.C. asked, catching a strange glare from the warrior.

"I don't know," Red Hawk replied. "I don't speak Cheyenne." He signed to Lizard, asking him to give his daughter permission to translate. Lizard grunted at her.

Rabbit raised her head and looked at the men in her father's tepee, her eyes lingering on the stare of N.C. "My father said he knows who you are, Eagle-on-the-Ground. Your father is a great warrior, and has killed many human beings. But he is possessed by demons."

Lizard spoke again, brushing his finger across the scar on his cheek, and the deep gash in his ear.

"He said you must be careful that the demons do not possess you, too." She paused in her translation. "And thank you for giving my necklace back."

"He said that?" N.C. asked.

"No, I said that."

She-Rabbit bowed her head again, and Caleb helped N.C. out of the tepee with a shove.

TWENTY

"THERE'S YOUR DADDY," Amelia Holcomb said, trying to sound cheerful as she turned the baby toward the gravestone. What a ridiculous thing to say, she thought, feeling grateful that Little Pete couldn't yet understand her words.

It was true that they had buried her late husband's thawed-out body here on the hill overlooking Holcomb Ranch, but the soul of Pete Holcomb was on high somewhere. They had thawed him out because he was twisted hideously from falling down the face of that bluff Whiplash had pitched him over, and had frozen like that. The cowboys, and Ab, had tried not to let Amelia see him until he had been thawed out and straightened, but she had pushed her way past Buster, and she had seen him all contorted. It didn't really matter, looking back. It was just a frozen corpse. Pete wasn't any more in there than he was under the grave marker now.

At the time, she hadn't questioned Ab's decision to bury Pete up here on the hill, even though the Holcomb burial plot was down by the cabin, where Ella and Matthew had been lowered. It wasn't until later that she realized why Ab had done it. That was before the barbed-wire telephone. When Caleb and the old man were yet unable to speak to each other—when Ab would not even speak to Caleb to tell him another brother had died.

Caleb always came back to Holcomb Ranch this way, by the old Arapaho Trail that ran over the Rampart Range. By burying Pete here, Ab had fixed it to where the trail and the gravestone would tell Caleb. And that was how it had happened. Caleb had come home to visit Pete and found Pete's name chiseled in stone. A hard way to learn it. Even harder than seeing Pete twisted and frozen from that fall, she suspected.

Amelia knelt by the grave and placed the cut wild flowers against the stone. They were insignificant here, seeing as how living wild flowers sprouted all around the grave where Caleb had seeded them. There was only one piece of ground where they failed to grow: a blackened circle where Caleb made his campfires. He still came home this way. And he would camp here upon the evening of his arrival; and he would tell stories to Pete, and play songs and sing. Below, she would hear the mournful violin, and look up to see Caleb between the fire and stone, and she would smile, though tears misted her eyes. Perhaps it was well that Ab had buried Pete here after all.

She spread a blanket in the sunshine and lay Little Pete there on his stomach. Immediately, he began to crawl. He had the same spunk all the Holcomb brothers had shown all along. Matthew, the oldest brother, had been the wildest. It was Matthew who had first courted Amelia, and brought her here to the ranch from Colorado Springs. His reckless streak had killed him by the age of twenty: shot dead at a sawmill dance in old Colorado City.

By contrast, Pete had channeled his energy to far greater advantage. He had won Amelia's hand, taken over the ranch, brought religion to the cowboys by establishing a bunkhouse Sunday school. Then he, too, had died, thrown off the bluff while deer hunting alone, leaving Amelia a widow with child.

Now Caleb, the third-born of Absalom, was out there somewhere riding the same stallion that had thrown Pete into Cedar Root Canyon. What was he doing out there? Why couldn't he settle down? What could he possibly be looking for?

When she tried to conjure memories of their faces now, it was Caleb's who came most readily to mind. This had shamed her at first. Shouldn't Pete's memory have been strongest to her? Pete had been her husband, after all, the father of the son he never knew. In time, though, she had come to understand that Caleb's memory was strongest to her because he was the one left alive. Her mothering instincts were reminding her that Little Pete needed a man to take the place of his father. Caleb was blood kin. He was the best candidate. Certainly that was all there was to it.

A memory came to her. One that had been cropping up a lot lately. It was of the first time Matthew brought her to the ranch. The first time she met Caleb. Yes, the first time she met Pete, too, but it was Caleb who dominated the memory, even though she had married Pete. What if Caleb and Ab had never had that falling-out? What if Caleb had never started to drift? Would she have married him instead of Pete? Would Caleb have even wanted to marry her? Why was she even thinking of it?

"Oh, good heavens," she said. "Am I in love with Caleb Holcomb?"

She looked at the circle of charcoal and ashes where Caleb made his fire one night each spring; and where he warmed himself to talk to a departed brother. They had been so close, even beyond the miles and the months apart. Caleb had promised her just last winter that he would quit drifting and stay home to help raise Little Pete; yet he was out there again, wandering. She knew he hadn't meant to lie. It was that damned fiddle. Caleb forever craved a new audience. That was the thing that galled him like a spur. Amelia desperately wanted Caleb to stay here, and yet she knew a settled life would spell misery for him. Who would listen to the music? Who would dance? Laugh at the stories? Who would beg him to play on, sing one more?

She glanced back at the blanket and saw that Little Pete had already crawled off and had a handful of dirt headed toward his mouth. "No you don't," she scolded. She grabbed him, dusted the dirt away, and put him back down in the middle of the blanket. Instantly, he was crawling toward the dirt again. She was going to need help with this one. Where the devil was Caleb?

Motion below caught her eye, and she focused on five riders trotting from Holcomb. They were too far away yet to recognize, but something about their pace told her they meant business. Maybe it was the whole specter of the dying town beyond them; and the distant smoke of the engine on the new tracks far to the east. The town of Holcomb was doomed—bypassed now by the railroad—and Colonel Ab had been brooding like some starving vulture over the whole affair. It was a bad time right now on what was left of the old Holcomb Ranch.

The riders were closer now, and Amelia could see that two of them were riding mules. One was Terrence Mayhall, his muscled outline recognizable even at this distance. The other Mayhall brothers certainly accompanied him. But who was the fifth horseman? Was he wearing a derby? Yes, he was!

Little Pete made a sound, and Amelia caught him too late this time to prevent the mouthful of dirt. "Oh, you!" she said, snatching him and the blanket up as a hawk would lift a mouse. She dusted the dirt away with the blanket and moved swiftly toward her mount: a ten-year-old Appaloosa mare, gentle and stolid, waiting with dumb glazed eyes near the gravestone.

Mounting with Little Pete under one arm, she looked again toward the riders. Already, Ab was coming out of his cabin, and Buster was coming in from his field to confront them. She nudged the mare with her heels and eased down the hill on the old Arapaho Trail. What could the Mayhalls possibly want here but trouble? Where the devil was Caleb Holcomb?

TWENTY-ONE

THE FIVE RIDERS stopped by the two-rut wagon road where Buster waited. "Howdy, Buster," Terrence Mayhall said, perched smugly on a large mule.

"Mister Terrence," Buster replied, bending the brim of his hat down in a greeting. "Can I help you gentlemen with somethin'?"

"What's that growin' yonder?" Frank Mayhall said. He was watching Ab approach as fast as the old wooden leg would allow, but he was pointing toward a ten-acre square to his right.

"Milo," Buster replied.

"What the hell is milo?"

"Sort of like sweet sorghum, but it's supposed to weather drought better. Figured I'd try me a little of it."

"Always tryin' somethin' new, ain't you, Buster?" Terrence turned to the man wearing the derby, a city-dressed man, clean-shaven, who nevertheless sat very naturally on a poor livery mount. "Now, Mr. Little, let me tell you about Buster, here. Once't he was a slave, but he ex-scaped and come out here to homestead. Beat all the other settlers, and got all this good acreage on the creek. Always tryin' somethin' new, like that milo there. I tolt him once't, I says, 'Buster, you must be the smartest nigger I ever heard tell of,' and you know what he said? He says, 'That's plumb right, Mr. Terry, and I's smarter than some white folks, too!' "

The Mayhall brothers burst into laughter over Terrence's impersonation, except for young Joe, who only seemed nervous waiting on his mule. Mr. Little did not smile, but neither did he regard Buster Thompson with any degree of interest.

"One thing I'll say for Buster," Terrence continued, "he proved up honest on everything he's got. He sure 'nough plowed and lived on his homestead, and you can see his pines growin' on his timber culture claim." He paused a few seconds, for Colonel Absalom Holcomb was just now limping within earshot, and he wanted the old man to hear this: "Buster ain't like some other folks along this creek. He never did get greedy and go to cheatin' the homestead laws to get more than his share."

Ab stopped in front of the five mounts and glared at Terrence Mayhall. He leaned on his walking stick with his left hand and propped his right fist on his hip, sweeping the tail of his coat back to reveal the gun belt, and the old Walker Colt, which he had taken to wearing almost everywhere he went these days. "Who are you?" he asked, his trouble-clouded eyes swiveling to pierce the man with the derby.

The stranger swung down from his borrowed horse and strode forward, removing his derby. "I'm Delton Little," he drawled. "General Land Office."

Ab shook the man's hand cautiously. The city clothes and the derby could not detract from the way Little had so naturally swung down from the saddle and met Ab at ground level as a man of the West would know to do. "What brings you to my place?"

"One of your homestead claims has been challenged," Little said, seemingly as unconcerned as if he were discussing the weather.

Ab glanced up at the mounted men. "By who?"

"By Joe Mayhall," Frank said, slapping his little brother on the back. "The boy's turned twenty-one, and he's old enough to file on land. The piece of land he wants is one of them with the little rotten shacks on it up the creek."

"These men insisted on coming along," Delton Little said. "You're welcome to come along, too, if you want. I have to investigate all challenges of this nature."

"Of what nature?" Ab said.

"Joe Mayhall claims that nobody ever lived on the particular quarter section in question; that a shack was thrown up to give the impression that somebody lived there, but that no crops were grown, and that the requirement for residence was never satisfied."

Ab glanced at the youngest Mayhall, who was staring at the cropped mane of his mule. "Joe Mayhall wasn't even born when I started homesteading Monument Park. His brothers have pushed him into this. They've been after my ranch and irrigated farms since the day they came here."

"You understand, I have to look at all sides. We will hold a formal hearing, if necessary."

"Which quarter section are they challenging?" Ab said.

Delton Little pulled a folded plat map from his pocket, squatted, and spread it on the ground. "This one here, on Monument Creek."

Ab could no more squat than he could wear a spur on his wooden leg, but he stooped over as far as he could and squinted at the map. "Buster, come look. I don't have my eyeglasses."

Buster glanced across his cornfield and saw Amelia approaching with Little Pete in front of her on the saddle. He climbed over the old rail fence and squatted beside Delton Little. Taking a few seconds to orient himself with the map, he found the quarter section in question. Taking a few more seconds, he tried to think of the best way to say it.

"Well?" Ab demanded.

Buster rose and put his hands in his pockets. "That's Matthew's claim, Colonel."

The wooden leg and the slack flesh on Ab's old face began to quiver as he felt a primal ire strike deeper than ever, deeper than fear or grief. His glare pulled by impulse to Terrence Mayhall, his rival now for almost twenty years on this range. Mayhall had cut fences and violated Ab's herd with mongrel bulls, but this was an outrage beyond all reckoning. "You will not live to own my son's claim," he said, his voice like a groan of agony.

Mayhall only shrugged. The name Matthew Holcomb meant nothing to him. He had come here the year after Matthew died, and had filed on a claim adjacent to the one Matthew had filed on, only to be forced out by grasshoppers, drought, and Ab Holcomb. "Just because your son couldn't prove up, doesn't mean my little brother can't."

Delton Little had picked up his map and moved to the edge of the road, pushed aside by instinct and experience. He was folding his map, but his eyes were busy looking for cover, finding it in the form of a pile of stones Buster had cleared from his field and neatly stacked.

Ab was walking stiffly backward, his mouth moving wordlessly in insensible anger. He was swatting at the coattail covering his pistol butt, trying to get at his weapon.

Frank and Terrence Mayhall were spurring their mounts to opposite sides of the road, spreading the field. Edgar was yanking vainly at the grip of a sawed-off shotgun he had tied to his cantle strings. Young Joe was staring, trying hopelessly to understand it all.

Buster stepped in front of Ab, grabbing the colonel's right forearm and pointing toward the cornfield. "Look yonder!" he shouted. "Yonder comes Miss Amelia, holdin' that baby 'cross her saddle." He said it like a warning, as if the woman and child would whip them all.

The men shot glances toward the cornfield, and back at one another, each holding his weapon, like holding ground. A mountain chinook came down ahead of Amelia, sweeping all bravado and threat of rash acts eastward with it. Terrence reined his horse back onto the road, as did Frank, and Buster released his grip on Colonel Holcomb's arm.

"I've changed my mind," Delton Little said, only two steps away from the pile of stones. "I'd rather go look at this claim on my own. I suggest you men all go back to your farms. Except for you, Buster. You come along with me to make sure I've located the right quarter section."

The men said nothing, each refusing to be the first to turn.

Amelia trotted up on her spotted mare, her smile fading as she regarded the expressions on the faces of the men. "Good morning, gentlemen," she said, cautiously.

The Mayhalls removed their hats, attempting gallantry. "Mornin', ma'am," Joe said, his voice a nervous squeak.

"Would you gentlemen like to come up to the house for some coffee or something?"

Frank Mayhall placed his sweat-stained felt back on his head. "We was just headin' back to our place, ma'am. Thanks, anyhow." He turned his horse. "Come on, boys."

The Mayhalls wheeled and rode back up the wagon lane, taking turns watching each other's backs.

"Colonel?" Amelia said. "What's going on?"

"They're tryin' to get it all," the old man said, still trembling. "They got my ranch. They got my town. Now they want all my irrigated lands, too."

"Who?" Amelia said.

"Everybody! They don't know what I've done here, all these years. They don't know what I've lost."

The chinook blew a thin loose strand of Amelia's hair across the curve of her cheek, and she looked hard at the stranger in the derby.

"Buster," the land investigator said, "let's go look at that claim."

"I'll go saddle a mount."

"You tell him, Buster," Ab said as they walked toward the barn, Little leading his rented horse. "Tell him about Matthew and Pete. Tell him about the dog soldiers we fought off, and the grasshoppers!" He was shouting now. "Tell him about Cheyenne Dutch, that old son-of-a . . ." He glanced at Amelia. "Tell him how that ridge log rolled off and crushed Ella, Buster. You were there! You've seen it all with me! She was just trying to look after Caleb!"

TWENTY-TWO

B USTER RODE UP the creek with Delton Little, giving the histories as best as he could remember, lending favor to Ab's title in any way he could, shy of outright lying. They held to the berm alongside the main irrigation ditch, Buster knowing all the best places to cross the laterals and avoid the mud. Buster himself had engineered and dug the main ditch with a mule team and a slip shovel. He had built all the sluice gates in his iron forge, and had surveyed and staked most of the laterals for sharecroppers to scratch with their plows.

Fields of corn, wheat, oats, alfalfa, and potatoes patched the landscape like a quilt, each with its own texture and color, each with its own whispered answer to the chinook wind.

"This here claim was made by a Texan name of Sam Dugan," Buster explained, as they rode past an irrigated field of onions now rented on shares from Ab by a homesteader. "Ol' Sam punched cows for Colonel Ab, when he wasn't workin' this here claim. After he proved up, he sold out to the colonel and moved east to make a book writer. Colonel bought a lot of claims like that, after these cowboys learned they didn't have no stomach for farmin'."

"So," Little said, "Colonel Holcomb used his employees to file on land, prove up on it, and then he'd buy their claims from them?"

"I'm the first hired man the colonel ever had. I been workin' for him nigh on to twenty-five years. I proved up on my own claims, and Colonel never tried to buy me out."

Little took his derby off and wiped a faded bandanna across his brow. "Your claims don't concern me, Buster. These others don't either, to tell you the truth. I don't care how Colonel Holcomb got his land. Ain't my business. It's just this one claim. The Matthew Holcomb claim. Those Mayhall brothers are making serious charges."

"Well, that's Matthew's old claim up yonder," Buster said, jutting his chin forward. "The one with the trees. Some homesteader done leased it from Colonel and put a fruit orchard in there a few years back. Bearin' fruit good this spring, I reckon."

When they got to Matthew's claim, Buster led the way through peach and apple trees, and reined his mule back at the rotten remnants of the log shanty in the middle of the orchard. "This here's what's left of Matthew's cabin."

Little got down and walked around the caved-in one-room structure. Some of the log ends still overlapped one another at the corners, but the majority of the walls had sagged and rotted back into the earth. "Did he ever live here?"

"I never got up this way back then," Buster said, avoiding the eyes of the investigator. "Matthew didn't stay around Colonel's place much back then. Rode up this way all the time. I guess he was livin' here, all right." He knew well enough that Matthew rode up this way because it was on the trail to the Denver whorehouses.

"I don't see any shingles on those rafters. Did the place ever have a roof on it?"

Buster shrugged. "Like I said, Mr. Little, I never did get up this way back then. Busy workin' my own claim, and Colonel Ab's, too. Matthew maybe had a sod roof on it, and somebody done come along and taken the sods off, I reckon. Could have had a canvas roof, too. I don't know."

"He built the place hisself?"

"I guess. His brothers maybe helped him some."

"Where are they?"

"Pete's buried back yonder on that hill, and Caleb . . . God knows where that boy is. He don't drift by here too often."

Delton Little nodded, and repositioned his derby. "The Mayhalls told me Matthew Holcomb died before he could prove up. What happened to him?"

Buster sat on the overlapping ends of the rotten logs, feeling them give under his weight. "We was all down at a dance at the sawmill in old Colorado City. Me and Caleb and the ranch manager at the time—a Mexican name of Javier Maldonado—we was playin' music for them miners and cowboys and them whores that used to work down there. Well, Matthew was drinkin' whiskey with this old mountain man used to drift up and down here, name was Cheyenne Dutch. They got in a scrap over somethin', and Matthew pulled his gun on old Dutch, and Dutch shot him dead, right between the eyes. Javier put his guitar down, pulled out his pistol, and shot at Dutch six times, and finally got him."

"And then the claim was transferred to Colonel Holcomb's ownership?"

"Yessir. I believe Pete saw to it."

"What year was all this, Buster?"

"I believe it was seventy-one."

Delton Little squatted, flat-footed, and gazed absentmindedly out under the branches of the young fruit trees. There were several ways to look at this claim. From a legal standpoint, Matthew Holcomb had obviously thrown together a fake cabin of rotten logs to make it look as if maybe he had once lived here. No doubt witnesses besides the Mayhalls could be dredged up to testify that Matthew had only played at satisfying the homestead laws. This claim could be wrenched from Colonel Holcomb's grasp, and given to Joe Mayhall, orchard, irrigation ditches, and all.

But, lordy, Delton thought, imagine what chaos that would create. Every father's son without a warrant would begin to challenge Ab Holcomb's old claims, and a land rush would begin. Right now, Ab—mainly through Buster Thompson—had dozens of irrigated farms running smoothly because they were all under his control. But let twenty-some-odd different landowners get ahold of this valley, and they would start squabbling over water rights. The courts would be clogged for years with litigation, if they didn't just take to outright shooting each other over which sluice gate was opened when. Delton had seen it happen before.

There was enough bad blood between the Mayhalls and Ab Holcomb already. Hadn't Ab almost pulled his old Colt on the Mayhalls just this morning? Let the Mayhalls get their hands on the Matthew Holcomb claim, and Ab would shoot at one of them, sure as hell's hot. Then one of them would kill old Ab, then that drifting Holcomb boy, Caleb, would come along and kill a Mayhall . . .

Colonel Holcomb was an old man, and the Mayhalls had plenty of land already. Not as much as the colonel, but the colonel had beat them here, fought Indians, seen a wife and two sons die. Let the Mayhalls lease an irrigated farm from the colonel like everybody else if they wanted one. Ab's lease fees were not unreasonable, although that was probably because Buster set them.

Delton Little's legs began to cramp, so he sat down on the ground, in the scarce shade of a peach tree, and propped himself up on his elbows. There was, of course, the most important issue yet to be considered:

What was in it for Delton Little?

Who had the most money? Colonel Ab Holcomb. The old man was desperate. His town was dying because of the new railroad route. His bank was failing as loans defaulted, businesses closed their accounts, and land values sank. His ranch was down to just a couple of thousand acres. His daughter-in-law was doing better with the Appaloosa horses than Ab was with his cattle. The only thing the old man had left was some cash and his irrigated farms.

The Mayhalls, by contrast, were in debt. That just about cinched it.

"You know what bothers me, Buster?"

"No, sir."

"This old cabin ain't got no doorway cut in it. How the hell does a man live in a cabin that ain't got no door? Climb down the chimney? This ain't gonna be easy. We let this thing get to court, and the Mayhalls have got us."

"Us?"

"Hell, yes. They've got witnesses who will testify that Matthew built this cabin of rotten logs and never lived in it nor plowed so much as a kitchen garden." He got up, dusted his hands, and took his reins. "Then there was the change of ownership after Matthew died. That sort of thing always makes for legal trouble. What those Mayhalls want more than this one cotton-pickin' fruit orchard is to gall the old man, and they'll go to any length to do it. Why do you think they picked Matthew's claim to challenge? I just wish I had the resources to steer this thing clear of the courtroom."

Buster stood and brushed the flakes of rotten wood away from the seat of his trousers. "Resources?"

"Hell, yes. It takes time and money to fight a claim challenge like this." He looked Buster in the eye. "Especially money."

"How much money?" Buster said. He wasn't surprised. Nothing much surprised Buster anymore.

"I can push this thing through a formal hearing before the Mayhalls know what hit 'em, and save this place for the colonel, but you gotta understand arrangin' that sort of thing costs money, Buster. Risky, too. Nobody takes risks without expectin' some sort of reward."

Buster nodded, and walked to his mule. There was nothing more to say. He and Delton Little understood each other. You didn't have to paint a picture for Buster Thompson.

TWENTY-THREE

So often had he dreamt and thought of the boy hiding near the falls that he could see it true from any facet or slant. Now he dreamt of it as if floating on the river herself, the rain-charged stream rushing under him as the fog of time curled back against the current. There, on the bank, the boy waited, the big Colt in his hand, the hat brim pulled low over eyes that shone with tears held back.

Everywhere were the sounds of rushing water: the river churning over the rocky ford; the falls plunging from the creek above. The boy lay prone under a low branch of willow, the Colt—already cocked—before him on a crumbling hollow of deadwood. So completely was he hidden that had not the dreamer once lain there in his place, he would scarcely have known to find him.

The boy was trembling like the wind-stirred leaves around him, but suddenly his shaking ceased with a shock that could still even the deepest rigors of fear, and the dreamer knew the riders were coming.

He saw it now—remembered it—as if through the eyes of the boy. Three riderless horses had rounded the bend from the pecan grove. The boy did not breathe until the four mounted Indians appeared behind them, and then he gasped. He was trapped now. To run was to die. To shrink back under the log was to rot inside with cowardice. The only course was to use the Colt, and to use it well.

Gradually, it became easier. The painted riders came nearer, their posture jaunty on their Comanche saddles. The leader carried the lance high and forward, and from it dangled the scalp that reminded the boy of their cruelty. He remembered what they had done. He remembered how he had watched from the sumac, unable to act, horrified to the point of sickness. To see the same butchers and torturers now, riding smugly home with grisly trophies, made his rancor impossible to contain in one boyish body.

The exception among the riders was the fourth. This young brave slumped in the saddle as if ill. He was not much more than a boy himself. The dreamer tried to shroud him in fog—for the memory of this warrior pained him—but the haze of time swirled where it would, and some things could not be veiled, no matter how long ago seen.

It was the bloody scalp and the proud visage of the leading warrior that gave the boy his will. His heart pounded like surf in his chest, and he could hear it, even above the loud rush of falling water. He waited, and waiting here was as excruciating as twisting flesh.

The three stolen horses reached the ford, stopped to look at it uneasily, though they had crossed here before, even in swifter currents. The lead horse sensed the boy somehow, even above the din of cascades, even against the flow of scented breeze. The horse looked at the boy hiding there, took a step toward him with muzzle nodding.

The boy knew this horse; had ridden him often. This was the horse who would steal up behind him and nudge him hard between the shoulder blades; who would blow warm breath in the face of the young rider who felt as light as a cowbird on his back; who would mouth the boy's hair as if it were turf. They thought as one—this horse and this boy—and the dreamer remembered the fear that his horse-friend would reveal him. But even this the animal could sense, and turned to step into the river as the Indians swung behind him.

The lance carrier pushed the stolen horses into the water at the ford, and another brave came beside him to help. The third warrior let his mount drink at the shore, and the youngest came up last, slumping on his pad saddle.

Now the boy had only seconds to wait, but they crawled like days of summer. He had to let all four Indians wade in, for the water would slow their attempt to escape. At the same time, he had to hope they would all remain in range of the big Colt, and in this, his horse-friend seemed to be helping: balking knee-deep in the water, causing the four Comanche to come up together behind the stolen stock.

And now it was about to happen, as it had happened in one never-ending dream-memory since the day of this nightmare. The boy, by logic and instinct, had numbered his targets. The youngest brave would be last. The lance bearer would die third, as he was deepest into the river. Of the other two warriors, the one farthest from the bank would fall second, and the one nearest would fall first. This first target was already aligned in the irons of the Colt revolver, and the boy's trigger finger began to turn back like a coiling snake.

It was the way with this dream to take the dreamer's memory here; to cruelly cast him back into the body of the boy; to make him fear and hate; to make it happen again, the outcome unknown. The boy paused, almost balked. Then his horse-friend bowed his great neck, cocked his head, and looked back at the boy for salvation. A black-powder blast ripped through the singular roar of water endlessly flowing, pouring, falling . . .

TWENTY-FOUR

WALKER COLT KINCHELOE rolled out of his bunk and hit the wooden floor in the dark. The wind was blowing outside, fierce and loud through the tops of tall firs, like rushing water. He felt the Colt in his hand, as he had gone to sleep holding it. It was dark, and he did not know for a moment where he was, who he was—dream or dreamer, man or boy.

The fist pounded on the plank door again.

"Walker! It's Hiram Baber! Are you in there?"

Moons and winters flooded back, carrying with them years of great sorrow and beauty, and Walker sat up on the floor of his one-room cabin. "Hi?"

"Yes, it's me. Open up. I'm alone."

Walker winced at the stiffness sleep left him with these days and got to his feet. He took one step and lifted the latch on the door, cracking it to find Hiram Baber standing alone in the starlight, a thoroughbred heaving fog into the night behind him.

Walker kept behind the door as he swung it open. "Well, git yourself in," he said. "There's Bad Faces in them foothills."

Hiram stepped into the cabin. "Bad Faces? Walker, there isn't a Sioux within a hundred miles. They're all on the reservation."

Walker blinked hard, put the revolver down, and lit the coal-oil lantern. "They're in them hills."

When the light came up, Hiram chuckled at the comical sight of Walker C. Kincheloe in faded long handles, the rump flap hanging unbuttoned like a listless flag. "You're still half asleep," the New Yorker said. "The hostiles are all gone."

The big Texan rubbed his face, beard stubble scratching on rough hands. "Them Bad Faces dog me like buzzards on dead meat," he growled. "There ain't no head count on 'em, and never will be. They're in them hills."

Hiram felt uneasy. This wasn't the welcome he had expected, but he was on Walker's range now, not his own. This was a different Walker C. Kincheloe—one who would surrender nothing. "I didn't mean to startle you," he said, careful not to sound too apologetic.

"Well, next time, holler out from the oak motts before you go poundin' up again' my door. Men have met their maker roustin' me out of my bunk too sudden."

Hiram put his hands into the deep pockets of his blue woollen coat. "I'll remember that."

Walker smacked his lips, scratched his stomach, and looked vaguely around the cabin. "Hell . . . My manners come to me slow of a mornin', Hi." He shook Hiram Baber's hand. "I could use a cup of coffee with about two fingers of chain lightnin' in it."

"Sounds good."

Walker clamped the Colt under his arm and started groping at the front flap of his long handles as he stepped outside.

Hiram felt warmth from the small cast-iron stove, spied some split wood, and stoked the fire. It got cold up here nights, even this early in autumn. A pot hung from a peg on the wall, and a barrel of water stood in the corner, so he put four or five cups on to boil. Then Walker came in, shivering, and began to pull his clothes on.

"Guess you're wondering why I'd show up here this time of morning."

Walker shrugged. "I figure you either got lost huntin' elk, or you come to beg me to take my job back ramroddin' the TW."

"It's that horse. You remember my thoroughbred stud horse."

"What about him?"

"You're the only man I know who can shoe him properly. You know how his hind feet clip his forefeet unless he's shod well."

"Yeah, he'll forge all right. Hell of an overreach on that long-legged son of a bitch."

Hiram pretended to check on the coffee water, though he knew it could not possibly be boiling yet. "Could you shoe him for me?"

"Hell, I guess," Walker replied, buckling his belt. He picked up one boot and looked for the other. It took a while to find it, as it had been kicked far under the bunk, into the shadows. "Yeah, I'll shoe your damn thoroughbred for you—long as you don't expect me to believe you come all the way up here just for that."

Hiram's eyes met Walker's, and he smirked. "I've just come from Cheyenne. The Stock Grower's Association has acquired a warrant for your arrest."

Walker nodded. "Took 'em long enough to find the sand. What's the charge?"

"Rustling. It stems from that maverick you branded upside-down at the roundup. Your son and that fiddler were named in the warrant, too, but it's common knowledge that they've left the territory."

The Texan shook his head as he poured an unmeasured amount of coffee into the pot of heating water. "The country has gone to hell, Hi. A man's a criminal now for ropin' a maverick on free government range and puttin' his brand on it—unless he's a rich bastard from back east, or Scotland—then he can have all the damned mavericks he wants. I swear, Hi, you all in that rich man's club have taken away the little man's chance."

"There are a few of us in the association who are fighting this maverick law and everything that goes with it. Why do you think I rode all night to warn you?"

Walker lurched slightly with measured skepticism. "Who are they sendin' to collect me?"

"The association is calling in every one of its stock inspectors, and they've hired a new chief detective to lead the posse."

"Who?"

"Dave Donaldson."

"Well, I'll be jiggered," Walker muttered.

"He's still fairly aggravated at the way you split his scalp with that pothook at the roundup. He's made plenty of talk around Cheyenne lately."

Walker was strapping his shoulder holster on over his shirt. "If you think I'm runnin' just because Dave Donaldson's augerin' a big hole in the wind, you've got your boot on the wrong foot."

Hiram grinned with satisfaction. "I knew you wouldn't run."

"You're damn right. Got too much work to do. It's time I gathered my herd from the Bighorns and turned 'em onto winter range. I've got wood to split, pens to build, and horses to work. There's more work for me with N.C. driftin' around behind Hard Winter Holcomb. No bunch of hired regulators is gonna run me off my own homestead. They'll have to drag me out dead, but I won't be the only one wrapped in a blanket."

Hiram peered into the pot on the stove. His eyelids were sagging, and stout brew was what he needed. "There's another way, Walker."

The Texan looked surprised. "Hell there is. Run or fight, and Walker C. Kincheloe's done all the runnin' he'll ever do."

"There's another way to fight."

"How's that?"

"In court."

The big man let the idea soak in a mere second or two, then hissed and waved his hand at Hiram.

"Remember what the point is, Walker."

"What is the point, Hi? What's the point of anything anymore?"

"The point here is to rid Wyoming Territory of the cursed maverick law before a range war breaks out between the big men and the little men. Now, you can be the one to start them shooting, or you can be the one to kick the shell out of their chamber."

Walker judged Hiram's choice of vernacular. It was unlike him to talk in anything but varnished back-east English, and the Texan was impressed. Hiram must have rehearsed *kick the shell out of their chamber* all the way here from Cheyenne. "That seeds easier than it takes root, Hi. The big boys have got judges and juries on the payroll in Cheyenne."

"That's why you'll turn yourself in right here in Johnson County. I already spoke to Sheriff Durham over at Buffalo. He said he'll trust you to your own recognizance and you won't have to spend a minute in jail. I'll put you up in a hotel room, hire a lawyer from the States, and we'll set this maverick law back on its heels. There's no way a jury of twelve Johnson

County men is going to convict you for branding a maverick on the free range, Bill Maverick be damned.''

Walker noticed the coffee roiling in the pot on the stove and pulled two tin cups from the shelf. Taking his jug from under the bunk, he pulled the stopper with his teeth and splashed some whiskey in each cup. He wrapped a dirty sock around the handle of the pot and lifted it from the stove, pouring the brew, thick with coffee grounds, into the cups. ''What about my cattle?'' he said, handing one of the cups to Hiram.

''A couple of the boys from the TW are coming to take your herd down from the high country, and to start building your pens for you while you're gone.''

''I don't take handouts.''

Hiram gritted his teeth and shifted the hot cup in his hand. ''It's not a handout. I offered to pay the boys for looking after your place, but they wouldn't take my money. They said they owed it to you, especially since you're willing to fight the maverick law for every little man in the territory.''

''What makes you so all-fired concerned about the little man, Hi?''

''I was reared to respect democracy. Every man should have a voice and a chance. Some of these foreign cattle barons don't see it that way, and frankly neither do some of these back-east elitists. They truly believe they were born better than the common man.''

Walker blew across the top of his cup and slurped down a swallow of good, hot brew. ''What do you believe?''

Hiram stood for a moment, drew himself into the pose of a stumping politician. ''I believe Wyoming is America in boldface letters. I believe the Bighorn Mountains are hallowed ground, washed in ancient blood. I believe Thomas Jefferson had Walker C. Kincheloe in mind when he wrote 'of the people, for the people, by the people.' I believe a drop of sweat is worth more than a nugget of gold. I believe those of you who won the frontier ought to get first crack at its resources. And I've never been poor, but I believe a poor man ought to have a chance to get rich.''

Walker squinted at the New Yorker as he made more room in his coffee cup. He splashed another wave of whiskey into the cup, and offered some to Hiram, who declined. ''You've thought about this,'' he remarked. He looked at the cracks around the plank door, which were showing some vague suggestions of daylight now. He thought about Paterson, N.C., Hard Winter Holcomb, the dream he had dreamt before Hiram woke him. He looked again at the New Yorker.

''Best place for me to shoe that horse,'' said Walker C. Kincheloe, ''is at the blacksmith's down in Buffalo.''

TWENTY-FIVE

Walker C. Kincheloe's cabin stood at the upper end of a red-walled canyon, seven miles long, up to three miles wide. Hiram studied the place well as the Texan saddled his night horse, left in a thicket of evergreens near the cabin.

The red canyon walls rose fifty to a hundred feet on either side of the homestead, yet failed to box the place in above, leaving the cattle access to higher country through a pass at the head of the canyon. The canyon was narrow here, just a quarter mile across. Walker had already begun fencing the head of the canyon with rails chopped from straight young aspens.

Hiram had ridden here by the moon, but he remembered the lower end of the canyon, seven miles downhill, being as narrow as the head. With the rock bluffs shutting Walker's herd in along two sides, the canyon provided a perfect natural pasture, well chosen by a man who knew the cow business.

This was Walker's winter range. He had long advocated holding herds off parts of the range to be used for winter grazing. Though greed had driven the big outfits to drop the use of winter range, Walker still guarded this canyon as if he owned it, and let no cattle in from spring through fall. He let his small herd graze the mountains in the summer, and kept them in the canyon through the winter, where they found plenty of grass, thanks to Walker's territorial ways.

The stream that swerved across the canyon floor didn't carry enough water for trout, but for cattle it served well. Walker had known this place for years, and had seen it once in the clutches of a dry summer, when the stream quit running altogether during the daylight hours yet would spring to life again at night. This time of year, with rain falling regularly in the high country, it made a good noise running just forty paces from the cabin.

The cabin itself was a temporary thing. When a real house got built here, the cabin would probably become a shed or tack room. The altitude and the shade of canyon walls and tall trees made the place cool in summer, yet it was protected from north winds, and low enough to make habitation here bearable during the long winters.

"This is a good little house you've built here," Hiram said, as the big man led his horse down from the evergreen thicket.

Walker grunted as he slid his long-barreled Ballard into the saddle scabbard. "Too poor to paint, too proud to whitewash."

"Why did you have your night horse hidden up in that timber?"

"I grew up in Comanche country."

"So?"

"Stealin' horses to Comanches is like racin' 'em to you and me. Just somethin' they did for fun, and maybe a little profit now and then. Down in Texas I'd always have a lone mount tied somewhere in the oak motts—especially with the light moon—and it's a habit I still hold to when I'm camped alone."

Hiram was packing some biscuits and cured meat in the saddle bags. "What the devil is an oak mott?"

"Just one of them old Texian words, Hi. You know, a thicket of oak trees. I backslide and talk Texian sometimes. Let's go."

Hiram mounted and reined his thoroughbred down the canyon, the way he had come up.

"This way," Walker said, tilting his head sideways toward the pass at the head of canyon. "I'll show you the high north trail out. It's shorter."

They rode through the pass, Hiram smiling at the waterfall that twined like a ribbon of lace through a gauntlet of glistening rocks. The pass led to a steep divide that slanted up to the high country of the Bighorns, and down to the foothills over Buffalo.

"The town is just around them peaks yonder," Walker said, pointing northeastward. "If you look real hard, you can see the old Bozeman Trail like a snake track down on the prairie."

Hiram took in the view. "A hawk could fly to town in ten minutes, yet to get a wagonload of supplies here I bet would take a full day's time coming the long way up the canyon."

"That canyon's never felt a wagon wheel, but the day's comin'."

As they picked their way down through the evergreens, Walker went on about his homestead: how N.C. would file on the lower end of the canyon when he turned twenty-one, and how they would gradually preempt all the land between their homesteads as profits from the cattle trickled in.

"God made that canyon for cows," Walker said, "and made me to be a cow man. I reckon I was born to take up that homestead. It's a hell of a trail gettin' to where the Good Lord wants you."

"This is a hell of a trail," Hiram said, nervously eyeballing the steep drop below. "How do you know where to go?"

"I blazed all the trees," the Texan replied, touching a scar on a pine as he passed. "Don't you ever pay no mind to the sign around you?"

Hiram considered it a rhetorical question.

They stopped on the rim of a valley when Walker raised his hand, like a cavalry officer bringing the troops to a halt. "Listen," he said.

Down in the valley, Hiram heard the familiar strain of several bull elk bugling and wished for all the world he could forget this Bill Maverick nonsense and go hunting. The whistles and yodels, their echoes commingling against rocky places, sounded like whooping warriors, screaming women, and fluting cranes rolled together.

The relative warmth of the plains crept into their clothing as they descended, leaving the mountain forests for the grassy foothills. The trail broadened, becoming less intimidating to men and horses. Noon found them on Clear Creek, where they stopped to eat the cold biscuits and salt-cured meat from Walker's cabin.

"Is this meat from one of your beeves?" Hiram asked.

The big man snorted. "I don't reckon I've ever et one of my own beeves. Hell, that would gag me sure as arsenic."

"But it is beef, isn't it?"

"Slow elk," the Texan said, leaning back against a sun-warmed boulder and tipping his hat over his eyes for a nap.

"What the devil is slow elk?"

"What you're eatin'. Ain't that what you asked?"

Hiram mulled the matter over as he chewed the tough meat. "It's a maverick, isn't it?"

"That would run again' the grain of the laws of the great Territory of Wyoming." He smacked his lips, settled a little deeper into the dead grass matted thick beside the creek.

Hiram leaned over to drink some cold water off the surface of the creek, but he couldn't let the matter lie. "Is it somebody else's beef?"

Walker lifted his hat and let one eye shine a glare at the New Yorker. "Don't fret yourself, Hi. It ain't TW beef." He dropped his hat back over his face and chuckled.

"It's one of Shanahan's CU cows, isn't it? One you found ranging in your canyon?"

Walker crossed his legs, standing a boot on its spur rowels. "Slow elk."

The ride into Buffalo from Clear Creek took only two hours, the horses choosing the pace. As Hiram Baber and Walker C. Kincheloe neared the outskirts, Walker saw a cowboy getting on a horse on the rise between him and town. The cowboy disappeared behind the hill, galloping away toward Buffalo.

"That feller lit out like a rooster with socks on," Walker said, spurring his mount to a lope. He pulled up at the crest of the hill and saw the cowboy's dust trail streaking straight into Buffalo. "That don't sit with me," he said.

"Probably just some cowboy feeling his oats," Hiram said.

"Looked like he was waitin' on us."

"Relax," Hiram advised. "The sympathy is with the little man in this town. No posse would dare to come here looking for you."

Just the same, Walker reached across his buckle with his left hand, and tested the draw of the Colt strapped butt-forward at his right hip. Casually, he shifted the reins to his left hand, and with his right, tested the shoulder-holstered weapon under his coat.

Buffalo seemed caught up in its usual routines. As they rode among the buildings, Hiram pulled his watch from his pocket. "If I know Sheriff Durham, he'll be sipping whiskey at the Bighorn Saloon right now." He pointed toward the sign across from the courthouse and angled his tired thoroughbred toward the hitching rail.

"I thought you wanted me to shoe that horse."

"It will wait until we've had a drink, won't it?"

As he dismounted, Walker noticed a sweat-lathered horse standing at the rail, the cinch loosened. It could have been the horse he saw the cowboy mount beyond the edge of town. There seemed to be a normal number of saddle horses in front of the saloon, but when Walker glanced at the livery barn across the corner, he saw the ground at the gate cut up as if a whole herd of horses had just come through.

"Come on," Hiram urged. "I'll buy. That trail was dusty."

Walker stepped under the awning, ducked the high crown of his hat under the sign reading BIGHORN SALOON. The curtains were drawn as usual, for womenfolk often walked by here, but the Texan noticed someone peeking out. The piano was playing, but the saloon seemed otherwise quiet for the number of horses tied at the rail.

Walker hooked his coat behind the Colt at his hip, grasped his lapel with his right hand, ready to reach for the shoulder holster, as was his habit. Hiram Baber parted the double doors in front of him, and Walker came in close behind Hi, using the New Yorker as a Comanche would use a buffalo-hide shield. He came in wide-eyed, so he would be ready for the gloom of the smoky saloon, and he noticed every face in the room turning to look at him.

The piano stopped abruptly, then pounded a fanfare. Walker's hand was halfway into his coat when he saw the hats coming off all over the room. Smiles broke across sun-creased faces, and a swell of men's voices erupted in song:

"... for he's a jolly good fellow ... which nobody can deny!"

Walker grinned with one side of his mouth and pulled a cigar from inside his coat. He tried to say something, but a general yell drowned out his voice, and men began slapping his back as if it were on fire. Someone handed him a jigger of whiskey and Hiram pushed him toward the back corner of the saloon.

"A round on me!" Hiram shouted, and the way became clear as men lined the bar.

Sheriff Brownie Durham emerged from the dark smoky corner, a man of fifty, tough as a keg full of nails and built like one. He was known to be friendly toward small-time cattlemen and settlers, and rather cool toward arrogant back-easters and foreigners who owned huge outfits. His face revealed nothing as he shook the Texan's hand. "Walker," he said, "you're under arrest." He slapped the big man on the shoulder, and pushed his way out of the crowded barroom.

Hiram gestured toward a table, and Walker C. Kincheloe saw a stranger sitting there. The man was getting up in years, yet Walker suspected hard living had aged him fast. He had a skinny cigar between the fingers of one pale hand, a glass of whiskey in the other. A bottle stood on the table, half full.

His suit was black, and it slouched across sloping shoulders. His red cravat had a gold-and-emerald pin stuck in it. His hat was dusty flat-topped silk, and it shaded the sagging features of his pale face: the pendulous jowls, the quivering cheeks, the bruiselike bags under his shooting black eyes.

"This is your lawyer," Hiram said. "Simeon Baldwin, of St. Louis."

The Texan frowned. "How'd you get him here so fast?"

"I've been anticipating this maneuver on the part of the association."

Walker pushed his hat back and reached across the table.

Simeon Baldwin's right hand left its whiskey glass to shake with Walker like a cold dead fish. "Let's get one thing clear up front," the lawyer said. "I'm the only thing standing between your ass and conviction by a jury of your peers. I don't care if you rot in jail, but I'm paid to keep the likes of you out of jail, and I like getting paid. You don't have to like me, and I already don't like you. If you'll do what I tell you, we can stomach each other. If you won't, you can go to hell."

Walker sat opposite the lawyer, bit off the end of his cigar, and spat it over Simeon Baldwin's shoulder. He stared at the quivering mass of pale flesh as he reached for the bottle on the table. "Damn if this ain't the ugliest sack of stinkin' legalisms I ever laid eyes on," the Texan said. He drank from the bottle, though he still held a full shot glass.

"Then hire a more attractive attorney," Baldwin said. "You'll be the one looking like shit after your first week behind bars."

Walker smiled and looked at Hiram. "He's got a mean streak. He'll do."

"Good," Hiram said, breathing a sigh of relief. "Let's get right to it. Simeon."

"You'll be indicted by the grand jury tomorrow," Baldwin announced.

Walker snorted. "I thought you were paid to beat this case. Ain't you gonna put up a fight?"

The lawyer's growl evolved into speech: "Don't you understand? We *want* an indictment."

"What in hell's name for?"

"If they no-bill you here, it just means some trumped-up grand jury in Cheyenne can have at you later. What we need is an acquittal. Don't you understand double jeopardy?"

"I understand double barrels."

"You've broken a territorial law. To prevent another court in the territory from trying you on the same charge, we must have an acquittal here. Make no mistake about it, Kincheloe. You have broken the law. You are a criminal. You deserve to go to jail."

"Like hell," Walker said. "The bastards who writ that maverick law are the ones that should go to jail."

The lawyer's tufted eyebrows made devilish peaks that prodded his hat brim, and his whole face shook. "If you backward frontier illiterates would question your governmental officials, you wouldn't have unconstitutional laws beating you down into the dirt of your worthless homesteads."

Walker bit halfway through his cigar before he curbed his anger. Baldwin's talk galled him, but so did the bitter truth in his words. "Your Illinois advice dries up like a tulip out here, Baldwin. My worthless homestead don't leave me time to sit on my ass at every session of the legislature. If I don't like what the government says, I don't *question* it, I *fight* it. Hell, if one of our legislators caught the sickly likes of you questionin' somethin' they writ, they'd like as not shoot you and run for reelection on your carcass. We have a bounty on fat lawyers in this territory."

The lawyer didn't flinch. "Tomorrow you will be indicted, and then we will go to court, and you will curb that smart hole in your face, because if you don't they'll throw you so far back in jail they'll have to shoot beans at you with a Winchester."

Walker smirked with surprise and looked at Hiram. "He gives as good as he gits, don't he?"

Simeon Baldwin sensed an advantage, and seized it: "I've been shot by legislators and other species of subhumans before, Kincheloe—in pistol duels, ambuscades, and barroom shootouts from North Carolina to Texas. Every man who has ever taken aim at Simeon Baldwin has died in prison or is picking at vermin there now."

Walker drew the revolver from his shoulder holster like a greased snake. He poked the barrel hard against Baldwin's cravat, and cocked the hammer. "Your legal books and lawyer talk don't put much scare into me, Baldwin. I'll take aim at you when I please, and die where I please."

Baldwin tried to brush the pistol barrel aside, but Walker had him bested in arm strength, so the lawyer rose grunting from his chair, gripping the table to steady himself. "I'd better go prepare your case. Where's the whorehouse?"

"Ask anybody," Hiram Baber said.

"Just so we understand each other, Baber. I am not a crusader. If you're looking for someone to take this ridiculous case to the Supreme Court, look elsewhere. I acquit criminals. I could not care less about the constitutionality of your piddling maverick laws."

"Understood. All we want is an acquittal. That should send a message to the association."

The stoop-shouldered lawyer pushed his way through the barroom, and Walker C. Kincheloe put his pistol back in its holster.

"What do you think?" Hiram Baber said.

The Texan shrugged. "Hell, I like him."

TWENTY-SIX

CHAUNCEY SHANAHAN SAT fuming in the courtroom, the stench of cheap cigar smoke and whiskey crowding him like the lowly commoners he was forced to sit with shoulder to shoulder. The jury had arrived at a verdict, and would emerge any minute to deliver it. The five homesteaders, four cowboys, and three local entrepreneurs had deliberated only twenty minutes, and everyone knew what verdict they would render.

It had all happened too fast. By the time Shanahan found out Walker C. Kincheloe had been indicted in Johnson County, the trial was about to begin. He had scrambled to get a special territorial prosecutor assigned to the case and to secure subpoenas for witnesses who had seen Kincheloe rustle the maverick in broad daylight, but only one of the cowboys who had witnessed the incident could be found. The cowboy worked for Shanahan's own CU outfit, but his memory had proven useless. Realizing that the cowboy was protecting Kincheloe, Shanahan had fired him, and had had the association blacklist him, forevermore preventing him from earning a livelihood in Wyoming as a cowboy.

Dave Donaldson's testimony should have been enough to convict Kincheloe. He had stated quite clearly that he had seen Kincheloe brand a maverick bull with a *W* brand—actually the *M* maverick brand of the association applied upside-down to make a *W*. According to Donaldson's testimony, Kincheloe had then cut the rustled bull into his own herd and left the roundup.

But then that immoral pettifogger, Simeon Baldwin, of St. Louis, had succeeded in discounting Donaldson's testimony with his cross-examination:

Baldwin: Mr. Donaldson, where is this bull that the defendant allegedly branded with an upside-down *M*?
Donaldson: I don't know.
Baldwin: Then, what evidence do you submit before this court?
Donaldson: My word.
Balwin: Mr. Donaldson, what was your position, professionally speaking, at the roundup in question?
Donaldson: Roundup foreman.
Baldwin: Who hired you, and what was your salary?
Donaldson: The Wyoming Stock Growers Association paid me forty dollars a month.
Baldwin: And what is your position with the association now?
Donaldson: Chief detective.
Baldwin: And your current salary?
Donaldson: Two hundred fifty dollars a month.
Baldwin: No further questions, Your Honor.

The common folk in the courtroom had cussed Dave Donaldson down from the witness stand, outraged that a man could draw such a salary for beating honest men like Walker C. Kincheloe out of their share of the cattle business.

For a few tense moments, Chauncey Shanahan had feared that both he and Donaldson would be mobbed. And things had only gotten worse when Walker C. Kincheloe himself took the stand:

Baldwin: Walker, do you have a brand registered in the Territory of Wyoming?

Kincheloe: Yes, I do. The *W* brand.

Baldwin: Did you brand the maverick bull in question with your own *W* brand?

Kincheloe: My iron wasn't even in the fire. I asked the boys for Bill Maverick's iron.

Baldwin: By Bill Maverick, you refer to the *M* brand that the Wyoming Stock Growers Association uses on mavericks according to territorial law.

Kincheloe: That's right.

Baldwin: And did you use this *M* brand on the maverick bull in question?

Kincheloe: I did.

Baldwin: And did Chief Detective Donaldson enjoy an advantageous view of this branding?

Kincheloe: Well, he was three or four lariats off, laid up in the bed wagon, but I don't 'llow he enjoyed much of a view of nothin' with both eyes blacked and swole up like a snake-bit pup.

Baldwin: Why was the foreman of the roundup lying in the bed wagon with swollen eyes while the work was going on?

Kincheloe: Dave had him a kind of accident the night before.

Baldwin: What manner of accident?

Kincheloe: He run into a pothook.

When the laughter in the courtroom subsided, the questioning continued:

Baldwin: Chief Detective Donaldson alleges that you used the *M* brand of the Wyoming Stock Growers Association upside-down, making it a *W,* which would be *your* brand.

Kincheloe: Dave Donaldson's a liar. I used the brand right-side up.

It had been a simple matter for Simeon Baldwin to put the case away in his closing remarks. There was simply no evidence, other than Dave Donaldson's word, and he had been some distance away recovering from an accident that had left his vision temporarily impaired. In addition, Donaldson had a financial interest in seeing Kincheloe convicted—two hundred fifty dollars a month, more than eight times the salary of the average cowboy.

Now the gavel was banging on the bench, and the judge was asking for the verdict.

"We find the defendant, Walker Colt Kincheloe, not guilty!" the jury foreman shouted.

Benches rocked back in the courtroom as men sprang to their feet. Walker drew admirers like iron shavings to a lodestone, and Chauncey Shanahan found himself elbowed to a far side of the courtroom. He looked at Dave Donaldson, but his chief detective could only shake his head.

Suddenly, Shanahan found his Scottish temper too heated to contain, and he leapt onto a courtroom bench, shouting, "Stop! Stop this travesty!" as his thick brogue rode the deepest bellow his lungs could issue.

The crowd turned on him angrily, but Walker's voice shouted above the din:

"Wait, boys! Let Chauncey have his say."

The Scotsman threw his arm back as if to crack a whip, and leveled a damning finger at Walker. "You are guilty!" he shouted. "You are a thief, and a rustler of cattle, and the association will see that you are nevermore permitted to run stock on these ranges!"

"Not if I have anything to say about it!" a voice declared.

The gazes of all the overwrought men turned to find Hiram Baber stepping up on a bench in back of the courtroom.

"Men," Hiram continued, "do not take Chauncey Shanahan's opinion as that of every member of the Wyoming Stock Growers Association. There are those of us in the association who opposed the maverick law from the first, and I for one still oppose it. The issue is not the maverick. The issue is the range!"

"The issue is disregard for authority!" Shanahan bellowed. "You had better mind your tongue, Hiram Baber, or you will find yourself blacklisted and drummed out of the association!"

"You don't possess that authority, Chauncey. This is a territory of the United States of America, and as such it is a bastion of free speech and democracy; of majority rule, not elitist domination. This is still a democracy, and the Wyoming Stock Growers Association is a democratic institution."

"You are a part of the conspiracy," Shanahan hissed. "You are a sympathizer to thieves and maverickers!"

Hiram was calm, but his voice was rising, and he began to gesture with his index finger. "Your obsession with mavericks will destroy the Wyoming cow business for everyone, Chauncey. Again—the issue is not mavericks! It is the range! When was the last time you rode several days across the plains? There are places out there where a kid goat couldn't find enough to eat! The range is being used up, and all you can think of is adding more mavericks to your herd! If the Territory of Wyoming is going to claim mavericks as public property, then they should be sold on the open market, and the revenue used to benefit the people, not the association. That money could provide relief from drought or blizzard.''

"Hi's right," Walker said, stepping to the edge of the courtroom mob. "The range is overstocked. You rich men don't need more cattle, you need to cut your herds. What if we have a hard winter, Chauncey? Your cattle would starve by the thousands. The range can't take any more.''

"What we do with the range is the business of the association," Shanahan replied, shaking with ire, "not a mob of uneducated thieves. And you, Kincheloe, are a common criminal and a liar! You have wantonly defied the maverick law of this land, and gotten away with it. You used that branding iron upside-down, and lied about it on the witness stand, in the plain sight of God!''

Walker put his hand on the shoulder of his lawyer, Simeon Baldwin. "Should I tell him, Simeon?''

"Go ahead," the lawyer replied, a rare smile making the slack flesh of his face wobble. "They can't touch you now. The Constitution protects you from double jeopardy. You have been acquitted of this crime, and can never be tried for it again.''

"In that case . . .'' Walker took a step toward the Scotsman. "Chauncey, you're dead wrong about that brandin' iron bein' upside-down. I told the honest truth up there on the stand. I was holdin' that iron right-ways up, like an *M*.'' He paused, and grinned all around the room. "Nope, it wasn't the iron that was upside-down. It was the bull!''

Laughter actually shook the courtroom to the point that the stovepipe rattled, and let whiffs of smoke into the room. But Walker Kincheloe raised his arms to quiet his supporters.

"That ain't all," he said. "The reason Dave Donaldson couldn't find that maverick bull is because me and a friend of mine et the last of it a week ago on Clear Creek!''

"Thief! Criminal!'' Shanahan blurted.

"That I am, Chauncey. But in a country where the law's worse than the crime, a criminal's a hero.''

Chauncey Shanahan attempted to say something in return, but Walker C. Kincheloe was rising to the shoulders of strong men who made more noise than one Scot could rival.

TWENTY-SEVEN

H ARD WINTER HOLCOMB saw N.C. wince and flail his left hand, trying to fling free the pain. But so infectious was the old Mexican ballad that the young cowboy could not long keep his sore fingertips off the taut gut strings of the guitar. Caleb was pleased that N.C. had some musical senses about him and was going to make a satisfactory guitar strummer by the time his fingertips toughened.

The fiddler stroked his bow to the meter of "Los Barandales del Puente," and Javier Maldonado released a *grito* from his throat, a graceful high-pitched yell, musical even in its chaotic escape. Javier was doing the real work on the guitar, but Caleb's son, Angelo, ten years old now, was adding to the guitar music with his own instrument. With a familiar fiddle tag, Caleb cued Javier to repeat the bridge of the song, and the old ranchero belted the lyrics loud:

> *Dame la mano, morena,*
> *Para subir a tu nido.*
> *No duermas sola.*
> *Duerme conmigo*

Give me your hand, dark one, Caleb thought, as he struggled to translate this tune he had heard Javier sing several times, *to ascend to your abode. Don't sleep alone. Sleep with me.* He still hadn't figured out what all this had to do with "The Railings of the Bridge," which was the English meaning of the song's title, but at least the fiddle part translated.

They were gathered around a huge fire in the old *casa consistorial,* the large hall adjoining Javier's mansion that had once served as a town hall of sorts for the village of Penascosa, back when a hundred souls lived here. Now it was just Javier and his children by his late wife, Sylvia; Marisol and her three children by Caleb; a couple of old bachelor corn and bean farmers; and a few vaqueros who worked Javier's cattle.

Javier and Angelo, Marisol and the girls—all this had taken some advance explanation for N.C., and Caleb had broken it to him in easily digestible portions on the long trail from Indian Territory to the Sacramento Mountains of New Mexico.

It had first come up in Texas on a new ranch located along the south bank of the Prairie Dog Town Fork of the Red River. An English syndicate owned the ranch, and it was completely enclosed by mile after mile of barbed wire. The ranch headquarters sprawled just under the Cap Rock, south of Tule Canyon.

It was here that Caleb and N.C. had contracted to break and train a string of cow ponies. N.C. gladly did most of the rough riding, earning, he thought, the lost spirit from each horse he broke. Caleb finished the horses, teaching them to neck-rein and respond to spurs and bit, riding miles of fence while he was at it.

In the evenings, they would ride a pair of green-broke mounts up onto the Cap Rock, the escarpment that ranged for hundreds of miles, north and south. Once on top, they could overlook the rolling plains to the east, or watch the sun set across the table-flat High Plains that began at the top of the Cap Rock and sprawled across vast treeless spaces into New Mexico.

It was here, on the brink of the Cap Rock, that Caleb first mentioned his New Mexican brood. "I might try to swap the ranch out of one of these hosses," he said. "If we get one tolerable gentled, I'll take it to my little boy, Angelo."

"I didn't know you had a kid," N.C. said. "How old?"

"Ten."

"Where's he at?"

"He lives in Penascosa with his mother. We'll stay there a while this winter, maybe go huntin' in the Sacramentos."

He had left it at that, and spurred the bronc on back down the trail. "Let's have some supper, then I'll teach you a couple of new chords," he suggested, for N.C. had just taken up guitar playing.

Weeks later, with the cow ponies broken, they had drifted south along the Cap Rock to a road ranch at the head of Yellowhouse Canyon, on the military route between Fort Griffin and Fort Sumner. Caleb was swapping music for a few days of room and board, and N.C. was making himself useful around the barn and corrals, hitching stagecoach teams, feeding stock, fixing leaky water troughs and such.

"How'd you like to drift down to El Paso before we hole up at Penascosa for the winter?" Caleb asked N.C. one night, putting his fiddle aside to pick up a cup of coffee that tasted heavily of bourbon. "I'd like to buy somethin' for the girls."

"What girls?" N.C. had asked.

"Marta and Elena."

"Who are they?"

"My daughters."

N.C. picked up the guitar, attempting to remember the chord Caleb had taught him yesterday. "You got three kids? Their mama don't mind you stayin' gone all the time?"

"She used to, but I don't reckon it bothers her now at all."

N.C. strummed a while, but Caleb was offering nothing more. "Well, while you're shoppin' in El Paso, I might just buy somethin' for myself." He grinned.

"I expected you might."

A month later, in El Paso, Caleb bought some things for the girls at a dry goods store, and had them wrapped up in boxes.

"Ain't you gonna buy nothin' for Mrs. Holcomb?" N.C. asked.

Caleb didn't answer until they were in the bookstore down the street. "There ain't no Mrs. Holcomb. I had my chance to marry her, but I fooled around and let somebody else do it." He thought about adding something to the effect that N.C. could learn from his mistakes, but for all he knew the boy would take it wrong, go off half-cocked, and marry a whore tonight.

"What did we come in here for, anyway?" N.C. replied, suddenly aware of all the books stacked around him.

"I promised Kate Llewellyn I'd buy a Bible," Caleb replied, thumbing through a leather-bound one. Almost immediately, he came across several words he didn't recognize. " 'Scuse me," he said to the clerk, "but have you got a dictionary you'll throw in the deal?"

"Who was it, anyway?" N.C. asked, a short while later, while the two smoked cigars and sipped whiskey at the Acme Saloon.

"Who was what?"

"Who was it up and married that gal before you got around to it?" He wasn't about to admit it, but he could just imagine how awful it would feel to hear somebody had up and married She-Rabbit back in the territory.

Caleb sighed and threw back his whiskey. He didn't like talking about it, but it was high time he told N.C. the whole story. He brandished his glass at the bartender and braced himself to relate the memories that still galled him inside like a gut-ache.

"She married an old friend of mine named Javier Maldonado. When I was a kid, growin' up in Monument Park, my old man hired Javier out of New Mexico to be our ranch manager. Javier was the one who killed Cheyenne Dutch, right after Dutch killed my brother Matthew. Later on, he left our place to take over his uncle's spread on the east flanks of the Sacramentos."

With his forearms, he covered the face of the Bible he had just bought, somewhat embarrassed to have carried it into a saloon. "When I started driftin', about your age, I paid him a visit, and he'd let me winter at his rancho. There was a little Mexican village there at the time called Penascosa, but it's just about died out now, and Javier's ranch headquarters is all that's left of it.

"Anyway, I took a shine to this skinny little senorita who lived with her granny there in Penascosa. Her name's Marisol. There wasn't a priest around, so that was excuse enough for me not to marry her. We just sort of acted married whenever I come around to winter there, and them youngguns didn't care whether their folks was hitched or not.

"I wasn't there when any one of 'em came into the world."

He took the glass from the bartender. "When I got to Penascosa last year about this time, come to find out Javier's wife had died, and he'd up and married Marisol while I was gone."

N.C. stiffened, his eyes glassy from the one jigger of whiskey. "And you're still pals?" he blurted.

"Long as he's raisin' my kids. Hell, it's my own damn fault."

After El Paso, they had packed the presents for the girls on old Harriet's pack saddle, and, leading Angelo's gift mare, they had ridden north to the Sacramento Mountains, Javier's ranch, and what was left of the village of Penascosa. It had been a tense reunion for the adults, though the children had seemed overjoyed to see their father bringing gifts.

Now they had settled into an uneasy but tolerable familiarity in which they just didn't talk about the fact that Caleb and Marisol had spent some ten years as a man and woman coupled—at least when Caleb wintered there. And at night, they would gather in the old *casa consistorial* and play music—just like old times—though there were only a handful of listeners left in Penascosa, most of them employed by Javier.

There was one vaquero, about nineteen years old, who was dancing little Elena around the flagstone floor, whirling her in his arms until her feet and hair trailed out behind her. It made Caleb smile to hear her squeal with such delight.

The tune ended, and the vaquero returned Elena to the floor, bowing to her and sweeping his sombrero from his head with mock gallantry. Elena just put her hand over her mouth, pointed, and laughed.

This vaquero was named Lucero Dominguez. He was new to Penascosa, having drifted in from Arizona. But he was already a favorite among the vaqueros for his skill on horseback and the way he handled himself, mounted or afoot.

Lucero grew a thin mustache, heavily waxed to make two points. He wore two six-shooters of cap-and-ball vintage, converted to take cartridges. His gun belt also held an old hunting knife with the handle pieces missing, amounting to nothing more than a flat piece of steel, pointed and sharpened at one end. His outfit was that of a hard-riding tough: patched and practical in a land of cactus thorns and yucca spines; high boots with spur rowels like windmills; faded bandanna knotted tight around his throat; sombrero brim doubled over where his hand often gripped it to sweep it from his head.

Caleb could find nothing unlikable about this young man, but he didn't like him anyway. Lucero was a newcomer to Penascosa who had too readily gained acceptance. He was too flashy, even in his drab costume of a vaquero. Angelo was trying to look like Lucero these days, tucking his pants into the tops of his boots, tying his bandanna tight around his throat, the knot just under and to one side of his Adam's apple, the ends hanging down.

Angelo is supposed to favor me, Caleb thought, not some trail-dusted drifter come here to attract a bunch of attention. Then he realized they were the same—himself and Lucero—and his dread deepened.

One cold and sunny day, Caleb heard voices as he walked over the old footbridge crossing the Rio Penasco. Peeking around an adobe corner, he saw Angelo and Lucero facing each other by the corrals, standing several feet apart. Suddenly, Lucero threw his knife, sticking it in the dirt between Angelo's boots. Angelo couldn't help scooting just inches backward out of reflex.

"*Gallina!*" Lucero taunted the boy, hooking his thumbs under his armpits and flapping his elbows, fowllike. "Let me show you," he said, pulling a boot off and sticking his bare foot forward. "Pick up my knife and throw it. Stick me between the toes if you want to."

Angelo pulled the knife from the ground at his feet. He gripped it carefully by the blade, staring uncertainly at Lucero's foot.

"Hurry up! My foot is getting cold!"

Angelo threw the knife, and it stuck perfectly an inch from Lucero's little toe, surprising Angelo himself, and surprising Caleb who watched around the corner.

Lucero, who had not flinched, laughed and threw his head back. He let fly a yelp as he reached for his boot, then he pulled up the knife. "Now this time, don't move. It ain't gonna kill you."

Suddenly Caleb saw himself back at Monument Park, Matthew taunting him with some contest of nerves, Pete always taking up for him. He stepped long around the corner, wishing he had put his spurs on this morning, so they would ring now and announce his presence. "*¿Qué pasa?*" he said. "What are you boys doin'?"

"Practicing," Lucero said.

The answer took Caleb aback for a second, and he didn't reply until he reached the boys at the corral fence. "Nobody needs practice bleedin'," he said, "it comes natural." He turned to his son. "I thought you were supposed to be feedin' horses, Angelo."

Angelo, seeing that his father was displeased, turned to do his chores.

Caleb looked at the young vaquero, who showed no signs of intimidation. "Lucero, how come you to leave Arizona?" he said in English.

The vaquero shrugged and answered in Spanish: "Maybe I am just a wanderer like you. *¿Quién sabe?*"

TWENTY-EIGHT

ONE MORNING WHILE looking for goats in the pine forests of the high Sacramento Mountains above Penascosa, Javier heard the crack of antlers slamming together. He made his pony stand, and listened, squinting when the horse breathed deep and made the leather squeak. In a minute, it came again: a pop almost as loud as a pistol shot, followed by snapping branches, sharp hooves stamping for purchase, tined antlers gnashing like pitchforks used in battle.

Javier didn't try to locate the two fighting bucks. He forgot about goats and rode down to Penascosa to make preparations. It was time to clean guns and ride for the high country. The bucks were rutting: forgetting their camaraderies of the summer to wage mortal combat, head to head. The prize: a harem of young does in no way prepared to outlast the maniacal instinct of the male to breed.

In years past, Caleb and Javier had led twenty or thirty men on this annual hunt: cooks, woodchoppers, skinners, camp rustlers, dog handlers. Now there were only nine men, including Angelo, N.C., Lucero, and four other vaqueros.

On the hunt, Javier and Caleb managed to regain the easy companionship they had once known. Here, away from Penascosa, Marisol, and the children they now somewhat shared, it was as if nothing had ever strained their friendship. They just hunted, drank tequila, played songs at night in the cabin they had built years ago.

They even took equal joy in having Angelo along for his first hunt and alternated as the boy's guide. As it happened, they were both present when Angelo shot his first buck, a fork-horned deer that bounded unexpectedly into a clearing in front of them as they walked back to their horses after an unsuccessful morning's hunt. They both put their hands on Angelo's shoulders, but he had already stopped and was lifting his Winchester.

The buck, hit through the lungs, had to be trailed, and both Caleb and Javier wanted to find it as badly as Angelo. They got on their knees to search for spots of blood, marking each find by hanging kerchiefs or gloves or other articles on tree limbs above the tiny crimson specks. When finally they spotted the deer dead on the forest floor, the three of them stood in a circle, threw their shoulders back, jutted their stomachs forward, turned their faces to the sky, and whooped so loud and long that their throats hurt.

N.C. shot a yearling bull elk and a bobcat the first day of the hunt. The next day, he killed two wild turkey hens with one bullet by waiting for their heads to line up in his rifle sights. Even so, the cowboy was hard-pressed to enjoy himself in camp. As the only one who didn't possess even a rudimentary understanding of Spanish, he missed out on almost everything said.

When N.C. was around, Caleb took pains to speak English, even if spoken to in Spanish. Everyone else maintained that a man who didn't speak Spanish didn't really speak, and ought to learn. A couple of the vaqueros didn't understand a lick of English anyway, so N.C. was outnumbered.

Lucero Dominguez spoke English very well, but he refused to employ it, and N.C. got the impression that Lucero did it just to rile him. Finally one afternoon in front of the cabin, N.C. asked Lucero where he intended to do his hunting that evening so they could stay clear of each other. Lucero answered in Spanish, gesturing vaguely to the north.

"Goddamn it, Lucero!" N.C. blurted. "Talk English! Your people got their ass kicked down here in the Mexican War."

Lucero suddenly condescended to employ his second tongue: "Nobody told me," he said, imploring with gestures of mock surprise. "Why don't you show me how it happened." With two insolent fingers of his right hand, he invited N.C. to come closer.

The cowboy took one step when Caleb let a pistol shot fly into the pine branches above. "If you boys are gonna fight, put your guns down first."

N.C. slid his Winchester into his saddle scabbard, then unbuckled his gun belt and handed it to Caleb. While the fiddler turned his back to put N.C.'s pistols on a split-log bench, Lucero drew both revolvers, flipped them over, and handed them butt-first to a nearby vaquero. Caleb turned around just in time to see the two rush each other, and he noticed the throwing knife still in Lucero's scabbard on his gun belt.

It was too late to stop them. N.C. had managed to duck Lucero's first roundhouse attempt and butted the vaquero in the chest with the crown of his hat, driving him hard into a pine tree. He belabored his opponent's gut with punches, until Lucero hooked a thumb in his eye and gouged him back.

N.C. shook his head as if bee stung, then leaned ahead again, sneaking a punch between Lucero's fists to bloody the vaquero's lip. Lucero only laughed and spit blood, and when N.C. came at him again, the vaquero grabbed the cowboy's hat brim and pulled, taking N.C. off balance. As the cowboy stumbled past him, Lucero kicked him smartly in the rear, much to the appreciation of the watching Mexicans.

"Why don't you fight like you've got some guts?" N.C. said.

Lucero was beckoning with that pair of churlish fingers again, so N.C. waded in knuckle first, backing the vaquero up against the cabin wall. Taking a fist hard on the side of his head, Lucero suddenly hooked his boot over N.C.'s spur in a practiced maneuver and shoved the cowboy backward.

N.C. landed on his back and rolled instantly to his feet, gasping for breath. He was furious to see Lucero grinning at him, scarcely winded. He closed cautiously, hellbent on teaching Lucero a lesson now, his feelings hurt badly by the laughing Mexicans. "You fight dirty," he said.

Lucero wiped blood away from his mouth. "Fighting is a dirty thing." He circled away from the cabin, knowing the cowboy would pin him there again.

The Mexicans were urging Lucero on, but he refused to take the fight to N.C., preferring to taunt the cowboy with beckoning gestures of his fingers. This time N.C. watched more carefully, cautious of Lucero's trickery. He stung the vaquero with a punch, then backed out. A flurry of three blows, the last one to the stomach, caused Lucero to drop his guard, and N.C. rushed in, seizing his advantage.

He grabbed a handful of the vaquero's shirt to keep himself from being tripped again and viciously pounded away with a wild right fist, like his father had mercilessly beaten Dave Donaldson with the pothook.

Caleb caught himself watching with both fists clenched until he realized Lucero was groping for the knife in his gun belt scabbard. "Watch the knife!" he shouted.

N.C. pushed away and released Lucero's shirt just as the vaquero slashed crossway, slicing through the cowboy's vest and cutting him skin-deep across his belly. N.C. grabbed the wound and felt blood, staring with disbelief at Lucero, wondering how badly he was hurt.

"Come on," Lucero said, still beckoning.

"I'm unarmed," N.C. replied, risking a glance at the blood that had stained his whole palm.

"Then get a knife."

"Nobody said nothin' about no knives," Caleb said, boldly stepping in between the combatants and turning his back to Lucero to check N.C.'s wound.

"*Bastante,*" Javier added as he took Lucero's pistols from the vaquero and motioned for him and the others to be on their way. "That's enough," he told them in Spanish. "Time to hunt now. Put that knife away, Lucero." He handed the revolvers to the vaquero. "That's enough fighting." But Javier knew very well that this fight had only added to the tension, rather than relieving it as he had hoped.

Angelo was staring at N.C.'s belly wound with his mouth open. He glanced at Lucero, who raised his eyebrows and winked at the boy. As the vaqueros escorted Lucero away like a hero, Angelo stayed to see the blood.

"Sit down over here and we'll get you patched up," Caleb said to N.C. He stripped the cowboy to the waist, making his skin tighten in the high cool autumn air.

After Javier had sent Lucero away with the other laughing vaqueros, he brought some hot water from the stove. "Lay him down here on the bench," he ordered and drizzled the scalding water down the length of the knife wound, four inches across N.C.'s stomach.

"It's just a scratch," Caleb commented, getting a good look at the wound through the blood. "Barely got through the skin." He made N.C. wince by poking around the edges of the cut. As he and Javier doctored the cowboy, they exchanged knowing looks and agreed without speaking.

"Let it bleed," Javier ordered, and he went back into the cabin. From the rafters, the ranchero gathered spiderwebs into strands. He stood on a barrel to harvest the silk, carefully keeping bugs and dust out of the gossamer rope he twisted until he had a thread as long as N.C.'s cut. Laying the strand of twisted web carefully on his palm, he went to the fireplace and scraped soot from the inside of the chimney with his knife blade, stroking it upward so the soot would collect on the blade. He dusted the strand of spiderweb with soot until it was well blackened.

Taking the soot-stained web outside, the *curandero* meticulously lifted it with his knife blade, positioned it over N.C.'s wound, then pushed it, inch by inch, into the open cut.

"Sit up," he said, and they wound strips of cloth torn from a clean cotton shirt around and around N.C.'s waist until the wound was well covered.

"I have a vest I will give you to replace the one Lucero cut."

"I'll just patch this one, Javier. Thanks, but this is an old vest, anyway."

Javier shrugged.

"Well," Caleb said, looking grimly at the patch job he had done on the wound, bloodied now with a dotted line soaking through the bandages, "I guess me and N.C. better drift on a little soon this winter."

Javier nodded. "It is unfortunate, but you are right, of course."

"Why should we have to leave?" N.C. said. "I ain't afraid of Lucero."

Javier gauged the sky for light. "You should be."

"How come?" the boy said defensively.

"Because he is afraid of you. You would have beaten him if he had not used his knife. I think Lucero would rather shoot you in the back than be afraid of you, my young friend."

N.C. frowned. He wanted to show that he wasn't afraid of Lucero, but the truth was he would just as soon drift on, away from this band of Spanish-speakers. "He ain't got the guts."

"Have you heard why Lucero left Arizona?" Caleb demanded.

"No."

"He don't talk much about it, does he?"

"So what?" N.C. buttoned his shirt over the bandages.

"He talks enough about everything else."

"How would I know? He don't talk English."

"*You* don't talk Spanish," Javier said, punctuating his point with a disarming smile. "Anyway, Caleb is right. A man with a cloudy past comes right out of the storm."

Gingerly, N.C. tucked his shirt down into the front of his pants. "Well, I'd just as soon drift on to someplace where folks talk English, but it ain't because I'm scared of Lucero."

"That's plain enough," Caleb said.

N.C. set to work, lashing his outfit and Caleb's onto Harriet's pack saddle while Caleb spoke to Angelo.

"When I come back next year, we'll get you a bigger buck," he said to his son.

"Maybe Javier will help me get one this evening," Angelo replied, ignorant of how the comment would bite.

Caleb forced himself to grin through his shame. "I hope you shoot the biggest one on the mountain."

"I thought Lucero was going to kill that gringo," the boy said, still glassy-eyed over the fight.

Caleb's brow wrinkled in puzzlement. "Now, watch your mouth, son.

I'm a gringo, and that makes you half and half, yourself. Anyway, there wasn't gonna be no killin'. The fight just got a little out of hand.''

Angelo shrugged and looked off toward the trail Lucero had taken.

''Well, N.C.'s about got our rig packed. I guess I better go.'' He wanted to hug the boy, but Angelo was ten years old and had killed his first deer. He shook his son's little hand.

As they eased down the trail from the cabin, Caleb turned to wave his hat and yell, ''Adios!'' but N.C. was too busy thinking about his wound. He was awful proud of it, but it hurt, and that made him mad. If he ever tangled with Lucero again, he would know better than to take off his guns. That Mexican fought dirty.

TWENTY-NINE

THE BLIZZARDS HAD too long howled, and the snowdrifts collected dirt. Now was the time for fresh rain, green grass livening the plains, tender leaves dressing the bare white aspen branches in the mountains. And this was the time of wildflowers erupting like fire among the grasses.

Amelia loved springtime on the Front Range.

The native blossoms grew where they would, of course, but in Monument Park they had help. It had started years ago, when Ella Holcomb tried to plant a flower garden with tulips and lilies, irrigating it with a bucket. Dry winds and parching sun had shriveled the garden, so Buster Thompson had gathered some wildflower seeds for Miss Ella. In time, the wildflower garden had become her grave site, and that of Matthew, her eldest. And when old Ab Holcomb had buried Pete on the Arapaho Trail, Buster had scattered wildflower seeds there, too.

Buster kept the seeds in cloth tobacco pouches the cowboys saved for him, labeling each variety, scattering them in the springtime along irrigation ditches, across hillsides, down the lane that ran to the ghost town that was Holcomb, Colorado.

And when they bloomed—the coral bells and Indian pink; the wine-cups and paintbrushes; the firewheels and kittentails—they brought Caleb home. He would arrive in the night, a campfire next to Pete's gravestone signaling his return. And everyone knew—as if in some sad and famous fable—that Caleb spoke to Pete up there in the night; told stories; sang ballads. And he would stay on Holcomb Ranch for a time to play music with Buster, to sow more wildflower seeds, to work cattle and horses, then to drift again. Always to drift.

But this year, Caleb had come home with a young cowboy from the Wyoming Territory. N.C. Kincheloe was bright, a bit reckless, and painfully courteous to Amelia, refusing to even speak to her unless his hat was in his hand. N.C. was to meet his father here after almost a year adrift with Caleb. And the father, one Walker C. Kincheloe, was coming to look at Amelia's Appaloosa horses.

This was a fine springtime, indeed. It was rare that Caleb brought friends home with him, and this made Amelia hope. Maybe he was changing, needing friends more, needing some constants in his drifter's existence. Perhaps he would see his way clear to stay home longer this year, longer still the next, and eventually . . .

She dared not let the hope well too high in her breast, for Caleb had disappointed her before. But, oh, he was needed here! Everything was in peril about Monument Park. The railroad had completed its new line to Colorado Springs, leaving Holcomb to rot and die. The town had been deserted. The bank had failed, the land office had closed. Only Colonel Ab's office remained open, and he went there just to brood and fret and wallow in his misfortunes.

Farms had failed without the nearby rail service, their neighbors swallowing them to use as stock pastures. Fully a third of Ab's irrigated fields along Monument Creek went unleased this spring, and Buster was farming all of them he could on shares. Monument Park was shifting to a system of stock farming to supplement crop yield, and homesteaders who had almost made it were leaving, defeated.

The Mayhall brothers, while not wiped out, had lost the Ingram place they had tried to buy, and their front pasture, which they had put up as security—a half section in all. They blamed only Ab Holcomb for all their troubles and were bent on vengeance by acquisition. Young Joe Mayhall had filed on Matthew Holcomb's old homestead, challenging Ab's claim to it, and a hearing had been scheduled.

It was well that Caleb was here for this, for Amelia feared Ab would only inflame the issue at the hearing. She had seen the old man grope for his antique Walker Colt that day out on the road, when the Mayhall brothers brought the land claims inspector, Delton Little.

We need Caleb here, Amelia thought. But the needs she knew most were her own. She had been a widow long enough now. Buster's wife, Gloria, had suggested that she attend more social functions in Colorado Springs. But Amelia only thought of Caleb. Every touch he had ever tendered remained upon her skin like a sunburn—even from years ago, when she was married to Pete—and before that, when she briefly courted Matthew.

And so it moved Amelia with hope and pleasure to stand beside Caleb now on the depot platform at Colorado Springs as the train steamed in. Caleb was holding Little Pete, and Amelia could hardly contain her joy at the way Caleb made faces and tickled the toddler with his overgrown mustache. She was quite sure she was blushing, and the smile simply would not slip from her face, though she knew it made wrinkles branch from the corners of her green eyes.

Little Pete was laughing his toddler's squeal, reaching bright-eyed for the mustache that tickled so, oblivious even to the locomotive that hissed and chugged behind him. As the brakes screeched against steel, a shaft of morning daylight moved onto the boy and his Uncle Caleb, streaming between two cars. It made Caleb squint until he dipped his hat brim to shadow his eyes.

"All right, straighten up, Pete," the drifter said to his nephew. "Walker C. Kincheloe's fixin' to step down and he's liable to shoot you on sight if he don't like the looks of you."

"Oh, Caleb," Amelia scolded, but her face smiled on, and she was happier than she had been in months. She even went so far as to put her hand around Caleb's elbow, as if he were her escort or something, and she blushed ever deeper when he glanced at her and winked.

Buster came up silently from the landing, having left Amelia's two-horse carriage at the hitching rail.

"Where's he at?" N.C. said anxiously, as passengers began to disembark. "I don't see him nowhere."

"Probably down in the smoker," Caleb suggested.

But it was Amelia who saw Walker first, recognizing him instantly by the descriptions Caleb had given her and the resemblance he bore to his son, N.C. He swung out through the end door of the baggage car, his hulking shoulders cutting a swath through the dust and cinders like the shadow of a cloud moving up a hill.

"Hey, Daddy!" N.C. shouted.

Walker tossed a bag down the steps, picked up three others with one clench. "Howdy, son," he said, shaking N.C.'s hand before he stepped onto the depot landing. "I see you left him in one piece, fiddler!"

"How come you got all this stuff?" N.C. asked, still grasping his father's hand.

"Ain't mine, son. I brought y'all a little surprise." With a gesture, Walker C. Kincheloe turned back to the door, and Savannah Baber breezed onto the steps.

When the little sprite appeared, flipping her hair like the tail of a palomino pony, Amelia felt Caleb change in her grasp, as she still held to his arm, loosely in her palm. Like a thunderclap, he tensed, and Amelia looked up to find his mouth open, face blank, eyes locked. Without the least show of ceremony, the fiddler blindly shoved the wiggling toddler into the side of Amelia's face, like a sailor chucking freight to stay afloat.

"Let me help with them bags," Caleb said to Walker, but he was sweeping his hat from his head as he spoke and looking out from under one lifted eyebrow at Savannah, stepping forward to take the pieces of luggage that obviously belonged to her. "You're a sight," he remarked to her. "What brings you down here?"

Savannah shrugged and brushed past Caleb as if he were a stable boy. "I suppose I came to ride that horse," she said, and then she fell upon N.C., teasing him with little hands that groped playfully at his ribs. "Don't you look like the rake! You've grown up!"

N.C. stood firm, grinning and grabbing one of her cool hands while he took his hat off. He liked having her fuss over him, of course, and she looked prettier now than ever; but he was damned if he would blush or backpedal. He had whored around for a year, and the mystery she had once wielded over him was diminished. Moreover—and standing with Savannah here at this moment made him see this clear only now—he had fallen in love with a Cheyenne girl named Rabbit.

Standing awkwardly with Little Pete in her arms, her springtime joy all faded like sackcloth, Amelia caught the eye of Walker, whose big ivory smile broke like white water.

"Ma'am," the Texan said, placing his hat over his heart, "the sun falls on you and that baby like light through the wings of angels."

"Oh, sorry," Caleb said. "Amelia, meet Walker Colt Kincheloe and Savannah Baber."

Savannah deserted N.C. to flit Amelia's way, raking her fingers across Caleb's arm as she passed him. "Oh, you're the widow who raises the Appaloosas," she said. She chucked Little Pete indelicately under the chin. "Beautiful child. Is he your first?"

"Yes," Amelia answered, feeling haunted by vague echoes. Hadn't she herself once prattled moronically along like this little temptress? Hadn't she once been a flirtatious little rich girl, playing the Holcomb brothers against one another?

"Miss Amelia," Walker said, "I'd sure like to get aholt of some stock like the stallion Hard Winter straddles. Never thought much of them spotted Nez Percé horses till I seen ol' Whiplash."

Amelia sidled her eyes toward "Hard Winter," but found him admiring the little temptress. "I'd be delighted to show you what I have this afternoon. I hope you're planning to stay awhile. We've plenty of space in the house, and you'll want to ride some horses before you make up your mind.''

''As long as we don't put you out.''

''Not at all.''

''Oh, Caleb,'' Savannah said, turning birdlike with bright eyes, ''I took the liberty of asking some friends from New York to meet me here in a day or two. They want to see some of the real cowboys I've told them about. Would you mind terribly if they visited the ranch?''

''Of course not. Have 'em stay awhile. We'll put 'em up at the boardinghouse.''

''Nonsense,'' Amelia said. ''I'm sure we'll find room for everybody right on the ranch. I've rooms to spare in the mansion. We wouldn't want guests to stay in that gloomy abandoned town.'' She could feel herself putting on her old debutante airs. She was a ranch widow now, and Savannah Baber annoyed her fiercely so far, but the thought of having some of her old kind here for a visit lifted her spirits suddenly out of the doldrums.

''That settles that,'' Caleb said, remembering that Buster was standing aside, unnoticed. He put on a prideful smile and nudged the big Texan. ''Walker, this here's Buster Thompson, the man who taught me fiddlin' and all.''

Walker pressed his hat back on and took a firm hold of Buster's hand. ''Some of the best hands I ever rode up the trail with was colored boys,'' the big man announced, punctuating the remark with a nod of admiration.

Buster forced a smile, trying to keep the sarcasm out of his voice. ''Some of us learns to overcome,'' he said. He took the luggage from Walker and turned into the depot. He was pretty sure Savannah Baber wasn't going to speak to him.

As the party moved away from the train, Walker stopped Caleb with a big hand on the fiddler's shoulder. ''See that ol' boy down yonder,'' he said, jutting his anvil jaw at a silk suit lumbering down the steps of a passenger car. ''He's too damn fat.'' The big Texan snorted and shook his head as he judged the muddle of humanity surging through the depot. ''I wish you'd look at the gawks on some of these bastards' faces. If that ain't comical!''

THIRTY

IN HIS FOURTEEN years of drifting, strumming guitars, picking mandolins, sawing fiddles, and blowing harmonicas, Caleb had sung and played in saloons, cow camps, camp meetings, theaters, tent shows, parlors, whorehouses, bunkhouses, sawmills, barns, railroad cars, and even upon his own saddle. He had ridden grub line and played for breakfast and oats. He had stroked the hair of horses against the gut of cats while buffalo hunters jigged on flint hides staked to the ground. He had turned his hat upside down so drunken prospectors could pay his wage in pinches of gold dust.

Some audiences were oblivious, except when he stopped playing. Some were volatile as nitro, full of hard-set eyes and fists itching for impact. Some were happy as white-faced calves gamboling and cavorting before a blue norther. But this audience assembled in the mansion that Caleb's late brother, Pete, had built for Amelia beat all he had ever seen.

First there was Walker C. Kincheloe, standing next to the liquor caddy so he could refill his snifter with brandy, which seemed to have no affect on him whatever, no matter how much of it he drank. Then there was Amelia, and Buster's wife, Gloria, who were so busy serving things and picking up things and making a fuss over the six guests from New York that they might have been deaf to ten fiddles. Next was N.C., who had been asked, even begged, to play but had only shaken his head bashfully and remained sitting between Piggin' String McCoy and Dan Brooks, with whom he felt comfortable.

Tess was all dressed up in her best sack dress and even wearing her false tooth, which she had had made when she was whoring back in Texas. But only Caleb knew about that, and he had never told a soul in Monument Park—especially Tess's new husband, Piggin' String. The damnedest thing about Tess here tonight was that she had taken to the folks from back east, and they to her, and now she sat among them on the couch and led them in singing. Tess had always loved to sing and knew all the songs Caleb knew.

But it was Savannah and her friends from the state of New York who gave the crowd its unique personality. They took to western music like nothing Caleb had ever seen. It was the fiddle tunes that had started them. Buster and Caleb would trade off on guitar and fiddle, each challenging the other with the next tune. Buster had started with ''Paddy on the Turnpike," to which Caleb replied with "Snowbird in the Ashbank." Buster fluttered through "Sugar in the Gourd" before Caleb could, for he knew Caleb played it better. Caleb countered with "Done Gone." Then it was on to "Tennessee Mountain Fox Chase," "Three Forks of Cheat," and "Drunken Hiccups."

The New Yorkers clapped in time, grinning like scared possums; they stomped their feet, trying in vain to yelp cowboy vociferations. They nudged each other, scarcely able to believe they were in on this. The young women put their soft hands to their faces and the young dudes shook their red-cheeked heads with their mouths gaping.

"Let's do ol' Long Fingers' favorite song," Buster suggested, weary of competition. So he and Caleb joined forces, Buster taking a fiddle solo between verses, while Caleb strummed the guitar and sang:

> . . . *Old Dan Tucker and I got drunk*
> *He fell in the fire and kicked out a chunk*
> *The charcoal got inside his shoe*
> *Lord bless you, honey, how the ashes flew . . .*

"Who was Long Fingers?" asked a young dandy by the name of Gerald Dutton, when the song and ensuing applause had died down.

"Well," Caleb said, his face becoming serious, "he was a chief among the Arapaho who once lived upon this very land. He's gone now, but he gave Buster the name of Man-on-a-Cloud, and me the name of White Wolf."

And the visitors fawned all over each other to find themselves in the presence of real frontiersmen with authentic Indian appellations.

These "dudes," as they unabashedly referred to themselves, had landed in Colorado Springs about twenty-four hours ago, so fagged from traveling that they only wanted to retire upon their arrival. But with sunrise this morning, they were ready to experience the west of their wild imaginations. First, they met one-legged Colonel Ab, which deeply impressed and moved them all, but which had had the effect of driving the old man deep into hiding for the rest of their visit.

The party included three girls about twenty, fresh out of finishing school, and three twenty-two-year-old college graduates—parts of whom were boyish, while other features were manly. They were all accompanied by the aunt of one of the girls—a scatterbrained spinster who was rather useless as a chaperon.

Right away this morning, they had insisted on taking a ride "into the high country." Caleb, Piggin' String, Dan, and N.C. had saddled gentle horses for them and accompanied them up the Arapaho Trail. They all proved to be accomplished riders, though String said the men "rode stiff."

Late this afternoon, they had taken a tour of the ghost town of Holcomb, Colorado, strolling silently down the street, deeply awed, talking only in voices low and reverent. And this evening had brought them back to Amelia's mansion for a feast Gloria had prepared. Aunt Mable had gone up to bed, having become quite glassy-eyed on wine, and the musical entertainment had begun, of which the visitors now seemed so remarkably appreciative.

"Look here, Hard Winter," Walker said, leaving his snifter on the liquor caddy and taking the bottle to pass with String and Dan, "play some by-God trail songs for these young folks."

"I'll play along on one or two," N.C. suddenly offered, blushing as he took the guitar from Caleb.

A cheer went up, and N.C. could not let his eyes fall on a soul for all the self-consciousness he felt. But Buster and Caleb resolved to back him up, and they all three let loose with "Whoopie Ti Yi Yo Git Along Little Dogies."

The young Easterners went crazy with joy, and after just the second verse had memorized and would join in on the chorus, the college men singing with as much bravado as they could muster:

> Whoopie Ti Yi Yo, git along little dogies
> It's your misfortune and none of my own
> Whoopie Ti Yi Yo, git along little dogies
> You know that Wyoming will be your new home

"Where do they come from, Hard Winter?" said Gerald Dutton. His eyes widened at his own gall. "You don't mind if I call you Hard Winter, do you?"

"If it's good enough for Walker to style me, it's good enough for the world. Now, what do you mean? Where does what all come from?"

"These songs, these cowboy lyrics."

Caleb thought for a moment that he didn't know and started looking for some line of bull to mask his ignorance. But, as he began, he realized that he did know. Yes, he knew as well as any man alive whence these ditties arose.

"Well, they come from all over, I guess. The boys made 'em up out on the trail—some of 'em. Now, that particular one we just sang together, that was a made-over song from old Ireland. I know because an Irishman down in San Patricio, Texas—a town laid out by Irish-born settlers—well, this old Irishman sang me the way it went back in the old country. It was a lullaby they'd sing to their younguns there.'' He let his fingers fall into place without looking and strummed a chord.

> *EE-I-O, my laddie lie easy*
> *Perhaps your own daddy may never be known*
> *I'm weeping and weary with rockin' this cradle*
> *And mindin' a baby that's none of my own*

''That's about all I remember of what he sung, but it gives you the idea. That song must've been two hundred years old when some cowpuncher took a notion to make some trail words fit it.''

''I'll be . . .'' Gerald Dutton said.

''I told you it would be an education,'' Savannah said. ''I told you all two years ago you should come west with me, and now you see I'm right.''

As they celebrated their belated good fortune, Caleb felt his face making a silly grin, and felt his eyes lifting. He saw Amelia standing in the kitchen, her hands balancing cups and saucers. She looked unusually happy, though she had spent the entire evening in turmoil.

My God, she's beautiful, Caleb thought, for the light was striking her well. He remembered the day Matthew brought her to the ranch to meet the family: how awkward and bashful she had made him feel. He remembered the way a hope in his heart sank when Pete said he would marry her. He remembered his mind often drifting back to think of Amelia while he was out there on some windswept plain or snow-dusted mountain.

Oh, but she had loved Pete so much, and Caleb was no Pete Holcomb. He was just a drifter and a no-'count fiddler, and he was lucky Amelia even let him in the house. He had failed Marisol, the mother of his children, and now Javier—another man better than he—was raising his own flesh and blood. He would only fail Amelia, too.

Shaking his head, he let his eyes linger on the trim figure of his former sister-in-law. Imagine him even thinking that Amelia would give him the *chance* to fail her. She turned happily into the kitchen, and Caleb's eyes fell to find Savannah reading thoughts in his head even he barely knew existed.

''Sing something sad and romantic,'' she suggested.

And he found her request an easy one to fulfill, for his heart was churning with verses.

THIRTY-ONE

As I was out walkin' and ramblin' one day
I spied a fair couple a-comin' my way
One was a lady as fair as can be
And the other was a cowboy, and a brave one was he

Savannah felt as naught but a child to Whiplash as she held him to a sidewise trot over the bald hill above Holcomb Ranch. The stallion had seen Pete's gravestone many a time before, but made a show of fear, dipping his head with such force that the reins almost yanked Savannah right over the saddle horn.

"Don't let him boss you," Caleb ordered. "Rein him!" He spurred the old mare to stay nearby.

"I'm trying!"

Whiplash suddenly turned his tail to the gravestone, as if he feared the ghost of the man he had killed. He bolted, all the gathered muscles of his great hindquarters jerking as he ground iron against rock.

Savannah clenched both little fists on the reins and pulled the stallion's chin back, but still he charged down the slope at half speed. Caleb overtook them, belaboring the fat mare with spurs, and caught a rein.

"I've got him!" Savannah insisted. "Turn loose!"

The fiddler smirked and surrendered the stallion's head. It might have been much worse than all this, he thought. It was well that he had prepared for this ride.

He had risen early this morning to ride the bronc out of Whiplash. This had been before daylight; before Savannah would even stir. And just before she mounted, Caleb had ridden the stallion again, out of sight behind the barn, switching the stud with the ends of reins to make him buck now if he was going to buck at all. For his own mount, he had chosen an old mare who would in no way excite Whiplash to violence or passion.

Now Savannah had the stallion just under control, as she had once sailed a small boat in a wild wind off the eastern main. Whiplash was strutting like a fighting cock, refusing to stand, but he would go the way she willed. Her eyes shone with a fury absorbed from the beast below, and her mouth held a smile of half pride, half thrill.

"I told you I could ride this horse," she said.

"Never said you couldn't."

Where are you goin' my pretty fair maid?
Just down by the river, just down by the shade
Just down by the river, just down by the spring
See the wild ripplin' waters, hear the nightingale sing

"I want to shoot your pistol again," she said. "Will you let me?"

"I am at your service today," he replied, affecting a grandiloquent sweep of his hat. "Whatever you want to do."

They had tied the horses near a spring that issued from the flanks of the Rampart Range, two meadows north of the Arapaho Trail. The sun was warm and the air cool; a breeze flowed up the slope. Their glade was the size of a horse pasture, the pretty maid and the brave cowboy at its lower edge, where the spring ran among evergreens and scrub oaks of tender leaves.

"What am I going to shoot at?"

"Did you ever notice," Caleb asked, sauntering among cream-white tree trunks, "how the bark of these aspen trees stares at you?"

"What do you mean?" she said, playfully waving the pistol Caleb had handed to her.

"See here, where a little branch broke off and rotted away? That's the middle of the eyeball that stares at you. The curves above and below it shape it like an eye."

Savannah saw the squint in the tree trunk, then glanced around to find similar markings on other aspens: winking, staring, watching. "Do you want me to shoot at that?"

Caleb strode back to stand beside her. "Put his eye out."

The Colt bucking in her hand made Savannah's heart leap. "I'm getting better," she said.

"Yes, you are. Just a little low, yet."

"Is it true that a forty-five can knock a man down if it hits him in the little finger?"

He shrugged. "I reckon it would if he had his hand over his heart."

Her next shot came closer to her mark, but still the aspen stared innocently, until the next bullet drilled the white of its eye, blasting a chunk of soft wood to flying pulp.

"You're a dangerous woman," Caleb said.

Well, they hadn't been there but an hour or so
Till he drew from his satchel a fiddle and bow
He tuned his old fiddle all on the half-string
And he played his tune over and over again

He would hold the chin rest of the instrument against the crook of his elbow and bounce the bow on two strings, waltz time, while he sang the verses. Then he would clamp the fiddle between chin and shoulder to bear down on the instrument, making the wail of the strings fill the forest and cross the glade. It was an old Irish tune, reworded by cowboys, called "Wild Ripplin' Waters."

"Dance with me," Savanna said. "Put the fiddle down, for heaven's sake, and just hum a waltz to me."

He leaned his fiddle and bow gingerly against a deadfall. "Never did much dancin'. I was always on the other side of the music."

She took his hand, draped her wrist across his shoulder. "Does it frighten you to hold a woman instead of a violin?"

He hummed a little, then said, "Dangerous woman like you? Makes my heart beat faster. Reckon that's fear?"

She didn't seem to hear. "What about the Widow Holcomb?"

His hum broke. "Amelia? What about her?"

"Have you held her? Danced with her?"

"She's my brother's widow, for heaven's sake."

"She's in love with you."

Caleb threw his head back and laughed. "She loved Pete. I ain't the man he was. All she wants from me is to help her raise that boy."

"You're wrong. She wants you."

He looked down at the certainty glaring in her eyes. "How do you know?"

"Because she hates me." She smiled as if she enjoyed being hated. "It's obvious."

He walled his eyes and hummed on, and Savannah pressed her smile against his shirt. They trampled the grass in a circle the size of a good loop. Finally he just quit humming, but the waltz took its time finding an end. They stood feeling each other's warmth until Savannah pulled away and looked up at the cowboy.

He had kissed her before, that day in the Bighorns. And now they were on his home range. With any other endeavor, he would have felt an advantage, but with Savannah he could not tell. He leaned toward her and saw her eyes close halfway.

When he put his lips on hers, he felt her hands move, one pressing across the small of his back, the other taking in the hair that fell on his neck. He could hear the breeze in the treetops, and Savannah's breath, scarcely aware of where one left off and the other began. What might happen next mystified him. He knew women well enough, but this one was a puzzle unto herself.

She twisted her face away suddenly and stepped back, panting with her mouth open, saying nothing.

"Is it time we went?" he asked, just in case she expected him to play the gentleman.

She glanced at the sky. "There's plenty of daylight."

"What am I gonna do with you?"

"Have any ideas?"

"Yes."

She waited. "Well?"

Love of risk surged through him like lightning. "I could throw my sougan down and spread my blanket where the shade dapples the tall grass."

> *Then said the cowboy I should have been gone*
> *No, no, said the pretty maid, just play one more song*
> *I'd rather hear the fiddle just played on one string*
> *See the wild ripplin' waters, hear the nightingale sing*

He was hatless, and leaning back on his elbows when Savannah joined him on the blanket. She grabbed his shirttail and pulled as she threw one leg over him and let her hair fall in his face. Caleb lay back and slid his hands up her thighs, into the ample folds of the riding skirt. The rough calluses of his palms snagged silk like a harrow dragged across the virgin sward. He noticed that her stockings ran high, very high, finally embracing her leg without benefit of garters, as only a good leg and a very fine stocking in combination could achieve.

"Hum that tune again," she suggested, whispering in his ear.

Caleb scarcely had the breath, but he did hum. And he would have robbed a bank just now if Savannah had suggested it. He was thirty-one years old and felt like a schoolboy with a Blue-back Speller. It mattered not to him that the eyes of a hundred quaking aspens gaped upon them.

> *Just down by the river, just down by the spring*
> *See the wild ripplin' waters, hear the nightingale sing*

THIRTY-TWO

TESS PULLED THE shawl around her shoulders and stepped out into the deserted dirt street of Holcomb, Colorado. Circumnavigating a large mud puddle, she turned back to look at the front of her erstwhile boardinghouse, now serving as quarters for Tess and her husband.

String had left before dawn as usual, and had ridden to the ranch to get the horses up from the pasture. Tess had lain in the bed alone, shivering in the large boardinghouse, listening to the sounds of whipping wind and rattling windowpanes.

Now she looked up at the same windowpanes from the outside, her arms crossed, eyes squinting against the backlighting of morning sun. She shook her head. The boardinghouse was too big. She and String would never have children anyway, so what was the sense in choosing a place that would need that much upkeep?

Turning south down the one-street ghost town, she came to the Dannenburg Café, once run by a German woman of the same name: a fat, laughing, red-faced woman who had moved on to California since the town died. Mrs. Dannenburg had been a friend, and Tess missed her. Everyone had moved on. Tess stayed only because her husband managed the Holcomb Ranch—what was left of it.

She stepped up on the boardwalk in front of the café, peered through the dusty windows, then opened the door. A rat scuttled for cover, and Tess slammed the door again, pulling her shawl tighter against a cool spring breeze hissing up the street. The café was a little small anyway, and even during the brief life span of Holcomb, Colorado, it had been used hard, with grease slung everywhere and things spilled. Besides, Tess detested rats. Snakes ate rats. She had once been bitten by a rattler that had the bulge of a rat still visible in its gullet. She cringed. Thinking of it made the fang scar on her leg ache all over again.

She strode on down the street, a lone browser in a canyon out of place. She judged the buildings on either side of her as she walked, dismissing most on sight, stopping to consider a few. Approaching the brick veneer of the failed bank, she slowed her pace, noticing Colonel Ab's horse and buggy around the corner, and beside them a saddle horse from the livery stable in Colorado Springs. What business the colonel could possibly be conducting in there mystified Tess. What was the use of meeting in a place as dead as this—an infant town doomed before the paint could peel from its new facades?

As she stood there and looked at the bank, its door opened, and Delton Little stepped out. He was smiling smugly and tugging at the tails of his vest. When he spotted Tess standing alone in the street, his wind caught in his throat, and he flinched. Seeing that it was a woman, he tipped his derby, the smile gone from a face suddenly pale. He turned the corner to mount his horse and trot away.

She knew vaguely who he was: a government man who looked into disagreements over land claims. She could only imagine why he would be meeting the colonel here alone, but Tess had an adequate imagination.

She wandered on down the street, stopping finally to linger in front of the abandoned general store. It was roomy, but not too much to look after. For some reason, the carpenters had neglected to build a false front on this building, so it looked as much like a house as a place of business. It stood alone, sharing no wall with any adjacent structure.

She stepped up to the door and cautiously entered. The only light came from the glass storefront. It would need windows added. She paced the length and breadth of the floor, figuring how many rooms could be partitioned off inside. There was space for a parlor, bedroom, library, dining room, and a spacious hallway. The storeroom in back would provide ample kitchen space.

Feeling suddenly excited, Tess burst out of the building and turned back up the street at a fast walk. She slowed a little in front of Ab's office, but decided it was not her place to bring the subject up to the colonel. Her stride hit a long rhythm as she struck out for the ranch. String had said something about working in the pens today, and that was only three miles from here.

Halfway to the ranch, she heard the rattle of Colonel Ab's outfit and stepped out of the road to let him pass.

"Good morning, Mrs. McCoy," Ab said, with strange humor. "Do you need a ride?"

"Don't need one," Tess said. "I can walk."

"Where are you going?"

"Over to the pens to talk to my husband."

"You might as well ride, then. I'll pass just by the pens on my way home."

"Well, all right," Tess said.

She got in, hoping the colonel wouldn't ask what she might need to speak with her husband about in the middle of the day. The colonel didn't.

In fact, he didn't say a thing. He just drove on as if nobody at all sat on the seat beside him. It was nice to ride up off the ground, though. Tess was still feeling snakey on account of seeing that rat.

Ab let Tess McCoy out at the lane that led up to the pens, and she walked the rest of the way. Buster had built the pens on his homestead when he acquired his first few head of cattle. Included in the set of pens was a narrow branding chute.

As she approached the pens, Tess could hear the cattle bawling. A cowhand would whistle, another would yell, and the bellow would come as the hot iron was applied to the shoulder or hip of a frightened bovine. Tess came to the outside fence of split pine rails and climbed onto it to look for String.

Piggin' String McCoy was inside the pen on horseback, pressing the last dozen head of cattle into the funnellike opening that led to the branding chute. He stood guard behind the cows, turning them back into the funnel as they tried to escape. Along one side of the chute, on foot, Buster and N.C. stood ready to hold each unmarked calf in the branding chute by means of two sliding gates, one in front and the other behind the unfortunate beast. Once the calf was trapped between these two gates in the narrow chute, a branding iron could be applied quickly between the planks of the chute.

In Buster's mind, this was more efficient and easier on the stock than roping and throwing each head to be marked. "What do you think about my pens?" he had asked N.C. earlier.

N.C., who considered this whole process a devious threat to the quality of his life, had replied, "I imagine this was once a good place to stake a horse."

Once released from the chute, the cattle would lower their heads and trot out of the pen to the open pasture, where Caleb and Walker held them, and cut them from the herd if they wore Buster's brand. Buster's cattle would remain here in his pasture. The colonel's stock would later be pressed out to the larger Holcomb Ranch pasture.

As the last yearling felt the agony of the hot iron, Tess noticed a lone cow standing with her rear end to the corner of the pen her husband rode across. Bones rose on the old cow's back and hips like sand dunes. Her head was low and panting, a string of saliva hanging from her mouth. Her every breath moaned a warning.

"All right, ol' cow," String announced, approaching cautiously on his horse, "now you will git!" He spurred suddenly, hoping to spook the cow out of the corner, but the old girl only returned the charge, coming after the horse's flanks with her short curved horns. String barely managed to avoid her by doubling back. He galloped a circle as wide as the pen would allow and tried again to push the cow into the funnel of the chute. Again she lowered her head and charged, this time hooking String's horse around the gaskin, and tearing the skin as she wrenched her head violently to one side with a blast of breath from her nostrils.

"Damn you!" String shouted, spurring his wounded horse away and untying his rope from the leather strings on the forks of his saddle.

"Hold on, String," N.C. shouted, bounding over the branding chute, landing inside the pen with a ringing of spurs. "You don't want to get your horse ahead of that cow in that damn chute."

The cow was in the middle of the pen, breathing like a locomotive, slinging her head to look alternately at String's horse and the young cowboy on foot.

"What do you think you're gonna do?" String said.

"She wants to chase somethin'. Let her chase me into the chute. Just have that loop ready to drop over her horns in case she gets me down."

Buster climbed up on the rails of the branding chute for a better view. "You watch yourself, Navy. That ol' cow's so mad she'll bite your spurs off."

N.C. only grinned. He liked the way Buster had decided on his own to call him "Navy," which was, after all, his name. He took four steps toward the cow and waved his arms at her. "Boo!" he said.

The old cow answered with a menacing toss of her head. Her eyes glared red and glassy. Her tongue probed nostrils, as if to taste her own suffering fury.

Piggin' String McCoy was laughing. "Hell, she's smarter than that, son. You ain't close enough. Give her a chance to catch you."

N.C. tested his boots for traction in the dirt-and-mud pen. He took three more steps toward the cow, glancing back at the chute to judge his chances. He was standing sideways to her now, ready to double back for the funnel the instant she made her rush. "Hup!" he shouted, flailing his arms.

The cow swaggered like a drunk, recognizing the challenge, daring the cowboy to come closer.

N.C. responded, taking two more steps toward the cow. It was almost as close as he would dare to go. Glancing back at the chute, he wasn't sure anymore that he could make the fence before the cow overtook him.

"That's too close," Buster warned. "She may be sick, but she's light. She'll git on you quick as corn goes through a goose."

"Come on, cow," N.C. growled, kicking a spray of dirt at her. He heard the hoofbeats of a lope and looked over the fences to see his father riding up.

"Git out of there, son!" Walker ordered.

The cow chose this moment of distraction to charge, and N.C. dug his heels into dirt, making his break for the chute. Within two strides, he was stepping long, the awful rattling bellow behind him closing like a hawk on a rat. He leapt a puddle of mud through which the cow slipped, daunting her pace enough that the swath her horns cut through the air missed N.C.'s rump by inches.

He could feel the blasts of her breath as he hurdled into the funnel and reached the corner post that turned into the chute. The men were yelling, and the moan of the crazed cow kept him from slowing down as he hooked an elbow around the corner post to turn his flight at full speed. He expected to gain some ground, but only recovered a step as the cow planted and cut up the chute like a wild cat.

N.C. could feel seven steps ahead of him to the first sliding gate, and there was a rattle in the throat of the sick cow that made his arms pump furiously for speed. If she caught him in this chute, he would be better off lying down than letting her get a horn in his crotch.

He made the gate in six steps and saw Buster ready to close it behind him. He heard the iron fittings slide, and saw the impact of the cow shake the lumber on both sides of him. Still, he took no chances, leaping over the left side of the chute with a bound that would have rivaled a deer's. The cow, seeing daylight at the end of the chute, forgot about the cowboy, and escaped to the herd, trotting stiffly with exhaustion.

"You like to have pissed in your own cistern on that one, son!" Walker growled. Then he looked across the pens and saw Tess McCoy. "Pardon my lingo, ma'am," he said, taking his hat off.

String followed Walker's eyes. "Woman, how come you ain't home?" It embarrassed the fire out of him to have his wife show up where he was supposed to be boss. Riding to the fence, he stepped from the stirrup to a rail, climbed over, and walked across the adjacent pen to the place where Tess perched. "What the devil is it?" he said hoarsely.

"I don't wanna live in that big ol' boardin' house no more."

"Huh?"

"It's too big, String. It's cold and lonesome, and it takes me all day to sweep cobwebs out of all them empty rooms."

"Well, I guess you better move on back to Arkansas where you come from, then. That's the house the colonel give us. We don't git our pick."

"I don't see why not. There's all them empty stores and things in town now. Why cain't we have one of them?"

String beat his hat against his thigh and hissed. "I swun, woman, I cain't believe you walked all the way down here to bother me like this."

"I didn't walk all the way. Colonel Ab give me a ride."

His eyes almost popped. "You didn't tell him you wanted a new house, did you?"

"I ain't stupid," Tess growled.

"I wonder. Now, you git on back home and be satisfied with what you have."

"No! I ain't gonna live in that dead town, String. That place has got haints in it. I want Buster to move the old general store down to the ranch and make a house of it with a big watch-it-rain porch all the way around."

String was about to choke on his chaw of tobacco. "Move? Woman, a house don't move 'less a twister sucks it up."

"Buster can move it."

"You gonna get Buster to spirit you a twister? Only thing that needs movin' around here is your hind end movin' on back home."

"Hey, Buster!" Tess shouted, waving him over.

"Just stay where you're at, Buster!" String shouted.

"Come here!" Tess demanded.

Buster approached and leaned an elbow on the fence rail. "Mornin', Miss Tess," he said, smiling. Tess was one of the best white women Buster knew. She always gave him the impression that she looked level at him.

"Never mind, Buster," String said. "Let us be."

"Now, String, these here is my pens, and I reckon if the lady wants to tell me somethin' in my own pens, I got a right to hear it." He gathered his eyebrows to show his interest and listened to Tess explain what she wanted and why.

"There," String said. "Now, would you set her straight and tell her to mind her place from here on out."

Buster was stroking his chin, gazing at the terrain between the ranch and town. "I got some freight jacks that'll lift it," he said. "Back a couple of drop-tongue wagons under it, and I don't see no reason why it won't just up and roll wherever you want it."

"Oh, I swun!" String moaned, walling his eyes. "You two will get me fired botherin' the colonel with your Mexican oats!" He jammed his hat down onto his ears and stormed off across the pen like a sick and angry cow.

THIRTY-THREE

BUSTER HAD ACQUIRED the four jacks one at a time over the years. The old Murphy and Conestoga freight wagons that passed through before the railroads tended to wear out while the jacks used to lift an occasional axle were still in good repair. With hickory handles long enough to produce ample leverage, each could lift a ton or two.

By the time the morning sun hit the back door of the erstwhile general store, the four jacks were in place under its corners. Buster manned one, while Piggin' String, Dan Brooks, and Tess handled the others.

"One, two, *three*!" Buster would sing, "one, two, *three*!" and all four jacks would rise a notch on the third beat. Almost without thinking about it, Buster fell into a work song he hadn't sung in twenty-five years:

> *Haul on the bowline*
> *The ship she is a-rollin'*
> *Haul on the bowline*
> *The bowline, haul.*

He stopped to let Tess catch her breath. She was a strong woman, but smaller than the men, of course, and she needed almost all her weight to bring the jack handle down. Buster saw Dan Brooks gawking at him around the corner and wished he hadn't strayed from a simple count of three.

"What was you singin'?" Dan demanded.

"Old sailor's song," Buster said.

"You was a sailor? I thought you was a slave back east."

This was the reminder Buster tried forever to avoid. "I sailed the Chesapeake regular," he said.

"In a slave boat?"

Tess came to Buster's rescue. "Dan, has your corner come up off the blocks yet? I want it kept level. I don't want my house to rack."

"It's floatin'," Dan said. "I hope it don't fall off and kill String and make you a widder."

"It ain't fallin' nowhere," Buster said. "Y'all ready?"

Dan Brooks went back to his jack, Tess nodded, and String hollered from the far corner of the frame building. Buster sang out one, two, three, and the hollow shell of lumber rose by notches. When the jacks rose as high as they would go, the laborers had to stack foundation stones, let the building down onto them, put other stone blocks under the jacks, and raise the building ever higher.

"I swun," String complained, sitting on the ground and tugging a large cube of granite out from under the raised building, "I ain't made for this kind of work."

As the old store rose to metallic clicks and human grunts, a procession appeared on the town's street, led by Colonel Ab Holcomb's one-horse gig. Behind him rode Caleb with Walker and N. C. Kincheloe.

"Hold up," Buster ordered, and he waited for Ab to look approvingly at the work. It had been a simple matter to convince the colonel that the building should be moved. When he mentioned that String was riding all the way to town every day for dinner, and really should have a house on the ranch, closer to his work, Ab readily agreed. If the moving of the store proved easily enough accomplished, Buster had ideas about moving other abandoned buildings from town to the ranch, and dismantling still others for their lumber.

When Ab reached the store on stilts, he drew rein and stared for a while.

"Buster," Walker remarked, "I sure hope a chinook don't git up and blow it sideholts. Might have to prize it up off of somebody."

"I believe he's thought of that," Caleb added. "That's why he put Dan and Piggin' String downwind of it. We can bear the loss of them."

As Caleb and Walker chuckled, String came around the building, dusting off the seat of his pants. "You want me to go with y'all to the hearing, Colonel? There's four of them Mayhall boys, and they might bring friends. I got a gun in my saddle pocket."

"Stay here," Ab said. "It's to be your house, isn't it? Besides, those Mayhalls won't try anything in broad daylight."

String spat a brown stream into the dirt street, grown up now with weeds.

Buster smiled, half amused at String's attempt to get out of work and half gratified to see Caleb and his father riding together again. Maybe they weren't talking a blue streak, but there had been a time when they wouldn't even cross each other on the road, much less ride the same direction together.

"Get on with it," Ab said, as he shook his reins. He really expected Buster to have had the house halfway to the ranch by this time in the morning, but he hadn't given much thought to the details. He had other matters on his mind. This morning in Colorado Springs, Delton Little would quash Joe Mayhall's challenge to the Matthew Holcomb claim. The Mayhalls

were going to be furious, but they had asked for it. Ab was wearing his
Walker Colt, and was happy to have Walker Colt Kincheloe along, too,
whom he could tell understood the stakes.

He had opposing feelings about Caleb riding along. On the one hand, it
was tonic to his sore aching heart to have his wayward son taking an interest in the home place for a change. On the other hand, he didn't relish the
thought of tangling Caleb up in this trouble with the Mayhalls, even
though it couldn't possibly be more dangerous than the messes Caleb must
have survived out there doing whatever it was he did with his life.

After the Holcombs and Kincheloes rode on toward Colorado Springs,
the jacking continued until Buster measured the underside of the building
against his chest and deemed it high enough to get the wagon boxes under
it.

"Let's get the rest of them blocks out from under the middle," he suggested, anxious to have the building stabilized on the wagons.

"I ain't crawling under that thing jacked up that high," String said.

Tess grabbed a rope and dove under the building. "I swear, String, you
have cried like a baby all morning long. *I'll* crawl under it."

"Here now, Tess, you git out of there!"

But she disregarded her husband and looped the rope around a foundation block for the men to pull out of the way. When the blocks were
cleared, Tess left for the boardinghouse to make some dinner for the men.
Dan and String pushed the first of the three wagons backward under the
lifted store while Buster steered it with the tongue. The edges of the wagon
box passed just inches under the floor beams. Buster had considerably bol-
stered the boxes of the wagons with beams and iron fittings, so they would
carry the weight of the building.

After backing the second wagon carefully into place beside the first,
Buster set to work making them one unit, fastening them in tandem with
beams bolted across the front and back of the wagon beds. The third
wagon went in front of the first two, its front wheels under the front door
to allow for turning.

Tess rang the dinner bell about noon, so Buster left the old general store
suspended over the wagons and walked with the two cowboys down to the
boardinghouse. They ate quickly, drank some coffee, and returned to their
work site.

Lowering the jacks, the workers let the building settle by degrees as the
wagon boxes complained with creaks and groans. Finally, Tess's house
had wheels, and was ready for the three-mile pull to Holcomb Ranch.

While they fitted Buster's four teams of draft horses with harness,
Buster heard String's saddle horse nicker. He looked toward Colorado

Springs to see four men coming at a trot. He recognized the Mayhall brothers at a glance and wished suddenly that he had loaded a shotgun or a rifle with his tools this morning.

The brothers slowed to a walk by the building on wheels, but none of them spoke. The three older brothers looked mad, while young Joe only appeared to wish he were somewhere else.

"Evenin', gentlemen," Buster said.

Joe Mayhall touched his hat and started to speak to Buster, but the silence of his older brothers gave him cause to hold his tongue.

Piggin' String McCoy came to the front of the building. He grinned smugly at the angry faces of the homesteaders. He had nothing against the Mayhalls personally, but they were nesters and had led the fence-cutting in years past that had broken Holcomb Ranch down to nothing, ending the glories of String's cowboy days. "How'd everything go in town today?" he asked.

Edgar turned his mule to face the cowboy. "You know damn good and well how everything went, McCoy. You, too, Buster. All you that work for old Holcomb is in on it, far as we can see."

"That's enough," Frank said, his war-seasoned gaze looking calmly over the house movers. "Don't make no never mind now, anyways. Let's git."

They rode on up the deserted street, and Buster went back to hitching horses, his heart thumping hard in his chest. This had been building for years. The Mayhalls were born of violence. Buster knew he had better watch out for them. They had just let on that they considered him an accomplice to whatever Ab had cooked up in secret with Delton Little. And Buster could not blame them. He knew very well what was going on. For years he had tried to keep things smooth between the Holcombs and the Mayhalls. But Ab had grown too old and hardheaded, and the Mayhalls had grown too numerous, too strong, too angry. They would do something to get even.

By the time he had the trace chains hitched and the reins run through the rings in the horse collars, he could see Colonel Ab's buggy coming in the distance from the direction of Colorado Springs, his escort of horsemen flanking him.

"Now, when me and Colonel Ab laid this town out," he said to the cowboys, "I tolt him we ought to make this-here street wide enough for freight wagons to turn in. Good thing, too, else we couldn't turn this-here house down toward the ranch."

"Damn, he talks like he's half owner and founder of this place," String said to Dan.

"He can be full owner and founder for all the good it'll do him now. Mayor of a ghost town don't pay much."

String chuckled and spat, wiping his sleeve across his mouth. "I reckon me and you can be the ghost town council, Dan. Tess says this place is full of haints, anyhow."

"All right," Buster said, taking the jibes with good humor. "Let's git this-here load started before Colonel Ab comes by."

Buster climbed up to the front door of the building with the four sets of reins while Dan, String, and Tess walked alongside the first three teams of horses. "Git up," Buster said, and the horses stepped forward. Double-trees and singletrees rose from the dirt on tightened chains, and the eight big beasts ran dead into the weight behind them, leaning reluctantly for a second. "Hup, there!" Buster growled, shaking the reins.

The horses bowed their necks into the collars, strained together, and began to move the burden they would pull three miles down to the ranch.

"Easy all the way," Buster said. "Them wheel hosses is all that can slow your house down, Miss Tess, so don't let 'em go faster than you can walk 'em."

The house turned onto the street to the caterwauling of straining wood in the wagons and in the building itself. Tess looked uncertainly over her shoulder, half expecting to see the whole thing list and fall onto the board-walk of the abandoned land office, but it rode level and made the turn.

Ab's gig overtook the moving shell in the street, and he looked around the corner of the store to find Buster driving from the front door. "I expected you'd be farther down the road by now."

Buster only shrugged, noticing that Delton Little had joined the group of horsemen.

"Have the Mayhall boys been through here?" Caleb asked.

" 'Bout half an hour ago."

"They stomped out of the courthouse plenty riled."

"They was still riled here," Buster said.

Ab lashed his horse with a buggy whip and trotted to his bank office, followed closely by Delton Little. The rest of the mounted men followed at a walk and waited in front of the office while Colonel Ab and the government man finished their business inside.

The old general store lumbered through the town, Tess walking with the lead team. Piggin' String and Dan had doubled back on foot to get their saddle horses for the long slow ride to the ranch. Buster drove on, watching Walker, N.C., and Caleb laugh about something in front of the failed bank.

This would have been a happy day if not for the danged squabble over land. The Mayhalls had shaken Buster, even more than that day when Delton Little first showed up in his idiotic derby and Ab tried to pull his old Walker Colt.

The erstwhile store rocked through a rut, and Buster's shoulders bounced against the doorjamb. He braced himself fore and aft by putting one foot in front of the other, a long step apart. Once out of town, he could sit down in the doorway and take it easy, but for now he wanted to be ready.

Ready for what? The horses were well trained, pulling fine. Tess was still coaxing the leaders on, and Buster reckoned she'd walk with them all the way to the ranch. Dan and String were coming up now, one on each side of the big draft horses. They had everything well under control. What could happen?

The low rooftop of the shut-down laundry shed afforded Buster a narrow view northeastward across the plains. He saw the road leading to the Mayhall brothers' spread. The bank door opened, just two doors up the left side of the street, and Delton Little stepped out, tugging at the tails of his vest. The bank was in the middle of town, the only brick building. It stood at the corner of the only intersection, the side street leading nowhere but to the livery stable, east.

Buster looked over the laundry roof again. This wasn't right. No dust. No Mayhalls riding in the distance. "Miss Tess," he said. He could feel it going wrong as his team drew nearly abreast of the bank. "Git back!"

Caleb and Walker heard Buster's order and looked up. Caleb was puzzled, for he could see nothing amiss about the team. Buster was shaking the reins, whistling at the horses. Walker put his hand over the grip of the Colt in his shoulder holster and cut his eyes up and down the side street.

"They didn't go home!" Buster yelled.

Ab stepped out of the bank door, and a roar of gunfire ripped into the group of men in front of the bank. Delton Little slammed against the red bricks and slumped onto his side. Ab fell facedown, his wooden leg shattered by a bullet. Mounts reared and bolted from the hitching rail. The team of draft horses ramped and stalled. Tess screamed.

Another volley made the red brick wall of the bank spout dust. Walker was holding his frightened horse by the reins while N.C. took cover behind Ab's buggy, holding the buggy horse. Caleb ran for his father as buckshot shattered the boardwalk under his feet. He lifted Ab, who drew his antique Colt, the black powder roar hurling a bullet vaguely down the side street.

Buster yelled fury at the draft horses and they jerked the moving store forward with a lurch. String was probing his saddle bag for his pistol when his horses screamed and fell on him, pinning his leg.

Tess ran for String's horse and pounced on the wounded animal's head to keep it from thrashing or rolling on her husband.

Delton Little's dead body jerked with impact of wasted slugs and Walker C. Kincheloe got mounted. Bullets ripped around the big Texan, but he returned them, spying a gunman behind an empty water trough down the side street in front of the livery. Ab's buggy splintered like timber in a tornado as the three men taking cover behind it set up their own barrage, though none had found a target yet.

The draft horses were pulling hard now, Dan having joined Buster in driving them into the cross fire with yells, and the store moved down the street like a man-of-war sailing into battle at sea.

Walker had driven off the man behind the water trough—that young Mayhall boy, he thought—and now the big man took cover behind the moving store, leaping from his horse so he could spring around the corner and fire at a smoking muzzle he had spotted on the café roof. Dan was with him but had no weapon with which to fire, so he stayed mounted.

The moving building splintered now, shielding the buggy. N.C. and Caleb rushed to join Walker behind the store, leaving Ab to hold the buggy horse.

Tess's shrill voice came down the street: "My house! My house!"

"My leg, goddamn it!" String replied, his voice breaking with pain.

Buster was judging his position, ready to rein in the draft team, when a jolt kicked him high in the rib cage. The reins he clenched kept him from falling backward; horses balked and the store stopped rolling; Buster pitched forward and saw the wagon tongue coming up at him. He hit the tongue and bounced under the right wheel horse, who kicked him and vaulted forward.

"Buster!" Caleb hollered. "Roll!"

Buster was in a blur, but he rolled under the tongue as the store started moving again, and the front wheels of the lead wagon straddled him. Caleb dove under the building, wrapped his legs around Buster's bloody chest, latched onto the running gear with his hands, and dragged Buster down the street to keep him from getting crushed by the wheels of the two following wagons.

Dan Brooks had spurred his mount into the gunfire to catch the lead team of draft horses, while Walker and N. C. Kincheloe fired over the withers of the big animals, peppering the rooftops with bullets. Their weapons clicked against spent shells, and the roar of gunfire ceased.

The Mayhalls were hollering at each other on the rooftops, inside the abandoned buildings. Boots scuffled on lumber. Above his ringing ears,

Caleb heard horses beating the ground at a gallop. Tess's house stopped rolling, and he felt blood like scalding water on the legs he had wrapped around Buster.

Buster wheezed as Caleb released him. "Better git me to a doctor, son. I'm shot pretty bad."

"All right now, hold on." A hundred thoughts milled in his brain at once, and the sight of blood moving down Buster's shirt made his stomach turn cold and heavy as an anvil. He put his hand over the wound, trying to stanch the flow.

Walker had reloaded and ridden down the side street and was emptying his revolver at the fleeing Mayhall brothers, who were far down the abandoned narrow-gauge tracks.

Down the street, Caleb could hear String's pained yodel:

"Damn it, Dan, come pull this hoss off my leg!"

THIRTY-FOUR

WALKER CAME BURSTING out of the doctor's office and leapt into the bullet-splintered buggy, where Caleb cradled Buster on the seat. "The doctor's up at Manitou, but they said there's another sawbones down at Old Town." He shook the reins and turned the tired buggy horse in the street. "Is he still alive?"

Caleb cupped his bloody hand over Buster's mouth. "He's breathin'." He had ridden all the way to town with his hands pressed over the wound the bullet had made.

"Can he hear us?"

"I can't tell."

Walker shook the reins and turned the buggy horse in the street. "Buster, just so you'll know, we got one of them, too," he said in a loud voice. "When they was ridin' away, I saw two of 'em holdin' a third one in the saddle. He was floppin' around like a rag doll, so I know he was hit bad. Bad as you, or worse."

Eyes followed them out of town as they drove to the neighboring settlement of Colorado City. The old frontier town, founded as a jumping-off place for prospectors plying the Rockies, was beyond reach of Colorado Springs' local ordinances against the sale of spirits and it tended to attract a harder set of folk.

Cussing the buggy horse down among the rotting shanties, Walker spotted a painted shingle reading DR. KETCHUM—PHYSICIAN hanging over the doorway of a building of weathered rawhide lumber. The horse was so tired that Walker didn't bother drawing rein, but growled "Whoa," and jumped out in front of the door under the shingle.

"He's over here," a voice said before the big man could get all the way through the door.

Caleb turned to see an ancient prospector smoking his pipe on a bench in front of a saloon.

"Get him inside, Hard Winter. I'll fetch the doc."

Walker trotted down the rotted corduroy walkway, entered the saloon, and gave his eyes a few seconds to adjust to the smoky gloom. "Where's Ketchum?" he said.

A man at a lone poker game looked over his shoulder. "What do you want?" He was middle-aged, and pale. Oil plastered his hair, and a set of frayed suspenders traversed his hunched shoulders.

"A man's been shot."

"Where is he?"

"In your office."

The doctor cussed and turned back to his cards. "How bad is he?"

Walker descended on the poker table, judging the three other card players, all of whom looked like meek townsmen to him. "He's real bad. Shot through one lung, I'd say."

The doctor threw back a shot of whiskey and turned up the corner of a card on the table to size up its worth. "How long ago?"

"Monument Park at a long trot." Walker was standing at the doctor's shoulder now, making sure he could see the hands of all four men around the card table.

The doctor sighed and studied the fan of playing cards held close to his chin. "Well, I guess he can wait till this hand's played out. Anyway, I don't treat much in the way of gunshot wounds."

Walker drew his weapon from the cross-draw holster at his hip and yanked the man to his feet by the shirt collar. "Where's your bag?"

"In the office," the doctor said.

Walker covered the startled men at the table and dragged the doctor away, but not before Ketchum could grab a bottle of whiskey to take with him.

"You don't need that forty-rod," Walker said.

"Whiskey's got medicinal properties, sir. Easy, now! Let me go!"

The big man hustled Dr. Ketchum out of the saloon and shoved him into his own office, where they found Buster lying on a table that Caleb had cleared of dirty dishes and utensils.

"My Lord!" the doctor said, seeing the bloody black man on the table. Suddenly he began to chuckle.

"What's so damn funny?" Caleb demanded.

"I was hoping for another spade back there in the saloon, and look where one turned up." He stuck the spout of the bottle in his mouth and turned the bottom up.

"He's drunk as a pissant," Caleb said.

"Best we got," Walker replied. "Get on with it, sawbones." He pushed the doctor toward the table.

As Ketchum approached the patient, a sudden coughing fit doubled him over and seemed about to drop him to his knees.

"Hell, he looks like he needs a doctor his own self," Caleb complained.

Ketchum propped himself up with his hands on his thighs, then looked at Caleb with watery eyes. "Consumption. Do you think I came west to live in this hellhole by choice?"

"Get on with it!" Walker repeated.

Caleb had lain Buster on his side and now lifted the blood-plastered shirt from the bullet wound for the doctor to view.

"Oh!" Ketchum cried, wincing and turning suddenly away. "I'm no good with blood."

"A doctor that cain't stand blood?" Caleb blurted.

Impatiently, Walker jabbed Ketchum in the ribs with the muzzle of his Colt. "Make medicine, damn it!"

The doctor took another swig and risked one eye in examination of the patient. "He's got a hole through him you could stick your fist into! If he's got any blood left, it isn't enough to fill a thimble."

"Do *somethin'!*" Caleb ordered, feeling his worry turn to anger.

"All right," Ketchum said, stooping in front of the patient's face. He opened one of Buster's eyes, as if to examine it. "Can you hear me, boy? You might as well give up the ghost. You don't need a doctor, you need a grave digger." He took his hand from Buster's face, squinted with merriment, and wheezed a hoarse chuckle with his elbows on the table and the bottle in his hand.

Caleb's hands became fists as he trembled with insensible ire. But as he came around the table, Buster's eyes opened and his lips formed a snarl. With one excruciating heave, his chest drew air and then he spat, spraying the face of the drunken doctor.

"Son of a bitch!" Ketchum rasped, raising his bottle to strike as he wiped his face with a cuff.

Caleb swung around the corner of the table and jabbed Ketchum with a hard left fist, bowling him over backward and sending the bottle scuttling across the floor, spinning, slinging whiskey in arches on the rough wood. He descended on the doctor as he rolled to all fours and kicked him through the door that Walker had opened.

"Get out, you quack!" he roared, then turned back to Walker, who was putting his revolver in its holster.

"Looks like it's up to us, fiddler," the big man said.

Caleb looked at Buster, found one side of his mouth smiling. He could hear Ketchum coughing uncontrollably outside. He looked at Walker, nodded, and clenched his tingling fist around Ketchum's black leather medicine bag.

Joe Mayhall scooped up a shovelful of dirt and threw it into the hole containing Edgar's blanket-wrapped body. He could no longer hold the sob back, and it burst from his lips as his eyes gushed tears.

"Quit blubberin'!" Frank said. "If it was Edgar buryin' you, he wouldn't be blubberin'!"

"I wish't it was!" Joe said.

"Both of you shut up!" Terrence ordered. "We ain't got time for it. They'll be comin' for us by now. Whose side do you think they'll take?"

Joe sniffed back his fear. "I knowed we shouldn't have done it."

"You didn't do nothin,' Joe," Frank told him. "Blasted a brick wall is all."

"Don't matter who done what now," Terrence said. His burly muscles strained at his clothes as he pushed dirt into the grave, using his shovel as if it were a broom. He could hear the womenfolk wailing in the house. "We don't stay together now, we'll die together on the gallows."

"Hadn't been for Buster movin' that damn house, they'd all be dead," Frank said.

"I wish't we'd got the colonel is all," Terrence said.

"He went down."

"I shot him in the leg, that's why. The wooden one is all. Lucky old bastard."

They finished shoveling dirt, watching the road from Colorado Springs for trouble.

"We'd better git," Frank said. "The boys have got the fresh horses saddled for us."

"Did you tell Mary to pack us some eats?"

Frank nodded.

"Then let's git."

Joe threw his shovel down. "Where we goin'?"

"Over the mountains," Terrence said. "We got cousins at the copper mines in Leadville. If we git split up, that's where we'll meet. We'll leave things settle here for a piece."

Joe stood by the grave as his brothers turned away. "Somebody ought to say some words over Edgar." He felt sick. He had never wanted that Matthew Holcomb claim in the first place. Never even wanted to farm. He dang sure never wanted any of it bad enough to shoot at somebody. He felt cowardly for letting his brothers drag him into this, yet if he had refused, they would have made him feel lower than a coward.

"Oh, all right," Terrence said, taking off his hat. "Say some words, Frank. Quick."

Frank dragged his hat from his head and raked the sweaty hair back. "Lord, this here's our brother, Edgar. He done good. Fought good, and died good. Heaven or hell, it won't make much difference to Edgar, but I guess he was God-fearin' as the next man. We'll git them that laid him low, Lord. 'Eye for eye,' like the Good Book says. 'Tooth for tooth.' Brother for brother. Amen."

THIRTY-FIVE

THE SPECIAL BOARD meeting took place on the second floor of the Cheyenne Club. Hiram Baber sat along one long flank of the meeting table. He was listening carefully, digesting every word, but his eyes kept drifting to the view of the plains through the cut glass of the double French doors, then back to the hardwood file cabinet where Secretary Sturgis kept all association documents.

The cabinet was usually locked, and Sturgis carried the only key in his pocket. But it was open now, and Hiram ached to peruse the files.

"My conclusion is a natural one," Chauncey Shanahan was saying. He was standing near one end of the table, his weight leaning on knuckles that whitened against the polished oak surface. "Because of the severe winter and the reduction in cattle prices, we must agree across the board on two items. Number one: Reduce the wages of all cowhands. Two: Abolish the tradition of free board for cowhands at ranch houses."

Judge Carey, president of the association, nodded as Shanahan sat down. "Anybody else have anything to say?"

Hiram hesitated for a dramatic moment, then rose in silence. "Yes," he said, pausing again for suspense. "I don't know what brand of logic Chauncey has applied to our situation. Perhaps it is a Scottish brand, but it is not a western brand. If we adopt the two measures Chauncey is calling for, the cow business as we know it in Wyoming will be doomed."

A grumble ran the length of the table like a telegraph message up a wire. Chair legs rattled against the imported oak floor as men turned to better hear the argument of Hiram Baber.

"In the first place, we have not had a severe winter. If you would listen to men who were living here years before any of us came, you would know that. Most of the men in this room didn't even stay in Wyoming for the winter. The cattle fared poorly through the winter not because the weather was harsh, but because the range has been abused. If we had experienced a truly severe winter, most of us would have lost fifty percent of our herds, and some may have lost as high as ninety percent."

A few incredulous scoffs turned to chuckles, but Hiram strode resolutely around the table, to the French doors. He turned the polished brass handles, flung the doors open, and took one step out onto the balcony.

"Do you see that bunch of cows out there a half mile or so north? The whole time Chauncey was speaking, I watched those cows plod. No matter how cloquently he spoke about wages or free board, those cows kept moving. They did not pause to switch their tails contentedly, nor to lie down, nor to chew their cuds. They have nothing in their stomachs with which to make cuds. They are looking for grass, gentlemen, and there's none to be found!" The cool bite of early spring was tightening Hiram's flesh, working the way rawhide shrank to strengthen a saddle tree.

Shanahan rose. "The reason there is no grass is because we've allowed the peasant classes to maverick their way into our domain!"

The French doors rattled behind Hiram as he came back into the room. "Chauncey, how many head of cattle did you add to the range before winter set in? Five thousand? Ten thousand? Henry, I've heard you brag that you bought twenty thousand head in Nebraska and turned them out on the Sweetwater. Twenty thousand! The little men own herds that number in the dozens. The pressure they put on the range is insignificant. We haven't addressed the real issue in this meeting, gentlemen. It is not wages of cowhands, nor free board at ranch houses. God knows the issue is not mavericks. The issue is greed. We'll all be wiped out if we don't agree to reduce the size of our herds by as much as half."

"That is not possible!" Shanahan said. "Prices are far too low for us to start dumping cattle on the market."

"Prices are low because cattle are declining in quality, and the decline is caused by lack of nutrition. Besides, the price you'll get now is better than what you'll get for a carcass. We've all made obscene profits on this range for years, but now it's time to take our belts up a notch and cut back. We're going to have to take a loss sooner or later and get the range back in shape. To think that we can make up our losses by cutting wages is ridiculous. I for one will not go along with any wage cut. I have already lost my best men to Montana, Colorado, Idaho, even Canada. Some have gone back to Texas, where they are *encouraged* to own cattle instead of blackballed for it. Why? It gives them a vested interest in the range.

"Anyway, the men won't stand for a wage cut. You've seen what the people of this territory did to your Bill Maverick law. Every man brought up on charges of mavericking has been acquitted. No jury in the territory will convict. This association's power is all on paper, gentlemen, and nowhere out there among the people.

"As for this 'free board' Chauncey speaks of, it's real name is the *grub line,* and it is the only thing keeping our work force here through the winter. It is a tradition of the range as old as the frontier. We can't offer these cowboys seasonal wages, then tell them to starve through the winter!

"Chauncey, you don't want these cowhands to own cattle, you won't let them buy mavericks, you don't want to pay them enough to live on year-round, you don't want to offer them an occasional meal in the off-season. You don't want them filing homesteads on the public domain, but you've given them no choice. They must homestead land and maverick cattle in order to survive. Because of your ridiculous Bill Maverick law, mavericking cattle is the same as rustling cattle now. You've driven them to a life of crime. What you fail to understand is that the sympathy of the common people in this territory lies with the rustler now, not with this association. We have devastated this once prosperous land. When the lynch ropes uncoil, whose necks will be in the nooses? Those of men you have driven to rustling cattle? Or your own?"

Judge Carey called for a recess before asking for a vote, and the men rose to fetch drinks downstairs.

"I'm with you," one of the members said quietly to Hiram. "I've got good men working for me now who know the business, and I don't want to lose them."

Hiram shook the man's hand and sensed the division in the room, a majority grouping around Chauncey Shanahan, Secretary Sturgis, and Judge Carey. But the men who came to Hiram's side were ever increasing in number, making him hopeful of eventually controlling some influence in the association and in the whole territory.

Hiram Baber had come to Wyoming for two reasons: to get rich in the cattle business and to experience some western adventure before settling down with some debutante to run the family export businesses back east. But now, something new had begun to germinate in his ambitious mind. Folks listened to him out here. Not just his own kind, but the common western folks, as well. It had started merely as an attempt to keep his friend Walker C. Kincheloe employed in the cow business, but it had grown beyond anything he had planned. He had taken a stand, and men were expecting him to carry the fight to the finish. Lately, he had caught himself rehearsing stump speeches, looking forward to statehood for Wyoming.

He was in perfect position. Twenty-eight years old, book literate, trail hardened. He could combine horse sense with common sense, lace vernacular with verse, ride point or shape policy.

"I wish we had voted right after your speech," one of the more moderate cattlemen said. "You would have won a majority to your side."

Another moderate put his hand on Hiram's shoulder. "That's why Judge Carey called for a recess, so he could whip up support downstairs before taking the vote."

"Doesn't matter," Hiram said. He watched as Judge Carey urged Sturgis downstairs. "No matter what the vote, I won't cut wages. The men won't work for less than they're getting. And no man has the right to tell me whether or not I can feed a drifting cowboy in my kitchen."

The hard-liners were all in the stairwell now, and Hiram realized that Sturgis had forgotten about locking the file cabinet. "We'd better get to the bar and whip up our own support." He gestured toward the stairs, urging the men to go ahead of him.

Halfway down the stairs, Hiram felt his breast pocket. "I've left my cigars, gentlemen. Pour a brandy for me, and one for yourselves, and I'll be right down."

He turned back up the stairs alone, paused to make sure no one would follow, and made a line for the file cabinet. This was the first chance he had had to get into the files without anyone knowing, though he had tried for almost a year whenever he came to Cheyenne.

The first drawer opened quietly, and he thumbed through the folders, not really sure where to find the records he sought. The second drawer stuck, then squeaked, but the men were making too much noise downstairs to notice. He thumbed through folders until he found a thin one labeled "MAVERICKS, SALES."

Yanking the file, he opened it on top of the cabinet, keeping one ear trained for footsteps in the stairwell. There were only a few sheets of paper in the file, and he rifled through them until he found one labeled "Roundup 17" at the top. Following his index finger down the hand script, he found the date—May 19—and beside it Chauncey Shananhan's name. In a column to the right he found a line that read, "3 head, $10 each, total, $30."

Hiram took all the documents from the file, closed the empty folder, returned it to the cabinet, and closed the drawer. Again he looked at the pages he had lifted, his heart pounding. It was all that he had hoped for. So much so that he hadn't even thought beyond acquiring it. What would he do now?

These documents held proof of corruption in the highest levels of the Wyoming Stock Growers Association. Specifically, one entry proved that Chauncey Shanahan, in cooperation with the roundup foreman, Dave Donaldson, had conspired to outbid all small operators at the roundup. Hiram remembered being present when Chauncey bid fifty dollars to keep Walker C. Kincheloe and Jack Flagg from buying a maverick branded *M* by the association. But Chauncey had not paid fifty dollars for that beef. He had paid only ten, as the official document indicated, signed by Secretary Sturgis. This was proof of a conspiracy intended to keep cattle out of the hands of anyone save the very wealthiest and most influential members of the association. Hiram had to wonder how widespread the practice had become.

Hearing footsteps, he quickly folded the sheaves of paper and slipped them into his breast pocket. Taking a cigar from the same pocket, he bit off the end and met Secretary Sturgis at the top of the stairs.

"Did I leave the files open?" Sturgis asked.

Hiram looked back. "Perhaps you did. That drawer's open a bit."

Sturgis grunted and took the filing cabinet key from his pocket. "Hell of a speech you made, but I don't agree with you. There will be plenty of grass with the spring rains."

Hiram looked through the French doors. The cattle he had watched had now trailed completely out of sight. "Rainfall doesn't blanket Wyoming. The herds congregate where it has passed and eat every blade of grass before it can grow stirrup high. Anyway, what if the rains didn't come at all this spring?"

Sturgis shook his head and strode as if exhausted toward the filing cabinet. "When did you become such a pessimist?"

"I'm a realist."

Sturgis locked the cabinet and turned back to Hiram. "Well, it was a nice speech, and a good try, but you don't have the votes.''

"Probably not," Hiram conceded, and he smiled.

"You'd make a good politician. Come on, I'll buy you a drink.''

Two days after losing the vote, Hi was cutting into a rare steak in the restaurant of the Cheyenne Club when he sensed someone approaching. Looking up, he found Chauncey Shanahan, the smug grin still on his face.

"Hiram," the Scot said with a nod.

"Sit down, Chauncey," Hi said, a smirk of his own beginning to form.

Shanahan sat across the small table and laced his fingers together between the clusters of shining silverware. "You made a valiant effort, Hiram, but it was misguided. You'll see that the wage cut will benefit you in time.''

Hiram grunted and gestured with his fork as he chewed a tender morsel of beef. He swallowed and said, "I'm not cutting wages. My men make forty dollars a month. And the latchstring will always be on the outside of my door for a drifting cowboy.''

Shanahan stiffened. "You can't enjoy the benefits of this association—like that steak you're eating in this club's dining room—if you don't follow the rules of the organization." His knuckle rapped against the table in cadence with his harsh words. "A vote was taken and recorded. Now you must comply, or I personally will see that your name is stricken from the rolls. You will not be allowed to attend the roundups, nor to work your cattle. Your unbranded calves will be claimed by the association as mavericks and sold to the highest bidder. You will be drummed out of the beef industry in Wyoming, Hiram. You will be blacklisted.''

"I don't think you want to do that, Chauncey." He let his silverware rest and leaned against the chair back. "Let's go back to that one point you made about my unbranded calves being sold to the highest bidder. I suppose that if the highest bidder bids fifty dollars a head, he will still pay only ten?''

Shanahan's eyes darted. "What the devil does that mean?''

"I lifted some documents from the association files the other day. They are now in the possession of a friend of mine who has instructions to turn them over to the newspapers should anything happen to me. Those documents prove that you and several other high-ranking members of the association have been conspiring to buy mavericks at a price fixed under the highest bid. You can bid as high as you like and beat the little men out of the mavericks because you know you will pay only ten dollars a head anyway. If you were to blacklist me, Chauncey, I would be forced to make this information public.'' He took up his knife and fork and resumed his meal.

Shanahan's mouth gaped for a long moment, and he trembled with rage. ''Blackmail,'' he said.

''Blackmail . . . blacklist . . . It's all pretty ugly, isn't it? Now, there's one other thing. I'm putting Walker C. Kincheloe back to work as my ranch manager. If the blacklist against him is not lifted for his crime of owning his own herd, I'll be forced to give those documents I mentioned to the newspapers.''

Shanahan suddenly sprang from the table, his chair scooting away behind him. ''You've joined them, Baber. You're one of them now.''

Hiram jutted his head forward. ''One of whom?''

''The ring of thieves. You've stolen documents from this association, and now you would help them rustle our cattle.''

''I just want everybody to have the same opportunity to succeed. That's the only way to protect the range from greed such as this association has fostered. Think about it, Chauncey. I could have just exposed you. I'm giving you the chance to work with me.''

Shanahan fumed and stalked away.

Hiram noticed the bartender and a few cattlemen staring from across the room, wishing they had heard what had been said. He went back to cutting his steak. Now he had some leverage, but he had to wonder if this was the best way. His first inclination had been merely to expose Shanahan and the other conspirators. But the graft was so widespread among the leaders of the association that release of the information was likely to promulgate a range war between the big men and the small operators. Perhaps this way he could hold the documents over the heads of the conspirators and force some change. It was a distasteful business, highly political and scandalous. But business was business, whether it was on the cattle ranges or in the shipyards.

He stabbed the last piece of his steak and lifted it to his lips, but paused before he wolfed it down. He turned it on his fork and regarded it curiously. Strange to think that this was what it was all about. All the graft, corruption, and greed. All the ill feelings and hot tempers. It all boiled down to this. A piece of meat.

THIRTY-SIX

CALEB HAD THOUGHTS of dread and wonder coursing through his mind. He sat upon Kate Llewellyn's wood pile, the ax handle against his knee. The tin cup in his hand felt warm, good against the chill of open plains before dawn. It was dark. No moon shone. Clouds scattered in the sky were invisible, but he knew they were there by the stars they obliterated. The big dipper was upside down.

All this he noted and appreciated. All this he measured against what it would mean for the coming day, and the trail ahead. The dark was full of sights to work his mind. But past images of broad daylight were what made him *feel,* made his heart ache and throb, made his skin writhe around stirring guts.

He had slept just three steps away last night. His bedroll was barely cool. His fire had wakened neither Walker nor young N.C., who had camped with him under the stars. He was waiting to hear a board creak inside. When Kate Llewellyn arose, he would chop wood, and things would begin. Kate was in the cabin, but she was not alone. Savannah lay there as well.

And now the memory of love under aspen leaves seized his heart and lifted it on a string. Then, the guilt of hiding it all from Amelia. Next, silent gunshots swarmed like bumblebees and Buster's blood felt hot as the cup in his hand. Buster was there, grimacing, his wound like that of a hunted deer. Caleb's heart sank to the pit of his stomach to recall the bits of bone he had picked away, the torn flesh against Buster's black skin, the scalding water and bandages, and the desperate prayers he had felt unworthy of offering.

And yet, Buster had stood to see him off—stood beside Colonel Ab Holcomb on his splinted peg leg, which he'd wrapped with rawhide. And again his chest swelled to think of these men he had left behind again. Every word his father had said came back:

"Son, I never asked you for much. Maybe I never had the right. But please . . . Please, do one thing for me."

"What?" he had asked, dumbfounded to hear the old man speak to him this way.

"I know you've got to drift. But for a time—just this year, son—stay close to Walker and his boy. Stay together until you hear something."

Caleb had glanced at Buster, who was nodding, that dreadful look of wounded and shattered men yet on his face. "Until I hear something about what?"

"About *them*," the colonel had answered. "We killed one of them. Buster and I will look after one another here. You've got to stay with Walker and his boy. Until you hear the law has them, stay close to your friends. Don't let them catch you alone, son."

The cup was cool in his hand now, the battle back on his mind. He had lifted his father, and helped him to safety. He hated the memory of cowering behind the buggy, but every shot he had loosed, however desperate, gave him pride. They had been lucky. They might have all been shot dead as Delton Little in his bleeding derby. That Buster had survived was a miracle.

A small cool hand touched his neck and he flinched. It was Savannah, silent as the clouds above, her body now pressing warm against him from behind.

"They'll be awake soon," she whispered, her lips touching his ear.

The trip from Colorado Springs had been strange with Savannah always near. They had made a pact under the aspen leaves to keep their affair a secret one. Sneaking in and out of her arms only amplified Caleb's lust. Yet, Amelia knew.

When the women came to drunken Dr. Ketchum's office, it had revealed itself momentarily—whatever the thing was between them. While Gloria shrieked maniacally over Buster's prone form—shrieked to the point that Buster, weakened as he was, put a hand over his ear—Savannah had come to Caleb and embraced him, leaving Amelia standing there, feeling like the outsider. He was pretty sure Tess suspected, too. Tess knew Caleb's weakness for flesh from her own days of ribald survival.

Yet, Savannah had ignored him well enough through other long hours. Traveling by rail, and camping two nights on the way here to Kate Llewellyn's, she had treated him as if he were a common pack mule, or at best one of the dozen Appaloosas Walker had bought on credit from Amelia. Come to think of it, Savannah held Amelia's Appaloosas in lower regard than pack mules, merely because they were Amelia's. Caleb didn't quite understand why Amelia and Savannah harbored such a primal dislike for each other, but a blind man could feel it whenever they were in a room together.

It was not just Savannah's ability to ignore him that galled so. It was also just annoying to have a woman in camp all the time, to constantly mind his language, to keep his shirt tucked in, to ride two miles merely to piss out of sight on the open plains.

Yet other times, when he expected it least, she would steal up behind him and retrieve his affections with a touch, as now she placed her lips against his ear.

He craned his neck, and his mouth met hers, but then she was gone. A skillet rattled in the house and N.C. rolled in his blanket. The Appaloosas grumbled at Savannah as she passed their corral. Caleb threw the cold dregs aside and found a good round log to split.

THIRTY-SEVEN

THE BOY HELD his pony to a walk. He would rather gallop, of course, but that would come soon enough, and he needed to save his mount for the chase. Today he would help the old man hunt wild cattle, and plenty of galloping he then would know.

He felt the dreamer watching, sensed the dreamer's fear. There was something out there in that fog that made the dreamer tremble, but the boy knew no cares this morning. He was going to meet the old man, and then they would kill big moss-backed longhorns and skin them for hides. The old man had promised to show him how to kill one by pouncing upon it with a bowie knife.

The boy held to the trail, well worn between his cabin and the old man's. He stopped here, on the bluff, and the fog parted for a moment as the dreamer remembered the view across the river. The dreamer's memories were all the view this boy possessed, for his life was this dream, lived over and over again, and it always started this way; carefree, comfortable, innocent.

The boy heard an old tom gobble down in the pecan bottoms and wished he had a gun. But hunting cattle was better than hunting turkeys, and the old man would let him carry a gun to protect himself, in case a bull turned to gore his horse. The boy used his spurs, and the dreamer cringed, knowing now the boy's life would begin to change to one of lasting haunted horror.

Gunfire popped in the distance, and the boy drew his reins tight. He peered through the fog, and something strange emerged. It was the way of the dream to make the boy live it as if it were the first time, every time, though this dream had cycled a thousand times, as the earth turning, the moon rising, the sun setting. When the fog parted, the boy knew, somehow only now, that he should have seen the old man running from the Indians. Instead, he beheld something highly peculiar.

A town stood below in the valley where no town could have lain. Men were firing at each other there. One in a derby had fallen in front of a red brick building. Across the one long street, others fired in ambush from rooftops and windows. And the boy looked on in wonder and confusion, for a building was floating down the street, drifting like a cloud on the wind.

Now a big man was on his horse down there in the town, and the boy could not say why, but he felt so sad for this man—so very sad. The big man was shooting a pistol, and the building was floating down the street to shade him from bullets, yet in a way the boy thought it would be kind for a bullet to catch him, kill him clean, set him free.

The boy blinked, and the town vanished. He heard more gunfire and whirled his mount to see the old man he knew so well galloping a horse through the dream-haze, four warriors on his heels. And the boy spurred his horse down the steep bluff. He rode hard to the river, hoping to help the old man swim it and escape.

Low branches of pecan came out of the mist to whip the boy's face and the dreamer tried with every morsel of will he owned to make the boy stop, to wake himself, to end the dream, but it came on anyway. It came on.

That scream echoed through the bottoms, through the mist, through the mind of the tortured dreamer, through the cursed life of the mounted boy. The scream came. And as if it were no more than the hoot of an owl, the caw of a crow, or the bray of a hobbled jackass, the turkey gobbler—so near now in the pecan bottoms—answered it. Answered it like a challenge from some strutting jake.

Then the old man screamed again, and so unearthly was his voice that the whole valley sank into cold bloody silence. Then it came again, and again, and again. And it would always come. When the dreamer slept, it came. The old man screamed.

Walker Colt Kincheloe sat upright in his blankets and heard boots scuffling near him. "Is that the old man?" he said.

"By God, that's a panther down in the bottoms!" Hard Winter Holcomb replied.

Walker gasped and found the fiddler's outline against the pale eastern horizon, an ax in his hand. He was here, at Kate Llewellyn's. "Panther?" he said.

"Yeah." He cupped his hands around his mouth. "Savannah! Better get back to the cabin!"

The light footsteps padded quickly to the woodpile, and Walker could see the little sprite seek protection under Caleb's arm.

"What *was* that?" she said.

"Panther. Wish it was light, we'd go huntin' him."

"I have to pee!" Savannah said.

"Go behind the house," Kate Llewellyn said, standing in the open doorway.

Savannah sighed. "Witch," she hissed, just loud enough for Caleb to hear.

She stalked around the corner, and Caleb took his first swing at the piece of wood. "Miss Kate, did you hear that panther?"

"I heard it."

He muscled the ax head from the log. "They come around here much?"

"Hardly ever."

He took another swing, splitting the log cleanly. "We'll go run it down after daylight."

"Leave it be. It ain't killed no stock." She turned back into the cabin.

When the fiddler brought his first armload of wood into the kitchen, Kate spoke to him from the stove. "I see you carry a Bible now in with your fiddle and things."

"Yes, ma'am."

"Do you ever read it?"

"I've read a little of it. Got me a dictionary to try to make sense of it, but it still sidesteps me in places."

She wrapped her apron tail around the handle of a skillet. "You're not supposed to understand ten thousand years of wisdom in one reading. Life will make it clear quicker than that blasted dictionary."

"Yes, ma'am," he said, anxious to get another load of wood.

"Hey." She glanced out through the open door and beckoned him closer with a toss of her head. When he came near, she said, "Did Walker ever tell you?"

"About what?"

"About Paterson."

"No, but N.C. did."

"Walker still have them dreams?"

"What dreams?"

"How should I know? I can't read a man's dreams. Any fool can see he don't sleep well. Never has. Lordy, poor Walker. Poor, poor Walker. He's had a hard life, Caleb Holcomb. Don't you forget it."

"No, ma'am. I better go look after them horses."

She caught him by the sleeve. "If you ever find out what them dreams are about, you tell me, you hear? I have a right to know. Walker's eased my sufferin'. Why, after them Cheyenne done me that way, Walker sure was kind. I owe him that, so you tell me what you know, hear?"

"All I know is, Walker C. Kincheloe is much a man, Miss Kate." He smiled and tried to touch her hand upon his sleeve, but she drew away. "Well," he said, "I'll just go help with those horses now."

THIRTY-EIGHT

P OWDER RIVER RAN low the first day of roundup twenty-three. Walker C. Kincheloe sat astride his Holcomb Appaloosa and frowned at the blowing dust, the cropped brown grass, and the spare flow of water down the half-naked riverbed. Directly, he saw a man riding toward him at a lope and recognized Jack Flagg by the big black hat he wore.

"Howdy, Walker."

"Jack."

"Dry, isn't it?"

"Like a Baptist camp meetin'."

"The heart of a haystack gets more rain than we've seen lately. You can just watch the cows draw up around their bones."

Walker grunted, and they looked over the valley in silence while the plume of dust Jack Flagg had raised blew away to nothing.

"Good-looking Indian pony you got there," Flagg said.

"Didn't pay nothin' for the looks." He smiled, the stubble bunching on his ample jaw. "Bought him down in Colorado from Hard Winter's sister-in-law."

"Who?"

"The fiddler, Hard Winter Holcomb."

Flagg nodded, chin high. "He's a pretty good hand, and a hell of a fiddler. He back again this year?"

"Yep. Down Powder River with the TW wagon."

Flagg reached into his saddle pocket for a plug of tobacco. He bit a corner off and offered some to Walker. "This your brand of chew?"

"Spits brown, don't it?" The big Texan took a large bite from the plug and handed it back.

"You here on your own?"

"I'm back with the TW, but I'm workin' my own stuff, too. How 'bout you?"

"I'm still with the Bar C." He worked the chaw in his mouth, trying to get around to the reason he had ridden out. Finally, he decided just to say it. "Some of the boys with the big outfits have had their wages cut."

"That's what I know."

"Me, I'm still getting forty a month. Boss wouldn't go along with the Cheyenne Club. But a lot of these other boys with the bigger outfits have been cut back to thirty." He spat, and not because he needed to.

"It don't sit with me either, Jack. Man eats out of the same pot of beans I do ought to draw the same time."

"I was thinkin' . . ." Jack Flagg left it at that.

"Me, too. Uppity bastards. Time we started standin' up again' 'em."

"Standing together is what it will take."

Walker knotted his reins and dropped the knot on the mane of his horse. He hooked one leg over his saddle horn and turned more toward Jack Flagg in the saddle. "You hear what happened 'while back on the Union Pacific?"

Flagg contemplated what Walker might mean, for a lot of talk circulated about railroad matters. "You mean the wage strike?"

Walker nodded. "It worked for them."

The sun set brownish red beyond the Big Horns, and men began to gather at the TW wagon after chuck with their own outfits. Caleb loaned guitar and mandolin to whomever could play and got the boys singing a few favorites. About a dozen men clustered around him, while the rest sat on the ground or leaned on the wagon or squatted or stood. Talk was low and vague.

"Play one more fiddle song, Hard Winter," Walker suddenly bellowed, and men drew nearer to the musicians, sensing that something more than toe-tapping was soon to come of this meeting.

Caleb stood and swung the fiddle up under his chin. " 'Billy and the Low Ground,' " he said to Woody Fletcher, who had been backing him up. He launched the old Scottish reel, grinning and strolling among the punchers. As he played, his eyes swept the crowd, and he saw faces familiar and strange.

Walker was there, bouncing to music beside Jack Flagg. N.C. sat on the tailgate of the chuck wagon, pining as he had been for some time over some girl he had met out there adrift. Caleb figured it had to be a whore, for he couldn't recall another eligible female N.C. had come upon. The only exception was that Cheyenne girl, Rabbit, and certainly he wasn't fool enough to think his father would allow any of that.

Some boys from the CU were frowning over the wood fire. Caleb stepped up on the tongue of the bed wagon for a better view, but couldn't see Chauncey Shanahan anywhere. Also absent was Dave Donaldson, whom the association had probably sent to run some other roundup this spring to avoid the risk of fighting another pothook. It made Caleb play lighter to see these men missing, knowing Walker and Jack Flagg had cooked something up in protest of the wage cut.

Turning his shoulders, and swinging the fiddle head west, Hard Winter Holcomb caught sight of Hiram Baber, who was nodding to the music, but judging faces in the crowd, like the fiddler himself.

Glancing again at Walker, Caleb read the subtle nod. He raised one foot—a sign to the guitar player—and ended "Billy and the Low Ground" with a flourish, leaping from the wagon tongue and kicking dust from the parched ground with the last stroke of the tune.

Walker threw his head back and loosed a coyote yell that caught on quickly and grew like an ocean swell. The punchers squalled like pack hunters, yipping at the sky, feeling worry fade behind the moment of release. Then the howl died, and the eyes turned under hat brims, turned toward Kincheloe and Flagg, turned in their sockets like swivel guns.

"Boys," Walker said, "the roundup foreman ain't in camp yet, but Jack and me thought we'd git a little business over with. Who all's had their pay cut by the Cheyenne Club?"

The punchers stood like cigar store Indians.

"It's none of our business," Jack Flagg said, "and I know you boys don't like to complain. But they're deciding down in Cheyenne how much you ought to get paid, and some of them have never turned a cow. Nobody asked you, nor even told you it was coming. Well, I say it's time you got to say your piece."

"Jack and me didn't get our time cut," Walker said. "The owners of our outfits wouldn't go along with the Cheyenne Club vote, and they're liable to git blackballed for it, unless we back 'em up."

The camp lay quiet until one young puncher cleared his throat and raked his heel across the dust. He was a rep from the Laramie Plains, and as such was the lone man from his home outfit. "My boss cut me back to thirty dollars a month. Said he didn't have no choice."

"We want to give him a choice," Jack Flagg said.

Walker noticed the men from the Long X Ranch talking among themselves. They seemed to come to an agreement on something, and one of them stepped forward. "We all got busted back to thirty," he said. "Even me, and I'm the foreman. Boss said wasn't nothin' him or us could do about it."

Hiram Baber was listening anxiously, about to burst with flowery speech. But he held his tongue and curbed his ambitions. This was Walker's moment to lead. This action would mean more if the working men arrived at it themselves.

"I'll tell you what I aim to do about it," Walker said. "I ain't roundin' up squat until every man gits his pay put back where it was before the Cheyenne Club vote."

Men began grumbling.

"Me, too," Jack Flagg said. "You boys who got cut back to thirty a month can ride back to your own headquarters and ask for the raise."

"Hell, don't ask for it," Walker said. "Demand it!"

"Right. And the rest of us can just lay up here in camp and listen to Hard Winter and the boys play music. We won't brand a single head until every man gets decent pay."

"Man eats out of the same pot of beans I do ought to draw the same time!" Walker shouted. He had liked the way that sounded earlier when he said it to Jack, and now it just reeled from his tongue.

Hiram could no longer contain himself: "Walker, you can't feed an outfit like this on beans alone. What these men need is slow elk."

The cowboys raised eyebrows in silent amazement to hear a member of the Wyoming Stock Growers Association advocate the hunting of mavericks. Even a member as moderate as Hiram Baber.

"Damn right!" Walker said. "We'll kill us some slow elk and have us a feast. And, Hi, seein' as you're the only member of that goddamn association who had the guts to show his face at this roundup, we'll need you to carry the news to the Cheyenne Club while the boys go get their wages set right. Will you do it?"

"I'll do it if the men vote for it," Hiram said, thrusting his fist before him.

"Who all votes to go on strike?" Walker said.

Before a man could raise hand or voice, Hiram was stepping forward waving the suggestion away. "Hold on, now. It's got to be done right if you want it to carry weight in Cheyenne. First, you men need to organize. Somebody has to nominate a leader."

"I nominate Walker C. Kincheloe!" said Jack Flagg.

"Somebody has to second it."

"I second it," Caleb cried, pointing his fiddle bow at the big Texan. He had held back, never before having been interested in anything political like this. But this was something he had seen develop from the inside since last year's roundup, and the excitement was drawing him in.

"Any other nominations?" Hiram said, pausing. "All in favor of Walker C. Kincheloe representing this group of men, say 'aye.' " He waited as the cry went up. "All opposed?"

"Now, just a goddamn minute!" Big Tom Foutts, foreman of Chauncey Shanahan's CU Ranch, pushed his hat back on his head. "What in the hell are you gittin' us into, Walker? If we go back to the ranch and tell Shanahan to up our pay, we might just as soon ask the devil to give back Pilate's soul. I've worked for Shanahan goin' on seven years now, and he don't make a move without the association backin' him up. He'd sooner sass his mammy than go again' the Cheyenne Club vote."

"That's what I'm talkin' about, right there," Walker said. "Chauncey Shanahan's got his association backin' him up, but what do you got? Who says you can't have your own damn association? Like Hi says, let's organize!"

"You're gonna organize me right out of my job."

"Excuse me!" Hiram Baber said. "We were in the middle of a vote. All opposed to Walker Colt Kincheloe representing this group of men, say 'nay.' "

"Nay, goddamn it," Tom Foutts said. "Nothin' personal, Walker, I just don't see any sense in it all."

"The ayes have it!" Hiram announced. "Walker, you're in charge."

"All right." One of his big hands wrung the other. "What the hell do I do now?"

The men laughed, feeling joyful about something they really didn't understand.

"What's the purpose of this meeting?" Hi asked.

"To get the boys to go on strike till everybody gets their wages put back where they were."

"Then somebody has to make a motion to propose a strike."

"I move that we strike," Jack Flagg said. "Who will second it?"

Walker turned to Flagg. "Hell, you understand this stuff, Jack. You should be the leader."

Flagg grinned. "Damn right I understand it. Why do you think I nominated you before somebody could nominate me? Now, who will second the motion to go on strike?"

"I second it," said the rep from the Laramie Plains.

"Do we vote now?" Walker asked.

Jack Flagg nodded.

"Everybody who wants to go on strike say 'aye.' "

A resounding reply sprang like pheasants flushed from hiding, a hearty melding of voices—voices of men hardened by work and worry, of boys indifferent to danger or authorities, of shiftless souls feeling a moment of direction.

"Everybody again' it, say 'nay.' "

"What damn good would it do?" said Big Tom Foutts. "You've already made up your minds."

Walker smiled and tucked his thumbs under his belt. "That settles it. Hi, you carry the news to Cheyenne. You boys that got your time cut head on back to your home outfits in the mornin' and get your wages put back where they was. Tell your bosses if they won't do it, we won't work their cattle. Will you go along with that, Tom?"

Tom Foutts frowned. "Hell, I guess. But Shanahan ain't gonna go along with it."

"He will if he wants his cows worked. Anybody else got anything to say?" Walker looked across the weathered faces, some a little dazed, some defiant, some apparently amused. "Meeting adjourned! Fiddler, play 'Bully of the Town.' Step back boys, and watch me clog!"

THIRTY-NINE

THE YEARLING HEIFER of slick ears and hide had wandered over the rise one morning and trotted toward Powder River. Seven boys had ridden like Indians and, conveniently mistaking the heifer's horns for the spike antlers of a young bull elk, had downed her with numerous shots from carbines and revolvers fired from the saddle, running, at a range close enough to produce powder burns on the brindle hide. Her meat was tough, for she had not fed well in months. But diced to small chunks and boiled like hell among potatoes, onions, a few carrots, lots of salt and pepper, and what little tallow could be found on her, the stewed slow elk had made passable fare, sopped with hot sourdough biscuits.

After a few days, men and boys began filtering back to the roundup grounds in triumph, celebrating restored wages. Hiram Baber returned, having ridden hard to report the stunned looks on the faces of the association members at the Cheyenne Club. Even the reps from far-off ranges made their way back, one by one, laughing about how readily their bosses had given in to the demands for higher pay; how they had been hailed as heroes by their compadres for bringing home the benefits of the strike from far-off roundup twenty-three.

In time, all the punchers returned, with the notable exception of Big Tom Foutts and his boys from the CU. The CU was one of the spreads nearest to the roundup camp, so much speculation spread about what might be holding the CU boys up. The popular theory held that Chauncey Shanahan had refused to raise wages, and Big Tom was waiting him out to the bitter end.

A lone rider appeared one day to break the monotony at the TW wagon. Caleb was lying in the shade of the wagon about midday when he saw the rider stop at the next wagon up the river. The rider talked with the leader of the wagon a while, then rode on toward the TW wagon. Caleb's first thought was that one of the Mayhalls had come to get him, but when the rider got close enough, he realized he'd never seen the man before. The rider stopped near the TW wagon and swung down from a horse that had been used too hard to hold its head high.

From his napping place under the wagon, Caleb watched as Walker and Hiram stood to greet the visitor. Caleb's hat was low over his eyes, affording him the opportunity to size up the stranger without seeming to stare.

The man was hard-bitten, his outfit dusty from hat to boots. His old bat-wing chaps were stained with the grease of many meals taken in camp. The holster on his gun belt was empty, and Caleb assumed the man had put the weapon in his saddlebag to protect it from dust. His clothes were faded and patched, his face pinched and mean, with intelligent eyes, a week-old beard, and a nose that had been broken and set a little crooked.

"Howdy, Milo," Walker said. The big Texan let no joy fill his voice.

"Walker," the man said, nodding. He smiled at Hiram, revealing a gap in his teeth. "I'm Milo Gibbs, Mr. Baber."

"Pleasure," Hi said, shaking the stranger's hand.

Walker shot a critical glance at the jaded mount Gibbs had ridden in on. "That your horse?"

"Why else would I be ridin' him?" Gibbs answered.

"What do you call him?"

Gibbs glanced over his shoulder and smirked. "Call him? I call him mine."

"He ain't got a name?"

"What the hell good would a name do him? He ain't a dog. Wouldn't come if I called him by name."

"Mine will," Walker said. He pointed to his top horse, Ol' Shine, who was staked some forty paces away.

"Like hell."

Walker whistled through his teeth, and Ol' Shine raised his head. "Ol' Shine! Come here, boy!"

The saddle horse took three steps, until he tightened the halter rope tied to the wooden stake driven into the ground.

"Come here, Ol' Shine!" Walker growled.

The horse walked back to the stake, muzzled it, curled his lips back, and felt the hard wood between his teeth. Taking a bite on the stake, Ol' Shine pulled up on it until it slipped from the ground, then he ambled eagerly toward Walker, taking care not to step on the stake rope he dragged.

"See there, Milo," the big man said, chuckling. "If you'd take time to learn a hoss somethin', instead of just ridin' him into the ground, you'd find givin' him a name useful."

Milo smirked. "I keep a horse to work, not learn tricks."

Walker patted Ol' Shine loudly against the side of his neck. "What brings you by, Milo? Huntin' cow work?"

"That's right."

"Well, you might as well drift on. We got all the help we need."

"I heard about y'all goin' against the Cheyenne Club. Thought you might be hirin' some hands like me."

"We ain't hirin' nobody."

Gibbs nodded. "Well, I'd be obliged for some chuck. Y'all are welcome at my camp anytime."

"Where is your camp, Milo?"

Gibbs smiled. "Well, it floats, Walker. You know."

"Yeah. Maybe the cook will find somethin' for you, but then you'd better drift on to some other roundup where you can find some work."

Gibbs turned back to the tired horse and mounted. "Never mind about the grub. I carry some beans, and I always find me some meat about suppertime."

After he rode away, Walker said, "Now I know there's trouble comin'. When the likes of Milo Gibbs starts showin' theirselves and offerin' to hire on, the air just smells like trouble."

The CU crew finally returned in time for dinner one day, two days after the last rep had come in from the farthest range. Big Tom Foutts led the CU boys straight to the TW wagon, where Walker Kincheloe was filling his plate with slow elk stew, beans, and biscuits. Caleb, N.C., and the rest of the TW boys were there, as well as several men from other wagons who had been sharing the stew.

"Howdy, Tom," Walker said, poking his finger into a pie made from dried apples. "Any sign of rain out there?"

Tom just shook his head.

" 'Bout time you got back. Taken some augerin' to make Shanahan cough up the raise, I guess.''

Tom swung slowly down, his weight in one stirrup causing the horse to lean. "He wouldn't cough it up. All the augerin' in the world wouldn't change his mind."

The friendly welcome left Walker's face as he approached Foutts with his plate in his hand. "Well, you better have somethin' to eat, then git on back to the ranch and tell him again. Lay down the law this time. We'll start roundin' up, so you and your boys can get in on the brandin' when you come back with the raise."

"Goddamn it, Walker, we ain't comin' back with no raise. Shanahan told us either collect our time and get the hell out of the territory, or go back to work the roundup. Said he'd blackball us all so's we'd never work Wyoming again. Me and the boys talked it over. We're satisfied with what we're gittin', and we'll just work the roundup at thirty dollars a month."

"You know we can't do that, Tom. If one outfit breaks this strike, the rest of these boys'll go back and they'll just be gettin' thirty a month, too. We voted to stand together, and that's what we'll do."

Big Tom's lips bunched in frustration. "This is bullshit. I didn't vote for any such goddamn thing. Where's the roundup foreman?"

"He showed up a week ago, and I busted him back to keeper of the tally books. We don't need no Cheyenne Club foreman tellin' us how to work cows on our own home range. I'm roundup foreman now, duly elected."

Tom kicked a pile of horse dung. "You and your damn votes, Walker. You've voted me and my boys out of our jobs!"

"You'd have lost your jobs anyway, the way things are goin'. Most of us probably will. Why do think Chauncey cut your wages? Because he's too damn greedy to cut back anywhere else. Keeps overstockin' the range—look at it! Nothin' but dust and cow tracks. Beef keeps lookin' poorer, prices keep droppin', but the damn Cheyenne Club won't cut back their herds. Hell no, they cut your wages. Another year like this and we'll all be out of a job. Now, you've got two choices. Go back and get the raise out of Chauncey Shanahan's tight Scottish asshole, or hitch your chuck wagon and leave this roundup."

Big Tom Foutts fumed and mulled over his options. He gave some consideration to kicking the slow elk stew out of Walker's hand. It would bring on one hell of a fight, but there was no match for Walker C. Kincheloe anywhere in the territory, and Big Tom knew it. He was tired of riding back and forth, but there seemed no other way to go. He simply sighed and got on his horse, outnumbered and outvoted.

Walker watched the CU men ride away, hazed in dust. He put his stew down on the tailgate of the chuck wagon, no longer having an appetite for it.

Hiram Baber took the coffeepot from the bank of coals on which it rested and poured a helping that still boiled momentarily in the cup. He took his cup to the tailgate of the chuck wagon, removed a small bag of sugar from a cubbyhole, and poured a little in his coffee. "I think you did the right thing, Walker. It gets tough sometimes."

"Tough, hell. Things are gonna have to get a damn sight tougher." He was glaring at Hi's cup of sweetened coffee with disdain. "It ain't right that the CU boys catch all the crossfire. Everybody ought to give a little, and I aim to do my part."

"How?"

"What have you been preachin' about the range for the past year?"

"That it's overstocked. That everybody ought to cut back their herds."

"By how much?"

"By half. That's what I told the owners at the Cheyenne Club."

"By God, you've won me over, Hi. After the roundup, I'm gonna cut a hunnerd head out of my herd of two hunnerd, and I'm gonna drive 'em to Ogallala. I don't care how low prices are; I'm aim to do my part. How 'bout you?"

"I'll match your one hundred with one hundred of my own."

Walker laughed and clapped his big hand on Hiram's shoulder. "My drift was, do you aim to cut your herd by half, or just talk about it?"

Caleb and some other men around the wagon looked up from their plates.

"Well, Walker, half my herd would amount to several thousand beeves. My losses would be twenty times what yours would be."

"Hell, you're twenty times richer than ten of me. Now, do you want to ease the pressure on this range or just talk about it?"

"You know I do, but I'd take a loss on every head, the way the market is."

Walker stuffed a wad of tobacco in his cheek and packed it with a frown. "Talk don't grow much grass, Hi."

FORTY

CALEB TIPPED HIS head forward to watch his mount drink, and dust cascaded off the front of his brim. Water in Powder River ran so gritty that the horse shook his head and mouthed the bit in protest. A bandanna tied tight around the bridge of Caleb's nose seemed only to slow the cloud of dirt down some, and it was itself cloaked in brown.

He sighed—snorted, really—and swept his dust-galled eyes across the valley. A general bank of fine dirt hung everywhere, yet rose denser from the herd of ten thousand beeves, strung all along the valley. It was like mist on the shore of a sea pounded by roaring surf. It sprayed from the hooves of every horse that cut to turn a cow, spouted from the trail of every trotting steer, exploded like black powder smoke from everything that gouged, raked, stabbed, scraped, or chopped into the land.

He probed inside his ear and heard it grind; blinked and felt it scratch. He tasted it on his tongue, smelled it through his bandanna. It was like life in an hourglass, for the whole world had turned to sand.

Trotting back to the herd, he came across a bull calf standing alone outside the rolling sea of horns and hides. It couldn't have been more than two weeks old: tired, lost, hunched pitifully; motherless. Caleb reined in, the calf too exhausted to run. Looking up, he saw Walker C. Kincheloe loping his way.

"Seen N.C.?"

"He went after a bunch that broke."

Walker shook his head, feeling the frustration of everything. "What's wrong with that boy, Hard Winter? He ain't said two words in two weeks. If I didn't know better, I'd say he's pinin' for some gal. What did you learn him out there?"

Caleb noticed the black dirt gummed around Walker's eyes and knew his must look as ugly. "Didn't have to learn him nothin'. He just kind of went into rut."

Walker had been studying the lost calf since he rode up. "Well, I wish he'd git over it. I liked him better when he used to foller me around sayin' yessir."

"He's just feelin' his oats. Won't last forever." He stared at the calf with Walker for several seconds. "What should we do with this bull calf?"

"Cut his throat probably. He's starvin'. Cookie's already butchered three dogies today. This roundup's got too damn big. Kills too many calves.''

"Well, I ain't cuttin' his throat. You go ahead."

"Let's see if we can make him bawl his mama out of the herd."

The big man dropped his loop over the calf's neck, and jerked it a few times, but the calf offered no complaint. He stroked the flanks of his horse with spurs, and dragged the calf. It released a half-hearted bleat.

"Hell, he ain't got the strength to say mammy."

Walker hoisted the calf up to his saddle, lifting it hand over hand. Placing the limp foundling across his thighs, he reined toward the herd and let out an imitation calf moan that was so real it made Caleb look. He worked the edge of the herd, fifty yards away, the suckling bleat coming impossibly from his barrel chest.

After covering a furlong, an old cow came bellowing out of the herd at a trot, head low. Walker let the calf hang by its hind feet, then dropped it on the ground. It bounced up, wobbling on weak legs. The cow stalked up to the bull calf, sniffed it, and stared menacingly at the cowboys as her calf began to probe for milk.

They watched in silence as the little bull found the udders and rooted hard with his nose, causing his mother to lurch.

"Hell," Walker said, "he's still starvin'."

They turned back toward the branding fires and found Hiram Baber waiting to join them, his mount daubed all over with sandy sweat from a day of labor in the cloud.

"The books are all tallied, Walker. The boys have worked everything. Except for the CU herd, of course."

"It'll take two weeks just for the damn dust to settle," the big man grumbled.

"My TW tally is up to thirty-five hundred."

"So what?"

"You're my ranch manager. I pay you good money for good advice. If you say to cut the herd in half, I'll do it, and then some. I'll throw eighteen hundred head in with your hundred, and we'll make a big drive to Ogallala. If we don't get some rain soon, they'll all starve anyway. We might as well cut out the ones we want to market and put road brands on them while we've got them bunched."

Walker pulled the bandanna from his face so Hiram could see his smile, the first one he had found reason to fashion all day. "You're gonna make a fine cowman, Hi. And you might just save the whole territory from all-out war." He pulled the bandanna back over his smile, unsure why he had chosen those words. He had seen ranges turn to dust before, but never quite this badly. He had seen the looks on good men's faces go black and foreboding. He had seen the humiliation of hunger drive honest souls to vice and bloodshed. Walker C. Kincheloe had seen too much for his own damn good.

The market drive shaped up the day after the tally books shut. Nineteen hundred head of mixed cattle turned south for the railroad, the TW crew pushing them away from the main herd with some difficulty.

"Hey, Walker," Caleb said, joining the drive from the roundup grounds down the valley, "the boys want to know what they should do with the CU cattle."

"They still bunched?"

Caleb nodded.

"Scatter 'em. Big Tom and his boys'll be here to work 'em soon as we clear out. Make 'em earn their thirty dollars a month."

Caleb puckered his mouth and stared at the saddle horn. "You sure you want to do that? It ain't Big Tom's fault."

"I'm sure I *don't* want to do it. But how in the hell is Chauncey Shanahan gonna learn, unless we hit him in the payroll where it hurts? We leave them cows bunched for Big Tom and Chauncey will get more out of the strike than anybody."

Caleb nodded and looked everywhere for a break in the dust cloud, finding none. "Did you ever think you'd see the day when a bunch of cowpunchers had to go on strike?"

"I never thought I'd see a cow man put sugar in his coffee."

The drovers let their herd walk easy up the valley of Powder River, three days to the mouth of Salt Creek. There they found three other outfits road-branding herds of five hundred each. The word had spread that Hiram Baber was backing up his talk about thinning herds, and three of his followers had decided to join him in the drive. They hadn't cut their herds by half, of course, but they had contributed a token five hundred each to the cause.

Walker decided to drive the combined herd of thirty-four hundred up Salt Creek to its head, then over the divide and into the Platte Valley.

"It'll be a long day without water once we cross the divide. Hope you boys don't mean to strike for more sleep."

But after one day south, Salt Creek had ceased to run where it usually flowed that time of year. It dried up into a series of pools, each smaller and more bitter than the last. After two days, the pools had become so tainted with alkali that the horses wouldn't drink from them. The water barrels on the chuck wagon ran dry quickly once the remuda had to be watered, and the cook tried making coffee from one of the alkali pools.

"I've drunk mule piss out of cow tracks that tasted better than this slop!" Walker slung the coffee out on the dusty ground. "Saddle up, boys! We'll drive all night and all day until we hit the Platte."

They crossed the divide about midnight and started the long plod downhill. Morning came, and one of the boys fell out of his saddle, asleep. The cowboys shredded tobacco to rub into their eyes, the fire perking them ramrod straight on their horses for a time. At dusk the cattle were so tired that most of the men had to drop back to ride drag, constantly harassing the poor suffering beasts to keep them moving.

N.C. drained his canteen after dark, and his mouth turned to cotton. He ran out of spit to swallow, and his tongue began to grow so numb that he couldn't speak, though he hadn't done much talking all day, anyway. When he realized that his tongue was actually swelling in his mouth he almost panicked, but reminded himself that there were other men in the same fix with him and none of them had resorted to hysterics.

At dawn on the second day, the wind shifted, and a chinook hit them in the face, bringing the smell of Platte River water to the nostrils of the lumbering beasts. The drag riders swung to point, but any attempt at holding the cattle back proved futile. They stampeded the last five miles to the river, all thirty-four hundred head. Even the remuda broke away. Only the saddled horses could be held back by the bit. Three steers fell and were crippled so badly that Walker just shot them.

The leaders fanned out at the riverbank and many of them bogged. Hundreds of dumb brutes pushed from behind, crazed by the smell of cool fresh water. Three cows and a yearling steer drowned, trampled under, and dozens became mired in quicksand, too weak and bloated with water to pull themselves free.

When he got to the river, N.C. jumped off his horse and stuck his face in the water. His tongue had swollen to the point that he could barely close his lips, and there was little room left in the back of his throat to swallow. He more or less soaked his face in the water until his father came along.

"You all right, son? Don't drink too much all at once. N.C.?" Walker realized how dried out his son was now and leapt from his mount to pull him from the river. "Easy, now. Just sip some till your tongue goes down. Why the hell didn't you tell me you was thirsty, boy? I'd have shared my water with you."

Caleb roped and pulled cattle from the bogs until his mount barely had the strength to take the slack out of a lariat. All the horses were exhausted, and the cowboys pulled the last few beeves out by hand, six men to a rope.

They camped on the Platte for a week. Men and horses rested while the cattle grazed the riverbanks bare. They moved eastward on the eighth day, along the north bank of the river, secure in the knowledge that they would have water all the way to Ogallala, a good three weeks' drive away.

On the fifth day traveling along the Platte, a cloud came up in the west and by nightfall had consumed half the sky. "Keep your slickers and night horses handy, boys," Walker said. "Double up on guard tonight."

It was two-thirty in the morning when the storm struck. Caleb was just about to wake his relief after a two-hour shift riding night guard. It was plain he would get no sleep this night. As he rode back to the bed grounds, big drops began to hit his brim. The cattle were on their feet when he got to the herd, and rain was coming down harder. Lightning was all in the clouds, the thunder muffled, the flashes shadowed.

Caleb swatted at something pale on his brim that he thought at first was a moth. It fluttered next on the ears of his horse: an unexplainable spark; a gyrating worm of foxfire. It rose and danced upon the horn tips of three thousand cattle, and Caleb felt hair standing on the back of his neck.

In one magnificent moment, a shaft of pure light struck like all the brilliance of the sun in one beam. Its roar alone jolted Caleb from his seat and he felt himself sliding in mud, his horse dragging him by the rein he had managed to hold. Blinded, he heard only a ringing in his ears but felt the ground quake with twelve thousand hooves.

Pulling himself up, he saw his horse silhouetted against a ripple of sheet lightning in the clouds and managed to get his foot in the stirrup as the mount wheeled. Looking around, he regained his bearings, saw three dead cattle on the ground. There was a horse on the ground, too, and nearby its rider, facedown in mud.

Fifty-some-odd cattle came boiling over a swell in the ground, and Caleb tried to turn them, but they dashed all over and around the body of the fallen cowboy. His ears were working better now, and he sensed groups of cattle scattering in every direction. The near bunch ran past him, and he went to the corpse of young Billy Owen, an Oregon boy on his first summer away from home.

He jumped from his horse, rolled the boy over, and shook him. He smelled the stench of burned flesh and decided that young Billy had been dead even before the cattle stampeded over him. He would take the boy's body to the wagon, wrap him in a blanket, then go chase cattle. They would bury Billy later, on the lonely banks of the North Platte.

* * *

N.C. had seen it from three hundred yards away. He had noticed the balls of fire on the horns of the cattle first, then he had seen the bolt of lightning strike and branch into five long fingers that lashed like snakes' tongues over the whole herd. A split second later, some one thousand crazed beeves were coming his way, and all he could do was stay ahead of them.

The blasts of lightning made things clear only a few leaps ahead, for rain obliterated everything farther on. N.C. could not tell where the thunder left off and the rumble of hooves took up. The cattle were so close behind him, and so tightly bunched, that he could hear hundreds of horns rattling against each other in a primitive warning. His fear of being trampled underfoot kept him galloping, while his terror of the unknown terrain ahead made his eyes strain and his fists clamp tight on the reins.

The storm made time and space immeasurable, and it seemed to N.C. that he had been running an hour when he realized that he could no longer hear the rattle of horns. He pulled his mount back to a walk, listening for cattle or riders above the sound of rain that beat his hat. He knew he must keep moving to prevent his horse from dying of chills, so he pointed away from the driving rain and walked.

At dawn, N.C. was still alone. When the clouds broke and he saw the sun he turned south, hoping to find the outfit, and breakfast. Fatigue overwhelmed hunger, and he lay down on his slicker to sleep. Waking a couple of hours later, he mounted again, his horse stiff and rough to ride. Everywhere the range was scarred, cut deep by running water. He followed one rivulet to a stream that boiled with churning mud. Figuring it for Rawhide Creek, he followed it downstream.

About three hundred scattered cattle turned up over a rise, so N.C. bunched and pushed them back toward camp, though his instincts and rational thoughts grappled with each other about in which direction camp might be. His rational thoughts won out when he found the North Platte running almost out of its banks. He trudged on upstream until he saw the wagon, and about a thousand cattle. He threw his bunch in with the others and rode to camp in time to hear the boys singing "Rounded Up in Glory" over the grave of his friend, young Billy Owen.

Three days later Hiram Baber and Walker C. Kincheloe placed themselves a hundred yards apart and let the cowboys walk the entire herd between them. Their counts matched: 3,284.

"I wonder what happened to those hundred and nine head," Hiram said.

"Probably fell off in the river and drown't." The big Texan began to laugh. "Hell, they'll beat us to Ogallala!"

The rest of the drive was dry, and dust began to blow again. What grass there was produced fresh sprouts for a time, but much of the growth had been parched, grazed, and eroded away beyond restoration. The rain, it seemed, had cut away as much grass as it had nurtured. At least the cattle were trail-broken now and hardened to the routines of the drive.

Just two days west of Ogallala—with morale beginning to rise near the end of the drive—Hiram came loping back to camp after dark, his face clouded with worry. The camp was several miles from the river, and the cook had just pointed the wagon tongue at the north star so he would know which way was which in the morning. Hiram left his top horse to stand and joined the men in the chuck line.

"You look like you just swallered spoilt milch," Walker said.

"There's another herd five miles east of here." He held his plate as the cook filled it, declining the second helping from the ladle.

"I seen the dust cloud hangin' over 'em. Who is it?"

"A bunch of Texas cowboys hired to deliver a herd."

"Deliver it where?"

Hiram looked across the faces of the tired men and boys. "The CU Ranch."

"Damn!" Walker barked. "How big of a herd is it?"

Hiram crushed a biscuit in his hand, letting the crumbs sprinkle the top of his beef stew. "It appeared to hold five thousand head or better."

"Hell, Chauncey done that 'cause we done this." The big man gestured toward the cattle on the bed ground.

"It's only the first herd," Hiram said. "The cowboys said they were turning back to Texas to bring up another herd before winter set in." He walked away with his food and sat on the ground alone, some fifty yards from the wagon.

Caleb asked a friend if he had any cigars, but his friend had been fresh out for five days. One of the younger hands who had been riding drag the entire trip offered Caleb the makings of a cigarette, and the fiddler figured he'd accept, though he didn't think much of hand-rolled smokes.

He went to the fire, pulled out a stick, and touched the orange brand to the end of his cigarette. He replaced the stick carefully, for the cook had situated it there for the purpose of lighting smokes. He walked fifteen paces from the wagon, stood flat-footed, and smoked his cigarette with his back to the boys.

This was a hell of a note. He hadn't minded so much driving cattle to market to sell at a loss so long as a point was being made and he was getting standard wages. But to have Chauncey Shanahan come along and mock them so sure hobbled a man's spirit. They had lost a good young boy, Billy Owen, for nothing. The range was going to be harder abused than ever.

He scorched his lips smoking the last sliver of tobacco, then ground the butt into the dirt. Looking back, he saw heads hanging all around the campfire. Well, this was where Hard Winter Holcomb earned his keep. He twisted his belt around and made for the side of the chuck wagon where his mandolin was stashed.

He knew just how to work a bunch like this. You start out with something subtle—something in a minor key to match the glum mood, but paced quick enough to keep the mood from sliding lower. Then you slip into some sing-along the boys can't resist joining in on, and before you know it you're stroking the fiddle and daring somebody to do a jig.

In half an hour he swung the souls of twelve jaded men so skillfully that they didn't even realize he had headed them off. Before they knew it, he had them singing, and he had chosen a tune calculated to stir their pride in who they were and what they did. It was ironic that the song rang with an old bagpipe lilt, like Chauncey Shanahan's voice, but the men didn't know the tune's origins and didn't care. It was a cowboy's song now, and it said what they knew, what they felt, what they needed to hear:

> *. . . So tie up your kerchief and ply up your nag*
> *Come dry up your grumbles and try not to lag*
> *Roust out your steers from the long chaparral*
> *The outfit is bound for the railroad corral . . .*
>
> *Come shake out your rawhide and shake it out fair*
> *Come break your old bronco to takin' his share*
> *Roust out your steers from the long chaparral*
> *The outfit is bound for the railroad corral . . .*
>
> *Come flap up your holster and snap up your belt*
> *Come strap up your saddle whose cantle you've felt*
> *Say goodbye to the steers from the long chaparral*
> *The outfit's arrived at the railroad corral . . .*

* * *

The outfit arrived at Ogallala without any further trouble. Hiram Baber paid off his hands, and they had a spree in town. Walker got into a fight, won, bought drinks for the man he had knocked down, and they both ended up shooting their guns at the stars. Caleb doubled his wages fiddling in a barroom with his hat turned up, and N.C. just disappeared.

The next morning the men from Powder River rolled out of their cots and counted heads. One was still missing, and it turned out to be N.C. They combed the town for him, but couldn't flush him out.

"How do I know the goddamn Mayhall brothers didn't git him?" Walker complained.

"Oh, hell," Caleb said, "I don't reckon you ever drifted none when you were his age. You've seen the way he's been mopin' around. That's what it is. He's cut loose and gone out to see the country."

But Caleb himself was not at all at ease about N.C. until he opened his fiddle case that afternoon and found the note:

> *White Wolf,*
> *Gone south Rabbit huntin.*
> *Eagle-on-the-Ground*

FORTY-ONE

BIG TOM FOUTTS strode slowly up to the gate of the picket fence. He hesitated before stepping into the yard. The sun was at his back, glaring in a legion of windowpanes and arresting his view of whatever went on inside. Tom usually stayed clear of the big house. He and Chauncey Shanahan both liked it that way. Whenever Shanahan called for him to come up to the house, it generally meant that something had gone wrong.

He stomped loudly when he got to the porch, hoping someone would open the door for him so he wouldn't have to knock. When he knocked, a housemaid whom he didn't know opened the door, and a cat ran out. The pretty little maid looked at him and shut the door in his face without speaking.

Tom waited. The door opened again, and the housemaid let him in. He knew the way to the study, the only room of the house in which he had ever sat himself down on a chair. He found the old Scot smoking his pipe there.

"Sit down, Mr. Foutts. Hang your hat."

Big Tom prized his hat from his brow and hung it on the turned hard-wood knob of a high-backed chair facing Shanahan's desk. "I'm supposed to meet some boys on the North Fork this evenin'," he said, his weight stretching the overstuffed leather upholstery.

Shanahan glanced at him. "I'll make my point soon enough, Mr. Foutts." He tapped the ashes from his pipe bowl and set it aside. "Roundup twenty-three. You were there. You know who the leaders of the strike were."

"Ain't no secret."

"Name them."

Tom probed his cheek with his tongue, wishing he had a big quid of tobacco there now. "Jack Flagg and Walker C. Kincheloe got it started. Kincheloe was elected captain. That fiddler, Hard Winter Holcomb, seconded some of the motions. They did it all by popular vote. Nobody tried to scam nobody."

Shanahan nodded. "The Wyoming Stock Growers Association intends to file charges against the men you just named for committing a breach of peace. You'll need to stand before a judge and swear out a complaint."

"Complaint?" Big Tom shook his head. "I ain't complainin'. Just sayin' what happened."

"Your complaint will reference the fact that you were not allowed to work your employer's cattle in a public roundup controlled by an association granted authority by the legislature."

The leather protested under Big Tom's shifting weight. "The hell I wasn't allowed. I worked the cattle, all right."

"But not during the roundup."

"I ain't complainin' about that. Dusty as that damn roundup was, I ought to thank them boys on strike for beatin' me out of it."

"The fact remains," Chauncey said through gritted teeth, "that a breach of peace was committed. Now, you will ride to Buffalo in the morning and issue your complaint with the justice there. It is your duty as a citizen of this territory."

Big Tom checked his ire for several seconds, lest it should explode all over the study. "Mr. Shanahan," he said, pulling himself to the edge of his chair. "You tell me to ride up into the Bighorns and fetch you a canteen of ice water, and I'll saddle up. Tell me to shoe your favorite mount out in the pens and help you up in the saddle, and I'll oblige. You tell me to round up ten thousand of your blasted cows and drive 'em to Moose Jaw,

Saskatchewan, and I won't even ask you how come it. But don't you tell me I've got to go somewheres and complain. I don't collect wages to moan and whimper.''

Three knocks on the door down the hall punctuated Big Tom's speech, and Chauncey Shanahan bolted upright from his chair. The old Scot threw a blanket off what had appeared to be a lamp table to reveal an iron safe. He stooped to work the combination and the little housemaid appeared at the door to the study.

''Mr. Hiram Baber,'' she announced with a timid Scottish lilt, her eyes cast down at the floor.

''Bring him,'' Shanahan ordered, taking a bundle of greenbacks from the safe.

''Yes, m'lord.''

Big Tom twisted. Never had he heard a man called 'lord' before. Who the hell did this Scot think he was? God? A stack of bills slapped the desk in front of him. ''What's this?''

''Your pay through the end of this month.''

Big Tom stood, put his hat on, and hitched his belt higher around his ample girth. He reached for the money and peeled several bills away, letting them scatter on the desk. ''I'll just take my time up through today.'' He heard footsteps and knew Hiram Baber was standing behind him in the doorway to the study.

''Do not expect evermore to work cattle in Wyoming, Mr. Foutts.''

Big Tom stuck the money in his coat pocket. ''Kiss my ass, you uppity Scotch bastard. You better hope to hell you never cross my path outside of this territory.'' He turned and strode past Hiram Baber without meeting his gaze.

Chauncey was shaking his head. ''These cowboys have no grasp of their station. No respect for their betters.''

Hiram beat the dust from his hat and sat in the chair Big Tom had vacated. ''They're not peasants, Chauncey, and they won't be treated as such.''

The front door shook the whole house when Big Tom slammed it.

''They won't be treated as royalty, either. Not by me.''

Hiram smirked. ''What did Big Tom do to warrant your blackballing him? Buy a milk cow?''

''He refused to swear out a complaint against your foreman for breaching the peace at roundup twenty-three.''

''What good would that have done? You couldn't find a jury anywhere in the territory that would side with the association against Walker C. Kincheloe. You're beginning to make a hero of him, Chauncey.''

Shanahan looked through the window and scowled as he watched Big Tom Foutts stalk down to the bunkhouse to gather his belongings. "And you are beginning to make a nuisance of yourself, Hiram Baber."

Hi pulled himself straighter in the chair. "Is that what you invited me here to say?"

"Not at all. You are here to be granted one last chance. You will remove Walker C. Kincheloe from your payroll and he will be placed back on the blacklist."

Hiram scoffed. "You're forgetting those documents in my possession. You wouldn't want me to release them, would you?"

Chauncey placed his knuckles on his desk and leaned toward his visitor, glaring. "Who do think you're foolin' with, you dashit little twit? You are no more than a bug to me, and I would just as soon crush you flat. The documents you stole have been replaced by new ones. Yours will be dismissed as forgeries if you release them. However, it would prove rather embarrassing to the association, so I have come up with an incentive to keep you from releasing your illegally obtained documents."

Hiram brooded in anger. "What incentive could you possibly offer me?"

"Your family's reputation."

Hiram stood, fed up with Shanahan's looking down at him. "What the hell does that mean?"

Shanahan looked outside again and saw the boys down at the bunkhouse standing in a group, watching Big Tom roll everything he owned into one blanket. "The fiddler at your ranch—Holcomb. Hasn't he taken quite a shine to your sister?" It was worded as a question, but spoken as a fact, in the Scottish way. "I have it she visited the fiddler's family ranch in Colorado, traveled with him by train and in camp."

"Escorted all the while by Walker C. Kincheloe, my ranch manager."

"Known cattle rustler and gunman. Imagine how the society editors would treat that shoot-out in Colorado. Your sister's chaperon and her bordello-fiddler beau spilling the blood of good, honest farmers."

"You don't know what you're talking about. They were caught in an ambush and defended themselves."

"Aye, but every story has its darker side. Your folks will not long admire the way you have looked after your baby sister, Hiram Baber." He shook his head and made sounds with his tongue, as if shaming a child. "Little Savannah Baber in camp with gunmen and thieves."

"You're more of a thief than those you accuse."

"Not according to the laws of the Territory of Wyoming, or the State of Texas."

"Texas?"

"You don't know?"

"Know what?"

"You should be more careful of whom you employ. Walker Kincheloe left Texas years ago to escape prosecution on a charge of cattle rustling and murder. Now your baby sister consorts with this fugitive, and especially with that gun-wielding whorehouse fiddler, in a most untoward manner. Are you the only one unaware of it? The scandal will tantalize the entire eastern seaboard."

Hiram felt as if unarmed and looking down the barrel of a gun. He should have suspected something like this. He felt like a rank amateur. "What do you want?"

The ride from Shanahan's CU Ranch to Hiram's TW headquarters was twelve miles, and he changed his mind every mile as to what he would do. At mile eleven, he had decided just to tell Walker everything Shanahan had said. But Walker was liable to ride straight to the CU and rough Chauncey up a bit. Maybe even kill him.

By the end of mile twelve, the ranch house in sight, Hiram knew what he would do. He also knew what he should have done. He should have exposed Shanahan when he discovered the association's corruption. Too late for that now. Now he was nothing more than an accomplice for not blowing the whistle. Now he was lying to cover his own tail.

He found Walker and Caleb in the corral, working with last year's broncs. "Walker," he said, his boots making little dust clouds drift across the ground, "why the hell didn't you tell me you were wanted in Texas?"

Walker turned as if ready to fight. "Who says I am?"

"Bounty hunters are asking about you all over the territory."

The big Texan sighed deep and rolled his eyes. "It rears up to gall me now and then. Talk about hair in the butter!"

"What's it all about?"

Walker sauntered to the rail and hooked his arms over it. He pushed his hat back and smiled as if he enjoyed the telling. "Happened years ago when I was maverickin' in Blanco County, just a strappin' kid is all I was. I roped a heifer and was heatin' a runnin' iron when this feller comes along and says that heifer belonged to his boss. Said he'd seen it suckin' one of his boss's cows the year before."

"And you disagreed, I take it."

"She was a long yearlin', Hi. This feller'd had plenty of time to put a brand on her. I just picked up my runnin' iron to make my mark and he come at me with a gun, so I shot him.''

''Dead?''

''I ain't no wing shooter. Anyway, I went about my business, till this ranger showed up at my camp. Said the dead feller's boss wanted me hung or run out of Texas. I picked runnin' over hangin'. Nobody liked that boy anyway, and he didn't have no family. If it wasn't for the bounty on my scalp, I'd have been governor down there by now.''

Hiram stood with his thumbs in his vest pockets for a long time. ''You better go up to your place in the foothills and hide out until this matter settles itself.'' He turned to Caleb. ''Holcomb, you'd better clear out, too. That scrape you two had in Colorado has got people calling you both gunfighters.''

Walker C. Kincheloe rode to his spread in the foothills of the Bighorn Mountains. Caleb Holcomb decided to drift south, promising Walker that he would look for N.C. And Hiram Baber went to bed sick to his stomach of lies; sick with worry about his sister. He had watched Caleb mount that day. He had watched Savannah chase him down, overtaking the fiddler a quarter mile from the ranch house. He had watched them embrace and kiss, each in the saddle.

FORTY-TWO

M AWL KNEW HOT and cold. He knew darkness, moonlight, and sunlight; wind, rain, and hail. Mawl knew eat, drink, and fight. Fight made Mawl a monster. Fight brought pain, and pain brought rage, and rage made Mawl a victor. Mawl knew the pleasures of a victor's loins.

Mawl knew fear, though he feared none of his own kind. Not even the old ones, who could wheel, and gouge, and make him run from pain they piled upon pain. Mawl challenged them time and time again and sensed one day he would beat them. Mawl's horns were long and his head was hard, and he feared no amount of agony the old ones could make him suffer.

But Mawl feared the scent of those who ate meat. They were wolf and coyote, lion and bear. They were wild dog, and jaguar, and others too small even to bother him, but he feared them all the same, for their scent made a terror seize him all over and made him flee.

But these eaters of meat were never Mawl's master, for he could kick and wield his hard horns; he could run and join many of his kind, which the meat-eaters feared. Once, he had found meat-eaters all around him, and he had fought them, and heard them squeal, and made them fly and roll. They had hurt him, and he feared them, but they failed to master Mawl.

Mawl knew horses, and Mawl knew men. Horses alone, he did not fear. He could fight them, and they would run. They would kick and bite, but Mawl was their master. Men on the ground, though they stank like meat-eaters, were not to be feared, only hated. They were small and weak, and he had once proven it by knocking one down.

But a man together with a horse was a thing to be feared. Mawl didn't understand it, and didn't try. Sometimes man and horse simply became one. It seemed like a long time ago when Mawl learned this. It happened back when he knew the taste of milk, back when he still followed his mother.

The horse-men came, and his mother called his name, and he ran with her in terror, bunching with others he knew. One of the horse-men had caught him somehow by his legs and dragged him, and men on the ground had pounced all over him and made a horrible pain seize his flank. It came with an odor more horrible than the pain—the odor of Mawl himself burning. He had escaped somehow, and had run back to his mother, back to his kind. But in that bunch, the smell of burned hair and flesh and the smell of blood made Mawl fear the men who became one with horses.

After that, Mawl ran when he saw horse-men. After the first time of bitter cold, when his mother made him quit sucking and play turned to fight, the horse-men came again, and there were too many for Mawl to escape. He was bigger now and battle had made him less afraid; he decided he would fight a horse-man, for he didn't want to feel their pain, or smell himself burn.

When Mawl charged the horse-man, it ran like a horse alone, but always came back when he quit chasing it. It was afraid, but it was quick. He went after it again and again, and hated it because it would not fight. Mawl thought he was its master.

But then the horse-man did something that no horse alone or man on the ground could do. It caught him somehow by his head, and threw him sideways upon the ground. It did this though it was not even near enough to touch Mawl. When he got up, it threw him down again. It threw him time and time again, until Mawl was too hurt and tired to get up. A horse-man was a thing to fear, and more. It was Mawl's master.

Now the long hot time had come again, and the horse-men were back. They made Mawl crowd together with his bunch, and made others of his kind join the bunch, though Mawl did not know them all, for some had come from far away and were tired when they joined the big herd, and easy to fight. Mawl found he had a lot of fighting to do, and he bellowed out his name as a challenge until it became a whistling scream in his throat.

Mawl was large and strong now, and he loved to conquer challengers. He knew the sweep and power of his horns, for he had felt them crash through brush when he ran from the horse-men and the meat-eaters. He had learned how to twist his head and wrench his great neck and make his foes moan with pain. Mawl feared none of his own kind, not even the old ones. He would conquer them all one day, for every fight he won made him more the master of his own kind.

But he would not try to fight the horse-men who swarmed around this great herd. He stayed away from them. Everywhere in this herd was the smell of burned and bloody ones, and Mawl knew the horse-men were making themselves masters of his kind. One day a horse-man in the middle of the herd made Mawl leave those of his kind. Alone, away from the herd, the horse-man caught him somehow around the neck and choked him. Another caught his legs that kicked, and they were his master. A man on the ground pulled him down by his tail, and made that same terrible pain shoot across his flank again. The same pain and the same stench made Mawl's rage consume him until he was blind. A man on the ground sliced through part of his ear, and Mawl could feel it dangle, and he smelled his own blood. Then he escaped somehow and ran back to the great herd. The pain and the stench made him hate and fear his masters.

The great herd was in the place Mawl knew as home, where thorns and needles stuck his knees and snout and water flowed below. Where grass came green in bunches, and meat-eaters prowled among shadows. Where sunlight scorched his back, and bloodsuckers galled his flesh. Where Mawl lived, and ate, and drank, and fought, and felt the pleasures of a victor's loins.

But then the horse-men made the great herd leave this place, and Mawl could not see the mountains of home against the sky. He could not smell the trails he had traveled since he followed his mother. He could not hear the water that ran below. But Mawl felt his home place behind him, and knew where it was.

It was the time of moonlight when Mawl felt the call of his home place most, and he would moan out his name in sorrow. The time of moonlight in this strange land made Mawl know fear, and he could not lie down to rest. He plodded away from the herd, feeling his way home. But the horse-men would not let him go home.

Then one night, when moonlight came pale, Mawl saw something move on the ground and snuffed at it, and it rose like a stick and made the noise he remembered from when he was small. It was the thing that sang and struck and made pain, and he ran from it suddenly, his tail rising high to warn the others. And in his instant fear, Mawl decided to run all the way home, and not even the horse-men could turn all those who followed him. And though he ran on until the time of sunlight, the horse-men got ahead of him, and turned him away from home, and made him go on to other strange places with the great herd. And Mawl began to know that his home was nowhere now that the horse-men were his masters.

He walked on, ate grass, drank water where he found it. He went ahead of the others, for he was strong, and walked faster. Mawl came to water that ran, and felt the ground drop out from under his feet, and found that he could move through this water.

He saw men on the ground sometimes, and often wanted to make him-self their master, but always horse-men were near, who would protect the men on the ground. Then he saw a man on the ground with no horse-men or even horses around. And Mawl put his head down and trotted, and growled his name at the man on the ground. He felt like the man's master and ran with all his great strength and anger and hatred. The man was weak and slow, and Mawl tossed him easily into the air and came to crush him against the ground.

Then a crack hurt Mawl's ears, loud as the light that made him fear the time of darkness and rain and hail. He shied and circled the man on the ground, and the sound came again, and Mawl felt pain stab him low be-hind his front legs, and he ran in fear and anguish. That pain grew and spread, and Mawl let the others pass him, for he was sore now, and slow, and the days smelled like dust. But the pain made Mawl wiser, and he knew he would never again challenge a man on the ground. He would fight his own kind, and that would make him master enough.

So Mawl healed, and moved to the front of the herd again, and chal-lenged any one of his own kind who cared to fight. And then he met the strongest of the old ones, who had beaten him time and time before. But this time Mawl went blind with rage and felt the monster possess him with quickness and power. He hooked the legs out from under the old one and drove him to the ground and made him moan with pain. And as the old one hobbled away in defeat, he grunted out Mawl's name.

Now Mawl was master of his own kind, and he knew the pleasures of a victor's loins. And even the horse-men gave him respect as he learned he could walk with them, so long as he led his herd where the horse-men wanted to go. Mawl led his herd across waters that moved, over hills and strange plains. In time he came to know one of the horse-men apart from the others. The horse part of this master changed with each new sun, but the man part made a noise that Mawl came to recognize as the great herd went on without a home.

By day, Mawl would walk near this horse-man he knew and listen to the noise he made. He began to like the noise, and he walked nearer to the horse-man. He respected this master, and this master respected him. One day the horse-man came very near, making that noise Mawl liked, and Mawl felt the horse-man catch the end of his horn. He was not afraid, and he let the horse-man hold the point of his long horn and listened to the good noise his master made as they walked on, far away from the home place Mawl could scarcely remember.

One night Mawl awoke with a strange man smell in his nostrils, and he rose to his feet to find the strange man. He walked into the wind, toward the smell. He hooked others out of his way as he moved, and they began to rise around him, for Mawl was their master. Coming to the edge of the herd, he smelled the strange man stronger, and moaned his name as a warning.

Now Mawl saw something that made his heart lunge in his great chest. A man on the ground was coming at him in the moonlight. Mawl gouged the ground with his hoof, but the strange man was not afraid. Then something flew all around the man, catching the bright moonlight like wings of an eagle coming to kill something on the ground, and Mawl was afraid of this strange man-bird and remembered the time lightning shot from the man on the ground.

The great herd spread far across the strange land when Mawl started running. He felt fear of many strange things, and ran, leading many of those who knew him as their master. He ran until his lungs ached; then he heard the horse-man he respected and felt the comfort of that good noise.

Mawl made the others stop running and led his bunch whence they had fled and felt well that the good noise of the horse-man stayed with him. When the time of sunlight came, the horse-man came to him, and rested upon the end of his long horn, and Mawl listened to the good noise of his master. The man-bird of the night was gone, for his master had protected him, and Mawl knew peace. No longer did he fear or hate his masters. He respected them, and they him. He was ready to go to strange places, and cross moving waters, and eat, and drink, and feel fight make him a monster, and know the pleasures of a victor's loins.

Mawl was master of all his kind.

FORTY-THREE

SHE-RABBIT TRUDGED absentmindedly up the banks of the river, her meager burden of firewood barely felt across her forearm. Sometimes she had to walk a long way up the timbered bottoms to find enough wood for the coming day. The wood along this stretch to the Washita had almost been used up, and she suspected her father would soon move their village to another place where there was more wood, more grass for the horses, more small game to kill. But her father would never tell her until it was time to take down the tepees.

Finding wood had been made even more difficult since Eagle-on-the-Ground had come back for her. In fact, it was hard to concentrate on anything. Her father had noticed her absentmindedness and had scolded her for it. She just couldn't keep her mind on her chores anymore.

A good limb cracked under Rabbit's moccasin. "You do not see wood unless you step on it," she said, admonishing herself. She picked up the limb, broke it into pieces short enough to carry.

She could not imagine why a white man was taking up so much space in her head. Since she had gone away to school at Carlisle, Pennsylvania, Rabbit had arrived at the opinion that not all white people were all bad. Her father had not wanted her to go, but Red Hawk had convinced Lizard that it would be well to have a daughter who could translate English and knew the ways of the whites, so her father had allowed her to go away for a year.

She had learned the ways of white people and had come to like some of them, but Rabbit was Cheyenne, and her father was the great warrior-chief Lizard, and she would marry a Cheyenne brave whenever her father told her to. She had no business thinking so much of Eagle-on-the-Ground.

She knew how the whites married. They were different. Often, they made up their own minds about whom they would wed, and she thought that was good. And the men took only one wife, and she thought that was good. But she was not a white girl.

Rabbit's father had always made her decisions for her. Even when she was away at the white man's school, her father's will had guided her every move. There had been a time when she would have thought it impossible even to have a conversation with a white man, much less to think of marrying one. When and how things had changed, she could not say, but Rabbit was beginning to have strange thoughts.

These foolish thoughts took her away from wood gathering and other chores. She thought about how it would be to live as a white man's wife. She had seen white men's wives smile and laugh and dance in their husbands' arms. They were weak and pale and didn't know how to straddle a horse, but they owned shiny things to wear, and a different dress for every one of their seven days.

She cautioned herself as she trudged on up the riverbed. Was she imagining what it would be like to serve a white husband? Yes, and worse. She was not thinking of just any white husband, but the one Chief Red Hawk of the Arapaho had named Eagle-on-the-Ground. Oh, she wished he had never come back, but she didn't wish so very hard. What if she were to run away with this young white man? Could they escape her father?

Eagle-on-the-Ground could terrorize and enthrall her all at once. Since he returned to the reservation, he had hunted her like a deer, and would appear at the river when she came to get water, or emerge from the shadows as she went to move the staked horse at night. He had told her from the first word that he intended to marry her, and that was why he had come back.

Rabbit found herself sitting on an old deadfall, daydreaming. A noise on the bank above made her whirl, and she saw cattle plodding. Standing on the deadfall for a better view, she saw the mounted cowboy, and recognized him instantly as Eagle-on-the-Ground.

Her heart leapt like a lion going for the kill, and her first thought was to hide behind the fallen tree she was standing on. Then another thought struck her. She would pretend not to have noticed Eagle until he was upon her, then she could let her eyes meet his again. It was a lame ploy, pretending not to notice all the squeaking saddle leather these white men burdened their horses with, but Rabbit decided upon it. She leapt from the deadfall and made as if looking for wood to gather.

"Well, lookee here," N.C. said, drawing rein. The three beeves were grazing calmly ahead of him, so he turned his horse into the river bottom and ducked branches as he approached the Cheyenne girl.

"Go away," Rabbit said. "You will make trouble for me."

N.C. swung down and looped his reins loosely around a hackberry sprout. "Don't want to make no trouble for you. You know what I want." He saw her eyes flash to meet his and took it as a good sign, though it was only a glance. With her armload of wood and her hair over one shoulder, she was the prettiest thing he had ever seen. She wore an ankle-length white cotton dress with long sleeves, and over it she layered a blanket as a knee-length skirt, wrapped around and tied with a horse-hair rope around her thin waist. She seemed poised, graceful, and forbidden, and the fact that his father was a hater of Cheyenne was nowhere in N.C.'s thoughts right now.

"I don't know what you want," she said, but in truth she did, for she wanted to hear him say it again.

"I want you to marry me."

She looked away. How much longer would he tell her these beautiful things if she continued to show no interest? "I don't believe you. The old women told me you only want to wrap me in your blanket one night. Then you will be gone."

"I wouldn't treat a lady like that."

"I am not a lady. Just a squaw." She glared, but anger melted from her face when she saw his smiling blue eyes.

"You're a lady to me. Why do you think I have those three steers yonder?"

She looked at the cattle and shrugged.

"I'm takin' 'em to your father so he'll let me marry you. That's the way y'all do it, ain't it?"

"Don't. You don't know what you're doing."

"I want to make life easier on you, Rabbit. Don't you want a house, and a woodstove? When you marry me, you won't have to pick up wood, or haul water, or skin carcasses. I'll give you your own horse, and all the clothes you want."

"Don't ask my father. He will kill you."

N.C. caught the sincerity in her warning. "See there. You don't want me kilt, do you? I guess you care somethin' about me. Now, I've looked into it, and the only way to git married white-man legal in the Indian Territory is to ride over to . . ."

She turned away and kept walking. She hoped he wouldn't actually take the steers to her father, and if he did, she hoped he wouldn't be foolish enough to ask for her hand in return. Her father might surely kill him. Eagle-on-the-Ground didn't know much about the old ways.

N.C. got back on his horse and pushed the three steers down the river. He was certainly not about to give up on his plan at this point, now that he had started a stampede and stolen another white man's cattle.

He had gotten the idea yesterday. Lizard and a bunch of Cheyenne braves had gone to confront a herd that was crossing the Cheyenne-Arapaho reservation. Red Hawk had gone along to translate and to keep things from getting out of hand. Red Hawk had asked the drovers for a beef in exchange for taking the herd across the reservation. The trail drivers almost always had a few head too crippled to go on, and he had figured they wouldn't mind getting rid of one.

But the trail boss of the outfit was a hard bargainer and had told Red Hawk that the Indians would have to wait for a second herd the same owner had coming up behind, because they had let the second herd pick up all their slower drag cattle before crossing into the territory.

N.C. heard all this at Red Hawk's house yesterday, and decided to investigate. The Arapaho under Red Hawk were doing well at reserving their own stock for slaughter, but Lizard's Cheyenne were down to eating their pet dogs, and N.C. figured Lizard would be awful grateful if he could round up some meat for Lizard's village.

So he had ridden to the herd for a powwow, and found his friend, Hard Winter Holcomb, riding swing, resting his wrist on the horn tip of a big motley-faced lead bull, all battle-scarred and road-branded, a chinga'o flickerbob dangling from his right ear. Hard Winter was singing "Whoopee Ti Yi Yo" to the bull when N.C. rode up.

> *It's your misfortune and none of my own*
> *Whoopee Ti Yi Yo, git along little dogies*
> *You know that Wyoming will be your new home*

"Red Hawk didn't tell me you was riding with this outfit."

"Didn't tell me you was stayin' at his house, either. That's just the way he is, Navy. Says no more than he figures you need to know."

"Who's bossin' this outfit?"

"Blocker." Caleb pointed to the man riding a quarter mile ahead of the herd.

"Where y'all takin' it?"

"Chauncey Shanahan's spread on Powder River. They hired me, seein' as how I know the country and all. I come down here to look for you, mainly. Surprised you ain't got yourself lanced by old Lizard yet."

N.C. grinned. "I'm playin' my cards careful."

"You want to join up with this outfit? I'll vouch for you."

"I think I'll hang around here for a while."

"Figured you might."

N.C. shifted in the saddle, looked over the plains, and scratched the back of his head. "Anyway, Red Hawk said there's a second herd comin' up behind."

"Ain't no second herd. Blocker was bluffin'."

N.C. shook his head. "Red Hawk says the Cheyenne are liable to stampede this whole herd if y'all don't pay up with a drag steer.''

"I don't believe I heard what you just said."

"I said, Red Hawk told me . . ."

"And I said I don't believe I ever heard what you just said." Hard Winter glared at the young man to his off side, and broke the glare with a smirk.

They rode on another furlong, until N.C. spoke: "How's Daddy?"

"Fine, I guess. Hiram run us both off."

"What for?"

"Me for sky-larkin' with his baby sister. That ain't what he said, but I know that's the reason why."

"Why'd he run Daddy off?"

"On account of bounty hunters from Texas bein' after him, he said, but I think the Cheyenne Club's the one that's after him. He went up to his homestead in the foothills. Said he'd had it with the TW and was just gonna run his own herd from now on."

"He ain't in no trouble, is he?"

"No more than usual. That strike he and Flagg started has stirred things up some. I guess it'll settle out."

N.C. grunted. "You ain't seen no Mayhalls, have you?"

"No, and I ain't huntin' any."

They rode on quite a little ways, until N.C. realized he had finished all his business. "How come you hold hands with that bull?"

"Me and him's pals," Caleb said, smiling. "When I joined this outfit in Texas, this bull was meaner than eight acres of snakes. He caught our night wrangler, Gregorio, away from his horse one mornin', draggin' some wood up, and like to have killed him. Gregorio had to shoot him through the brisket to keep hisself from gittin' mashed.''

"He don't look mean now."

"I took to singing to him on the trail, and I believe that's what tamed him. I still wouldn't git off my horse and piss on him, though."

N.C. had said his farewells, promised to watch out for himself, and had ridden back to Red Hawk's village, his mind already made up.

Last night, he had ridden back to the herd on a fresh horse, crept near on foot, and while the night guards were out of sight, he had waved a slicker at that motley-faced bull Caleb had tamed with singing and stampeded the whole herd across half the Indian Territory.

Once the stampede started, he had mounted and chased three two-year-old steers down into the Washita bottoms, where he had held them until daylight. He figured the drovers would give up searching for them after a while and get the hell out of Cheyenne country. He also figured Lizard would be pleased enough over the gift of three beeves to start thinking of him as son-in-law material.

Lizard's village was all cluttered with bones and burnt rocks, and strung out over a good half mile of tablelands overlooking the river bottom. N.C. herded the beeves to Lizard's tepee, which he recognized by its markings and larger size. Starving dogs hazed his cattle and nipped at the heels of his horse, and squaws stood to watch him pass. He did not look back to see the braves who ventured out of their lodges to investigate the commotion.

He saw Lizard emerge as he neared the big tepee, and loped to the front of the steers to hold them. The chief tossed his head in a demand for information.

"I brung you these beeves from that herd," N.C. said, gesturing at the cattle, then at the chief, as if giving them over.

Lizard glanced at N.C.'s weaponry, then checked the cattle for road brands and marks, recognizing the flickerbobs of the outfit that had refused to pay in beef. Why this young white buck had brought them was a puzzle. Lizard remembered "Eagle-on-the-Ground," as the Arapaho across the river in Red Hawk's village were calling him. He knew Red Hawk liked to make and use white friends, but Lizard had no use for the boy at all. The beeves probably were Red Hawk's doing, and Red Hawk had sent this cowboy to deliver them for whatever reason. Probably Red Hawk's braves had stampeded the cattle last night and cut a few out.

"I want to marry your daughter. That's why I brung 'em to you. I've heard tell that's the way to do it."

Lizard turned away from the prattling white gibberish and walked to his horse, which was staked in the shade of the trees at the riverbank. Swinging bareback onto the pony, he grabbed a handful of mane and rode to the handiest lodges to shout orders. Three Cheyenne warriors mounted and headed for the open flats beyond the village. Lizard cut in front of N.C., released a squall that made the cowboy's flesh crawl, and started the three beeves running.

The warriors out on the flats had their bows strung and arrows notched. Letting the cattle run by them, they leaned ahead on their ponies, and yelped for joy, giving chase. Each singled out a steer and shot arrows into the terrified longhorns until they collapsed and bled to death on the ground. Each warrior rode around his kill as it died, holding bows, arrows, and reins together in one hand.

Women with knives in their hands trotted toward the dead beeves, and N.C. caught sight of Rabbit returning from the river bottom with her wood. Lizard, too, was coming back to his lodge, and the old chief could not miss the expression on the cowboy's face when N.C. looked at She-Rabbit. He loped his pony to the white man, rode in between Eagle-on-the-Ground and She-Rabbit, and gestured for him to leave.

"Well, hold on, chief," N.C. said. "You took the beef. Don't that mean I get to marry your daughter?" He pointed at Rabbit.

"You're going to get killed," she said, under her breath.

Lizard heard her and silenced her with a fierce glare, the scar on his cheek writhing over jaw muscles.

"Ask him for me," N.C. suggested. "Ask him when we can set up our own lodge."

Rabbit risked a glance at him. "Get out of here, you fool. Don't you know he could kill you, and you would never be found?"

N.C. sighed with impatience and tried to form words with his hands, the reins draped over his open palm. "Listen, Chief Lizard. You get the beef." He gestured toward the dead cattle, then the chief. "Now, I get Rabbit." He made the appropriate gestures.

Rabbit looked at the ground in fear and embarrassment.

Lizard thought he could only have misunderstood, so he stood frozen between rage and confusion. Once more, he tried ordering the white man away with a gesture.

But N.C. was untying his blanket from the saddle strings. He shook it out, causing his horse to spin once before he could tighten the reins. "See here," he said, making the logical gestures. "Me and Rabbit want to wrap the blanket." He draped the blanket over his own shoulder, but made room to his left side for another under the blanket. "For good."

Rabbit put her hands over her ears, unable to listen to anymore.

Lizard was sure he understood now and turned to stalk immediately toward his tepee.

"Go, now!" Rabbit urged. "He's going to get something to kill you with."

"Oh, he is not," N.C. replied.

Rabbit dropped her armload of wood, but held on to one piece about as thick as her wrist, and hard. She used it to beat N.C.'s horse until the animal shied away. N.C. complained, but Rabbit chased the kicking horse, raising welts on its rump with the stick. N.C. galloped thirty yards just to get away from her, and when he turned back, he saw Lizard emerge from his lodge with a bow.

The old chief put the end of his bow on the ground, hooked the bow behind his leg and bent it, hitching the loose bowstring over the end, stretching it tight. N.C.'s horse whirled, still excited, and when he came around again, he saw Lizard notch an arrow and draw the bow. Rabbit threw her stick at the horse, and N.C. started away, seized suddenly by a fear of being run through with an arrow shaft.

He had made only three leaps when he felt the impact and heard the pop of the projectile slamming into the cantle of his saddle. He craned his neck and arched his back to look over his shoulder, his eyes walling in terror as he focused on Lizard drawing another arrow.

The timber engulfed him, and he galloped headlong into the river bottom, his spurs hooked like claws into the flanks of his mount.

FORTY-FOUR

RED HAWK AND N.C. sat astride good Arapaho paints, their vantage a high knoll between the Washita and the Canadian. To the west, a long line of bare fence posts, like sentinels for the white man, faded in a veil of dust that gathered with distance. To the east, Red Hawk's crew of Arapaho workmen labored in white man's clothing—leather gloves, colored shirts, vests with watch chains, canvas work pants, and suspenders. But long hair gathered and trailed out from under their felt hats, and beaded moccasins tracked the ground. They were taking down the four strands of barbed wire that stretched away to the east as far as the eye could see.

"Lizard wouldn't miss low," Red Hawk said. "High, maybe, as you were running away, but not low. He was probably trying to cripple your horse."

"You mean just to warn me, so's I'd get away all scared."

"I mean so he could chase you down on foot and kill you with his knife. Lizard likes to count coup on you before you die. It gives him power."

N.C. swallowed. "But he seen I had my sidearm."

"Lizard doesn't fear bullets. They go around him. He has medicine."

The cowboy crooked his lip and raised one eyebrow, not knowing what to think. The arrow tip he had pried from his cantle, made of filed iron from a barrel hoop, had given him a new perspective. Before, he had assumed that every warrior who submitted to living on a reservation had been tamed. Now he gathered that some were just biding time, eating Uncle Sam's beef while they waited for the first sure opportunity to kill a white man.

For some time, Red Hawk and N.C. had been observing the approach of a rider beyond the crew of men removing the wire fence. Now the man was near enough that they could recognize him as Ball Grimes. He had stopped to watch some workmen coiling barbed wire into a loop the diameter of a washtub. When he spoke to the men, they just shrugged, and pointed to Red Hawk on the knoll.

"Well, we had us a sweet deal for a while, Red Hawk," said Ball Grimes before he even drew rein. "Now, I reckon the boomers'll beat us both out of a livin'. Goddamn tater-grubbin' punkin' rollers."

"What'd they do?" N.C. asked.

"Do? Hell, boy, they got the government all stirred up about openin' the unassigned lands to homesteaders, and the first step is to git rid of us cattlemen. And hell, I don't even run no stock on the unassigned lands. I was leasin' from Red Hawk. Paid up front. They out-lobbied us, Red Hawk, plain as day. Caught us nappin' under the bed wagon."

"You want the wire?" Red Hawk said.

"What the hell am I gonna do with it? I ain't got no pastures to fence no more. Hell, we had this reservation cut into the nicest half a dozen pastures you ever seen, and the goddamn boomers got President Cleveland to declare our leases null and void. When was the last time you seen President Cleveland in the Indian Territory?"

"Where you gonna take your herd?" N.C. asked.

"Ain't no place to go, boy. The range is taken up from the Gulf to Snake River. Ain't no grass left. I'm sellin' out and goin' broke."

Red Hawk looked at the rancher's face. "If you want to sell the wire, my boys will freight it to Caldwell for you."

"I can't afford the freight. I banked everything on this lease bein' permanent, and now the president's makin' me sell out with the market lower than it's been since ol' Socks was suckin'." He patted his gelding on the neck. "I ain't got a pot to piss in, nor a window to throw it out of. Sell the wire for yourself if you want to."

"I'll see that you get half the profit," Red Hawk promised.

"You better save it so's you can buy your own land back. There's already talk about bustin' up the reservations, after the unassigned lands. Them boomers'll git your land, Chief. Right down to the dirt under your fingernails, if you don't watch 'em. I just passed a bunch of boomers not five miles back up against the timber along the South Canadian. They was plowin' a big circle around their camp, and you know what that means. I tolt 'em Lizard's had war paint on all summer over boomers, but they didn't pay me no mind."

Red Hawk looked off toward the valley of the South Canadian, as if he might see the boomers from here. Old Long Fingers had always told him that one day Indians would have to own land like white people, in little pieces, as individuals. "Where do you want me to send the money from the sale of all this wire?"

Grimes spat. "I honestly don't know where you'd send such a thing, Chief. Where the hell am I gonna go? I don't know nothin' but cows, and never knew enough about that to make no money at it. Hell, just keep the money. Pull them posts up, too. Them are good bois d'arc posts, worth a nickel apiece. Hell, pull the postholes up and sell 'em for well shafts for all I care!" He smiled and chuckled, spurred old Socks westward. "Adios, Red Hawk. Don't let the boomers catch you with your pickets in."

After Grimes left, Red Hawk and N.C. followed his back trail to get a look at the boomers on the South Canadian.

"What did he mean about the boomers plowin' the circle around their camp?" N.C. asked.

"They'll plow up a firebreak, then set the grass on fire outside of the circle."

"What the hell for?"

"It keeps the herds away from their camp. They don't want to mess with any cattlemen." His heels urged the paint pony to a lope as they closed ground on the river.

When the timber hove into view, the first boomer they came across was pushing a one-horse walking plow about a half mile away from the river bottom. N.C. already knew about all he planned to learn of plowing, but could tell this boomer in striped city pants and matching vest knew even less than he did. The boomer couldn't seem to keep his weight on both plow handles without the reins falling off his shoulder. The horse, too, seemed unaccustomed to plowing and suited more to pulling a buggy.

So absorbed was the boomer in his plowing that he didn't notice the pair until they were upon him.

"You, there," Red Hawk said. "You are squatting."

The boomer wheeled, and his horse lurched, pulling the plow over sideways. He managed to catch the reins before the horse ran off with the plow. "What do you mean, sneakin' up like that?" He saw the chief's long hair, the feather in the hat, the paint horse, and the moccasins in the stirrups, and he rolled his eyes hopefully toward his camp against the timber.

"Do you know where you are?" Red Hawk said.

The boomer gawked at the cowboy, then at the chief. "I know damn good and well where I am. This is my claim, and you're trespassin'."

"That river there is the South Canadian," Red Hawk said. "Both banks lie within the Cheyenne and Arapaho reservation. *You* are trespassing.''

The boomer appeared astounded with Red Hawk's statement. ''Are you Indian? You speak good English.''

''This is Chief Red Hawk of the Arapaho,'' N.C. said.

''Who asked you, boy? What are you, anyway, some half-breed?''

N.C. saw half a dozen riders galloping from the river. In the distance he could see tents, two wagons, and several horses tied at a picket line stretched between two trees. ''I'm a friend of Red Hawk's.''

''Well, here come my friends, so mind your manners.''

Red Hawk's pony heaved a huge sigh, but the chief remained stoic. ''Why have you come here?''

''You heard of the Oklahoma Colony?''

Red Hawk nodded.

''We're members of it. Me and my partners have thrown in together and formed a town company. This is gonna be our town. One of our men is an engineer and figures we can get a railroad bridge across the river here.''

The approaching boomers pulled their horses back to a trot and fanned out, flanking their friend and coming to a stop.

''This is not public land,'' Red Hawk said. ''You can't file on it.''

The man with the plow laughed, feeling bolder now with his partners around him. ''By the time Congress adjourns, we figure all of Indian Territory is gonna open up to settlement. President Cleveland has already run the cattlemen off. Why would he do that, except to make room for settlers? When it happens, we'll be ready to file, and we'll have the first town in this part of Oklahoma Territory.''

''This land was ceded to the Cheyenne and Arapaho by treaty. It can't be opened to the public.''

''You were ceded this land on condition that you established farms,'' said a man wearing a brand-new flat-topped panama hat. ''I haven't seen a farm one.''

''We have farms on the Washita,'' Red Hawk answered.

''That's right,'' N.C. said. ''Irrigation ditches, too.''

''Good for you,'' said the man in the panama. ''That means the Indian policy is working, and you're all becoming assimilated. Now, whatever land is left over can go to settlers.''

''Not under the law,'' Red Hawk said. ''Under the law, you are trespassing.''

''Laws change. We expect Congress to open Oklahoma by January.''

Red Hawk looked at each man down the line. ''I'm going to do you men a favor,'' he said. ''I'm going to ride to Fort Reno to tell the soldiers you are here.''

''Why the hell do you call that a favor?''

''Because if I don't tell the soldiers, Chief Lizard of the Cheyenne is going to find you here. Lizard hates nothing more than a white squatter, and he already has his war paint on. He's had trouble with some drovers, and I hear he shot an arrow at some fool cowboy just a day or two ago.''

N.C. squirmed a little in his saddle.

''We're armed,'' said the man with the plow, ''and a bunch of damned soldiers will play hell tryin' to remove us. Now, as for Injuns, I'd sure like to mix it up with 'em before they're all tamed.''

The man in the panama urged his horse forward. ''Look, mister . . .''

''Chief Red Hawk,'' N.C. said.

''Look, Chief. I think I have an idea that might change your mind about telling anybody we're here.'' He smiled and raised his eyebrows. ''Why don't we make you an honorary member of our town company? Better yet, why don't we name the town after you?''

''Why don't you name it after yourself? Call it 'Dead White Man.' That is what you're bound to be if old Lizard finds you here.'' Red Hawk turned south, and N.C. followed.

FORTY-FIVE

THE SUN SANK under a lone cloud—a mere wisp of vapor suspended like a frazzled feather, all pink, then red, then purple. A pack of coyotes began yipping like chirping birds down in the Washita Valley as Red Hawk led N.C. onto a well-beaten trail.

''We're below your village a fair piece, ain't we?''

''Below my house,'' Red Hawk said. ''I keep a lodge downstream. Sometimes I like to live like an Indian.''

Looking over Red Hawk's shoulder, N.C. saw flames flickering down the trail and made out three tepees in a little cottonwood flat above the south bank. A mongrel dog greeted them with sniffing nose and wagging tail, and two women took their horses as they got down. Red Hawk spoke to the women in Arapaho, then motioned for N.C. to follow him into the largest of the three lodges.

The cowboy took his hat off as if stepping into a house and let the low light from the fire shake his shadow across the inside of the lodge. He touched the wall and knew it was buffalo hide, not canvas like most of the tepees he had seen in the Indian Territory. An iron pot sat on flat stones in the fire, and some kind of stew simmered within. Smoke trailed quickly up like someone drawing a rope hand over hand.

A woman nudged N.C. away from the entrance and Red Hawk spoke to her, then began taking off his vest and shirt. He threw them aside, then dropped his pants, standing naked save for his moccasins. The woman brought a breechcloth, which the chief tied on with familiar ease. She put a supple robe across his shoulders and he sat on another rolled robe on the ground.

"Here, we live like Arapaho, Eagle-on-the-Ground." Red Hawk motioned for the cowboy to sit on the west side of the fire.

"Long as I don't have to git nekkid." He watched the woman go back outside, and said, "Who is that squaw?"

"My wife."

"I thought I met your wife at your house. That don't look like her."

"You met my house wife. This is my lodge wife."

N.C. sat on a roll of buffalo robes, his stomach growling as he smelled the stew. "Y'all can have more than one wife?"

Red Hawk smiled. "In the old days, a man could have as many wives as he could feed. Now, the Indian agents want us to have just one. One Quaker agent told me I had to choose one and let the other one go, so I brought both wives to the agency, sat them down in his office, and told him he was going to have to choose for me, and he was going to have to tell them. He looked at my wives a while and told me I could keep them both, but it would be better if I kept them apart. That was okay, because they never liked each other very much, anyway."

Red Hawk's lodge wife came back in and served the men stew in wooden bowls. They ate in silence with spoons made of buffalo horn, and the woman refilled their bowls until they could eat no more. Red Hawk groaned with satisfaction and reclined on his robes.

"Who lives in the other tepees?" Eagle asked.

"The sisters of my lodge wife. I would marry them all, but I'm not supposed to now. Still, I take care of them, and they help my wife."

The cowboy shook his head, feeling thrust out of place in Red Hawk's escape. "Did you live like this all the time when you were my age?"

The chief nodded. "I hunted. I sought battles. I looked for wisdom."

"I guess things have changed some on you."

Red Hawk caught a note of pity in the cowboy's voice. "Things will change on you, too, Eagle-on-the-Ground. Hold what you can, as I do here; but learn the new things, or you will lose everything."

The cowboy cut his eyes across the neat, level floor of the comfortable lodge, trying to understand what Red Hawk meant. Maybe it was some nugget of Indian wisdom he would come to understand later. ''Amazin' what all you've learned. Nowadays you're buildin' real houses and diggin' irrigation ditches.''

The chief peered out through the lodge opening. ''What I have learned from white men is no more a part of me than a single leaf on a whole tree. It is the white man who has much to learn. You know nothing of spirits; nothing of the circles. You think too much about machines and money and things. You read books, but you don't read what the spirits write in flocks of birds, or in clouds, or in things that grow from the land. You know nothing of the Arapaho. We can talk with the spirits and heal sick people. We can find things that are lost and stolen.''

N.C. sat quietly for a long time, watching the shadows pitch wildly across the bison hide. He felt ashamed and hated, but did not know exactly why. He knew his father would be ashamed of him now, squatting in this hide lodge, listening to talk of spirits and circles. The more he thought about it, the more indignant he became. What was a man supposed to believe? Walker C. Kincheloe could claim one thing and Chief Red Hawk another, but in the end, it was up to each man to render his own wisdom.

''Well,'' he said at last. ''If y'all are so good at findin' lost things, why don't you try findin' my brother for me? Maybe then my daddy could have some peace, even if all you found was bones.''

Red Hawk spread his robe and stretched out under it. ''There are those who know what happened to your brother.''

Eagle-on-the-Ground cocked his head and snapped his glare around on the chief. ''Who?''

''Cheyenne.''

The cowboy sat upright and felt the fire as he almost leaned over it, bending toward his host across the lodge. ''How do you know?''

''Every Indian old enough remembers those days. Maybe no one person knows everything, but there are those still living who are like the pages of some white man's book all torn apart and scattered on the winds. If you could put the pages back together, you would know what happened to your brother.''

''Well, how bad are the pages scattered?''

Red Hawk shrugged. ''It was your own father who helped to scatter them, and now he needs them together more than any man, so the demons won't possess him. Some professor would call that irony. I call it just a fact, because it is.''

Eagle-on-the-Ground squinted. "How hard would it be to find out, after all these years?"

"The Cheyenne are broken into northern and southern bands now. They are on different reservations and can't even camp together anymore. Anyway, who wants to help a white man? Especially your father. Among the Cheyenne your father is called Heap Killer. He is a bad man to them, like a devil. They would tell stories about him to their children, and the children would tremble in fear and have bad dreams about him.

"In the old days, your father searched hard for your brother, and he got a few white captives back from the Cheyenne. The way he would get them back was to ride into a Cheyenne camp and take the whites, killing any warrior who tried to stop him. He had medicine, like he was bullet-proof.

"I saw it happen once while I was camping with some Cheyenne in the Republican River country. A white girl in the camp had been caught and made into a slave. Heap Killer came charging a horse into camp at dusk, alone, and put the girl on his horse while she was gathering buffalo chips for the fire. Some warriors shot at your father, but he killed two of them and wounded two others. Then even after he had the girl on his saddle— her name was Kate Llewellyn—he kept riding all around the lodges, calling your brother's name."

Red Hawk closed his eyes and made his voice sound like a far-off echo: "Paterson . . . Paterson . . . Pat . . . Pat . . . Paaaaaaat . . .

"I thought it was his medicine, so I remembered how to say it, though I was afraid to speak it, fearing I would turn into a devil like him." The chief opened his eyes and sat up, looking out through the lodge opening. "Your father is hated by the Cheyenne, and feared, but he is respected. To count coup on him would mean great medicine."

Eagle-on-the-Ground heard the echoes of his brother's name drift far away and felt a morsel of his father's pain. "If you was lookin' to put the story of what happened to my brother back together, who would you start with?"

Red Hawk stared a long time into the fire, then let his eyes drift up to the cowboy's. "I would start with Lizard."

A horse nickered outside.

"Will you try to find something out? Will you ask some of the old folks?"

Red Hawk nodded. "I will do what I can for you, but Lizard is going to make it hard. He has much influence over all the Southern Cheyenne, and they won't talk if he tells them not to. I know you are going to take his daughter away, because I have dreamt about it. Lizard will not like that, and he will make it hard to get information from the Cheyenne. Maybe there are some old Arapaho who used to camp with the Cheyenne who saw something of your brother. I will try, but when you marry She-Rabbit, you may never know what happened to Paterson-Paterson-Pat-Pat-Pat.''

The dog began barking outside.

Red Hawk smiled. ''The spirits work tricks on people like that sometimes. Who knows why?'' He pinched some cedar shavings from a flat rock and offered them to the fire, making it flare. ''Did you know we all have the same god?''

Women were moving around outside, and Eagle-on-the-Ground heard hoofbeats.

Red Hawk lay back down and rolled in his robe. ''Go see who that is. I am one tired Indian tonight.''

N.C. heard the women chattering excitedly and rose to peer through the entrance hole. By the light of the risen moon, he beheld Rabbit atop her father's horse, and his whole chest throbbed with instant heat, like cedar offered to the god of fire. One of the women had the horse by the reins and was trying to send Rabbit away, so N.C. stepped out, catching her eye.

Rabbit slid from the heaving pony and ran to the cowboy. ''I'm ready,'' she said. ''Let's go.''

''To git married?''

She nodded. ''My father was going to make me marry someone else, so I ran away.''

N.C. smiled, his limbs seizing up like a dead man's. From inside the big lodge, he heard Red Hawk's voice:

''Take fresh horses.''

When they got to Fort Reno, dawn was breaking, and the stagecoach was about to leave for Kansas. The district justice, a young appointee from Illinois, refused to marry N.C. and Rabbit without authorization from the Indian agent, so N.C. pulled out his pistol and told the functionary he had better make exceptions. They were married and boarded the stagecoach just as it was ready to leave. They had to ride on top with the driver, for the passengers didn't want to ride with a squaw.

''Where will you take me?'' Rabbit asked, the wind from the ride making her hair trail across her face.

''I'm taking you to the mountains you remember when you was a little girl. I have friends there on the Front Range. We can buy a house cheap in an abandoned town called Holcomb, Colorado.''

FORTY-SIX

THE TOOLS LAY idle in Buster's hands. One was a draw knife, the other a wood chisel. He didn't even know why he was holding them; he just came out of his daze suddenly on his work stool and realized they were in his hands.

He had been thinking of that day in the abandoned town of Holcomb, when the Mayhalls started shooting. He had been thinking of the pain that had throbbed through and through when he spat in the face of that drunken doctor in Old Town. It was as if beating that bullet wound had taken all the fight Buster ever had or ever would have again, and now he was like a dead man occupying a live body.

He had harvested, but had done a sloppy job of it and didn't care. He had shipped a few steers through Colorado Springs, but he would just as soon have shipped the whole herd to be done with it, no matter how low prices had fallen. He had cut some hay on Ab's vacant irrigated plots up Monument Creek, but he had cut only half as much as he might have.

That Kincheloe boy, Navy, had showed up with a little Cheyenne wife, and Buster had helped them move the saddlery building to the ranch for them to use as a house. Navy was working for Amelia now, training horses, but Buster couldn't care less whether or not he stayed. He had moved the former laundry building from town for Lee Fong to use as a house, but moving houses just reminded him of how the Mayhalls had come near killing him in the first one.

He hadn't even taken any pleasures from Gloria in bed, and she was awful cranky because of it—even more so than usual. ''I didn't know they done shot your thang off, too,'' she had said to him the last time he pushed her away.

Buster's kids tended to put some cheer in him when they wanted to play, but for the life of him, he just didn't have the energy to laugh with them longer than fifteen minutes.

That bullet had wounded his soul, and now he just came to his old work shed at night to escape Gloria and the kids and to brood. It was cold and raining outside and there was no fire in the stove, but he was too lazy to stoke one. Winter was coming on, and Buster just didn't know what he was going to do. He was as good as dead.

He put the draw knife and the wood chisel aside and turned on his stool, the burlap carpet bunching under his boots where it had come undone.

There was something to fix. For twenty years Buster had kept this little log shop floored with sawdust covered by burlap sacks all sewed together. For twenty years he had kept his cash hidden under the sawdust in the middle of the floor, until Colonel Ab started that bank and Buster invested his thousands. He had lost all but four hundred dollars when the bank failed. It hadn't bothered him much at the time, for it was just money, but now he was sorely bitter about it and he caught himself cussing old Ab's name under his breath. Buster had never been one to cuss a man before that Mayhall rifle slug took him in the chest.

Colonel Ab was no better off, though. He hardly came out of his house at all these days. Ab was just like that. Over the years, Buster had seen him drift in and out of one blue funk after the other. He winced. "Blue funk" was a term a fellow slave had once used, and Buster had never forgotten it. He had thought more about slavery these past months than he had in decades, and he didn't know why. He had been a free man for twenty-five years and thought he had put behind him the resentment over the youth his white master had wasted for him. For the first time in years, he had visualized Master Hugh Arbuckle's sallow drunken face, and it made him seethe with useless hatred.

Now he knew how Colonel Ab felt in one of his blue funks. He was worthless. Everything he had done in life was meaningless. His eyes rose slowly to the wall, and a long shudder of guilt made him tremble. His fiddle was hanging there, dusty. He hadn't stroked one string or plucked a note since that day in Holcomb. The calluses had melted away from his fingertips. Buster was lying in that drunken doctor's office, bleeding, and racked with pain, and terrified of death.

The Mayhalls were coming back, and Buster didn't even care. He knew they would return. Maybe tonight, maybe next year. It was all he thought about, though it didn't scare him a lick. He wanted them to come back. Maybe they would blast some life back into him, the way they had blasted it out. He had tried everything else. He had attempted first to work himself out of the funk, only to wind up confused with exhaustion. He had tried to pray, but couldn't. He had even tried to die in his sleep—tried so hard that he would just lie there and sweat—but that, too, had failed.

The Mayhalls were coming back, and all Buster could do was wait. He kept a gun nearby all the time now, as he once had kept a fiddle or banjo handy. He ached for their return. He had gone unarmed the last time they shot him, but he would never get caught so again. He picked up the twice-barreled goose gun he had lugged down here from the house. That would make a mess of a Mayhall or two. He had turned out just like old Colonel Ab, mired in a blue funk.

He looked through the dusty windowpane and could just see smoke trailing from the chimney up at Ab's old log ranch house. He knew what it felt like to be Colonel Ab now. Lordy, at least Ab had built a fire. He was lower than Ab Holcomb.

"God help me," he said. "Bring 'em on, Lord. Bring on them Mayhall boys."

Colonel Absalom Holcomb finally had it figured out. Ever since Ella died back in '60—and he promised her as she left that he would make sure Caleb outlived him—he had been looking for a way to beat Caleb to the grave without dishonoring the Holcomb name. He had gone so far as to thrust himself into battle at Apache Canyon in '62, where the rebels shot his leg off. Over these many years he had often sat and moped for long spells with his old Walker Colt in his hand, wishing he could place its muzzle under his chin and join Ella. He had little fear of hell. *Life* was hell to old Ab Holcomb.

Now the gun was in his hand again, and he was almost happy. It was so simple that he could scarcely believe it hadn't occurred to him before. It was going to be an accident. He was just cleaning his gun—staying prepared for the return of the Mayhall boys—and it was going to go off accidentally.

Ab had had the big three-roomed log house to himself ever since Lee Fong had asked Buster to move the old laundry from town to the ranch. Tess McCoy had started a regular migration of wood-frame structures ever since she had moved the general store onto the ranch for her and Piggin' String to live in. It was well that Lee Fong had acquired a house, for now he wouldn't be underfoot asking for a bunch of explanations.

Ab had built a fire up in the big stone fireplace and had hung a lantern from the iron hook on the beam above. He had spread a rag on the table. He had placed the ramrod there with the little brass-wire brush he had bought from the gunsmith in Colorado Springs a while back. He had cut some patches from the rag to run down the barrel. The oil can was handy, and everything was ready.

He cocked the old Colt, held it backward in his hands, and put the muzzle against his chest. He came so close to pushing down on the trigger with his thumb that his heart throbbed like a gunshot in his chest. He put the pistol down and took one more look around. Was there anything he had left undone? He wouldn't be coming back.

He wished he could have written a note to Caleb, but that would hardly have made it look like an accident. Suddenly, something occurred to the colonel, and he marched across the room on one stocking foot and one peg leg. He grabbed the lantern on his way, strode into his bedroom, and opened a drawer on his writing desk. The letter Caleb had sent him from the Powder River country was there. He opened it and read it one more time:

> *Colonel,*
> *I have drifted up to Powder River country, east of the*
> *Bighorns. I am hired on for the roundup with a ranch*
> *manager name of Walker Colt Kincheloe. Walker has taken*
> *a yearn for a string of Nez Percé horses after watching Ol'*
> *Whiplash work. If you will tell Amelia to hold some good*
> *stock till spring, I believe Walker will pay top dollar.*
>
> > *Your son,*
> > *Caleb*

He folded it and put it in the breast pocket of his shirt. There. They would find him shot to death by accident while cleaning his gun, and they would find that letter in his pocket. Surely they would tell Caleb, and Caleb would know the colonel had held his son close to his heart when he died. Now he was ready. He had to do this, before the Mayhalls got Caleb. He could not bury another son. Not Caleb.

Back on his bench at the table, Ab considered how such a thing might happen. They would say that the colonel had been too lazy to unload the gun before cleaning it, but that was not so unusual with an old cap-and-ball gun like the Walker. It was a lot of trouble to load, so it made sense that he would have just left it loaded while he cleaned the barrel and wiped it down with a little oil. Yes, that would look convincing enough.

He oiled the pin around which the loads revolved, then ran an oiled rag down the barrel and set the ramrod aside. Now it was plain that he had actually done some cleaning on the gun. Using the remainder of the rag, Ab began to wipe down the old steel frame of the antique revolver. This was it.

It was better that he died, anyway. Ab was going mad. Since the scrape in Holcomb, he had begun seeing Mexicans. He hadn't conjured guerrillas since he lived in Pennsylvania right after the Mexican War. Now they were everywhere: peeking up from irrigation ditches, peering out through windows of abandoned buildings in town, lurking behind woodpiles and fencerows. The other day he saw not only a band of mounted Mexicans on the hill beside Pete's grave, but a Texan in rebel uniform and a Cheyenne dog soldier, all bristling with weaponry. Enemies from two different wars had come back to haunt him and drive him crazy. It was better to die while he still had some senses left.

He turned the muzzle to his chest, draped the rag over it. Now to press the trigger with his thumb. Now to die. To rest. Would Ella be there? "God, please don't make me go to hell for killing myself." Now to slip the weight of days gone by and trials too many to number. He held his breath, felt the tension of the trigger spring.

The latch rattled and the old plank door swung slowly open. Ab looked up, blinked the mist from his eyes. Were those Mexicans? They stood there under low-slung brims dripping with cold rain. Had they come to watch him die? One of them took a step inside, uninvited. The hat tipped back, and light struck the face.

The Walker Colt was shifting under the rag in Ab's hand, and his chest was throbbing like a boiler. "The Lord is merciful," he whispered.

"We come to kill you," said Frank Mayhall, as he opened his slicker to reveal a shotgun.

Ab smiled, pulled the cloth away with his left hand, and lifted the Colt with his right.

"Shit!" cried Frank, lunging backward into Terrence and Joe as he raised his shotgun.

The two barrels of buckshot hit Colonel Absalom Holcomb so hard that his finger pulled against the trigger of his Colt. The lead ball splintered the heavy pine doorjamb and caught Terrence in the throat as the Mayhall brothers scrambled into the rain. Ab's body slammed back against the table and recoiled, pitching forward onto the floor.

Frank Mayhall was pumping pistol slugs into the room, but it didn't matter. Absalom Holcomb was back in Mexico with Sam Walker, caught in the fusillade of some guerrilla lieutenant's ambush. His comrades were at hand, calling to him, and Captain Walker himself was trying to lift Ab up.

"Go on," Ab groaned, "I'm killed. Get to the horses."

But his comrades would not leave him to die alone. They gathered around him, bullet-proof, and lay their hands upon him. They lifted him high and carried him away.

FORTY-SEVEN

"Wake up," Frank said, putting the muzzle of his revolver against Dr. Ketchum's temple.

The doctor snorted, facedown on his cluttered desk. He had passed out there, too full of whiskey to lie down without getting caught in the drunk's whirlpool of spinning nausea. He coughed, his head feeling as if it were in a vise. "Who the hell are you?"

Frank lifted him by the collar. "Name's Mayhall. I have a patient for you."

Joe Mayhall turned the wick up on the lantern and began adding wood to the doctor's little cast-iron stove.

Ketchum focused his eyes and tried to make sense of everything. He saw the youngest brother shivering at the stove, looking cold and worried. He glanced up at Frank's face and felt fear overwhelm his intoxication. The wick was burning brighter now, and a wheezing sound drew his attention toward a third brother sitting on the examination table. Terrence Mayhall's neck was wrapped with a bloodied bandage, and breath rattled from his throat. His eyes were set hard and mean, and his lips smiled defiance.

The name Mayhall registered. "You the fellas who killed Colonel Holcomb?"

"We are."

"That was three days ago."

"Four, you drunk bastard." Frank pushed the doctor toward Terrence.

"What do you want with me?"

"Well, seein' as how you pulled Buster Thompson through after I hit him in the chest with a rifle slug, I figured you could handle Terrence's neck wound."

"I didn't do a thing for Buster Thompson. I told him he was fixin' to die, and he spit on me. Surprised the hell out of me that he lived at all."

"Well, you'd better hope Terrence lives, or you won't."

Ketchum swallowed, and searched the office for whiskey, finding only empty bottles. Terrence was unwrapping the bandage from his own neck.

"You reckon this'll be all right, Doc?" Joe Mayhall lifted his coat and shirttail to show Ketchum three puncture wounds in the small of his back.

Ketchum squinted. "What is it?"

Frank chuckled. "After we kilt the colonel, ol' Buster come out of his shack and fired two loads of bird shot at us in the dark when we rode by."

He yanked Joe's shirttail down. "You ain't hurt, boy. You don't hear Terrence whinin', do you?" He pushed Ketchum toward the examination table and gestured with his pistol muzzle at the neck wound, now exposed.

Terrence cocked his head to one side as the doctor squinted and swerved toward him for a closer look. The oozing wound made Ketchum's stomach churn, and his throat clamped down to suppress the gag. He opened a leather bag and picked out a pair of forceps. Kicking the door of the stove open, he held the instrument in the flames for a few seconds. His hands were trembling as he poked into the wound, his head throbbing with pain and his stomach barely able to keep the whiskey in. "Hold the lantern over here, boy. Lower. Lower!"

Deep in the wound, he could feel the rough edges of the bullet with the forceps. "Open your mouth and say 'ah,' " he ordered. "Give me that lantern, boy." The patient's throat was swollen almost closed, and though the light was poor, Ketchum could make out part of the bullet protruding into the back of Terrence's throat, all inflamed and swollen.

"Well?" Frank said.

"He needs to have that bullet taken out of there."

"What the hell do you think we come here for?" Frank bellowed. "You're a doctor, ain't you?"

"I never was much of a throat man. Likely that bullet's against his spine. One slip, and he could die." A hacking cough caught Ketchum unprepared, and doubled him over as sure as if he'd been kicked in the gut. He staggered toward the stove and spat in through the open stove door.

"Well, you'll be dead if you don't get that bullet out and get him ready to ride."

"It's all inflamed," Ketchum complained. "Why didn't you bring him here the night it happened?"

"We had a little ground to cover," Frank said. "Quit stallin', and git the bullet out."

Ketchum thought his head might explode with pain, but he could see Frank Mayhall meant business, so he kicked a straw-bottomed chair toward the examination table and sat down to go to work.

"Lie down," Ketchum ordered. The forceps trembled like leaves in a breeze as he inserted them into the wound. "You sure you don't want some laudanum or something?"

"Just do it," Frank said. "He won't flinch."

"Give me light, boy," the doctor said to Joe. "Hold the lantern just over my shoulder."

Ketchum could feel the bullet now with the forceps. His heart was throbbing so hard that his arms were virtually lunging, and it was all he could do to keep from jabbing the steel instruments through Terrence Mayhall's neck. "I've never seen a wound like this. It's a wonder the bullet didn't break his neck and kill him."

"It went through a pine wall before it hit him. You got it yet?"

"I've got ahold of it, but it's gonna hurt like hell when I pull it out. You better hold his head down."

Frank put the pistol aside on the table and put both his big hands on Terrence's forehead.

"Here we go," Ketchum said. He swallowed, put both hands on the forceps for a better grip. When he pulled, he felt the bullet come free, but then the jaws of the forceps snapped together and Ketchum staggered back.

Terrence gasped when the pain stabbed, and felt the bullet suck into his windpipe.

"You get it?" Frank asked.

Ketchum was peering at the ends of the forceps. "It came loose, but it must have slipped."

Suddenly, Terrence realized he couldn't breathe and struck Frank's hands away from his forehead. He sat up on the table, wild-eyed and scared.

"What's wrong, Terrence?" said Joe.

Terrence leaped from the table and slapped his own chest. He grabbed his sore neck and spun crazily around to glare at Ketchum. He dropped to his hands and knees and heaved grotesquely, like a dog trying to vomit.

"Help him, Doc," said Joe, coming to Terrence's side.

Terrence leapt up from the floor, pounding on Joe's chest. He pushed his youngest brother back against the wall and shook him, then grabbed his swollen neck again, his eyes crazed with his lust for air and life.

"He's chokin'," Joe said.

"Goddamn, what'd you do?" Frank said to Ketchum. He grabbed Terrence by the sleeve and began slapping him fiercely on the back.

Terrence felt the bullet lodge ever firmer in his windpipe, and he turned on Frank with his fists. He ran at Joe next as his chest began to burn for want of air. He pushed everyone away and looked at the ceiling, tears running from his eyes. He waved his arms and opened his mouth as if caught in a nightmare, unable to scream no matter how hard he tried. The room grew dark for Terrence, and he knew he was dying. He had one last burst left before he fell, and he released it at once, letting it go in a singular jolt of all his hard burly muscle.

Joe watched in horror as his brother leapt backward into the stove, knocking the stovepipe loose, spraying the room with flaming brands.

Smoke billowed up as Terrence flopped helplessly on the floor like a cat-fish trying to get back to water. Joe just stared at the bizarre scene, his stomach sickened.

"Goddamn you," Frank said, looking slowly up at Ketchum. "Now you'll die too, by God!"

But Ketchum had picked up the revolver Frank had left on the examination table. It was cocked and swinging upward in his grasp. "Like hell I will, you murdering sons of bitches." A rug on his floor was catching fire quickly, but the doctor ignored it as he tried to make his eyes focus over the pistol irons.

Smoke stung Joe's eyes as he pushed Frank aside and drew his own weapon from the waist of his pants. Ketchum missed, firing between the brothers, and Joe dropped to his knees to get under the smoke cloud. He missed as the doctor scrambled and fired again. A bullet sang off the top-pled stove, and Joe shot wild a second time, sensing that Frank was mak-ing a dash for the door and his shotgun outside. He felt a bullet clip his ear and fired a third shot as the doctor danced through flames.

Joe cocked the pistol again and hunkered ever lower under the smoke. Ketchum was screaming, his pants leg in flames. Joe found him in the sights and fired his last two rounds, watching as the doctor fell forward across Terrence's legs.

Frank's hand grabbed Joe's collar and pulled him outside.

"Good," Frank said.

Joe coughed out the smoke he had inhaled. "What about Terrence?"

"Leave him lay, boy. He's dead. You kilt one of 'em that kilt him, and that's a start." He slid his shotgun back into the saddle scabbard and mounted.

"What do you mean one of 'em?" Joe asked.

"Colonel Holcomb was the other. He put the bullet in him, didn't he?"

Joe was mounting, and he heard a door open somewhere along the main street of old Colorado City. "But we already kilt Colonel Holcomb, too."

"There's another Holcomb left yet. Them Kincheloes, too. This ain't over." He spurred his horse toward the mountain trail they had ridden in on.

Joe followed, whipping his tired horse with his reins as the cold wind tightened the grimace across his face and streaked tears along his cheeks.

FORTY-EIGHT

Now MAWL KNEW snow, for it had fallen, and fallen, and fallen, and piled upon his head and back, and driven cold through his mats of winter hair, through his hide, through his muscle, and into his very heart. So Mawl turned away from the stinging wind as his tail grew heavy with ice, and he walked. The world turned white as if Mawl had gone blind, and the grass—what grass there was, all dry and tasteless—vanished under the snow.

The snow became Mawl's terrible new world, for it deepened, and stung him on the wind, and hurt his feet and legs and ears; his nose and tail and hide; the snow gave Mawl a kind of pain he had never known before, and all he could do was walk.

When he came to a creek bed, Mawl would seek out the willow bushes and wrap his tongue around the cold frozen switches, for he was starving, and the grass was hidden under the world of snow. He would use his great horns to beat the willows down, and would turn viciously on any one of his kind who tried to steal his tasteless frozen morsels of willow bark and twigs.

The days blinded Mawl with a cruel dearth of color, and the nights were but a black and freezing void. The only escape was sleep, when the snow would blow and cover Mawl, and make him numb to the cold, but even his dreams were snow, and wind, and hunger.

The others began to weaken and fall around him, and the meat-eaters came. All day and all night, Mawl heard their teeth pop and their throats growl as they feasted on the ones that fell. To run from the meat-eaters in the snow was useless. He only trudged on with the wind, and when he would see a meat-eater, he would let it come very near, then charge and swipe at it with his great hard horns.

The snow came down and the cold got colder. Mawl felt his skin hanging on ribs, and his hunger gnawed at him like some enemy eating him from the inside. His tail dragged a ball of ice that bloodied his hocks. The willows were gone, and everywhere were the others of his own kind: stumbling, falling, dying, dead, devoured.

Then he came to a low place where water should have been moving, but there was only a great flat field of snow. Mawl saw something dark in the middle of the field, and knew it was water, so he walked toward it, for he hadn't tasted water since the world turned to snow. But he stopped and trembled, for his frozen legs could sense some strange horror beneath his hooves. Others ambled past him, toward the dark hole of water, and Mawl moaned his name as a warning to them, but they paid no mind.

One of the leaders reached the dark hole of water and drank. Then another, and another. They lined its edges as if coming to drink at a pool in times of warm rain and grass. And Mawl wanted to drink with them, but some unnamed fear kept him away, and he moaned his name again as others went to drink with the herd.

It was then that Mawl felt the flat field of snow beneath his hooves shudder, and a huge horrible voice growled slowly from the dark hole of water. The field of snow opened, like the mouth of a monster the size of the world, and swallowed Mawl's companions. Weak with hunger and cold, they could only bleat as they disappeared, and in the time it would take to switch his tail, they were gone.

Now there were fewer of his kind with him, and the skulking forms of meat-eaters moved with him almost all the time.

In a bunch of trees along the bank of a creek, Mawl came upon some spotted horses. He stopped when he saw them, for they were beating their hooves against the snow, like a challenger wanting to fight, and they were plunging their muzzles into the holes they made in a way Mawl had never witnessed. When he came nearer to learn more, one of the spotted horses rushed upon him with flailing hooves. Mawl made a charge, and smelled grass on the breath of the horse as it dodged and snapped its teeth at him.

Now the hungry enemy eating him from within became his ally and made Mawl go wild with power. The snow flew in clouds ahead of him as he charged. He ran his hard head into the shoulder of a horse and wrenched his neck, catching a flank with his horn tip. The horse screamed and ran with the others as Mawl probed with his nose and tongue into the holes the horses had pawed. He found grass that he pulled up crusted with ice, and consumed it as fast as he could.

Others came to eat with Mawl, but he fought them off with a fury he had never known. When he had eaten everything he could find in the snow holes, Mawl followed the horses. He found they had not run far, and they clashed again, and again Mawl won and ate from the holes they had pawed.

After that day Mawl went with the spotted horses everywhere, and soon the horses learned to move over when Mawl came to eat grass from the holes they had made in the snow. When the horses ranged among some hills and canyons, Mawl followed, though those of his kind who were still with him drifted away from the cold wind and disappeared from Mawl's world.

The meat-eaters remained, and grew bolder, and Mawl had to watch out for them as he plunged his whole head into the deep holes the horses pawed. The grass he found was just enough to keep him from falling, not enough to make him stronger, never enough to make him warm. Mawl could not even remember warm.

One day the scent of many meat-eaters woke Mawl, and he rose from his bed in the snow to hear the horses running away. The snow had fallen all through the night and fell away from his back as he struggled to make his frozen legs stand. A wolf made a feint toward him, bounding through the snow. Mawl lowered his head, then felt teeth tear at his flanks. Enraged, he kicked, wheeled, caught the wolf with his horn and heard it squeal.

The wolves came on, as if they were part of the world of snow. Mawl kicked and spun and wheeled and charged until he was dizzy. He ran across a path he had made before in the snow, and smelled his own blood, for the wolves had bitten his tail, his hocks, his flanks. One had even bitten his ear, and Mawl had shaken it off and heard it crunch between his hard head and a big rock hidden under the snow.

Rage consumed Mawl, and his breath blew blasts of snow far across the colorless sky. He was master of all meat-eaters, and his horns dripped with their blood. But they kept coming, and coming, and coming, as the snow kept falling, and falling, and falling. In time he grew bloody and tired. He had not felt as weak since he followed his mother—a small and frightened calf. The wolves were more than he had ever known, and they did not fear Mawl as their master.

A wolf had seized Mawl by the hind leg, and he was too weak to kick it away. He turned, and thrust his throat right into the mouth of another wolf—a large one. The scent of so many meat-eaters sickened Mawl, and he bellowed piteously. Now the wolves had mastered Mawl, and he could not move. He felt their teeth tear his cold and aching flesh with ripping pangs of agony. They all pulled down, down, down; somehow Mawl knew to fall was to die, and he sprawled his stiff legs.

But the wolves were relentless, and Mawl was weak. He felt a front leg buckle and terror gripped his heart.

Then lightning struck and made the wolf at his throat yelp and curl on the snow. Mawl saw his chance, and flicked his head, tossing the wolf aside with his horn. The lightning was roaring like a monster from the sky, and the weight of wolves fell away from Mawl. The meat-eaters yelped and cried in defeat as he turned weakly to look for them and crush them with his hard head.

Then he saw the horse-man coming. It was the one Mawl knew—the horse-man who made the good noise on the long trail from the old home place—who rested upon the horn of Mawl as they walked many days together. And Mawl sighed his name, and knew the horse-man had helped him master the meat-eaters and knew the horse-man possessed the power of lightning.

The horse-man made the good noise that Mawl liked to hear, and when he turned away, Mawl followed, walking slowly, arduously through the trail the horse-man broke for him. And Mawl felt something swell in his great chest that he had never felt before, and he was glad to find his friend here in this world of snow and ice.

FORTY-NINE

Caleb had taken to writing them down—"Mississippi Sawyer," "Black Jack Grove," "Eighth of January," "Red Wing," "Tennessee Wagoner"—and he would practice them one at a time and that way assure himself and Walker C. Kincheloe that he was giving no one tune too much play on the fiddle. He had just thought of a new one—"Tugboat"—and was sharpening his stub of a pencil with his pocketknife to add it to the list.

The pencil was already sharp enough, but there was time to kill, and every little chore had to be drawn out in the last detail to make full use of the day. A mere point on the pencil would hardly suffice. A blizzard such as this required a symmetrical point, a point so near perfection that it was a virtual cone. When finally the whittling had ceased, Hard Winter Holcomb licked the tip of his pencil and wrote "Tugboat" quite ornately at the bottom of his only sheaf of paper, just under "Choctaw" and "I Don't Love Nobody."

He opened his fiddle case, took out the bow, and tightened the nut that stretched the horse hair. Gingerly, he picked up his chunk of rosin and applied it to the bow. Replacing the rosin, he picked up the fiddle and spent some time tuning it, then finally lit into "Tugboat" about the time he heard Walker's boots stomping snow away outside.

The big man entered and threw an armload of wood on the pile. He shook wood chips from his coat and went to warm himself at the stove. Taking the broom he had made a week ago with straw, string, and a pine branch, he began meticulously sweeping up the loose pieces of wood.

"Which one was that?" he growled when Caleb had finished playing the song.

" 'Tugboat.' "

Walker shook his head as he looked at Caleb's list. "Sounds just like 'Sally Johnson' to me."

"It's a lot like 'Sally Johnson,' but it's got some different notes."

The big man opened the door and swept the wood chips out. "You can have 'Sally Johnson' or 'Tugboat' but you can't have both!" He slammed the door.

"But they're different," Caleb argued.

"Different, hell! They sound alike! They all sound alike anymore." The Texan grabbed the list of fiddle tunes. " 'Tugboat' sounds just like 'Rachel' and 'Jenny Lind' to me. Hell, they sound like 'Chicken Reel' and 'Cripple Creek' and 'Forked Deer' and 'Dinah Had a Wooden Leg!' I don't see how you tell 'em apart from one another. I'll swear you're lyin' to me, fiddler. You know three or four damn songs, and you just play 'em one after the t'other and make up them names while you go along. 'Irish Washerwoman!' What the hell's that got to do with a infernal fiddle?"

Caleb wisely put the fiddle away and slid it under his bunk. "You been out to the shed?"

"Out to the shed, down to the privy, over to the woodpile, around the corral. I been everywhere I could go without gittin' bogged in snow, and I'm still about to go nutty as a peach orchard boar cooped up here like a hen. I thought I'd seen winters, fiddler, but this one beats all."

"How's that motley-faced Texas bull doin'?"

"How's he doin'? He's eatin' all my hay! Every time I go out there and see Chauncey Shanahan's bull standin' in my shed eatin' my hay, I get a cravin' for tenderloin and beef tongue. Probably be the only damn bull Chauncey has left alive after this winter, and here I'm feedin' it for him."

"If it'd been Chauncey himself, I'd have let the wolves have him, but me and that bull is pals."

"Don't tell me again. I've heard a hunnerd times since it started snowin' how you rode a thousand miles with your hand restin' on that bull's horn. I don't want to hear it no more. Tell me one of them other wild-ass windies of yours."

Caleb fell back on his bunk and cracked his knuckles for a full minute, thinking. "Did I ever tell you about the winter I spent snowbound with Burl Sandeen?"

Walker's eyes jolted open. "The cannibal? Don't lie, Hard Winter. Sandeen would have et you sure as a jackrabbit if you'd been snowed in with him all winter."

So Caleb spent the better part of an hour telling how Burl had saved him from starving in the mountains, only to find out years later that Burl

Sandeen had a reputation for eating his camp mates in the dead of winter.

After that, Walker opened Caleb's dictionary to a random page and thrust his finger arbitrarily onto a word in boldface type. "Predestination!" he said, pleased with his luck.

"P, R, E . . ." Caleb said, then searched the ceiling and gnawed on his lip before picking his way through the rest of the spelling, one letter to a breath.

"Damn! Oh well, you're only halfway there. What's it mean?"

The fiddler stroked his winter whiskers for a while, then said, "It means whatever's gonna happen is gonna happen, and you ain't got no say-so over it because the Good Lord has already planned it out."

"Wrong! Says here, 'The doctrine that God in consequence of his foreknowledge of all events infallibly guides those who are destined for salvation.' I win. I'll contest you to another one."

It was a game of wits Walker liked, for he always won, by his rules. If Caleb did not know the definition word for word, he lost. In truth, the fiddler was getting pretty good at knowing what the words meant, even if he could not say so in dictionary parlance. Since buying that dictionary in El Paso, he had made a habit of learning a word or two every day, memorizing the spelling and the gist of the definition, though he often had to look up several words in the definition itself. (The Bible he had bought in El Paso seldom fell under his perusal.)

After Walker had won several rounds with the dictionary in his hand, Caleb was allowed to play some songs, so long as he left his "infernal fiddle" under the bunk. So he sang some ballads with his Mexican guitar, starting with "Mustang Gray" then moving on to "Utah Carrol" and "The Shortgrass Song":

> *The stallion was nervous to smell of the snow*
> *Whistled in by a norther beginnin' to blow*
> *When across a box canyon, the hunter, in luck,*
> *Leveled his sights on a wide-antlered buck*
> *The cloudy sky rumbled, the Winchester roared*
> *The cow pony stumbled, the freezin' rain poured*
> *The wide-antlered buck and the hunter both fell*
> *Into the box canyon, as deep as a well . . .*

"Never heard that one," Walker said.

"I made it up myself. It's about my brother Pete."

Walker stared a while and shook his head. "What are you doin' here, Hard Winter? You ought to be roastin' your shins at some whorehouse fireplace, singin' for the gals. You ought to be down south.''

"I wish I was. I used to winter down in the border country with my senorita, till my friend stole her from me.''

"Don't tell that one again, either. I've never heard the likes of a grown man whinin' over a Meskin gal.'' He restacked the firewood by the door again and swept up the wood chips he jarred loose.

"You reckon we could make it down to Hiram's ranch?'' the musician said, changing chords as he spoke.

"I reckon we will when we run out of meat, or burn the cabin down. Till then, I don't see that it's worth the risk. Freezin' to death ain't the way I want to go.''

"I sure wish we'd have gone down there when we could.''

"Well, fiddler, I'm sure I'd be welcome, seein' as how I talked Hi into sellin' half his herd that would have just froze to death otherwise. But I ain't so sure he wants you around since he figured out you been skylarkin' around with his little sister.''

"I don't see why not. Savannah don't even stay at the ranch come winter.''

"It's the principle. He don't want you gittin' comfortable around his place.''

Caleb struck the first sour note he had hit all day, and grinned. "Amelia tolt me last time I stopped by home that she had invited Savannah and all her friends from back east to come stay at the ranch again come spring. Says she'd like to have 'em come every year.''

"It ain't my business, but you're loco for lettin' them two squaws in the same room together, both of 'em sparkin' for you in their own way.''

"Sparkin'? Amelia? Hell, she's my sister-in-law.''

"That ain't no blood kin. Are you blind, or just stupid? If you had any sense you'd be down there with her right now. Savannah, on the other hand, now there's trouble. I've warned you, fiddler, she's just like a . . .''

"Just like a three-year-old,'' Caleb said.

"Damn right. Anyway, you may not live to see either one of 'em. Hell, there's seven or eight weeks of snow left out there. A man would have to be part polar bear to git through this blizzard. You might as well git comfortable and wait for a chinook.''

They sat in silence for uncounted minutes, Walker sharpening a knife and Caleb trying to shake a rattlesnake rattler from the F-hole of his fiddle.

"What's that doin' in there?'' Walker asked.

"Keeps spiders out,'' he replied. "I think it makes it sound better, too. This one came off the rattler that bit Tess when I was helpin' her pick buffalo bones down in Texas.''

"You've already tolt that one, too."

"I wasn't gonna tell it again. I was just sayin', this is the tail end of that snake."

Another several minutes crawled by.

"Somethin' I been wonderin', Hard Winter. What give you the idea to train that pack mule of yours to trail without a lead rope?"

Caleb lay back on his bunk. "Wasn't my idea. Buster trained her that way, mainly because she learned to untie her own lead rope, anyway."

"Don't bullshit me," the big man warned, shaving his arm with the knife he had honed.

"I'll bet you a dollar on it. She'll untie herself, then move down a hitchin' rail and untie every horse alongside her."

"You got a bet. Let's go see."

They put on coats and gloves and ventured out into the world of blinding whiteness. Once inside the barn, Harriet was haltered and tied to a rail beside Whiplash and Old Shine, the other horses having been turned out to fend for themselves. The motley-faced CU bull watched from his pen, great clouds of warm vapor billowing from his nostrils.

It took her the better part of an hour, for Walker tied the half-hitches rather tightly, but Harriet eventually loosed her own rope and the reins of the two saddle horses.

"Son of a bitch," Walker muttered, smiling all the same. He handed the dollar to Caleb.

The roar of wind paused outside and let the long moan of a wolf pierce the sky full of snowflakes.

The two men looked at each other, then Walker burst from the barn and ran back to the cabin for his rifle. Caleb met him on the path they had stomped and shoveled day in and day out since the blizzards began to howl. Turning from the path and slogging through waist-deep snow to the corral, they climbed the rails like a ladder until they could see high over the four- and five-foot drifts gathered everywhere in the head of Walker's canyon.

"You see him?" Walker whispered, squinting at the frozen world of white.

Caleb shook his head. "Sure sounded like he was huntin' somethin', though, didn't it?"

Walker cocked his rifle. "There goes somethin'!" He pointed with the muzzle of the weapon.

The fiddler narrowed his eyes and could see the dark form appearing and vanishing in the blowing snow, like a trout hiding beneath the froth of white water in a clear mountain stream. Whatever it was floundered clumsily through drifts about three hundred yards down the canyon. "Wait. That don't look like no wolf."

"By God, that's somebody! Who in the name of sweet Jesus would be away the hell up here in this weather?"

Caleb ran into the barn to saddle Whiplash. He charged down through the deep drifts, finding the trail he had made a few days before covered over with fresh snow. Walker guided him by waving until he found a man kneeling in the snow, exhausted, covered with hat, scarf, coat, blanket, and gloves.

"Hey!" the fiddler shouted. When the man looked up, Caleb saw Buster's face, and the eyes closed, and the head bowed as if a prayer had been answered.

Buster was too cold to speak or to grasp the saddle horn, so Caleb helped him mount and laboriously led Whiplash back up the trail they had broken.

Walker caught Buster when he fell from the saddle and helped him into the cabin. After Caleb put the horse away, he trotted back to the cabin and found Buster shaking so violently that he could barely keep coffee from sloshing over the rim of a cup only half full.

"My mule give out a mile below," Buster was saying. "The wolves was on him before I was fifty yards away. They didn't mess with me none, but they sure skeered me."

Caleb squatted beside his oldest friend in the world. "What the hell have you come here for? Are you crazy?" He put his hand on Buster's shoulder and smiled.

Buster did not return the smile. He reached inside his vest and took a folded piece of paper from his shirt pocket.

When Caleb took it, he stopped breathing, for there was a hole torn all the way through the folded, bloodstained leaf of paper. He opened it slowly and found the note he had written to his father before the town of Holcomb died. He hadn't seen that note since he had posted it in Buffalo, but it was as familiar to him now as if he had just written it, and for a moment he shot back to that warm Wyoming day and felt the way he had felt when he first read over his letter, all full of hope for a new start with his father.

Buster watched as Caleb's eyes clouded over. His face and hands and feet were hurting fiercely now, and he took it as a good sign. "I brung *good* news for you, Walker."

"For me?"

Buster nodded. "Navy's stayin' with us now, workin' for Miss Amelia." A smile cracked the black man's lips. "You're gonna be a granddaddy. Navy done brought him a pretty little Cheyenne wife out of the territory, and she's gonna have her a little half-breed come spring!''

The fiddler heard the news and knew he would have tried to break it some other way to Walker. He would have started by telling the big man to brace for bad news, then he would have virtually apologized for it. In fact, he had been trying since it started snowing to find a way to tell Walker that N.C. was sweet on a squaw maid.

Buster had just blurted it out like good news, and indeed, Walker seemed to be taking it all right. He looked relieved. He'd been worrying about N.C., and to hear his son was safe on the Holcomb Ranch made the blizzard somehow easier to endure.

But all this just flitted over the surface of Caleb's thoughts, in the way a man could drive a six-mule team for an hour down the road and not remember a thing he had passed, his thoughts away somewhere else.

Caleb's thoughts were back in Colorado, twenty-five years ago. His mother was nearby, watering some flowers she was trying to grow. His father had two good legs under him and was plowing with a yoke of oxen. He was far away, but Caleb remembered how large the man seemed. Large as the country.

He remembered the way his mother addressed his father as ''Ab, honey.'' He remembered his father calling her by name: ''Ella.''

Caleb was sitting on the roof of the dugout he would live in until a cabin was built. He was six years old, whittling with the pocketknife his father had given him. Then his father took the knife away from him for whittling on the edge of the roof, where he might have fallen off and stabbed himself.

''Is that a safe place to use a knife? I thought you were old enough to have it, boy, but I guess you're not. I'll keep it for you, and you can have it when you learn to use it right. Now go in the house and think about that.''

Caleb reached into his pocket and felt that knife, warm against his palm. He was six years old again.

Suddenly, he found himself standing in the blizzard. The letter with the bloodstained buckshot hole was in his left hand. He tipped his head to look at it, and when he did, an avalanche of snow fell from his hat brim and landed on the letter. He didn't even remember walking outside.

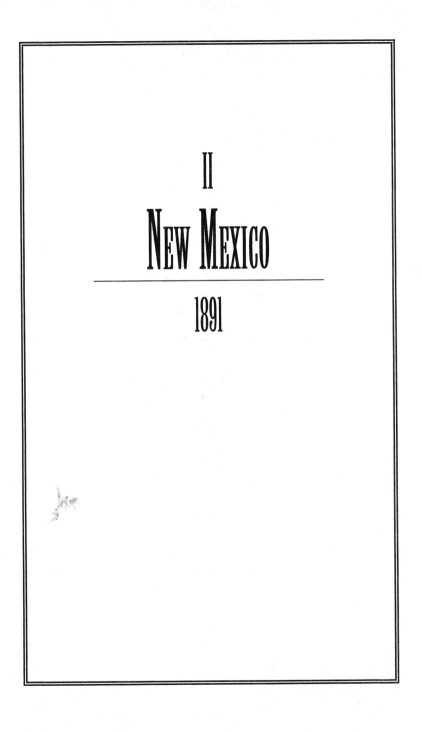

II
NEW MEXICO

1891

FIFTY

"It's been four years, but I still shiver when I think about it. How Buster even made it is a miracle to me . . ."

N.C. heard those words and knew Caleb was telling the story of the blizzard again. He led his night horse to the chuck wagon, wrapped the reins twice around a wheel spoke, and scratched the gelding on the withers.

Javier had a guitar on his knee, and Caleb was gesturing with a fiddle bow as he spoke. Angelo was listening to his father tell the stories of faraway places. At seventeen, he was on his first cattle drive, night-herding the remuda and helping the cook. It was time for him to ride out and relieve the wrangler, but Angelo had picked up Lucero's bad habit of having to be told two or three times to take his shift.

Lucero was stretched out on the ground, his elbow on his saddle. He should have been straddling that saddle by now, for it was his night to take first guard and the two vaqueros holding the herd on the bed ground had not yet eaten supper.

N.C. took a beat-up Mexican guitar from the wagon. It was handmade, its neck carved from a beam so thick the player could hardly reach far enough around to make the chords. The hollow body was made of slabs so thick that they would scarcely vibrate. The instrument, strung with twisted catgut, didn't put out a lot of sound but was built stout enough to take the punishment of the trail and was small enough even to be carried in a saddle wallet made of an old feedsack. Hard Winter Holcomb had carried such guitars many a mile across the ranges behind his cantle or on his pack mule.

On the way to join the circle of drovers, N.C. noticed that the fire had dwindled to flickers under the coffeepot. He stopped and looked around for the cook, finding the old *cocinero* quite a way off in the moonlight, tending the oxen that pulled his chuck wagon. N.C. took several steps back toward the chuck wagon, trying to keep the jinglebobs from tinkling against his spur rowels. The *cocinero* kept an old cowhide slung under the wagon bed, in which he hoarded precious firewood. N.C. snuck a couple of chunks out of the tarp, hid them behind his guitar, and walked unassumingly to the fire, where he placed the wood across the coals. He withdrew to an empty place on the ground and sat cross-legged.

"... I thought we had it bad in Walker's cabin up against the Bighorns, but it was down below where the winter was really bad ..."

The *cocinero* stormed into camp and shook his finger at N.C. "Goddamnee, you! I see you gettee my wood! You wantee eat *manana*, you gettee more wood!"

"All right," N.C. said, raising his palms in the air. "Damn, you'd think it was gold or somethin'." N.C. looked across the fire at Angelo as the cook stomped off. "The wrangler's waitin' on you, kid. He ain't et yet. Neither have them boys out there on the herd. I wonder who has first guard tonight." His eyes drifted toward Lucero.

Angelo stood and picked up his horsehair bosal.

"I have first guard," Lucero said, "but I am going to listen to the end of this story. Anyway, it ain't your business."

Angelo sat back down, emboldened by his idol Lucero.

Caleb went on with his story and tried to calm N.C. with a subtle shrug of one shoulder. "... and them cows would come up in the towns like in Buffalo and Douglas, and they'd just stand around the houses, nothin' but bones and cowhide, and they'd beller the most pitiful noise all night and all day. Well, the folks didn't have nothin' to feed 'em, so's they'd just drop, one at a time, till the streets was piled with dead cattle.

"Story was, one feller found a ol' cow in his horse shed and felt bad, so he fed her a pot of spoilt beans he was about ready to throw out. Well, that cow took the bloat from them beans and blowed up. They said she blowed clean open, like she'd swallered dynamite!"

Javier hissed and grinned at the starry sky.

"Some of the big outfits had strung drift fences, and the blizzards kept drivin' the cows south, right into them fences. They'd bunch up there, crowdin' tighter all the time, and they'd freeze to death pressed against the fence, sometimes standin' straight up! They'd pile so high that live ones would walk on top of the dead ones and fall over the fence, then keep driftin'. One of Walker's four-year-old steers turned up in the Laramie roundup, and we calculated he'd crossed three drift fences to get there.''

''If it's so damn cold up there,'' Javier said, ''why do you go back every winter? You should spend the whole winter with us on the Rio Penasco like you used to.''

''I know why he does it,'' N.C. said, ''but I ain't gonna tell y'all her name.''

Caleb tapped the bow against his knee. ''I'm spread kinda thin these days, Javier. I like to visit up there till the snow gits deep, then drift down to y'all's range for Christmas. Couldn't used to do that, but with railroads all over the place now, hell, I don't have to miss seein' nobody.''

''You forgot to tell 'em about how all them dead cows smelt,'' N.C. said.

''Oh, well, when there finally come a chinook and things started to warm some, the ice broke on the rivers and the snow run off and there was thousands of dead cattle floatin' downstream. They'd pile up in the eddies and rot and stink like nothin' you ever heard tell of. Buzzards got too fat to fly.

''A lot of them foreigners went back across the ocean, busted. This one Scotsman name of Chauncey Shanahan lost thirty thousand head. He'd brought 'em up from Texas just before the winter, and they wasn't much on cold. Me and Walker kept one of 'em alive for him in the shed—a tough motley-faced bull—and Chauncey didn't even say thanks. Just got more money from Scotland and started overstockin' again. I ain't never been out in his privy, but I hear he's got a stack of five spots where Javier would put last year's almanac.'' He paused to let the boys chuckle. ''Hell, he kindles his cookfire with ones and twos!''

''Tell 'em how Daddy come out,'' N.C. suggested.

''Well, Walker had a hunnerd cows before that winter and counted ninety in the spring. But he was smart. Him and some others sold half their herds before that winter come on and just kept their strongest ones. Sellin' half his herd give him some cash to buy a few more head when the grass started comin' back. And he cut hay in the fall and laid it up for feed. Also, Walker always keeps the stock out of this one canyon he lives in and holds it for winter grazin'. He knows what he's doin'.''

''Tell 'em how the Appaloosas fared,'' N.C. said.

''Oh, yeah. Walker had bought a string of saddle horses from Amelia, and every one of 'em come through that winter in fine shape. They'd paw that grass up from under the snow.''

''I told y'all we raise good hosses on Holcomb Ranch,'' N.C. boasted.

"Javier, you tell me when you want to buy a string of 'em, and I'll pick the best of the lot for you.''

Javier chuckled. "Buy? I'm selling horses, amigo. Selling cattle, selling horses, selling everything. Maybe I'll sell this one, next." He cuffed Angelo on the back of the head.

Caleb raised high his bow. "I'll bid on him, if he'll git out there and night-herd those horses like he's s'pposed to. Story's over, anyhow, boys. Go on, and you'll hear us play out there. N.C., do that one about the Colorado Trail."

Lucero left grudgingly, going out of his way to drag his saddle cinches through the dust upwind of N.C. N.C. began strumming chords on the guitar, and Javier just listened until he understood the structure of the song. N.C. had progressed well as a guitar player over the four years Caleb had been teaching him; this was one of his favorites and a most practiced tune:

> *Ride through the lonely night, ride all the day*
> *Keep the herd a-movin', movin' on its way*
> *Cry all ye little rains, wail, winds, wail*
> *All along, along, along, the Colorado Trail*

It was Javier's drive. Much of the range around his Penasco River ranch had been bought up and fenced. Where once he had grazed his cattle on open range, now cowboys from rival ranches rode fence and kept the wires taut. His range shrinking, Javier was having to sell cattle and let vaqueros go. He had already told Lucero and the others that they would have to find work somewhere else after this herd of seven hundred was delivered to a buyer at Granada, Colorado. How long he could remain on his deeded land, he did not know.

N.C. was here only because he had accompanied a carload of horses to El Paso. Working for Amelia, he bred Appaloosas not only for conformation, intelligence, endurance, strength, and size, but also for spots. Amelia had found that the showiest spotted horses brought a higher profit margin. When N.C. identified a horse that would not reproduce spots regularly, he sold it. Such comprised the carload he had shipped to a buyer in El Paso. They were good horses, and well trained, but did not possess the tendency to produce spots.

> *Eyes like the mornin' star, cheeks like the rose*
> *Laura was a pretty girl, God Almighty knows*
> *Cry all ye little rains, wail, winds, wail*
> *All along, along, along, the Colorado Trail*

While he was down El Paso way, he decided he would stop at Javier's ranch, where he had visited once before with Caleb. Caleb was due to ride back to Holcomb Ranch soon, for Amelia had planned the fifth annual western reunion of Savannah Baber and her socialite friends from back east. Come to find out that Javier was putting this drive together to sell most of his stock, and N.C. could help out on the way north.

The only hitch in the deal was Lucero. The vaquero had not forgotten the fight he and N.C. had gotten into at the hunting cabin up in the Sacramentos, and he took advantage of every opportunity to goad N.C. further. It was just a matter of time till they came together like fire and gunpowder, and everybody knew that Lucero fought dirty.

> *Ride through the lonely night, dark is the sky*
> *Wish I'd stayed in Abilene, warm and safe and dry*
> *Cry all ye little rains, wail, winds, wail*
> *All along, along, along, the Colorado Trail*

The cook roused the boys before dawn and reminded N.C. that he had better come into camp with some wood tonight if he expected supper. Caleb saddled a half-broke mount from the remuda and rode ahead to find water and a good bed ground for the coming night. N.C., because he was working without pay, got to ride point with Javier. This fiercely galled Lucero, who, as the top hired man, had to ride swing behind N.C.

Angelo helped the cook yoke the oxen to the wagon, then lay down on the ground as the sun came up and the herd moved north. He would get plenty of sleep, then catch up to the herd before dusk.

The cattle were broken to the trail and gave the drovers no trouble through the day. Grass was hard to find, being early yet in the spring, but that just tended to make the herd move a little faster.

Caleb came loping back to the point riders in the afternoon. "Better grass across the Canadian," he said. "It's runnin' cold, but it ain't deep."

When they got to the river, Javier approved of Caleb's crossing place. The river turned south here, so the low sun would shine on the hind ends of the cattle and they would easily see the way across.

"You see my tracks up and down the bank," the fiddler said. "The ground's solid. Just a little quicksand around the bend, and they won't drift that far."

The day being cool, and the water shallow, the drovers didn't bother to take their clothes off for the crossing. They got their pants legs wet crossing the channel, but the lead cattle swam nicely and got across to the bed ground without trouble.

N.C. scoured the riverbanks for timber, gathering half a dozen drifted tree limbs in his loop and dragging them back to camp to shame the *cocinero* for ever having doubted him. He had the first shift on guard, so N.C. ate while the other boys milled the herd and got it settled for the night. He caught his night horse from the remuda, saddled him, and rode to the bed grounds.

The sun was down now, the moon already hanging overhead, a quarter full. The cattle were lying down, their front legs first buckling at the knee and their hind ends following. It was a fine sight to a cowboy to see cattle chewing cuds and bedding down.

The High Plains chill crept in, and there was not a mountain or a windmill or a house marking the horizon. But N.C. knew the sky and found the Little Dipper. He knew how to align the two stars that made the edge of the dipper's cup and follow the line they described to the place where the Big Dipper would rise. About the time the Big Dipper's handle pointed straight up, it would be time for N.C.'s relief to come on guard. Of course, his relief was Lucero, and Lucero was likely to be late.

He sighed, buttoned his collar, thought of She-Rabbit and their little son, L.W. His name had started as a joke. N.C. had suggested to Rabbit that they name their firstborn for both his grandfathers: Lizard and Walker. Unfortunately, she had failed to see the humor in it and instead took to the name so tenaciously that no other would do. Now, Lizard Walker Kincheloe was fated forevermore to answer to his initials, just as his young father, Navy Colt Kincheloe, had done his whole life.

He was looking forward to getting back to Holcomb Ranch, his home now, even more than Caleb's. There was plenty of horse work to do. Rabbit was good to hold. L.W. was nothing but a joy, though something of a hellion. His mother, in the way of the Cheyenne, did not believe in spanking children, so the boy pretty much behaved as a wild Indian and got away with it.

Riding around the herd, he came upon one of the vaqueros, a young man named Guadalupe, riding slowly around the herd the opposite way N.C. rode. He just touched his hat brim, not knowing any Spanish and the vaquero not knowing English. Guadalupe was singing some Spanish ballad to the cattle, so when he passed out of earshot, N.C. began singing a night herder's song as well.

> *Oh, the years creep slowly by, Lorena*
> *The snow is on the grass again*
> *The sun's low down in the sky, Lorena*
> *The frost gleams where the stars have been*

N.C. knew the dumb cattle had no appreciation whatsoever for his vocal stylizations, but singing was a good way to maintain a constant drone of noise. An experienced night herder knew that absolute silence was a dangerous thing to allow on the bed ground. Should the silence be broken by the *cocinero* dropping a kettle, or a night horse shaking and flapping saddle leather, the sudden noise could cause the cattle to stampede. So he sang, and his singing drifted far across the herd, keeping the cattle calm if not entertained.

> *A hundred months have passed, Lorena*
> *Since last I held that hand in mine*
> *And felt that pulse beat fast, Lorena*
> *Though mine beat faster far than thine*

It felt good to be out here alone. The air was cool and fresh. Walker had forgiven him for marrying a squaw the moment he held L.W. in his big hands. They just didn't talk about Chief Lizard, that's all. N.C. was here helping a friend of a friend for no pay, and that felt good, too. His night horse was solid and agreeable. His conscience was clear. He was somebody. N. C. Kincheloe feared nothing, least of all Lucero Dominguez.

FIFTY-ONE

He hadn't been asleep a half hour when he felt the ground tremble and heard the low rumble of the stampede beginning out on the bed grounds. He sat upright and flung his blanket away as some nonsensical dream of spotted horses snapped. He shook his head, trying to gather some sense about him.

He was fully dressed and had only to slap his hat over his skull as he willed his tired body to rise. He kept telling himself that there were only seven hundred cattle and plenty of hands, and that maybe he would get some sleep tonight yet.

He stumbled the wrong way first, as vaqueros dashed for their mounts around him. Then he remembered having left his night horse staked west of camp. The old horse was head-high when he got there to tighten the cinch, and N.C. was a little ashamed to be the last man mounted.

''Come with me,'' Caleb ordered, holding a tight rein on Whiplash to keep the stallion in.

N.C. snorted the last grasp of sleep away and brushed his spurs across the ribs of his night horse. The moon was gone now, and the High Plains were black as the inside of a stovepipe.

"Help me find the remuda first. Might be rustlers."

The same thought had struck N.C., for why would the cattle, trail-broken as they were, stampede on a night as calm as this? "Last I seen of Angelo, he had the remuda up the river about a mile."

They rode together, trusting their horses to gallop into the black ink of the morning hours. After a ride of a few minutes, N.C. smelled dust and horses and knew they were near.

"Angelo!" Caleb shouted, having pulled rein.

"Over here!"

They found the remuda by starlight, the sounds of milling horses guiding them to the night herder.

"What happened?" the boy asked.

"Don't know," Caleb said. "The herd stampeded. You all right?"

"Yes."

"Can you hold 'em on your on?"

"Yes."

"You sure?"

"*Seguro que sí!*" Angelo insisted.

"If they break, just trust your horse to stay with 'em till daylight, then head 'em south till you strike the river. You'll know south because the sun will rise in the east."

"I know!" Angelo said.

N.C. grinned and let the silent chuckle shake his shoulders, knowing neither father nor son would see him in the dark.

"Let's git," the fiddler said.

N.C. and Caleb stayed together until they found the dust of the cattle herd, then drifted apart to look for loose stock. It was frightening to ride blindly into the night, but N.C.'s mount would break stride to jump and cut, so he knew the horse could see something of the terrain ahead. He just held the horn, gave rein, and stayed ready for anything.

When the fall came, it happened so suddenly that the rider only had time to point his toes to ensure his boots would slip free of the stirrups. He felt the horse hit on its knees, and he flew straight ahead, skipping across the ground so hard that he lost hold of the reins. He tried to get up, but stepped in a hole and twisted his ankle.

The horse had skirted a prairie dog town and tripped over one of the banked-up holes. The gelding was up and running away, which meant he was unhurt, but also meant he would be hard to catch. N.C. made a useless dash to try and cut him off, but tripped in another hole and hit the hard ground again. The sounds of hoofbeats faded, and he threw his hat to the ground.

Standing there, he began to hurt where the ground had chafed him. One shoulder felt as if the hide had been taken off, but his coat was not even torn through, so he knew it could not be too bad. He felt like the stupidest soul on the face of the plains, though there was little he could have done. He walked for awhile, then realized the futility of it. He would have to wait for daylight and trail his horse. For now, he might as well lie down and try to sleep.

Just as he rolled his hat to go under his head, he heard a horse running and skylighted a rider in a sombrero going south over a rise two hundred yards away.

When the first hint of daylight came, N.C. found the tracks his mount had made, then walked the two hundred yards to look at the trail made by the rider he had seen. He noticed the print of the unshod right front hoof and remembered Lucero's top horse having thrown that shoe a couple of days ago.

He followed his own mount's trail for an hour until he reached the river, and found his horse grazing in the bottoms. It took him another hour to catch the horse, as the gelding would bolt and run about fifty yards every time N.C. got close. Finally he pulled a big bundle of grass and talked the horse into coming close enough for a bite.

The horse had broken one rein off the bridle, so N.C. made one from saddle strings tied together. The gelding's head was sore from stepping on the other rein all night, but that only served him right for having run off.

When he was finally mounted, N.C. rode downstream and found the place where Angelo had been holding the remuda. What he found disturbed him. The tracks showed that Lucero's thrice-shod horse had joined the remuda and crossed it back over the Cimarron.

N.C. loped to the chuck wagon and found the *cocinero* there alone. "Any sign of the boys?"

The cook shook his head. "You no gottee no cows? You no vaquero."

"Listen, Coci. Lucero's stolen the remuda. My horse is fresh, so I'm goin' after him."

The cook's mouth dropped open. *"Ay-yi-yi."* He looked around for more riders. "You no go. You waitee for Javier. Waitee for Feedler!"

"They'd just slow me down. I got the only fresh horse left." He wasn't sure the *cocinero* understood. "Anyway, adios."

"Pendejo bolillo," the cook muttered and handed a couple of cold biscuits up to the rider.

N.C. crossed the river and followed the plain trail of the remuda due west across the plains. He started figuring. Lucero knew he was through working on Javier's ranch, so he must have decided to steal the horses, sell them somewhere quick and cheap, and escape among the Spanish-speaking communities between Santa Fe and Old Mexico.

It was a pretty good plan. First, stampede the cattle so all the boys in camp would wear their night horses out chasing longhorns. Then steal all the fresh horses. There was not even a mule left to ride, seeing as how the cook was using oxen.

The only thing Lucero had not figured on was N.C. getting thrown off his horse. Instead of chasing cattle all night, N.C.'s mount had loafed along the river and grazed. He would catch the horse thief in camp about dawn tomorrow.

Or was it *thieves?* N.C. didn't like to think about it, but Caleb's boy could have been in on the plan all along. Angelo sure looked up to Lucero. Lucero had a lot of dash about him, and he could have put a lot of adventurous notions in Angelo's head about senoritas and dances and the wild life of a *pistolero.* Then again, he could have just forced Angelo to go along.

There was only one way to find out, and it had been a long time coming.

FIFTY-TWO

ANGELO WAS TIRED and afraid. His heart felt like a rock sitting right on top of his guts. His father was going to think him a horse thief, and so was Javier. He looked over his shoulder, almost wishing to see them coming. The sooner he could explain himself the better.

Lucero's quirt cut him across the neck, and the boy reeled to the off side of his horse.

"Quit looking back!" the *pistolero* said. "Keep your mind on the trail ahead. I told you, if they catch up, I'm going to kill you, and I mean it!"

Angelo felt the tear break from his eye.

"You cry like a little baby!" Lucero said, taunting him. "I should have shot you back there. Maybe I'll kill you right here!" He drew his nickel-plated Colt, cocked it as it came out, and pointed it at the boy. "You want to die right here?"

Angelo shook his head and tried to look tough.

"Then keep these horses moving, boy!"

Angelo spurred his mount back up to a lope and waved at the tired remuda to keep it moving. He had always thought he was pretty tough up until now. Now he was just afraid. Lucero had been his friend, he thought, teaching him how to throw knives, and fight dirty, and shoot from the hip. But the moment he helped Lucero cross those horses over the river— doing what he was told without questioning—he had become a slave to his fear, and his desire to live to see his eighteenth birthday.

They came to a small river called the Gallinas and turned upstream. In the middle of the afternoon, they arrived at a corral built down in the brush of the river bottoms, out of sight. To Angelo, it looked like an old mustang trap. They herded the stolen horses into it.

Lucero jumped from his mount and took the saddle off, telling Angelo to do the same. They threw their saddles and blankets over the corral rails. Lucero pushed his sombrero back and blew two short whistles followed by a long one through his teeth. In about a minute, five riders came down through the underbrush from farther upstream.

In silence, they drew rein at the corral fence and looked over the stolen horses. They were the meanest-looking set of men Angelo had ever seen.

"Any trouble, Lucero?" one of them said.

He shook his head.

"Who is that?" said one built like a bulldog.

Lucero grinned. "He's a bad one. He likes to fight, so watch out."

The bulldog ducked between two corral rails. "You look a little pale, boy," he said to Angelo.

"His father is a gringo," Lucero announced.

"So, you like to fight, boy?"

Angelo backed up a few steps, but the bulldog shoved him in the chest.

"Leave him alone," said an older rider with a gray mustache. "We have no time to pick on little boys."

"Sure we do," Lucero said. "I got all the fresh horses."

The older rider frowned under his gray mustache and pulled Angelo aside. "Look, boy, you better go ahead and fight him now, while I'm here. I won't let him hurt you too bad." He turned to the bulldog. "The boy says he's ready now."

Lucero laughed.

Before Angelo could speak, the bulldog began shoving him in the chest, backing him up into the herd of horses, which parted to opposite sides of the corral. Angelo tripped over his spurs and fell. The bulldog kicked him hard in the ribs, and the gray mustache stepped in.

"Let him get up!" He turned to Angelo. "Fight, boy. Are you a chicken?"

Angelo felt shamed into rushing the bulldog, but his flailing fists failed to connect, and the horse thief punched him in the stomach and slapped him across the face. Angelo felt the fist hit his nose. He heard a dull crack, and buckled. He was on the ground next thing he knew, with the bulldog sitting on his chest.

The horse rustlers were laughing, but Angelo heard Lucero's voice above the others: "Don't you remember a damn thing I taught you?"

His hands searched the ground around him, until he felt a warm fistful of horse dung. Grasping it, he caught the bulldog gloating, looking back at his friends, and jammed the load of manure into the bulldog's open mouth.

The bandit sprang and spat, then drew his knife as the gang howled with delight. The gray mustache stepped between Angelo and the offended rustler.

"Move," the bulldog ordered.

"Enough. We have to get going."

"I'm going to cut him up!"

"Not now." The mustache drew his revolver and waved the bulldog out of the corral. "Catch yourself a horse," he said to Angelo.

Angelo wiped the blood away from his nose and mouth and got his rope to do as he was told.

The bandits made Angelo split the rustled herd into small groups, and each man drove a group away in a different direction. All the time, Angelo was wishing his father or Javier would come to rescue him, and he began to think of how they would trail him. He noticed the horse Lucero had ridden last night and remembered that it wore only three shoes. This horse he held back, hoping he and Lucero would take it with them. Maybe the rescuers would notice the track and continue to follow it.

The bulldog left threatening to kill Angelo the next time they met. Lucero and Angelo were the last to mount, and the thrice-shod horse Angelo had held back was still with them.

"That was pretty good with that horseshit," Lucero said. "But next time don't wait until he has your ass on the ground. Open the gate now, and let's go."

"I don't want to go," Angelo said.

Lucero drew his pistol. "Do you want me to kill you?"

"No."

"Then you better get moving. You have seen a lot of faces today, my friend."

It was something of a relief to be beyond reach of the bulldog and the rest of the gang, so Angelo counted his blessings and mounted. He drove the horses out of the corral with Lucero, feeling the fatigue of many sleepless hours pile up on him now. He knew his nose was broken, for it was swollen and aching.

"You are in it pretty deep now, boy," Lucero remarked. "If you ever tried to get away, the others would come hunt you down. I would hate to think of what they would do to you. I don't think they would kill you very quick, the way I would. Some people like to kill very slow, like a Comanche. You are better off just staying in it with us now, but you better learn to fight."

They herded the horses out of the pens and headed northwestward along the bank of the Gallinas.

"I see you put my horse in this bunch," Lucero said. "You think I don't know he has only three shoes?"

Angelo pretended not to understand.

"It was a good try, but your gringo father doesn't have fresh horses to catch us with, so it won't work. It's all right to think you are pretty smart, my friend, but don't think I am so stupid."

When N.C. got to the corrals, his spirits sank. He wasted a lot of time just sneaking up on the place, fearful of an ambush, and the sun was getting ever lower. Tracks ran everywhere, and he noticed a lot of boot prints around the corrals. Now it was plain that Lucero had planned the theft of the horses in advance and had arranged to have friends meet him there.

N.C. wasn't much of a sign reader and at first didn't know what to make of all the tracks. But after half an hour, he began to identify the six trails the thieves had used after breaking up the herd. He decided to follow each about a hundred yards from the corrals to analyze it.

The third trail he followed included the thrice-shod horse he had been behind all day. It also looked as if two horses were riding behind the others, perhaps meaning that Angelo and Lucero were still together. He wished his father were here. No one could read sign like Walker C. Kincheloe.

N.C. sat on the ground and cradled his head in his hands. He almost fell asleep in a moment, so he rose quickly and shook his head. He was not cut out for trailing outlaws.

He walked back to the corral to get his gelding and made the weary mount trot out of the river bottom. The sun was almost gone behind some low-ranging hills far off to the west. Picking up the trail of the horse with three shoes again, he made his gelding lope.

Dark was coming soon, but N.C. had decided just to ride on up the river, even after he could no longer see the trail. If he was going to catch them, it was going to have to be tonight. He was too tired to go on much longer.

FIFTY-THREE

THE MOON HEADED downhill among herds of stars. The wind was cold out of the northwest. Horse and rider reeled with fatigue when the smell of wood smoke knifed into N.C.'s nostrils and made him jerk the reins. He dismounted and led his horse into some brush along the river. He slipped his rifle from the scabbard, took his spurs off, and eased into the wind.

Down in a little flood plain on a bend of the trickling river, N.C. saw smoke streaming just above the ground, trailing from a bed of embers. Two dark forms lay rolled in blankets, and the stolen horses stood like sculptures inside a rope corral. What he would do next, N.C. could not say. He thought about sneaking down to the camp to catch Lucero sleeping. The trouble was the moon was slipping fast, and he didn't know which one of the blankets Lucero was rolled in. He didn't want to shoot Angelo by mistake after all this.

He wondered what his father would do. Probably gallop into camp and pounce on Lucero as he rose. N.C. was no Walker Kincheloe, and he knew it. Besides, he was just so tired; he didn't think he could put up much of a fight.

The obvious thing to do was get some sleep and catch the horse thief by the light of day. He had a good Winchester and was sure he could pick Lucero off from this distance. The decision made, N.C. lay down on his stomach, put his face across the back of his hand, and drifted instantly off to sleep.

A whistle woke him, and N.C. realized he had slept right through Lucero and Angelo's breaking camp. They were already mounted and pushing the stolen horses up out of the river bottoms.

He sprang, grabbing his rifle as he rose. A bad taste was in his mouth, and his heart hurt from having to pound so upon waking. Breath was short, but N.C. sprinted through the brush and up the bank, trying to get onto the open plains where he could get a clear shot at Lucero.

He broke into the open about the time the horses did, and spooked them, as he had come out of the brush only thirty paces from them. He squared his shoulders, cocked the Winchester, and aimed it at the trail rising from the bottoms. The startled horses were breaking upstream, and Angelo came out first, spotting N.C. there with his rifle. Surprised to find any human standing there, he jerked his horse to a standstill. N.C. motioned for Angelo to ride toward him, and as the boy broke downstream, Lucero came out of the brush.

"*¿Dónde vas?*" he shouted, then spotted N.C.

"Give up, Lucero!" N.C. blurted.

Lucero reached for his pistol and N.C. fired. Lucero's horse shied and N.C. fired again. Lucero shot back and smoke began to taint the air. N.C. fired his third, but still hit nothing. He decided that he had better not let Lucero escape, so he started shooting at the horse instead of the rider.

The first round made the horse hunch like a wounded deer, and a second made its hind legs buckle. Lucero leapt free as the horse fell, then used the dying animal as his shield as he drove N.C. and Angelo into the brush.

N.C. peeked over the rise and fired a quick shot toward the dead horse, just to keep Lucero down. Angelo was off his horse and kneeling at N.C.'s side.

N.C. took off his gun belt and gave it to the boy. "Take my pistol," he ordered. As N.C. reloaded the Winchester and looked over the situation, Lucero suddenly rose up and fired two rounds that rattled through the brush near him.

"He made me go along," Angelo said.

"I know that," N.C. said, irritated. "You ready to use that pistol?"

"Yes."

"Keep him worried with it, but don't show yourself. I'm gonna sneak up the riverbank where I can get a clean shot at him."

Angelo nodded as he cocked the sidearm.

"Hey, gringo!" Lucero shouted. "You better take the boy and get the hell out of here."

"Go ahead and fling one at him," N.C. said.

Without raising his head to see, Angelo held the pistol in the air, pointing it generally out over the plains. He fired a round that made the big Colt recoil a whole foot in the air.

"You ain't even comin' close!" Lucero said. "You better get away while you both got horses."

"Maybe he's right," Angelo said. "Let's just go."

"The hell I will," N.C. replied. "I ain't lettin' a damned horse thief go when I got him pinned down. Keep shootin'."

N.C. skulked off into the brush as Angelo fired another blind shot across the plains.

"That one hit a hundred yards away!" Lucero shouted, and laughed. "I think I'm coming out to kill you both in a minute, if you can't shoot no better than that."

But N.C. had the angle now, crawling on his belly up the riverbank, where he could see Lucero lying behind the horse. He silently cocked his rifle, put his elbows on the ground, and found the bandit in the sights, only thirty paces distant. He almost fired, but decided to give Lucero one last chance to surrender. "Give up, Lucero!" he shouted. "I got you now."

Lucero wheeled and fired, coming close with his shot. N.C. ducked as he fired and rifled a slug into the body of the dead horse. Lucero made a dash for the brush, firing both nickel-plated Colts as he ran, but N.C. paced him with the irons and caught him with a shot that went through both ribs and made Lucero's legs flail as he flew sideways through the air.

N.C. kept low for the moment, mixed feelings of confidence and horror swelling within. He poked his head high, birdlike, for a quick glance and saw Lucero lying, writhing on the ground.

"Goddamn it!" he shouted. "You kill me, gringo!"

Carefully, N.C. made his way to the bandit, his nerves wrought like fire consuming him from inside. Did he have cause to do this? He kept the irons on the wounded vaquero as he approached and saw that Lucero still had a Colt in one hand, the other palm covering the bloody wound in his side.

"Let that gun go," he ordered.

Lucero rolled halfway and glared. "I just wanted the horses. Why the hell you gotta kill me?"

"Let it go!"

"You ain't gonna hang me. Goddamn it, you shoot me, but you ain't gonna hang me, son of a bitch!"

"Just let the gun go, or you won't last to hang."

Lucero showed his teeth. *"Verdad!"* He rolled toward the cowboy, laboriously swinging the shiny Colt around like a load of something heavy.

The Winchester jolted N.C.'s shoulder. Then, as he worked the lever, he saw Lucero arching his back on the ground, all expression gone from his face. The bandit's body went suddenly limp, and he lay all dusty and alone on the bloody ground.

FIFTY-FOUR

"I TOLD HIM twice to give up," N.C. said. "He didn't give me no choice."

Walker nodded his head. "You just took a little more hair off the dog, son, that's all. It'll serve you when them Mayhalls come to call."

It was springtime in Monument Park, and Walker was sitting on the high rail of a corral fence, his hat back on his brow and a large quid of tobacco making a procupine bulge of his whiskered cheek. His spirits were about as high as they ever got. Grass was sure to come up thick from here to Powder River this spring.

"Daddy, it's been four years since anybody heard from a Mayhall. You don't think they'll crop up again, do you?"

"They seen brothers die. They'll be back. They could come after me up north, or they could hunt you and Buster down here, or they might try to waylay Hard Winter out on the trail somewhere."

N.C. shook his head, more out of disbelief than fear. "Javier told me and Caleb and Angelo not to go back to New Mexico, or Lucero's gang might git us."

Walker chuckled. "That damn fiddler can't light without somebody wantin' to kill him. I will say this for it: Hard Winter seems to like havin' his boy driftin' along with him."

"I had my share of fun when I rode with Caleb, but it'll wear on you always movin' like that."

"Better you to settle here, son, like you done. With a good string of horses to work and L.W. and that little wife of yours, I guess you done all right."

"Daddy," N.C. said, sitting on the rail next to him, a stalk of straw sticking out of his mouth.

"What's on your mind, son?"

"Not sure how to say it."

"You must've started tellin' me four times today. Don't let somethin' stick in your craw, boy. Git it out."

His son sighed and nodded to bolster himself. "It's about Red Hawk, in the Indian Territory."

"What about him?"

"A few years ago—the year I married Rabbit—I asked him to do somethin' for me. Seems like he's about gittin' around to it."

Walker let his eyes drift across the mountains and foothills; Buster's irrigated fields, fresh plowed; Amelia's large stone mansion; and the spire of marble Hard Winter had erected as the tombstone of Colonel Absalom Holcomb. "Gittin' around to what?"

"I asked him if he could find out what ever become of my brother."

Walker darkened, and the view in front of his face vanished. He was back on the plains, years ago, storming a Cheyenne camp, calling Paterson's name. And yet a new hope rose in his chest. He suspicioned all new hopes, of course, but at least gave them the same chance he would give a man to prove himself. "I thought Red Hawk was Arapaho. What the hell would he know?"

"I think it's because he's Arapaho that he's been able to find some things out. Cheyennes won't talk about it, because you're a bad subject to them. They call you Heap Killer."

"Give me a name, did they? I must be the devil to them. They're the devil to me."

"Well, the Arapaho got their own devils, but you ain't one of 'em. Red Hawk wrote a letter to me this winter and said since the old Arapaho used to camp all the time with the Southern Cheyenne, well, they seen some things."

Walker jumped off the corral rail and started walking slowly toward Monument Creek. "Things like what?" he said, when N.C. came to his side.

"There was some white boys taken into captivity now and then by the Cheyenne. This one in particular some of the old Arapaho seemed to recollect. They said he was the boy Heap Killer always come lookin' for. He had a scar on his chest about long as your finger. Said it looked like a burn."

Walker stopped and stared at the mountains in front of him. The new hope in his chest grew, and his suspicion slipped in spite of himself. Walker looked at his son.

"When your brother was just a snot-nose kid down in Texas, I had some wild cows in the pen next to the house one day, and I was brandin' 'em. It was his job to bring me the runnin' iron and put it back in the fire when I was done with it. Well, he tripped bringin' it to me, fell on it, and burned hisself. He squalled so loud that the cattle got spooked and pushed the fence down and got away. I had to sit him in the water trough to make him quit hollerin'."

N.C. smiled. "You reckon Red Hawk's onto somethin'?"

Walker nodded. "I ain't never told nobody about that scar. I hoped some day I might find him by it, but I didn't want the damn Injuns burnin' some other kid to pass him off as Paterson for the ransom. How much does this Red Hawk know?''

''He knows the Cheyenne moved Paterson around to several camps, tryin' to hide him from you. They would trade him for horses and robes and stuff. Well, this one warrior ended up with him, then the Arapaho never saw him around the camps no more.''

''What warrior?''

''That's just it,'' N.C. said. ''It could be the luckiest thing yet. Hard to say.''

''What warrior?'' Walker demanded.

N.C. made a ramrod of his spine and braced himself to blurt it out. ''Rabbit's daddy. Chief Lizard.''

Walker's eyes darted around for several long moments, and his face changed expression more than a few times. ''Well, how come Red Hawk don't just up and ask him what he done with Paterson?''

''Red Hawk's already got a pretty good idea that Lizard traded him to some other tribe, but before he goes to ask him face-to-face, he thinks it best that we settle some things.''

''Like what?''

''First, he thinks me and Rabbit ought to go back to the territory and show him his grandson. L.W. bein' your grandson and his, too, might help. Then he's got this other idea.''

Walker's fists clenched, and he spat on the ground. ''My idea is to send the army after him, throw him in the guardhouse, and hold hot coals to his feet till he tells. Goddamn it, he took my boy away!''

N.C. looked at the ground as if he had been scolded. ''I know you don't have much truck with Indians, but Red Hawk's been fair by me. I think we ought to do it his way.''

The big man sighed. ''Well, what does he want us to do?''

''Well, ever since the government opened up the Oklahoma lands, them boomers have been tryin' to get the Cheyenne and Arapaho reservation opened up. Red Hawk thinks it's just a matter of time before it happens. He wants us to get in on the land rush, then sign over whatever claim we stake to Lizard in exchange for whatever he knows about Paterson. Red Hawk says if we give him land, he'll be more likely to help us. Of course, Red Hawk wants an extra claim, too, so I've got Caleb and some other fellers ready to make the run with us: Buster, Javier, Angelo, and Piggin' String McCoy.''

Walker crossed his arms over his chest and glared. It galled him in a tender spot to have to treat with Indians. If he thought he could ride to the territory right now and beat the information out of Lizard, he would do it.

But N.C. had found out more in the last few years than Walker had in two decades of hating and hunting Indians. One painful lesson he had learned over the years was patience. If Red Hawk could find something out by swapping favors, fine. If not, he could always scalp Lizard later.

Walker swore a solemn and silent vow under his breath: If ever he found out Lizard had caused any harm to come to Paterson Colt Kincheloe, he would wring that Indian's neck with his bare hands.

"I'm gonna do it, Daddy. I'm gonna leave next week for the territory and plan the whole thing with Red Hawk. I'm gonna get my father-in-law a farm. If you'd come with me, I think we'd stand a better chance of findin' out whatever become of my brother."

Walker swept his hands down to his hips. "They say it was one hell of a land rush when they opened up the Oklahoma lands. I don't give a damn for some heathern Indian's farm, son, but I ain't gonna let it git between Walker C. Kincheloe and a land rush. I'll see you there."

FIFTY-FIVE

A MELIA TURNED THE team of spotted horses onto the abandoned main street of what had been Holcomb, Colorado. A few black-and-white dairy cattle looked up from their grazing, the novelty of the three-spring buggy bouncing over cow chips attracting their attention.

"Whose cows?" Caleb asked. Little Pete was scrambling all over the buggy seat as Caleb held the seven-year-old by the belt to keep him from falling out.

"Some homesteader who runs a dairy."

"Does he lease from somebody?"

"The town is all tied up in shares of the old Holcomb Town Company. I think the gentleman just grazes his herd here because nobody complains."

Caleb watched the weathered buildings pass by the buggy. Grass stalks and weeds were sticking up between planks on boardwalks. Signs hung slanted, faded, and peeling. The former bank building drifted by, and Caleb noticed how the bullet holes from the shootout with the Mayhalls had wallowed out and crumbled the red brick. This place made regrets well up in him like the warped places sticking out all over the wood-frame buildings. It was funny how neglect could drive a place so quickly to ruin. The soul was gone from this town, if indeed it had ever possessed one.

The steel rails of the abandoned railroad line had been pulled up to lay elsewhere. Settlers had lifted the old railroad ties, one at a time, to use in various enterprises. Only the grade of the road ran by the depot now, like the track of some prehistoric monster. Caleb had helped Buster build that depot with his own hands, before he left home to drift at age seventeen. Now a town had sprouted and died around it, and it stood useless, waiting for passengers, freight, stock; waiting for the long lonely whistle of a train that would never return.

"This is what I wanted to show you," Amelia said, drawing rein in front of the old Holcomb Inn. She looped the reins around the awning support of the buggy and stepped out.

"I believe I've seen the inn, Amelia." He grabbed his nephew's wrist and swung the boy out of the buggy like a menagerie chimp.

Little Pete stormed the dairy cows and stampeded them down the lane. He doubled over as they fled, his whole little body shuddering with delight as he crouched with his elbows on his thighs.

"Atta boy, Pete! Put a nine in their tail!"

"Don't encourage him, Caleb. You always get him worked up, then leave for parts unknown."

Caleb laughed. "He's the one gets *me* worked up!"

"Well, try to keep your mind on business just for one morning, would you?" She stepped onto the gallery and tested the front door of the inn.

"Business? And here I thought you was takin' me out for a pleasure ride."

"I brought you here to interest you in a business venture. In his will, the colonel left you all his holdings in the Holcomb Town Company. That includes this inn. I'm interested in it."

He gave a sarcastic grunt. "You plan to speculate in the kindlin' market?"

"I want to open it back up."

Thoughtfully he put his hand on his chin. "Well, it is the first hotel all them passengers see when they come through the depot."

She narrowed her eyes at him and bent her mouth into a snide smile. Just as suddenly, her eyes caught a spark of something down the street and the smile became genuine. "Good, here's Albert."

Caleb frowned a little when he saw Albert Farnham loping a spotted horse up the street. Farnham had a tendency to make a complete idiot of himself when he was around Amelia, going on and on with the most elaborate niceties and compliments. He was a family friend of the Babers who had come west looking for investment opportunities. He was of Hiram Baber's Ivy League fraternity and about the same age as Caleb and Amelia, making him older and more established than most of the guests Savannah had recruited for the springtime holiday on Holcomb Ranch. There was something suspect about a bachelor of that vintage, Caleb thought, though he realized he belonged in the same category himself.

Suddenly Savannah Baber flung off the wet blanket of Farnham's arrival by galloping around the old bank building on Whiplash. Caleb's heart fluttered to recall her fleeting embrace of just last night, and he jumped off the Holcomb Inn gallery to grab Pete and shove him off in the direction of his mother.

"Yes, I see," Albert Farnham said, taking up some former conversation. "Your description could not have been more accurate. I knew the place a mile from town." He got down from his horse and actually kissed Amelia's hand, as though he hadn't seen her in years.

Caleb ignored Farnham and took the reins of Whiplash as Savannah came to a thundering stop at the hitching rail. She teased him with a glance and sprang from the stallion without speaking to him. "Good morning, Mrs. Holcomb," she said to Amelia.

"Good morning, Savannah. So glad you could join us." She didn't sound glad.

Caleb entered last, still uncertain as to why this meeting had been called. But it was Savannah who attracted his attention, though he was just as concerned with whether or not Amelia realized that his eyes would not turn loose of the sprite, and perhaps equally as concerned, again, with how shamelessly Albert Farnham fawned all over Amelia. In such an atmosphere, which included the guerrilla antics of Little Pete, Caleb found himself wholly incapable of judging business prospects.

"Plenty of room for the stage, just as you described it," Farnham was saying to Amelia. "The dining facilities are adequate for a beginning, and the accommodations would certainly make the venture pay even at fifty percent capacity overall."

"Do you think so?" Amelia asked.

"Oh, it's a remarkable opportunity! Even if one were to build a facility like this from the ground up. But to have access to the building in this condition will cut the overhead of the entire operation to the point that it is simply impossible to pass up as an investment venture." He smiled and made his eyes twinkle at her.

"What do you think, Caleb?" Amelia asked.

He caught himself trying to figure out how Savannah's dress came off. "Huh? I don't even know what we're talkin' about."

Amelia rolled her eyes. "Albert has interests in several resorts on the

Atlantic seaboard. Albert thinks we could make the inn work as a kind of cowboy resort if we moved it onto the ranch.''

Caleb shrugged. ''Well, if *Albert* says so, why are you askin' me?''

''Because you own the inn.''

''If that's all you wanted, why didn't you just say so? You can have it.''

''No, Pete!'' Amelia said, scolding the boy for swinging from a dusty curtain. She turned back to Caleb. ''I don't want you to give it to me. I want you to invest it as your share of the venture.''

He adjusted his hat, as if to take some squeeze off his brain. ''Well, I ain't up on runnin' no hotel. I've camped in a few, but only occasional.''

Farnham chuckled for some reason. He always seemed to chuckle when Caleb spoke, no matter how much humor the fiddler intended. ''No one would expect you to concern yourself with running the resort, Mr. Holcomb. Your inn and your music would represent your share of the partnership.''

''Music? Partnership?''

''You would want to entertain the guests, I suspect,'' Amelia said. ''Whenever you were around, anyway. Along with Buster, of course, and N.C., and maybe even Little Pete, someday, if *someone* would give him musical lessons.''

Now the fiddler took his hat completely off and scratched his head with a certain vigor. Albert Farnham had leaned up against the dusty old lobby desk, at a proximity to Amelia that assumed far too much familiarity in Caleb's opinion. Little Pete was hugging Savannah's leg like a bear cub, and Savannah seemed to regard him as just such.

''Pete!'' Amelia scolded, and went to tear her son away. The boy ran toward the old stairway in a cloud of dust.

''So, Mr. Holcomb,'' Farnham said, ''when might we close a deal to include your building in our little enterprise?''

''Hold on, now.'' The fiddler slapped his hat back on. ''I've rode grub line many a year, and wherever I've lit, the latchstring has hung on the outside of the door. Except for them highbrow cattlemen in the Wyoming Stock Growers Association, I've never been turned away from a meal or a place to spread my cotton. Now y'all want to turn my old home ranch into a resort, pull the latchstring in, and swap wages for room and board?''

Albert chuckled heartily.

Caleb wheeled. ''Just what is so all-fired funny about any of that?''

The smile fell from Farnham's face, and he apologized. ''I simply admire your western speech, is all. It's like gold!''

''Nobody but you rides the grub line anymore,'' Amelia said. ''We're talking about taking honest pay for lodging in a resort atmosphere.''

He shook his head. ''We've had Savannah and her friends come visit as guests for five years. It don't sit right with me to start makin' 'em pay.''

Savannah raised a dainty finger as a signal to Amelia that she would handle this aspect of the negotiations. She breezed across the slick wood floor, steady and graceful as a boat under sail, leaving a wake of dust. She took Caleb by the arm and led him a few steps away, as if for some intimate consultation.

Amelia charged the stairwell to prevent Little Pete from climbing onto the banister.

''Now, Caleb,'' Savannah began, ''if some cow puncher drifts through your ranch, no one is going to ask him to pay for a meal or a place to sleep. He can stay in the bunkhouse just the same as always. Why, it would even lend authenticity to the resort atmosphere. But we're not talking about taking money from cowboys, we're talking about a bunch of dudes from back east who don't know how to experience the cowboy life on their own. We just want to allow them a taste of it. I've already queried all my friends who have visited here the past few years. They've all assured me they would gladly have paid for the experience.''

''This is the perfect setting,'' Albert added. ''Rail transportation is as near as Colorado Springs, yet those remote mountain trails lie just an hour's ride from your ranch. You've got Indian horses, cattle, log cabins, authentic western music. Even that Indian girl the young man is married to. That is, I assume she really is an Indian and not just pretending.''

''Who'd be fool enough to claim they was Indian if they wasn't?'' Caleb asked.

Savannah turned him away from the aggravating influence of Albert Farnham. ''Everything about you and your ranch is authentic, and that's what will make it work. I've thought about trying the same thing with Hiram's ranch, but it's too far from the railroads, and what on earth would we do for entertainment?''

''There's the thing right there. You all expect me to *entertain* folks.''

''Oh, well, let's not put you out any,'' Amelia said, dragging Little Pete down from the stairs. ''It's not as if you enjoy being the center of attention, or singing songs, or playing dance music, or telling your tall tales as they all crowd around you at the fireplace or the campfire. It's not as if you enjoy showing off that wild stallion of yours, or your guns or your . . .'' She looked at them standing there together—Caleb and Savannah—and suddenly lost her train of thought. ''Whatever!''

''Well, what about the ranch?'' Caleb complained.

"We will continue to operate it, of course," Amelia said. "My horses, and your cattle. You'll have the guests help you with the cattle work if they wish, like always. They enjoy it, for goodness' sakes. Don't you get it?"

Caleb straightened as if struck by something akin to lightning. "I git it, all right. You want to make me a dude wrangler!"

Amelia continued, undaunted. "We'll start the resort on a seasonal basis, next spring being the first season. The only difference from the past few years is that we'll put the guests up in the inn instead of in my house."

"And take their money," Caleb added. "I swear, I never thought I'd collect my time wranglin' dudes."

"Come on," Savannah said, leading him by the arm. "You ride with me back to the ranch and we'll discuss it. You'll see that it will be just business as usual, is all. Albert, may we take your horse?"

"If Miss Amelia would allow me to ride with her," Albert said. His eyes bulged, and he drew back in fear of Little Pete, who was storming around him, trying to catch a moth he had stirred up somewhere. "I'll drive, Amelia, and you can hold the little tyke."

Reluctantly, Amelia gave the signal for Savannah to put the finishing touches on Caleb.

"Now, how are we going to move this huge building to the ranch?" the sprite asked the fiddler.

He made a muscle for Savannah's little hand to hold on to, and relented, seeing that it had all been decided without him. "I don't know. Put it up to Buster. He's about ready to move somethin' full-growed."

Albert Farnham waited until Caleb had left before he allowed himself to laugh. "Amelia, you do understand that your brother-in-law is the key to the success of this enterprise. Without his stories and songs, I don't see that we have anything unique over the dude ranches of Estes Park or Manitou Springs. The Negro fiddler and that young guitarist just don't possess the showmanship Mr. Holcomb does."

"Mr. Holcomb doesn't know he possesses any such thing, Albert, and if you told him he did, you'd scare the wits out of him. You just leave him to me. I'll get him in on this if it's the last thing I do." She heard a piece of wood crack. "Pete! Little Pete Holcomb! You get your head out of there!"

As his mother hauled him out from behind the counter by the arm, Little Pete made his legs buckle just to make it tougher on her. "Uncle Caleb!" he screamed.

Albert grimaced and heard hooves beat the ground outside. "Ingenious of you to invite Savannah. She has quite a lot of influence over him."

A determined scowl bent Amelia's mouth as she popped the seat of Little Pete's britches once with her palm. "I didn't invite her."

FIFTY-SIX

THE STAMP OF COW sign laced a web around the old buffalo wallow water hole. Walker found a pile of manure so fresh that it hadn't even crusted over yet. His eyes swept the horizon, taking particular time in picking out individual objects against the backdrop of the Bighorns. It was one thing to look, another to see.

A track on the edge of the manure pile gave him direction and told him more than one head had left here not long ago. He went the way of the wild cattle and kept his senses honed. Crossing a high ridge, he saw the five head of longhorns grazing against the side of a roll in the plains. They were quite a ways off yet, and from here he couldn't see any brands, ear-marks, bobbed tails, jug-handled dewlaps, or anything else to suggest ownership.

A chinook spoke like a barroom whisper in Walker's left ear. He could ride two miles out of his way and sneak up on the cattle downwind, or he could charge head-on like a shot from a gun. Walker C. Kincheloe never went out of his way when a straight line would get the job done.

His mare raised her head when she felt Walker reach for the rope, for she had already seen the cattle. She made a lunge, but the rider held her back.

"Stand," Walker ordered, making the end of the rope fast around his saddle horn. He tied his leather reins together with a quick overhand knot, fixing them short so he could drop them on the mare's mane if need be. He tugged once on his hat brim, said, "You're fixin' to earn your oats, gal," and lay spurs to the mare's flanks.

The charge down the slope was like hearing thunder, feeling an ava-lanche, tasting wind, and watching the ground go by through the eyes of a hawk. Walker saw the heads of the dumb brutes rise, saw them signal fear with their high tails, and watched them disappear over the next rise.

An instinct threw his weight into the off-side stirrup, and before she felt the rein, the mare read Walker's mind and angled her charge. Coming over the rise, she saw the wisdom of her master, for the cattle had used the ridge as cover to break east for the ragged banks of a coulee, and she had gained many a stride by angling eastward behind the crest.

Walker could see brands now on two four-year-old cows, and the brands gave ownership to the CU Ranch and Chauncey Shanahan. But that big drag heifer was slick as a brass doorknob and looked about ready to drop her first calf. This was a stroke of luck, for Walker's herd had the potential of increasing by two this very day, if he could catch the heifer before she got into the coulee ahead.

The rope let out a coil, then another, and the loop took shape. Walker's spotted mare yearned to pull against the weight of a cow brute and somehow found another inch to add to her stride. The gap closed on the lumbering heifer; the circle of hemp whirled as horse and rider winked at dust; the rope sailed, flipped over a horn, figure-eighted across the far tip, and whirred tight.

The maverickers planted their feet—Walker's in the stirrups, the mare's on solid ground—and leaned back against the coming shock. Walker felt the hemp stretch through the saddle tree he straddled as a rumble of hooves faded down the coulee. The fat heifer whipped around the tether on her horns and bawled for help. He was glad he had horn-roped her, as he didn't expect he'd have to choke her, young and pregnant as she was. She made a charge at him, but the spotted mare knew some tricks, dodged, and jerked the heifer dizzy, like the popper on the end of a bullwhip.

This wasn't the place to throw her, as Walker needed fuel for a fire, so he reined the mare west with the heifer in tow to find a bunch of trees he recalled having seen around here before. A short ride over the ridge brought them into view, and Walker made the place at a lope, his horse heaving now from hard work.

When he saw dry grass, twigs, and cow chips, he turned on the heifer, made her run, flipped the rope over her quarters, angled quickly away, and slammed her sideways to the ground. Leaping from the mare, he yanked the pigging string from his belt where he had tucked it and fell on the heifer as she lay kicking on the ground. She was big to hog-tie, but dazed from the fall, and Walker had little trouble gathering a hind foot together with the front ones and making fast his string.

While the rope was still taut and holding the heifer's head, Walker drew his big knife from the belt scabbard, grabbed the tip of the right ear, and lopped about an inch of it off. The heifer bawled, reeled in pain, rolled her eyes, and slung saliva, but Walker already had the left ear in hand. Starting at the base of the ear, he sliced the underside toward the tip, leaving the part he had cut away attached to dangle from the end of the ear.

The mare slacked the rope on command, and Walker removed the rope from the heifer's horns, leaving her hog-tied. He coiled the rope and hung it over the saddle horn. The mare heaved in appreciation as Walker loosened the cinch. He tied the end of the old lariat she always wore around her neck to the stake pin he drove into the ground with his boot heel. She was a good Holcomb mare and wouldn't pull the pin out in a buffalo stampede. He let her graze in the bridle with the reins tied out of the way around her neck.

Gathering fuel, he stoked a tight fire, adding twigs, branches, and cow chips as the flames licked higher. As the big stuff caught fire, he returned to his saddle and took a corncob and a piece of iron rod a foot long from his saddle bag. He swept his eyes across the surrounding ridges before he squatted by the fire, and that was when he saw the rider.

He dropped the piece of iron and the corncob, for the rider was coming at a lope. He looked toward his mare—and the rifle booted in the saddle scabbard, ten long paces behind him—but decided to rely first on his handguns if he needed them.

I am afoot, he thought, and he mounted. If he rides up, I'll stand my ground. If he cuts behind timber or dismounts at a distance, I'll go for my Winchester. If he minds his manners, I'll mind mine.

The man raised his hand as he approached. He came straight on, until Walker recognized the young homesteader everybody called Ranger Jones, who recently had taken a legal claim on range nevertheless claimed by the CU Ranch and Chauncey Shanahan.

"Well, howdy," Ranger said, briefly riding out of his way to examine the hog-tied heifer. "Right ear crop, left ear flickerbob. I reckon you're fixin' to run a big *W* on her, too." He smiled and swung down from his mount. Ranger Jones was known as a tough youngster and a big talker, but he generally minded his manners around Walker C. Kincheloe.

Walker squatted by his fire and placed one end of the short iron rod among the coals of his fire. "Pleasure ridin', Ranger?"

"I seen the smoke. Figured I'd visit."

"Glad you did."

"What's that you're fixin' to brand with?"

"Piece of a brake rod off an old buckboard."

"Kinda short, ain't it? I know you're a damn tough Texan, Walker, but I want to see you hang on to that when it gits hot."

Walker picked up the corn cob and tossed it to Jones. "Reckon you ain't heard how smart I am, too. See that hole bored in the end of that cob? The cooler end of that iron slips right in there, and it makes me a pretty good handle. Learned that from Oliver Loving before the Indians kilt him.''

''You knew Loving?''

''Him and Goodnight, too. I'd go back to Texas and work for Charles Goodnight tomorrow, if I thought they'd let me back in the state.''

Impressed, Ranger Jones tossed the corncob back to Walker. ''I've branded with everything from a horseshoe to a half-breed buckle, but I ain't never seen the likes of that.''

When the end of the rod turned red, Walker slipped the corncob over the opposite end and marched to his tied heifer like a king with his scepter.

''Don't run it upside down,'' Ranger said, making sure to smile as he spoke.

Walker traced his large *W* brand on the hip of the bawling and kicking heifer. He sniffed the burnt hair—a pleasurable aroma to him—and left the heifer tied there. He walked back to the fire and stuck the hot end of the iron into the ground to cool it.

''I guess the Livestock Commission would frown on a little runnin' iron like that,'' Ranger Jones suggested.

''That outfit can kiss Walker C. Kincheloe's ass. It ain't nothin' more than a false front for the Wyoming Stock Growers Association.''

''I hear where they're callin' the likes of you and me rustlers nowadays.''

Walker stretched out in the sunshine and propped himself up on his left elbow. ''They've been callin' me a rustler since eighty-four, but there ain't a honest jury in the territory would convict me.''

''I've thrown a loop on some long-eared stock myself,'' Jones said, squatting west of the fire smoke, ''but I ain't never blotched a brand or killed a cow to get the calf.''

''I know you haven't, Ranger, and that's the kind the livestock inspectors ought to go after. There's rustlers, then there's rustlers. A man who'd change a brand or kill a branded cow to git her calf is a thief. A man who'd put his brand on a dogie calf or a slick yearlin' is just a hustler. It's root, hog, or die.''

''I've heard of Milo Gibbs and his boys splittin' a calf's tongue so it can't suck—weanin' 'em that way so's to maverick 'em.''

''Those boys are thieves. They ought to be hung with their own ropes. But maverickin's been the poor man's way into the cow business ever since the year of one, and now them big outfits want all the mavericks to theirself!''

Ranger Jones sighed. ''Still, I can see what they're thinkin'—them big outfits, I mean. They figure they got ten thousand head, and I got fifty. What's the odds on that heifer laying over yonder comin' from one of my cows again' the odds it come from one of theirs? Odds are, it's theirs.''

"A big outfit's got lots of boys ridin' for the brand. That evens the odds. Some of 'em pay a cowboy five dollars a head for every maverick he brands for the outfit. But let that same cowboy brand one for hisself, and they'll blackball him before the brand scabs over. It ain't a case of them wantin' their fair share. They want it all!''

Ranger spat in the fire. "Still, this Livestock Commission the legislature put in place of the association—looks like a better thing to me.''

"Ranger, you been readin' them Republican newspapers. Look who's on the Livestock Commission. There's only three commissioners, and they're all either members of the goddamn association or friends of members. Anyway, they all take their drinks in that rich man's club in Cheyenne.''

Ranger sighed again, this time adding a shrug. He believed in his guts that everything Walker said was true. But Ranger Jones had dropped by for more than just a visit. He was testing Walker's position on these issues, and he could not afford to be uncertain. "Yeah," he drawled. "Time was, a man wanted a maverick, he'd go out and rope one. Then that association come along and says you gotta bid on 'em at the roundup, only they don't let the little man git away with bein' the highest bidder.''

"Hell, now it's even worse!" Walker snapped. "Now they got a law says a man's got to put up a two-thousand-dollar bond before he can even bid! And the auction ain't at the roundup for each head of stock, it's at Cheyenne, *before* the roundup, for the *whole lot* of mavericks before they're even counted. Can you bid ten dollars a head on fifty or sixty head in one lot?''

Ranger searched his hat brim for a reply. "Hell, I can't even afford the trip to Cheyenne to bid, not to mention the two-thousand-dollar bond.''

"That's what I know, Ranger! And they know it, too. They've worked you and me out of a legal way to get mavericks.''

"But the association's shrivelin' up, ain't it? I hear they're down to less than two hundred members. They had twice that five years ago.''

"The smaller that outfit gits, the more powerful it gits. I been studyin' up on it. There's almost five thousand cattle owners in the territory, figurin' by tax rolls. Like you say, there's maybe a hundred and fifty members left in the goddamn Wyoming Stock Growers Association. But that hundred and fifty out of five thousand owns ninety percent of the cattle in the territory. It's a rich man's club, and they look out for their own.''

Ranger shrugged and rolled back on the ground. "Wonder what'll come of it all."

"Blood. Once was the day I thought the free range would last forever. Seemed like there was enough for everybody. But once the Indians was about whipped, hell, everybody come to get a piece, and there ain't enough to go around. But little men like you and me will be stepped on just so long before we rise up and fight. It'll come to shootin' before it's all over, and some good boys are gonna die."

"Well, Walker, I don't understand all I know about these laws and such."

Walker pulled his short running iron from the ground and found it cool to the touch. "They make it that way on purpose, so's to confuse you."

"The only thing I do know is that I got blackballed for legally homesteadin' land on range Chauncey Shanahan says is his and his alone, and he ain't even a citizen of the United States. They won't let me work my own cows in the roundup. Now the law says a man can't work cows unless it's in the roundup. So if I work my cows outside of the roundup, blackballed like I am, I'm a rustler. Well, to hell with that bullshit, Walker. They're makin' rustlers out of honest boys, and I won't stand for it anymore."

Walker could hold the smile back from only one side of his face. He turned the other side away. This Ranger Jones reminded him of himself, many years ago. "And just what do you intend to do about it, Ranger?"

The young stockman sat up and looked Walker in the eye. "I know what would git their dander up like a prodded rattlesnake."

"What's that?"

"A bunch of us small operators have got an idea."

"Does it go again' the law?"

"What if it does? You ropin' that maverick heifer layin' right yonder is again' the law."

Walker stroked his chin. "What's your plan?"

"We'll tell you, if you'll come by our camp tonight."

"Who all is in on it?"

"Nate Champion and Jack Flagg, to name a couple."

With his boot, Walker C. Kincheloe spread the coals of his branding fire. "So, you boys have been cookin' this up a while."

"We tried to find you and git you to throw in with us, Walker, but you're sure scarce of a springtime. Tell you what. My camp is just three miles or so from here. You come on with me and I'll feed you a bait of somethin' you ain't never et before."

"What's that?"

"A piece of your own beef." Ranger Jones grinned and rose.

"There's where you're wrong, Ranger. I et some of my own beef once't in a tight spot. Like to pizened me."

Walker tightened the cinch on his mare, jerked the knot from his piggin' string on the fresh-branded heifer, mounted quickly, and rode over the rise with young Ranger Jones. It didn't matter what Jones and Champion and Flagg had cooked up. Whatever it was, he had already decided to join them in it.

FIFTY-SEVEN

CALEB RODE OVER a range of hills called "The Horn" and found the herd spread out below. It wasn't much to look at compared to the huge round-ups he had helped work back in the eighties. Just a couple of thousand mixed cattle and a few chuck wagons. At a glance he could read how far along the work had come. About halfway, he reckoned, for half the cattle had been cut into smaller herds of the individual outfits attending the roundup.

Eight men rode up beside him, and his uneasiness mounted again. He could not even explain to himself what he was doing here. With the reins draped over his right palm, he ran his thumb across the calluses on the tips of his fingers, toughened by hour upon hour spent pressed against the strings of musical instruments.

Caleb had found Walker at his Red Fork camp just yesterday. There, he had howdied and shook with Jack Flagg, Nate Champion, Ranger Jones, John Tisdale, and three other blackballed cowboys. They had politely suggested he stay the night and play a few tunes, then ride on to Buffalo without asking questions or getting involved. But in spite of himself, Caleb had asked just enough questions, and now he was involved.

He sat astride Whiplash on the ridge of The Horn, not at all sure that he wouldn't be stopping bullets within the next three minutes.

Ranger Jones came up to one side of him and Walker to the other. Each man wore a brace of revolvers and felt a carbine through his stirrup leather. The other men in the party came up and fanned out on the ridge. They, too, bristled with blue iron; handles of pearl, hardwood, and ivory; magazines heavy with brass and lead. All had ropes looped fast around their pommels, ready for work that would cross over the line of the law in troubled Wyoming.

Ranger Jones looked down the line. "What do you think, Nate?"

"That nearest fire looks like the TW's. We'll use it."

"Now hold on," Walker growled. "No need to draw Hiram into this. He's more on our side than you boys know. We're here to make a point, ain't we? We'll use Chauncey Shanahan's fire. That's his outfit third to the south. I can see Dave Donaldson sittin' that big coyote dun from here."

Jack Flagg's black hat turned, and he briefly caught Walker's eye. "We'll make quite an entrance loping that far around the herd. But this is not the day for you and Dave to go at it, Walker. That would muddy the water."

"I won't start nothin' personal, and he don't have the guts."

Nate Champion smiled. "Well, all right," he said. "I don't know about you boys, but I'm gonna holler comin' down off this hill."

The men shifted in their saddles and the horses pranced, jostling the legs of the riders against one another. Whiplash felt the reins tighten, smelled the livestock below on a dusty chinook that tossed his mane.

Caleb clenched his teeth and felt his stomach churn. He didn't know what was coming over him, but this sort of thing was beginning to appeal to him. He told himself that it was a good idea to keep his hand in, for when the Mayhalls came back around. No, he hadn't heard anything from them since they killed his father. He had hunted them for two years, never getting close. But they would be back. Old Colonel Ab had killed Terrence—with the help of a drunken doctor, perhaps, but killed him nonetheless.

Yes, it was well that he temper his nerves on occasion for when Joe and Frank made their next call. But there was something else, too. Caleb had contracted the contagious indignation of men like Walker C. Kincheloe and Nate Champion. He was a little man himself. Always had been. It had taken years to get a grip on him, but there was an enemy on the rise here in Wyoming.

The association that Walker had come to habitually prefix with the term "goddamn" had outlawed the grub line. Even above all its other high-handed outrages, this one atrocity made Caleb hunger for vengeance. Those rich bastards had thumbed their long elitist noses at range hospitality. They had pulled in the latch string. They deserved to be taught a lesson. Caleb had to admit it. That was why he was here. He had chosen sides. He was going to take the big man down a peg or two. Of course, the big man was likely to lynch him from a dead tree in a lonely canyon someday. He was scared. He was mad. He was in the company of proud, indignant men. He was excited. He was about to bust loose with a war whoop and piss his pants all at the same time.

Suddenly the horse leapt, and Caleb had to clutch the horn to keep Whiplash under him. Nate Champion loosed his yell, and a half dozen others joined it. The roundup work below ceased at once, and even the dumb cattle broke their aimless mill and looked to The Horn.

Reins tightened, and the horses of the blackballed men fought their bits, slowed to a lope. A gallop would have looked too much like an attack. These boys were just going to work. When they decided to attack in earnest, they would leave no doubt.

Passing the TW wagon, Walker touched his brim in a subtle salute to Hiram Baber. Hi returned the greeting and watched with his mouth open as the party loped by. Since cutting Walker loose, Hi had taken over the management of the TW himself, and was looking almost like a regular cowhand these days. His herds had been severely diminished by the winter of '86 and '87, and the Baber family had cut funding for the cattle interests, leaving Hi to rebuild like a common settler. Where others like him had quit and moved back home, Hi had stayed, tightened his belt, cut his payroll, slashed his overhead. He was working now without salary and he was loving it.

The cattle bawled their protestations to the new riders but went unheeded, for the rumble of hooves overruled. The two minutes taken in closing ground on the CU branding fire twisted the air with a certain tension, and men caught working without guns felt naked.

Two hired hands at the CU fire stood and backed away when Walker C. Kincheloe lit nearby. Walker drew his running iron from his saddlebag. He marched forward as the unarmed cowboys made room for him. He thrust the end of his iron into the fire and looked out from the shadow of his brim at Dave Donaldson, sitting high on the coyote dun.

"What the hell are you doin' here?" Donaldson asked. "You're banned from roundups in this state."

Five of the blackballed riders had entered the herd of cattle and were cutting unbranded calves toward the CU fire.

"Hey, I'm talkin' to you, Kincheloe," Donaldson said.

Walker never thought much of a man who would talk down at him from the saddle. He ignored Donaldson and turned his iron among the coals.

"I'm foreman of this roundup, Kincheloe, and you're not to be on the grounds." Donaldson's eyes were darting, trying to take in the meaning of this visit. Did Walker mean to kill him, embarrass him, ruin him?

Nate Champion drove a calf at a dead run toward the CU fire, cut the air with his loop just three times, and threw, gathering in the hind legs of the calf as sure as if he had reached out and grabbed a bouquet of flowers with his bare hand. He was so close that he barely had to drag the calf twenty paces to come between Walker and Donaldson.

"Boys, get your guns!" Donaldson shouted. "These men are rustling in front of your eyes!"

As his horse kept the rope tight on the calf, Nate Champion leapt to the ground. He reached across the back of the bawling calf, grabbed the slack flesh at the flank like a handle, lifted, and threw the animal to the ground. He put his knee on a shoulder and bent a front leg to immobilize the calf as his horse quit dragging but kept the rope tight. Nate pulled a knife from his scabbard. "Right ear?"

"Crop," Walker said.

Nate sliced the tip of the right ear off and used his weight to hold the writhing calf down. "Left?"

"Flickerbob."

Nate made the mark with one pitiless stroke.

"You heard me!" Donaldson said, still keeping his hand well shy of his own sidearm. "Get your guns and disarm these rustlers!"

The two unarmed cowboys looked at each other, then at Walker and Nate. "I'll be damned," one of them said. "I'll be damned if I'm paid high enough to regulate."

"That might be that feller's calf, anyway," the other said, knowing very well what Champion's name was.

Jack Flagg and John Tisdale had added their irons to Walker's in the fire.

"Let's git us a drink of water," one of the CU boys said to the other.

"All right, and sit in the shade of the wagon a spell."

"Goddamn it!" Donaldson shouted. "Cut your horses out of the remuda while you're at it. You two boys are fired!" He spurred his coyote dun and rode off toward the TW wagon.

Walker judged the business end of his running iron and slipped the corncob holder over the other end. "The next will be yours, Nate."

Champion merely nodded as the hot iron traced a large *W* on the hip of the calf.

"Look at Donaldson giving Hiram what-for," Flagg said.

Walker glanced and saw Hiram standing there in the distance, just taking it. Hard Winter Holcomb was coming with another calf, so Walker went to get his iron back in the fire. Ranger Jones had headed a large maverick and would need Nate to do the heeling in about fifteen seconds, or there was going to be a wreck. Nate was already back on his horse and coiling his rope.

It was stupid to blackball men such as these; men who could work a herd like a gambler could shuffle a deck. He glanced back at the TW wagon and saw Hiram shrug and turn away from the roundup foreman, leaving Dave Donaldson there to fume over his own inability to act.

"Hey, fiddler," Jack Flagg said, "what's your maverick brand? Or do you have one registered?"

"My brands are registered in Colorado," Caleb said, dragging the calf up for Flagg to throw.

"Then what the hell are you doing here?"

Caleb watched John Tisdale holding the first of the rustled calves alone on the plains, expertly cutting back each break the calf tried to make to rejoin the big herd. "Everybody's got to be somewhere," he said.

Walker stood, his iron hot again. "Just run a fiddle head on that calf, Jack. That'll be Hard Winter's maverick brand. Hell, he didn't have sense enough to git when the gittin' was good, so he might as well go whole-hog outlaw with the rest of us!" He grabbed the big maverick by the tail and used his weight to pull it over.

Stretched helplessly by the ropes of Nate Champion and Ranger Jones, the beast lolled its dusty tongue and bawled for suffering mercy as the iron singed hair and blistered hide.

FIFTY-EIGHT

A BLACK SERVANT quietly entered the boardroom of the Cheyenne Club carrying a silver tray laden with toddies, sours, and smashes. Keeping as invisible as possible, he reached over the stuffed-leather backs of the big swivel chairs and placed each drink in front of the man who had ordered it.

"There were thirty head taken," Dave Donaldson was saying. He stood at one end of the table, behind Chauncey Shanahan, his hat hiding his belt buckle. "They were mostly calves taken from cows belonging to members of this association. They branded them with unregistered brands and drove them off over The Horn."

"You don't know which cows the calves came from," Hiram Baber said. "And not all the brands were unregistered. Jack Flagg's Hat brand and Walker Kincheloe's W have been registered for years."

Chauncey Shanahan ignored Hiram and gestured at Donaldson with the shiny chewed end of his cigar. "They were well armed, you say, Inspector Donaldson?"

"Yessir. Armed to the teeth. They caught us with all our guns in the wagons."

"You were wearing your guns, Dave," Hiram said.

He flinched, and his eyes flashed like lightning under the glare of the gaslight chandelier. "Well, how was I to take on nine rustlers by myself?"

"That's not what I meant," Hiram said. "I think you handled it the only way you could have. My point is that if they had come to steal, they would have shot you first and held the rest of us off while they took the whole lot of cattle. They didn't fire a shot. They didn't try to hide their faces. They didn't threaten anybody. They just went to work."

"Stealing cattle is not work!" Shanahan blurted. "It is theft, pure and simple."

Hiram turned his glass of straight bourbon in his hand. "Flagg's Hat outfit runs about five hundred head. Walker runs a couple of hundred, and the rest of those men probably average a hundred apiece. It's not inconceivable that they would claim thirty calves among them."

A grumble passed up and down the table. Some of the men glared at Hiram, while others pleaded with their eyes for him to drop the whole matter.

"It is not only inconceivable, but illegal. The thieves were blacklisted cowboys to the last man. They had no business even being at the roundup."

"It's just another example that the blacklist doesn't work. Men like Flagg and Kincheloe and Champion won't be forced out of their fair share of the cow business."

"Must you forever sing the praises of thieves and cattle rustlers?" said one of the foreign cattle owners.

"Let him speak!" said Chauncey. "Let Hiram Baber show his colors. Didn't Walker Kincheloe work for you as manager, Hiram?"

"Hell, he worked for you before he worked for me!"

"Briefly! And that itinerant fiddler, didn't he work for you as well? What is that fiddler's name?"

"Holcomb," Donaldson said. "Caleb Holcomb of Colorado. He goes by the handle 'Hard Winter.' He's been in shooting scrapes from here to Texas. Hired gun is all he is."

Hiram exploded in laughter. "Caleb Holcomb a hired gun? My god, Dave, he's a drifting fiddler!"

"But doesn't he court your sister," Shanahan said in his aggravating Scottish way of phrasing an accusation as if it were a question.

"My sister is none of your damn business."

"True," Shanahan replied. "But were she my sister, I'd caution her about traveling with and visiting the ranches of men associated with the rustler class. The scandal such a thing might cause in the newspapers!"

The man next to Hiram put his hand on Hiram's elbow. "We didn't call this meeting to discuss family members, Mr. Shanahan." He was a friend and admirer of Hiram, and he spoke rather sternly.

"Quite true," Chauncey conceded, raising his hands in the air as if surrendering. "Mr. Donaldson, you may take your seat."

The head stock inspector withdrew to a chair against the wall and hung his hat on his knee.

"We've called this meeting to deal with the issue of rustling. The livestock commissioners and I have been discussing the problem with Inspector Donaldson, and we've found a way to counteract this latest trend in theft. It's really quite simple and logical. We will sieze all cattle carrying the brands of known rustlers at shipping and market points. They will have no way to sell their stolen goods." He stood and walked to a map of the Western states and territories that hung from the wall beside Dave Donaldson.

"In practice, it will work this way. Our inspectors will observe all cattle moving through shipping points, not only in Wyoming but in surrounding states and territories—in Cheyenne, Ogallala, Great Falls. When cattle are found bearing the brand of the rustling element, they will be seized and held."

"Then what?" the man next to Hiram asked.

"The cattle will be sold. If the true owner can be identified, he will receive the proceeds. If not, the money will go to the Livestock Commission and be used to pay inspectors and cover like expenses."

Hiram looked up and down the table. Rich men were nodding their heads, stroking their neatly trimmed beards. Hiram Baber was ashamed to be sitting in the same room with them. He drank his whiskey in one swallow and stood, shoving his chair back behind him.

"I have a few questions, Chauncey. First, how are the inspectors supposed to determine which brands are the brands of the 'rustling element'?"

"We have a list," Chauncey said, slapping his hand down on a ledger book in front of his upholstered chair.

"What list? Where did it come from?"

"We compiled it."

"Who?" Hiram demanded.

"I, the stock inspectors, the livestock commissioners, and a few leading members of this association."

"Is Walker C. Kincheloe on the list?"

"Aye."

"Jack Flagg, Ranger Jones, Nate Champion, John Tisdale?"

"Aye, all four."

"Caleb Holcomb?"

"Aye, Holcomb's maverick 'fiddle head' brand is listed."

Hiram put his hand to his chin and paced along the side of the long table. He was the only man in the room wearing spurs, the emblems of the lowly cowhand, and they sang as he strode with a certain *shing*! "Let me give you a scenario, Chauncey, and you clarify for me how this new scheme of yours will work."

"That may prove enlightening," Chauncey said, beaming, standing ramrod straight at the end of the table.

"Let's say a yearling wearing Walker C. Kincheloe's duly registered *W* brand shows up in the railroad corral at Ogallala, Nebraska, and Inspector Donaldson, there, takes note of it."

"It will be confiscated and sold, of course. Kincheloe is a known rustler."

"But what if the yearling has already been purchased by a middleman, say, some settler dabbling in stock raising, as most settlers must do to supplement their farming income? What if this middleman, not Kincheloe, is shipping the yearling and has a bill of sale to prove his ownership?"

"Bills of sale are to be disregarded. The grangers are known sympathizers of the rustling element. They've been knowingly moving stolen cattle for the rustlers for years."

Hiram pulled at his earlobe. "And what recourse has Walker C. Kincheloe, or this middleman, or any other man got?"

"They can ride to Cheyenne and plead their case to the Livestock Commission. If they can't prove ownership, the yearling in question will be sold."

"Doesn't Kincheloe's registered *W* brand prove his ownership?"

"No."

"Why not?"

Shanahan smirked as if to belittle Hiram's inability to grasp the concept. "Because he is on our list of known rustlers."

Hiram shook his head. "All right, let's say that Dave Donaldson recalls that this yearling in question was one of the calves branded by Kincheloe and Champion and the others at the recent roundup they horned in on."

"Then the proceeds from the sale should go to whomever owned the yearling's mother."

"Let's just say, for the sake of argument, that Dave recalls that yearling being the calf of one of your CU cows."

"Then I would receive the proceeds of the sale, as well I should," Chauncey said, "but let me remind you, Hiram, that your herd, such that it is, was included in that roundup. If Inspector Donaldson identified the yearling in question as one belonging to one of your cows, *you* would be entitled to and would receive the proceeds from the sale."

The boardroom was so quiet for the next moment that a line of rail cars were heard jerking their couplings together at the depot far away.

"I would sooner kiss your ass than take that kind of filthy money," Hiram said.

A chorus of gasps made the room hum, and one half-drunken gentleman who had been nearly asleep looked suddenly sober, sensing the animosity that ricocheted off the walls.

"Mind your tongue!" Shanahan blurted.

"I will not mind my tongue, Chauncey, I will exercise it. And I will exercise my constitutional right to freedom of speech, though I realize full well that the Constitution is something this association holds in utter contempt!"

"Quiet!"

"With that outlandish list under your knuckles, you have set this country back over a hundred years!" Hiram's voice began to rise like a locomotive approaching through a tunnel. "The idea that your livestock commissioners, whose salaries come from taxpayers of this state, would conspire with you to label men criminals without the benefit of trial by jury, or any other constitutional provisions, is enough to make any lover of democracy want to burn this rich man's club to the ground!" His indignation burst out like a steam whistle.

"Enough! This is law!"

"This is a travesty! You have personally labeled citizens of this state criminals without due process and you are not even a citizen of this country! You have conspired to seize the property of hard-working men and you've claimed it as your own! You are elitism in its ugliest form, Chauncey Shanahan, and a danger to free enterprise."

"Get out!" Shanahan blurted. "Get out before you find yourself blacklisted for opposing the bylaws of this association."

"I'm gittin' out, all right," Hiram declared, drawling like a regular Westerner. "You can scratch my name from the rolls of this rich man's club and add me to your outrageous list of known rustlers, if you want! I will not belong to such an organization. I'm ashamed ever to have been a part of it! The biggest cowards in the state of Wyoming are sitting in this room!"

Hiram marched to the hat rack, snatched his big felt from a brass hook, and jammed it down on his head. "There's not a member of this association who has the guts to enter into honest competition with men like Kincheloe, Flagg, and Champion out in the sunshine of the open plains. Instead, you conspire in smoky rooms, behind closed doors, to compile secret lists and use the taxpayers' money to destroy your competitors and line your own pockets!" He grabbed the brass doorknob.

"Good-bye and good riddance!" Shanahan blurted. "You and your rustler friends will see soon enough who the cowards are!"

"If it's a range war you want, Chauncey, it's on your doorstep. If you want the blood of good young men on your hands, just push this sorry excuse for a law on through the legislature. They may be poorer than you, maybe less educated, less traveled. You may think they come from a class below yours. But if you ever find the guts to meet them on level ground, you arrogant Scottish bastard, they will cut you off at the knees before you can say 'God save the queen.' " He flung the door open, yearned for the pure air of real Wyoming to fill his lungs.

"Go to hell!" Shanahan said.

"I'll see you there!"

The room stood quiet after Hiram's boot heels stomped down the stairway. Only the hiss of the gaslight could be heard, and not even the cigar smoke moved. The man who had been sitting next to Hiram rose quietly and took his derby down from the hat rack.

"Where are you going?" Shanahan demanded.

"Back to Connecticut."

As the former member of the Cheyenne Club walked out, the black servant was returning with another tray of drinks. The Connecticut Yankee chose a shot glass at random and took it with him down the stairs. Another man rose, and another, and the membership roll of the Wyoming Stock Growers Association shrank by half a dozen before the night was over.

FIFTY-NINE

"WHOA," CALEB SAID, tightening the reins on Whiplash. Like Caleb, the stallion could sense a great gnash of voices and movement in and around El Reno. Having been cooped up for some time in a stock car on the Chicago, Rock Island, and Pacific railroads, Whiplash seemed anxious for action.

Suddenly the spotted horse lunged like a racer across the starting line and Caleb felt the cantle vault forward under his thighs. Pulling all the leather he could get his hands on, he managed to bounce off the saddle skirt and land behind the horn.

Some boys laughed outside the El Reno depot, but Caleb ignored them. With the spotted stallion under control, he realized that Harriet had plodded aimlessly into Whiplash's rear end after he had stopped, giving the horse just cause to spring.

"You pin-eyed ol' mule," he growled. "I swear, you must sleepwalk."

Harriet just blinked and twitched her ears to rid them of flies.

"Come on," he groaned.

Turning a corner in the booming town, the rider's blood began to flow like muddied waters in a swollen stream. There was music ahead, an occasional gunshot, hoots and drunken hollers; there was horse-race thunder, the recurrent knell of some smithy's hammer, and the tortured wail of grease-shy axles. Men and women surged through the streets like ants.

Skirting the edge of town, Caleb passed through a tent city where a man playing a squeeze box and another blowing a harmonica made dust clouds tapping their toes. Boys and dogs of various sizes and lineages chased one another among the guy lines, until one tripped and collapsed a tent. Caleb continued at a trot through the tent city, tipping his hat to some ladies he noticed darning clothing under a brush arbor.

The tinder-dry shanties and paint-starved buildings of El Reno came next. A fiddle wailed from a saloon across the way, and Caleb disapproved of a botched attempt to bow harmony out of the bridge to "Hell Among the Yearlings." The fiddler, he surmised, was either drunk or playing an ill-tuned instrument or both.

"Hey, Hard Winter!" somebody shouted.

He turned, saw a cowboy waving. "Oh, howdy," he said, returning the wave.

"Good to see you again."

"You, too," Caleb said, though he couldn't remember where he had met the cowboy, who turned into a doorway and was gone. This sort of thing was happening more nowadays, and Caleb had to admit he enjoyed being known all over but wished he could remember everybody's name.

Down the street, a group of men had cornered an army captain in front of one of the few brick buildings in town. The officer had his back to the wall, a semicircle of boomers holding him there.

"I don't make the orders," he was saying, "I just enforce them."

"Well, what's the holdup?" shouted an angry man wearing overalls tucked into boots that didn't match. "Congress done said to open up the reservation, didn't they?"

"Certain steps have to be followed," the captain explained. "First, the Indians have to take their cash payments, then they have to choose their allotments."

"They'll git all the best land that way!" one boomer cried.

"There's plenty of land, gentlemen. The Indians won't get it all. When they've chosen their allotments, then the Department of the Interior will set the date for the opening."

"It better be damned quick. A man needs the winter to build and fence so's he can plow and plant come spring."

"I'm not a farmer," the captain said.

"Well, can't we go in and look at the lands before it opens up?"

"No."

Caleb rode on as the boomers grilled the poor captain. He only hoped the soldiers wouldn't turn him back once he crossed the line to the Cheyenne-Arapaho reservation. He had come to meet N.C., Rabbit, Angelo, and Javier. Red Hawk had hatched a great scheme of some kind, and the first phase lay ready to execute.

He encountered no troops on the way to Fort Reno, finding the army post humming with even more activity than the town of El Reno, across the line. Hundreds of tepees stood around the fort and along the North Canadian. Wagons, travois, horsemen, and pedestrians flowed in and out of the fort, churning the air with dust and commotion.

Passing the first row of barracks, Caleb saw a buckboard pass, being driven by a smiling brave. In the bed of the wagon, several Cheyenne children and their mother played with silver dollars spread on a blanket. They tossed the coins to watch them glint, rolled them to one another, spun them on edge.

"Must be a thousand dollars layin' there," Caleb said to Whiplash. "What the hell does an Indian know to do with that kind of money?"

Not knowing where to begin looking for his friends and family, he rode to the parade ground and saw the Indians lined up, receiving the silver dollars. The Cheyenne and Arapaho chiefs had negotiated for silver, refusing to accept any other form of currency. Silver had heft, luster, integrity. It was of the earth. If the soldiers came and burned lodges again, paper money would go up like dead grass.

Harriet quit the ranks and sauntered to the water trough, so Caleb figured he might as well let Whiplash drink with her. He got down and loosened the cinch, planning to observe the spectacle at the fort for awhile, as he had never witnessed such a gathering. The Indians had been scattered across the reservation for years and some had never even come to the fort to put their names on the rolls. Word of the silver dollars had brought nearly every Southern Cheyenne and Southern Arapaho alive to this one place. They came in blankets and tattered buckskins, in broadcloth and overalls, in breechcloths and top hats.

In Texas, years ago, Caleb had once helped a settler spread a bunch of grain soaked in whiskey so that migrating passenger pigeons would feed on it and become too drunk to fly. They had been piteously easy to catch flopping around on the ground, and Caleb had pulled the heads off many a wild bird that day. He didn't know why he thought of that now, unless these Indians seemed drawn to the silver dollars as the pigeons had to the tainted grain.

He brushed some scummy-looking stuff aside on the surface of the trough and splashed the lukewarm water in his face. Maybe somebody would ask him to play a few songs. He was watching a brave strap a bundle of silver onto a travois when he felt the hand on his shoulder.

"Howdy, White Wolf," said Red Hawk.

Caleb turned. "Howdy, Chief."

They shook hands and exchanged genuine smiles, though Red Hawk seemed preoccupied.

"Come with me. We have much to do."

Caleb left his stock and strode for the lodges with Red Hawk. "Is my son here yet? And how 'bout N.C.?"

"They are all staying at my house on the Washita. Everybody is all right. We'll go see them tomorrow. First we have business to attend to here."

The fiddler's boots were badly run down at the heels and walking all this way didn't suit him, but he paced Red Hawk until they got clear of the government buildings. At the edge of the tepee village, they came to a group of about fifty Indians standing in a circle, hands clasped, singing. Their dress was all Indian, except for a couple who wore white men's hats. All at once, they began to shuffle, the circle moving clockwise. They continued the song, louder, and circled slowly, each left foot leading and each right foot following.

"Is this the Ghost Dance?" Caleb asked.

"Yes," Red Hawk said, continuing to walk.

"Hold on. Let me watch a minute."

The dancers moved almost shoulder to shoulder, and Caleb wished he had ridden to the village, so he could see over the heads of the dancers, into the middle of the circle. The occasional dancer would break free from the outer ring and cavort around inside, but he could not really tell what they were doing.

"What does the song say?" he asked.

"It says this." Red Hawk shut his eyes to listen, and to translate:

> *My children, when at first I liked the whites,*
> *My children, when at first I liked the whites,*
> *I gave them fruits,*
> *I gave them fruits.*

Caleb crossed his arms over his chest and stood hip cocked like a resting horse. "What's goin' on inside the circle?"

"The eagle feather of the leader makes the dancers shake and fall into a trance. They fall on the ground, and while they lie there, they visit the Shadow Land."

"You ever try it?"

"Yes, I have danced many times. At first, it didn't *take,* as you white men would say. Then I let the feather show me the way to the Shadow Land. I spoke with my daughter there. She told me I must not fight, that the spirits would look after the Indians. She told me I must protect the good white men I knew. That is why we must go to my lodge now. You will see."

Caleb watched the dancers circle a while longer. "If it's all about not fightin', how come it caused such a stir at Wounded Knee?"

"It was different there. The Sioux had their own additions to the dance, like the ghost shirt that was supposed to be bullet-proof. The Messiah has told all the Indians not to fight, just wait for the white men to disappear. But the Sioux didn't wait. They've messed up the religion for everybody."

"Who's this messiah?"

"His name is Wovoka. He's an Indian who lives in Nevada. He says he is Jesus Christ."

Caleb scoffed. "What's this about white men disappearing?"

"Wovoka says all white men will vanish from the old Indian lands, the buffalo will come back, and we will live as we once did. That's why we must go to my lodge now."

Caleb saw a woman's arms flailing from inside the circle, then she dropped out of sight. "You believe in the part about all the white people disappearing?"

Red Hawk looked at him. "I believe there are many ways to God. Come on."

They left the Ghost Dance as the chant of the song grew louder and made their way through the maze of tepees to Red Hawk's large canvas lodge. The chief's lodge wife was there, and he spoke to her, causing her to spring up from the fire she had been tending and the pot of simmering stew over it. Rushing to the deerskin bundle near Red Hawk's couch, she produced a pipe, stuffed it with tobacco, and left.

Red Hawk lit the pipe and motioned for Caleb to sit on the ground, facing him. When they were both seated, Red Hawk took a drag from the pipe. Caleb didn't feel much like smoking at the moment, but knew it had more meaning among Indians, so he accepted the pipe when Red Hawk handed it to him.

The chief blew smoke toward the light of the smoke hole and spoke: "When Long Fingers gave you the name White Wolf, he began what we finish here today. Actually, you began this thing yourself. By helping my people, bringing us buffalo hides to tan, giving us paint horses, teaching us to farm, you have made yourself as one with us. Now, smoke."

The Ghost Dance song rose to its highest pitch outside as he pulled smoke up the pipe stem. The still air in the lodge seemed to resonate with the song, as the inside of a fiddle must sound. He drew deep from the pipe stem and heard the Arapaho fire god consuming tobacco in the bowl.

"Now you are *Inuna-ina*. You are one of God's chosen children. As sure as if the blood of my ancestors moves in your veins, you are as much Arapaho as am I. Now, when the Ghost Dance makes its medicine, and the white men blow away like dust, and the buffalo return, your skin will darken like mine and you will ride with us in battle with Utes. And when you die, you will go to the Shadow Land and hunt with Long Fingers, for he is waiting to take you into his lodge and make you his grandson. White Wolf, you are my brother."

The song of the Ghost Dance ended abruptly outside, and Caleb felt the bite of smoke in his eyes. He passed the pipe back to Red Hawk. They sat in silence some minutes, until they had smoked the bowl.

"Now, we better get back to the fort," Red Hawk said and stepped through the hole into the world of fresh air.

"What now?" Caleb asked, catching up, feeling dizzy from smoking too fast and rising too quickly. He was blinded by the sun, winded from the trot to overtake Red Hawk.

"Now we stand in line with the others."

They passed by the Ghost Dancers, who had broken their circle and were resting, smoking, and sharing experiences of the Spirit World.

"What for?"

"The agreement with the Department of the Interior said adopted members of the tribe could receive payments and choose allotments. You need to get your silver, brother, so that I can use it to buy farm tools for your people.'' Moving and speaking much like a white man now, Red Hawk smiled and clapped his arm around Caleb's shoulder. ''Then, I will show you which piece of land to choose as your allotment—right next to mine.''

Oh well, the fiddler thought. He hadn't seen any other white men standing in line. It was still an honor to be adopted, wasn't it? Even if it wasn't, his mother would have approved. When Caleb was a boy on the Front Range, Ella Holcomb used to give old Chief Long Fingers cattle for his people to eat.

SIXTY

THEY COULD EYEBALL the wooden stakes like rifle sights and see them aiming at Red Hawk's front porch.

''How was I to know?'' the chief said. ''Though I was educated at Carlisle, I am still an Indian. I placed my house here because of the shade, the water, the pasture for my horses. How was I to know it would fall on a township line some white man with a compass and telescope would invent upon the earth?''

Caleb nodded, and recited something he had come up with recently:

> *We rode the ranges way back when*
> *The ranges had no fences*
> *So we took leave of our senses*
> *And we strung 'em all around*
> *Where once we used to parley*
> *With the Indians in their lodges*
> *Now the farmer's milch cow dodges*
> *As his harrow turns the ground*

Red Hawk looked at him and smiled. ''Is that some white man's song?''

''No, just one I made up.''

''It is a mystery to me the way you do that. The words you speak rhyme, yet they mean something, too. They sound good to the ear, but they tell a story at the same time. I know a lot of words in the English language, but I can't do what you do with them, brother. That is your medicine.''

He shrugged. ''For all the good it's done me.''

''It serves you. You eat good food and sleep out of the weather because people like to hear you speak and sing. But it serves you even beyond that.

It gives voice to your soul. Long Fingers was wise to name you White Wolf. The wolf has his own language when he sings. The words he sings mean something to him, and they move anyone who listens. That is how it is with you.''

Caleb rose from his squat where he had lined up the survey markers leading to Red Hawk's porch. He put his foot in the stirrup and rose smoothly to the saddle, his spine all atingle. "I dreamed of a white wolf last night."

"What happened in the dream?"

"Oh, nothin'. Just a white wolf runnin'."

"Did the wolf speak?"

Caleb laughed. "Lord, no. Just kept runnin' like a turpentined cat. What do you reckon that means?"

Red Hawk shrugged. "Means you're running away from something . . . maybe toward something. Your soul knows what it means, so don't think about it too hard."

The fiddler put his mind back on the business at hand. "So they told you to move your house off the township line?"

"Yes, but they don't have the imagination that you and I possess. I will claim the parcel under the east side of the house as my allotment, and you will claim the parcel under the west side as your allotment, and that way I will not have to move the house after you deed your house to me."

Across the pasture, N.C. stepped onto Red Hawk's porch with a coffee cup in his hand and immediately noticed the riders mounted near the river. "Hey, boys!" he shouted, waving. He turned into the house to spread the news.

By the time Caleb trotted up to the house, all the occupants were streaming off the porch to greet him: Javier, Angelo, Rabbit, and L.W. Little L.W. was especially conspicuous in authentic Arapaho garb including breechcloth, leggings, and moccasins.

"Howdy, son," Caleb said, shaking Angelo's hand before he paused to behold L.W. "Good heavens, look at this little savage."

"They dressed me up like an Indian, too," Angelo said, grinning. "They put my name on the rolls as Little White Wolf, and gave me silver dollars. Red Hawk let me keep one of them!"

"Well, don't spend it all on the same gal," Caleb said. "Did you get an allotment of land, too?"

"He got the parcel down the river where Red Hawk keeps his tepee and his lodge wife," N.C. said. "Rabbit chose the two parcels above it for herself and L.W. When we make the run, I'm gonna stake the one next to them, so we'll have three claims together."

L.W. was tugging at Caleb's chaps, so the fiddler lunged suddenly, caught the five-year-old, and hung him upside down. L.W. screamed with delight, pretending to plead with his father to save him.

"You got yourself caught, boy, don't holler to me!" N.C. said.

"You mean to tell me they're givin' allotments even to a little squirt like this?" Caleb said.

"One for every Indian," Red Hawk said. "Even for little half-Indians like this one. We are putting our parcels together to make bigger farms for ourselves when the reservation is opened up. It will be a race when it opens. You and your friends will have to ride hard to get here first and add your claims to ours, so that we will have big ranches and farms."

"How's Daddy?" N.C. said.

Caleb scratched the back of his neck, letting his hat fall over his eyes. "We stirred up a little trouble at the roundup with Nate Champion, Jack Flagg, Ranger Jones, John Tisdale, and some other boys, but Walker can take care of hisself. Things are gettin' mighty close up there."

"Is he still comin' down here for the opening?"

"He said to tell you he wouldn't miss another land rush for all the grass in Texas. You know how he likes to race."

"What about Buster?" Red Hawk asked.

"Buster said he'd be here. He's already got one of every kind of claim allowed, but said he'd make the run under a fake name to get you another quarter section."

"Piggin' String McCoy is comin', too," said N.C. "So is Dan Brooks."

"I'll tell you somethin' else . . ." Caleb grinned. "I stopped by the ol' TW before I drifted down this way. Hiram was away to Cheyenne, but Savannah was there. You ain't gonna believe this, but she said *she* would like to make the run, too."

"A gal?" N.C. said.

"Hell, she can outrace any man in this outfit, even Angelo."

When Caleb grasped his son's shoulder, the boy blushed with pride to think his father would label him the fastest rider among the grown men and an Indian chief.

"We're feeding a relay of horses and exercising them," Red Hawk said. "When the opening comes, we will have them positioned so that you and your friends cannot possibly be beat."

"What about sooners?" Caleb said. "I hear tell that when they opened the Oklahoma lands, a bunch of men had snuck in early and staked their claims before the others started."

Red Hawk flicked the suggestion away with a wave of his hand. "I will have an Arapaho guard posted at every parcel we want to claim, and they will keep the sooners away." He shook his head. "Boomers . . . Sooners . . . You white people have funny names for your tribes."

SIXTY-ONE

It was sad to see a river struggle so to make a noise. Lizard had seen the Washita roar where now it merely gurgled. The Washita would run free again come rainfall. But nothing that fell from the sky—nothing of this earth—would bring new power to the Cheyenne.

The chief drank from his cupped hand, then turned away from the Washita and mounted his horse, taking a handful of mane. He rode at a walk toward the top of the bank, where he could watch for trouble across the plains. Lizard had spent his life watching trouble come across the plains.

The Indian agent and the soldiers had told him to choose a piece of land too small to graze his horses. The white men thought Lizard didn't know that they would take that away, too, in time. Perhaps the white men themselves didn't even know they would do this, but they would. That was the way with white men. They took things: not through conquest and courage, but through trickery and lies that they as individuals were too dumb to invent, but which, as a people, just seemed to come to them.

If it was true that white men and the Cheyenne had the same god, then the Great Spirit was going to punish the white men forever in the Spirit World, and worthy Cheyenne warriors would pierce them with arrows and trod them under the hooves of warhorses in the world where they could only suffer and never die.

This Ghost Dance nonsense only disgusted Lizard. The so-called messiah in Nevada, the one named Wovoka, claimed he was Jesus Christ, but Lizard knew Wovoka had grown up among whites. The absurdity of it and the gullibility of the other tribes amazed him. Jesus Christ was a white man's savior. The Sioux had proven the uselessness of the Ghost Dance at Wounded Knee, so why were the others still dancing and falling into trances?

Why had Red Hawk and the other chiefs agreed to sell the reservation? Because of the Ghost Dance. Red Hawk truly believed that the whites would somehow be swept from the face of the earth, and the buffalo would return. For this reason, Red Hawk, and the other chiefs caught up in the twisted Ghost Dance logic, had sold the reservation for bundles of silver coins. Lizard knew the white men were here to stay. The Spirit World was the only one in which the Cheyenne would again reign supreme over lesser peoples.

He reached the top of the riverbank, and his horse stopped in the shade. The dozen tepees were formed in a rough circle, their entry holes facing east. The people here were Cheyenne to the last man, woman, and child. These were the proud ones who refused to take white men's silver and choose little square pieces of land. Lizard found it unthinkable that he, as a single human being, should own something belonging to spirits. The earth was intended for gods to own, not human beings. The idea that a godless piece of paper could somehow make a man possessor of the living earth was proof of how dim and shortsighted white men were.

The horses belonging to Lizard's band were scattered far across the plains, beyond the lodges, looking for something to eat. There was no escape from what the white man had done to this once-rich land. Even out here, where few white men ventured, their cattle had come, in numbers uncountable. In the days of buffalo, the grass had been tall, and the world had looked and even smelled better. Now it smelled like cow dung.

Why did the white man consider the great herds of cattle better than the great herds of buffalo? Why?

How long would it last? Would the soldiers come to fight? Lizard had been told that someone would choose an allotment for him if he didn't do it himself. Would they try to make him live on it? He would not be the owner of his own prison farm. These were the last of the free Southern Cheyenne here in his camp. Would they fight to remain free?

He had heard that She-Rabbit had returned to the reservation with her white husband, and a half-breed boy. Lizard missed She-Rabbit. She had always been a beautiful child, from the day she was born. She had been a faithful daughter, if not always obedient, until that white boy came. As white men went, the boy came from good warrior stock, being the son of Heap Killer, but he had stolen a good daughter.

Lizard lowered his eyes to the mane of his pony and his mind reeled to another day, long ago—a day that often came to him at odd moments. He had been lying outside his lodge, fanning himself with the wing of an eagle, when suddenly Heap Killer had thundered into the camp, calling his son by name: "Pat-Pat-Pat!" Springing to his feet and drawing his knife, Lizard had given chase to the mounted devil, only to see Heap Killer turn on him and fire a gun at his face.

The bullet had furrowed Lizard's face as sure as a white man's plow and jolted him into the world of evil dreams for seven sleeps. Yes, he had found this Pat-Pat-Pat among other Cheyenne, swapped a good horse and blanket for him, and made sure Heap Killer would never find him.

Red Hawk said maybe it was wrong to have taken Heap Killer's son away, and that the gods now were punishing him by having Heap Killer's son steal his daughter. The argument had not been lost on Lizard. It was strange that it should happen this way. He missed his daughter. He loved her. Heap Killer was a devil, but maybe a man could be made a devil when a son or daughter was taken away like that. Lizard would face death or deliver death if it meant that he could have his daughter back and have her love him again as a daughter should love her father. Heap Killer was not so very different.

Down in the lands the white man had given to the Comanche, Chief Quanah Parker had once told Lizard that Heap Killer had begun his life as a devil among the Comanche. It was taboo to speak of it in detail among the Comanche, but something very bloody had happened between that tribe and Heap Killer when he was only a boy down in Texas. Quanah Parker was half white, but he was all warrior, and Lizard regarded him highly and had fought with him against the buffalo hunters at Adobe Walls.

Now, Red Hawk was suggesting that a man-turned-devil could be turned back into just a man again. Red Hawk had said that if Lizard would help Heap Killer find out what had become of his lost son, then maybe Lizard could have his daughter back.

It was confusing. Was he still at war with whites? He knew it was useless to fight, for they numbered too many. But would the gods punish him in the next world if he helped an old enemy find a lost son? Were the gods punishing him now?

His eyes lifted, catching a glimpse of movement down the river. Horses emerged from the timber: three paints and a snowflake bay carrying riders, then four spotted horses like the Nez Percé had once bred far to the north. The paints had to be Red Hawk's, for he was partial to them and bred them well. But the snowflake bay drew Lizard's attention first, for a white man straddled it. A cowboy, it seemed, from this distance, with a big hat and a red silk neckerchief. The four Nez Percé horses were tied in a string, head to tail, led by the cowboy on the snowflake bay.

Now Lizard began to identify the riders. The large man on the paint had to be Red Hawk himself, though it had not occurred to Lizard right away because the rider wore Indian dress, and Red Hawk commonly wore the clothes of white men when in their presence.

The riders of the other two paints were small, one a woman, the other a mere child. The moment gripped Lizard's hardened old heart, for only a second had passed since the horses emerged and the hope was already upon him. Hope was a dangerous thing for a dissident Cheyenne chief to embrace.

The child left the group of riders suddenly and made his paint horse gallop toward the tepees. Lizard nudged his mount and rode to intercept the little horseman in front of the camp. He leaned forward and urged his pony on, for the little rider was coming like a hawk! The long black tail and white mane of the paint floated high with every leap, and a feather in the boy's hair fluttered crazily. Yes, it was just a little boy of maybe five or six winters, but how he could ride!

Men and women, and little children, too, emerged from their tepees as Lizard and L.W. came together at the outer edge of the camp. The boy slowed his pony to a trot, fearful of the stranger. He looked back, saw his parents coming, and felt more secure. Lizard was riding around him, glaring with eyes in which even the little boy recognized suspicion.

Except for the short brown hair, this little rider was the very image of a Cheyenne boy, and to see him on an Indian saddle, handling a horse so well at such a young age, made decades of anger lift from Lizard's tired shoulders in one breath.

The other riders came up, Eagle-on-the-Ground leading the four Appaloosas. Lizard saw She-Rabbit's eyes break away from his in the submissive gesture of a respectful daughter. She was even more beautiful now than she had been when she left, and pride swelled in the chief in spite of all that had happened.

Eagle-on-the-Ground submitted nothing and met Lizard's glare without a blink. He was a young man now, and proud, as the best of white men could know pride. One thing was good. This son of Heap Killer had taught Lizard's grandson to ride, and ride well; to manage and not fear his mount; to sit straight in the saddle and make the animal a part of himself.

"You know who that is, L.W.?"

The boy looked at his father. "Is that my granddaddy?"

"It is. Why don't you make a loop around the tepees and show him how fast you can ride."

L.W.'s eyes judged the course like those of a grown man, for riding to him was more than a boyish joy. It was the current that fed his young soul and powered his every dream. His mouth made a tough scowl and he willed the pony westward, around the southern curve of the circle of lodges.

It was good, Lizard thought. This was the way the sun circled the earth, the way the boy had chosen to ride. He loped his own mount a little toward the river to watch his grandson's paint pound the earth and disappear around the circle of lodges.

The people of the camp moved as one, like a flock of blackbirds, to see L.W. go around the western curve of the circle and start back. Lizard charged into the center of the circle to see the little rider appear between the lodges, then vanish, then reappear, the sound of the hooves rising with the boy in sight. How well he leaned into the mane that brushed his face and held the reins snug, moving with the horse's lunging head.

The people spilled out of the circle, to the east side of the camp, and rang with laughter long due for release. L.W.'s horse sensed the commotion, fed on it, and stopped in a rough four-legged leap and a single kick of a hind foot that actually made the little rider smile, though it would have made some grown men panic.

Horses pranced all around, feeding on the spirit of the romp. The spotted horses on the lead rope almost tangled, but N.C. straightened them out. Lizard came up to his grandson and caught the boy's eye. Smiling only with his eyes, the chief tossed his head northward in an invitation, and the boy understood. Together, they lunged, Lizard's poorly fed mount nonetheless running game. And as they rode abreast, they glanced at each other's form and admired. Once they caught each other's eye—this hardened old warrior and this innocent half-breed boy—and though neither knew the other's language, nor ever would, an understanding passed between them.

When they returned to the camp, Lizard reached out and touched the boy, grasping his arm and shoulder as if sizing him up for muscle. The chief glanced at Eagle-on-the-Ground, reined his pony away, leapt to the earth, and vanished inside his tepee.

"Get off your horses," Red Hawk said when Lizard came back out carrying a blanket. "Not you, little one. Only your father and mother."

N.C. and She-Rabbit obeyed.

"Stand close together," Red Hawk said, watching Lizard march toward them with the blanket.

N.C. put his hand around Rabbit's arm and squeezed. Her eyes remained on the ground, but her heart lifted.

Lizard strode long until he was directly in front of the young couple. He looked up once at his half-breed grandson and hoped the boy would remember him for this. He shook the folds out of the blanket and dust scattered. Wielding the blanket like some Spanish bullfighter, he made it encircle the shoulders of both She-Rabbit and Eagle-on-the-Ground, and he pulled it around them and made them hold it. Stepping back, he nodded once, then dismissed them with a wave.

"You are married," Red Hawk said. "Go on back to my house now, and I'll stay to talk to Lizard."

The young parents looked at each other, then remounted. N.C. untied the lead rope on the Appaloosas and let its end dangle in front of Chief Lizard. The old warrior watched it sway, then reached for it. He took it, tightened it between his grip and N.C.'s. Their hands were two feet apart on the rope, but they could feel each other's strength. At last the cowboy let the rope slip from his grasp and turned to ride away with his wife and son.

Lizard signed: *Why do you stay? I have no talk to make with you.*

Red Hawk replied: *I want to choose your piece of land for you, and give it to your grandson. It will lie beside the piece of land your daughter takes on the river, and they will have enough grass for their ponies.*

Lizard stood and thought and watched the three riders disappear. His hands made words: *I will not live there.*

I know.

Go back to your house. Lizard turned away, leading his new horses. The bottom of the canvas tepee cover was rolled up for ventilation, so Lizard wrapped the lead rope around the butt of a lodge pole, tightly enough so that the horses would think they were tied, but loosely enough to keep them from pulling down his lodge or hurting themselves should they shy at something. When they settled down some, he would turn them loose to graze with the other horses.

Red Hawk had followed, and waited for Lizard to look at him so he could carry on the discussion. *You maybe tell Heap Killer now where his son goes.* "Pat-Pat-Pat," he said. *Heap Killer and his friends will help us get more pieces of land for your daughter and your grandson.*

Lizard stood motionless a long time. *I must think about it.*

Red Hawk shook his head. *The time comes soon. You must not think long.*

Lizard turned away, ducked into his lodge, and pulled the flap over the hole.

SIXTY-TWO

"WHERE'S YOUR FIDDLE, Bitter Creek?"

Caleb Holcomb had been in Buffalo, Wyoming, no longer than twenty minutes and had answered the same question half a dozen times. "I left it with my outfit in the wagon yard." Some of his admirers had begun calling him "Bitter Creek" because he so frequently rendered the cowboy ditty "I'm a Wild Wolf from Bitter Creek, and Tonight's My Night to Howl!"

"Wagon yard?" the granger said. "Hell, I wished I had the hotel fare to loan you."

"Oh, I'm flush," Caleb said. "Just ain't a room to be had. Don't let it set heavy on your conscience, though; I've slept many a night on a bed of hay. It's cut fresh this time of year, anyway, and sure smells sweet."

"Where you playin' tonight?"

"Wagon yard, I reckon. Come on by."

He touched his hat brim and went his way. Around him, the town hummed with so much activity that a body would've thought court was in session, with a circus come to town and a hanging thrown in. Word had caught like wildfire, spreading out of Buffalo on the sagebrush telegraph, like ripples from a clod chucked into a buffalo wallow brimful with still water.

He had first caught wind of it all the way down in Indian Territory. Hiram Baber had sent him a cryptic telegram, requesting that he beat a hasty trail back to Wyoming for a "caucus." Caleb had looked the word up in his dictionary and lit a shuck for Wyoming.

He reached Cheyenne in a few days by rail. There, thousands of cattle belonging to "known rustlers" had been impounded and sold, the proceeds going to the Wyoming Stock Commission. A granger who had made the almost prohibitive journey from Johnson County to Cheyenne to prove his ownership on seized stock he had put on the market recognized Caleb and pulled him aside.

"There's gonna be a meetin' in Buffalo," he had said.

"That's what I've heard, but what exactly is the meetin' for?"

The granger had shrugged. "Just a meetin'."

"When?"

"I don't know, but it's bound to happen. Careful who you tell."

Later, at Casper, he learned more from a bartender who had worked the big roundup with the Bar C outfit in eighty-four and knew Caleb had raided this spring's roundup with Nate Champion and the others. "The meetin's set for around the end of October. They figure the settlers will have their harvest in, and the little outfits will be done shippin'. Not much shippin' goin' out anyway, since the Cheyenne ring started takin' cows."

"What's the meetin' for?" Caleb asked.

"Hell, I don't know." He leaned far across the bar to whisper even more softly to the musician. "All I know is, it's again' the rich bastards— fer'ners and all."

"Who's callin' this meetin'?"

The bartender shrugged. "I wouldn't have called it. Partial to my head."

The closer he got to Buffalo, the clearer the purpose of the "caucus" became. A homesteader and his wife on Crazy Woman Creek explained what they knew to Caleb the night he bunked with them.

"The thing is to organize," said the husband. "All these years, we been lettin' the big outfits boss us. They come here first, that's true. Hell, I come here with the EK, myself, and got fired and blackballed for homesteadin' this claim. Thing is, they don't want my kind runnin' cows. They still got the money, but now there's more like me and Sue than there are rich men. Time to organize."

"Yeah, but organize what?" Caleb had asked.

He shrugged. "I guess that's what the meetin's for. To decide."

"Well, who called this meetin'?"

The homesteader shrugged again, as if it didn't matter as long as something was happening. "We thought maybe you did, Hard Winter—you and your pals."

He laughed. "I've called a square dance or two."

"You don't have to make light for Sue. She knows it's serious. This impoundin' of our cows has got everybody het up. You know, I had eight old steers shipped to Cheyenne, and the stock inspectors seized 'em and called me a rustler, just because I was blackballed back in eighty-eight! My brand is registered, too. It ain't some maverick brand! Now, you tell me, which is the thief?"

The next day, Caleb could not resist stopping at the TW and was tickled near to tears to find Hiram gone and Savannah kissing him in plain daylight on the front gallery. That night, lying naked together on a grizzly bear rug in front of a roaring fire, they traded what information they knew.

"Hi's behind it," Savannah said, her eyes closed and her childlike smile making breath hard to come by for Caleb. "Since he quit the Cheyenne Club, he's been stomping around here, railing like a politician. All my friends went to Buffalo with him, but I've heard all I can stand about it."

"I'm glad you didn't go," he said. "I like havin' you here to myself."

Her eyes opened slowly and reflected the flare of a pine knot in the fireplace.

Caleb poured the bottom of a brandy past his tongue, felt its warmth vie with that of Savannah under the patchwork quilt. "You know I'd rather stay here with you, but I guess I better go to the meetin'. I'm in this deep as Nate Champion and John Tisdale since we raided the roundup."

She closed her eyes and smiled again, as if she really didn't care one way or the other. She drew a breath so long and cool that it seemed she hadn't breathed in ten minutes. The air almost sang across her shining lips.

By the time he got to town, Caleb was riding with blackballed cowboys, homesteaders, and an occasional hard case drawn by the smell of trouble. They moved toward Buffalo on foot, horseback, and in wagons. The meeting was set for the night of October 30, he learned, and its purpose was to establish an association of farmers and small stock raisers to rival the Wyoming Stock Growers Association, which had reined for years and currently had the governor, both senators, the state legislature, the U.S. Army, and 99 percent of the personal wealth of the state on its side.

"Hey, Hard Winter!" somebody shouted. "Where you keepin' that fiddle?"

He paused before stepping into the lobby of the Red Cloud Hotel. "Under my chin tonight, over to the wagon yard!" He waved, smiled at a face he couldn't place, and stepped in.

"There he is!"

Walker C. Kincheloe sprang to his feet to shake Caleb's hand. Jack Flagg thrust a cigar at him, Ranger Jones uttered an obligatory "Howdy," and Hiram Baber pointed at a vacant chair.

A dozen bentwood rockers had been set in a circle, each flanked by a spittoon and an ashtray. Caleb took the chair Hiram had assigned him, though he didn't like the fact that he would have to sit with his back to the saloon. He bit the end from the cigar, rattled it into the spittoon, and glanced across the faces of ten blacklisted cattlemen. He recognized John Tisdale, whom he knew none too well, but respected. One face was absent.

"Where's Nate?" he asked.

"He isn't coming in," Flagg said. "He and Ross Gilbertson are cow hunting down on Powder River. You know Nate doesn't care much for meetings and such." He smiled, propped a boot top on his knee.

"Everybody's here, then," Hiram said. "Let's get down to business so I'll have time to pen the documents before the meeting tonight."

Ranger Jones spat into a cuspidor and stood up. "Whose room we usin'?"

"We can make our plans right here," Hiram said.

"In the lobby?"

"We don't want to give the impression of any behind-closed-doors proceedings. Unlike the Cheyenne ring, we will meet in public."

Ranger Jones nodded as if he had come up with the idea himself and sat back down.

"Hey, boys," a voice said, coming from the saloon.

Caleb grabbed his gun grip and craned his neck to get a look over his shoulder, thinking a Mayhall had snuck up on him. But it was only Milo Gibbs, his eyes twinkling from drink. He leaned on the back of Caleb's chair, crowding the fiddler and making him uncomfortable.

"What do you want, Milo?" Walker asked.

"Just want y'all to know," he said, his words slightly slurred, "that whenever y'all git tired of *meetin'* and git ready to *do* somethin' . . ." He stood straight and thumped himself on the chest with a thumb. "Come see ol' Milo."

Walker frowned. "We'll bear that in mind."

Milo Gibbs swerved his way through the lobby, and the meeting began.

It was all a novelty to Caleb. He had no idea how Jack Flagg and Hiram Baber had memorized so much hullabaloo about parliamentary procedure, popular elections, nominations, and a whole mouthful of other high-minded notions. Hiram had been to college, of course, and Caleb had heard that Flagg had once taught school, but how they ever made sense of all that rigmarole was enough to baffle him on his best day. He finally satisfied himself with the idea that fiddle playing was probably a mystery to all of them and decided to just sit back and observe.

The dangedest thing was that Walker C. Kincheloe seemed to comprehend everything said, and even made an occasional contribution to the dialogue.

"Two points I want right at the top," he said once, though Caleb didn't know what this thing was upon whose top Walker intended to place his points. "First is the seizure of cattle in Cheyenne. We ought to petition the legislature to show how many votes we can raise again' 'em for goin' along with it. Second, we've got to show the newspapers that we're homesteaders and citizens, not just a bunch of rustlers like the goddamn Cheyenne Club keeps callin' us."

"How would you suggest accomplishing that?" Hiram asked.

"Set it down in the proclamation that this association we're fixin' to start aims to offer reward money for anybody caught shootin' cows out on the range, like some of these damn saddle bums have been doin'." He pointed the way Milo Gibbs had left.

"Unless it's some big outfit's cows," Ranger Jones said, only half in jest.

"Any cow!" Walker snapped. "A law ought to hold for any man, even a rich bastard!"

"Walker's right," Jack Flagg said. "We've got to class ourselves above the common thief and show the state—the whole country—that we're on the side of justice and fair play."

"Hell, I was just jokin'," Ranger Jones drawled.

A circle of spectators gathered around the leaders of the movement, standing three-deep in time and prompting Caleb to mind his mannerisms. He sat up straight, scratched only a couple of itches, belched only once, and didn't put a digit anywhere near a nostril.

Before it was over, the gathering of men had decided to style their proposed organization the "Northern Wyoming Farmers and Stock Growers Association"; to address all concerns of the region, even those unrelated to opposing the Cheyenne ring; to petition the legislature to cease all stock seizures called for by the Stock Commission; to offer reward money for the apprehension of real rustlers; and to discuss ways of holding large outfits accountable for crops trampled and otherwise destroyed by their herds.

"All right," said Hiram, rising from his chair. "Jack and I will draft the Declaration of Purposes and see the rest of you at the general meeting tonight."

"Ain't we gonna vote on somethin'?" Ranger Jones demanded.

"We'll follow the popular vote tonight," Hiram answered. "This association will be the true voice of the masses."

A meager volley of applause sounded throughout the lobby. Caleb had often heard ovations thunder twenty times as loud and as long for a good rendering of a tune. Yet that little rattle of clapping hands in the lobby chilled him. Maybe he had only sat with his mouth shut, dumbfounded and confused by the entire proceeding, but he could still sense that he had fallen into something more profound even than that which made people dance, which Caleb held nigh to holy.

As he turned for the door, he felt a hand on his shoulder and found Hi Baber nodding toward the bar, a grim look on his face. Caleb followed, proud to have been thus singled out and called aside. He took a seat with Hi at a remote table.

"I'll get right to the point, Caleb. I know you've been friendly with my sister. I've known it for some years now."

Caleb drank the whiskey Hiram poured for him and watched as the New Yorker poured him another. "I guess I knew you knew," he finally said.

"Do you realize Savannah is twenty-seven years old? She's virtually a spinster, for heaven's sake." He shot his own jigger of bourbon, his frustration showing.

"Well, I don't rightly know what a spinster is, Hi—I'll have to look it up—but whatever it is, Savannah makes a damn fine one."

Hiram's tired eyes glared at the fiddler and actually admired him a moment for his practical education and vagabond lifestyle. "Certain parties in Cheyenne would like nothing better than to embarrass me by smearing the reputation of my sister. You have no idea how highly you are envied in dark little rooms about Cheyenne, Hard Winter. If you're going to continue to see my sister, I insist you make an honest woman of her."

All of Wyoming imploded on Caleb with the suddenness of water hitting the bottom of a cascade. An image of Amelia flashed before his eyes, and a pang of guilt twisted him from within. He was scared. What if he did what Hi was suggesting? What if Savannah laughed at him? What if she didn't? Oh God, what if she had been waiting for him to ask all these years?

"You mean . . ." he said. "You mean . . ."

"I mean marry her, for heaven's sake. It's high time, isn't it?"

"You'd have her marry the likes of me?"

"She could do worse. You've got land in Colorado, haven't you? Not that Savannah cares about that. It's your image she wants. Or, her image on your arm. Do you have any idea how your fame has grown among dudes back east?"

Caleb shook his head, more baffled by this conversation than the one in the lobby.

"Even out here you're something of a celebrity, but back east the dudes you've boarded at your place in Colorado have inflated you into some kind of Western icon or something. Anyway, Savannah's worth more money than you've collected in twenty years of turning your hat wrongside up on the bar."

His eyes cut like a pair of pitchfork tines. "I don't care about that." The thing that hurt was the mention of twenty years.

"I didn't mean it that way. Look, you're a good man, Hard Winter. If you survive this range war you've likely gotten yourself into, I'd be proud to claim you as a brother-in-law. But if you're not up to it, turn my sister out for some other poor bastard to hitch in double harness."

SIXTY-THREE

SHE HUGGED HER knees and tucked the edges of the patchwork quilt under her toes to keep it in place around her. The sun had cast a shadow of the Bighorns across the man-made structures of the TW, so vain in their attempt at permanence. The cold would soon drive her into the house, but she would last as long as she could.

This loneliness appealed somehow. If only she had someone to share it with. Wasn't that incongruous? How could you share loneliness? Savannah had always wished she had a twin sister—someone just like her to keep her company.

With the limitless images of a Wyoming twilight flooding her senses, she suddenly caught herself thinking of Madison Square Garden. What was she missing? What was happening in Buffalo? Should she have gone with Caleb? Was he playing his fiddle somewhere? Could she be dancing? What about a nice opera? She hated the forced vocalizations, but peering across at the other boxes through her glasses almost always taught her something.

Vermont! Oh, the leaves!

San Francisco? No, not this time of year.

St. Augustine! Yes, the waves and the warm Gulf Stream.

She was alone here, and that was fine. But what was she missing? She should be dressing up tonight, feeling her corset pinch, turning heads, catching glances. Men should be stopping to watch her pass.

An image of herself lay like an opaque curtain over the hues of dusk. She had seen this image in a mirror at some hotel in Chicago. The chiffon dress in emerald, baring one shoulder a little more than the other; the string of pearls like a galaxy of planets, earrings suspended in orbit; the coils of sterling hair catching light, not so perfect that a few strands didn't stray. But her skin! Like milk, like cream, like marble warmed in the sun. Like wet silk draped and clinging to the curves of a goddess.

She smiled. How long would it last? This refuge embraced her like a cove. But shouldn't she be showing herself off somewhere?

The image of chiffon and pearls melted away as a horseman caught her eye. She knew in a moment that it was Caleb, his horse and mule stepping quick, knowing their way by now to the warm stall and the feed trough. She smiled. Here was someone with whom to share the solitude, for Caleb was alone even with a hundred faces staring up at him as he played. They complemented each other well. She fantasized about Caleb sometimes and knew his mind must reel often with thoughts of her, as did the minds of all men who had known her. But he knew enough to keep his distance. Caleb was a drifter. Would that all men she wanted were drifters.

As the rider saw her sitting on the gallery and angled toward the house, Harriet broke away from Whiplash's lead and made for the barn.

"Hey!" he shouted. "Harriet, you git over here!"

The mule trotted into the open barn door and disappeared.

"She's beginning to think this is home," Savannah said, almost accusingly.

"Buster would slap me sideholts if he could see how I've ruined that mule."

"I thought the caucus was tonight in Buffalo."

"It is, but your brother pretty much filled me in on everything that was gonna be voted on, anyway. I had more important business in mind."

She stood, and stepped to the gallery rail. "Come inside and get on with it, then."

Leather creaked as he swung down from the saddle, and spurs rang as he lit. "I don't aim to come in tonight. I'm bunkin' out in the barn."

She drew her lips together and raised an eyebrow. "That would be a nice change."

"That's not what I meant. Not in light of what I'm fixin' to do." He climbed two steps, until his eyes were just below hers.

That careless smile appeared, and she tossed her hair. "What on earth might that be? Something you haven't done before?"

He took his hat off. "Savannah, I've come to ask you if you'd marry me."

She almost laughed. She came so near, in fact, that she had to disguise it as a cough. She stared then with her mouth open and her hand against her throat. "Are you serious?"

"I am. I've thought about it hard. You could do worse. And I couldn't do no better." He had convinced himself of the latter, owing to the fact that Amelia would not have him as a husband—not after she had been married to Pete.

She took one step down and gathered him in the quilt. Whiplash was at the end of the reins in Caleb's hand and made a feint of shying. "You know I've never regretted one moment we've spent together."

He put his free hand around her waist. After riding so long in the wind, she felt warm as coals under the quilt. "That ain't exactly reason to marry a feller, is it?"

"You also know that I wouldn't give you an answer right here and now even if I knew what that answer might be."

"I didn't say you had to answer just now."

"Then come inside, and do your best to convince me I *should* marry you."

He drew back from the approach of her parted lips. "That wouldn't be right, Savannah. Not this time."

"You don't really intend to sleep alone in the barn?"

"Yes, I do."

"Oh, come on in with me. Please."

He could feel her breath as her arms drew him closer under the patchwork quilt. "Nope. I want you to think about it, serious."

She caught his lower lip between her teeth. "If you don't come in, my answer is no." She raised her lashes to catch the surrender in his eyes.

Caleb felt her tongue against his lip and relinquished all control. It was almost dark now, and the moon had yet to rise. Starlight showed him little enough, but his hands knew what he had ahold of. He smelled her hair, sweet with lilac. He had ridden at night and scented wildflowers he knew he would never pluck. This one was in his arms.

"Can I look after my stock first?"

"Would you be worth my consideration if you didn't?"

SIXTY-FOUR

CHAUNCEY SHANAHAN HATED the way the girl knocked. Barely audible at first, her fist on the closed door of the study was like a tree limb bumping a shutter in the wind. It came again and again before he even realized what it was. Why didn't she just rap three solid times on the door?

"What is it?" he shouted.

Her voice outside was like a muffled apology.

"Come in! I can't hear you!"

The door cracked, and her pretty little face appeared, eyes downcast.

"I'm attempting to finish my books, Claudia. I told you that. I'm going hunting tomorrow, remember?"

"Yes, sir, I'm sure I remember," she said timidly. "I would never be bothering you, sir, except that some visitors have arrived."

"Who?"

"Their names are Mayhall. They said they are brothers."

The name rang like a far-off knell, but Shanahan couldn't place it. He moved the curtain to see two hard-bitten characters standing in the sunshine outside. "Tell them there is no free board here. We don't recognize their so-called grub line."

"They say they have business to discuss."

"What manner of business?"

"They only said Mr. Dave Donaldson had sent them."

He jammed his pen into the holder. "Oh, bring them in, then. It's easier than trying to learn anything through you." She was a comely little Scottish lass, but as stupid as they came, he thought. And these Americans thought there was nothing to breeding.

"Howdy," Frank Mayhall said, entering with his hat in his hand.

Chauncey glared at both men, obviously brothers, though one was quite the elder. They sat down without waiting for an invitation to do so. "State your business, gentlemen. I have many things to do today."

"We're huntin' a couple of fellers you're after," the elder brother said.

"Are you lawmen?"

"Nope."

"Then why would you be hunting men?"

"Because they killed our brother."

The cattle baron's face did not change, but inside alarms sounded. He looked hard at the faces for the first time. The younger brother couldn't have been more than thirty, yet his features bespoke years of worry and hard living. The older one looked as tough as any man alive. "Who are these men you're after?"

"One of 'em's called Holcomb—the fiddler. The other'n's Walker C. Kincheloe. Dave Donaldson said they was rustlin' your cows."

Chauncey Shanahan had so many damning facts on Kincheloe and Holcomb that he had almost forgotten the story of the shoot-out in Colorado several years ago. "Aye," he said, "they are well known in the ring of rustlers about the town of Buffalo. In fact, each has taken a leading role in the organization of that illegal association there."

"So we've heard," the older brother said. "We've been bidin' our time for years now, waitin' to slip up on Holcomb and Kincheloe. Seems now they're on the wrong side of the law we might as well quit waitin' and just go git 'em."

"Fine," Chauncey said. "Good luck." He stood and gestured with one arm toward the door.

Neither brother moved.

"Well, is there something else?"

"It ain't as easy as all that," Frank said. "Fact is, Donaldson told us maybe you could help us out, and we could help you out. Huntin' costs money. When whatever you're huntin' can turn around and hunt you back, the price can git downright high as a cat's back."

The old Scot smirked. "You want me to fund your expedition?"

"Donaldson said the association was lookin' to hire men who could git the job done. We'll need two horses each, ammunition, grub, and suchlike."

Shanahan sat back down behind his desk. "The association is not hiring any such employees. And as for myself, I would hardly care to make it known that I had personally paid men to ride into Johnson County and . . . *arrest* rustlers."

The older Mayhall shifted in his chair, crossed one leg over the other.

"We keep our mouths shut, Mr. Shanahan. We ain't tolt nobody what Donaldson's tolt us. We make short cook fires and don't shoot unless we have to, then we just shoot once't. We stay shy of town and mind what brands we ride."

Shanahan sat like stone for several seconds, then rose from his chair. He lifted the Indian blanket that made his safe look like a lamp table and spun the combination with practiced facility. Tossing a stack of bills at Frank and a roll of silver at Joe, he shut the safe, and suggested the brothers leave. "If anyone were to ask, I would swear under oath that you men never took so much as a farthing from me. I don't know you, and I don't care to ever meet you again."

They stashed the funds in coat pockets and put their hats on as they rose. "Understood," Frank said.

"Don't trouble yourselves with the others."

"Others?" Joe Mayhall said, raising his stolid voice for the first time.

"Champion, Flagg, Jones, Tisdale, Baber. The other rustler leaders. Forces have been dispatched to deal with them. Until now, we've had no one show the guts to handle Walker Kincheloe. For your own sakes, be careful, gentlemen."

The Mayhalls left the study as Chauncey opened the door.

"Claudia! Show these men out!" He turned to his assassins. "This ranch offers no free board for saddle tramps. Your cursed grub line does not run here! Good day!"

Claudia walked before them and opened the door. Joe Mayhall snuck a gander at her as he left. She was pretty, timid. "Miss," he said, touching his hat. He wished he was just a cowboy here, instead of a paid murderer. It would be nice to see this girl sometimes. Joe Mayhall had never had a girlfriend.

The door shut behind him, and he shivered in the fresh air. "Frank," he said, as they walked to their horses.

"Yeah?"

"What the hell is a farthing?"

SIXTY-FIVE

JOHN TISDALE LEFT the general store with the Christmas gift for his wife in his hand. It was just a tortoiseshell comb, but it was all he could afford, and she would raise hell if he spent any more on her, anyway. It felt good just to get the shopping done. He had already bought toys for the kids and all the supplies they would need until spring.

Now he looked up and down the crowded streets of Buffalo for familiar faces. It seemed everybody from fifty miles around had come to town to lay in supplies before the snows started piling up. It was the end of November: time to catch up on news, time to shake some hands he hadn't gripped in a while. It was time to make some good memories to carry on the long drive back to the homestead.

In particular, he wanted to find Nate Champion and hear firsthand how Nate had managed to survive the assassination attempt. Two days after the big meeting in Buffalo, which had happened about four weeks ago, someone had burst into the cabin on Powder River where Nate and Ross Gilbertson lay sleeping. Shooting had started, and Nate had fought off the assassins. But that was about all John Tisdale had heard besides idle gossip.

Turning east, Tisdale came face-to-face with Dave Donaldson, who was turning into the general store he had just come out of. "Well, howdy, Dave," he said, careful not to sound too friendly. They had once been cordial to each other on the big roundups, years ago before all the maverick trouble and the blackballing began.

But now Donaldson made a strange face, as if he didn't know whether to be afraid or infuriated. He raked John Tisdale with a quick glance—the obvious precaution of one man checking another for weapons. "Tisdale," he said, returning the salutation.

This made John Tisdale mad—being called by his last name when he had addressed Donaldson by his Christian one—and he blurted out something borne of rumor: "Nate Champion is a friend of mine, Dave. I'd hate to think you were one of them that tried to kill him."

Donaldson looked right and left, to make sure no one would hear his answer. "He ain't dead, is he?" The stock inspector turned quickly into the store then, but looked over his shoulder for one last comment: " 'Bout time you got back to your wife and kids on Red Fork, ain't it, Tisdale?"

John Tisdale strolled on down the sidewalk, feeling disturbed over the chance meeting with Donaldson. These tensions between the little men and the big outfits were wearing hard on everybody.

He heard a fiddle in a saloon and looked over the swinging doors to see Hard Winter Holcomb standing on a crate. He paused, caught in the tune, even though he didn't recognize it. It was a slow waltz, and the fiddler was playing a beautiful harmony on the low strings, his fingers shaking to make the tones waver.

Without thinking, Tisdale walked in, though he wasn't much of a drinking man. Once inside, he noticed Walker C. Kincheloe motioning for him to sit at his table. Tisdale smiled, for Nate Champion and Ranger Jones were sitting with the big man, listening to Hard Winter play.

The song ended, and Caleb came back from the tune he had gotten lost in to see Tisdale taking a seat. He saluted the homesteader with his fiddle bow and struck up an old-world reel.

"John, you git uglier every time you shave," Walker said.

Tisdale sat and accepted the drink poured for him.

"Barmaid brought Ranger that glass, but he wouldn't drink with me," Walker complained.

"I was raised among Baptists," Ranger said.

"That means he just drinks at home," Walker replied.

Nate Champion smiled.

"Don't drink at all, damn it. Anyway, John, I was just tellin' the boys how I run onto Chauncey Shanahan in the foothills yesterday, comin' down from a big elk hunt. So I says, 'Chauncey, I know you hired them boys to try and kill ol' Nate Champion and Ross Gilbertson 'while back!' He didn't say nothin'. Didn't even deny it. So I just set my mind to makin' him fight, and I even called him a son of a bitch, right there in front of his whole huntin' party, and damned if he didn't crawfish!"

Walker's shoulders were shaking with mirth. "Ranger, you've got the biggest mouth I ever seen on a man that don't drink!"

"I swear to God, I called the son of a bitch a son of a bitch right to his face, and he wouldn't fight me. All he said was, 'You homestead on Red Fork, don't you?' Well, I says, 'What of it?' And he says, 'That's CU range.'"

John Tisdale slurped his whiskey and felt a pang of fear. "What did he mean?"

"Hell, he means he thinks he owns the government range, I guess. Who knows what that bastard means?"

Tisdale looked at Nate, then at Walker. "But I homestead on Red Fork, too."

"What are you tellin' us for, John?" Ranger leaned toward Tisdale and squinted. "We're your damned neighbors!"

Tisdale blinked. "I got a bad feelin'." He drank the whole shot of whiskey, a thing he had seldom done. "I just saw Dave Donaldson down the street, and he said somethin' about Red Fork, too. And, well, you didn't see the look he give me."

Ranger snorted. "Hell, what did you expect?"

"You'd better mind what he's sayin', Ranger." Nate Champion spoke as gentle as ever, and the other three men at the table leaned toward him to hear over the fiddle. "I overheard some folks talkin'. Seems Shanahan's bunch has spread it around that the Red Fork settlements are the center of rustlin' in Johnson County. That includes your place, Walker, since it empties into the Red Fork when it's runnin'. Also counts Jack Flagg, John, and you, Ranger. You and your brother."

"They'll play hell comin' to git me on my own claim," Ranger growled. "Look what you done to 'em when they come after you, Nate." Champion only bothered to shrug one shoulder, and that one just slightly. "All I did was broke 'em from suckin' eggs. I don't reckon they'll jump a man in his bed no more. They'll find other ways."

Tisdale felt an unexplainable fear seize his guts, and he poured himself another shot. "What happened up there, Nate? All I've heard is stories."

Ranger stood suddenly. "Sorry, Nate, but I've heard you tell it too damn many times."

Walker laughed. "He don't even have the decency to stretch it a little every time he tells it, does he, Ranger?"

"Where you goin', Ranger?" Tisdale asked.

"Home. My brother's waitin' on me. I've got lumber to haul, and a house to finish out."

"Hell, that's right!" Walker said. "You're fixin' to make some poor gal miserable the rest of her life, ain't you?"

Ranger Jones slumped with his thumbs tucked behind his broad cartridge belt. "She's got guts, ain't she? Tryin' to halter break a thing as wild as me?" He grinned, waved at the fiddler. "Adios, boys!"

John Tisdale looked across the table at Nate and urged him to get on with the telling.

"Well, you know Hall's cabin on Powder River?" Nate said.

"Yeah, seen it."

"Well, you know how cramped it is. Just before sunup, the door busts open and hits against the foot of the bunk me and Ross was sleepin' in. There was four of 'em, and they said, 'Got you, Champion,' and started shootin.' Well, I'd gone to sleep with my gun under my piller and my hand was on it when they woke me up. So I started shootin' back, and they run off. Wonder I wasn't hit. Guess they'll come after me with a scatter gun next time."

"And you recognized 'em?"

"No, but they left a blood trail, a gun they dropped, a jacket, and a horse. Sheriff Durham's trying to track 'em down."

Walker wasn't laughing anymore, and John Tisdale seemed mired in apprehension.

"Was Dave Donaldson in on it?" Tisdale asked.

Nate shrugged the one shoulder again.

"What the hell difference does it make?" Walker said.

"It's just the way he looked at me back yonder. And Ranger talkin' about what Shanahan said about the Red Fork settlers."

The fiddle had ceased, leaving a void in the saloon. Caleb switched quickly to guitar and began leading a group of former cowboys in singing "The Zebra Dun."

"It was just the look on his face," John Tisdale said. He threw back another jigger of whiskey.

SIXTY-SIX

R ANGER REINED IN the team and rode the brake down the grade to the bridge over Muddy Creek. The black horse sighed in gratitude, but the bay still acted wild and rattled the trace chains in a useless attempt to be free.

Glancing over his shoulder, Ranger saw the ends of the long boards scrape the ground where they sagged far over the tailgate of the buckboard. The ends of those boards were going to be splintered pretty bad by the time he got home, but he would turn them down in some dark corner of the house he was flooring, and no one would ever know.

He tightened the brake and smiled. She was going to marry him as soon as he finished the house. There were going to be kids crawling across that lumber in due time.

Ranger shuffled his feet in the loose hay on the floorboard. He had stopped at the wagon yard and asked for an armload of loose stuff just to keep his feet warm. Getting mighty cold nights, lately. It would be nice to have that warm young body to sleep with, just as soon as the house was finished.

The hooves clopped against the weathered boards of the Muddy Creek bridge. Ranger released the brake and shook the reins, making that fool bay shy. Thank goodness the black had sense. The bridge was short, and the road pitched up and veered west on the other side. Ranger turned to make sure his load of lumber was going to clear before he attempted to turn the wild horse.

His eye caught motion. A man stepped out from under the bridge he had just crossed. Dave Donaldson was lifting a rifle, recognizable even though he had a scarf across his face. Ranger stood to get at his pistol strapped on under his coat, his heart telling him he was beat. The reins hindered him, for his coat was buttoned, but he couldn't give the wild horse rein.

The blast came, and smoke shrouded Donaldson like a black saddle blanket thrown suddenly up before him. A jolt almost pitched Ranger between his team. It hurt, but he wasn't dead! The bullet had struck the cartridge belt around his waist and glanced away! He reined in the gun-shy bay and clawed again at his coat to get at the revolver. Another shot roared, and Ranger twisted as he felt it go all the way through. The next one hit between his shoulder blades, and he slumped down into the hay on the floorboard as the wild bay bolted.

The fear that gripped John Tisdale was nameless. He wished he had never bumped into Dave Donaldson outside the general store. Why had Donaldson looked at him that way? Why all the talk about Red Fork? What was going to happen? How were they going to do it?

He had waited in Buffalo several days, drinking. It was not his custom to drink that much, but it had taken some of the edge off the fear. Now he was sober, a day and a half south of Buffalo, alone and scared.

He had been scared enough to purchase a shotgun in the hardware store, and the gun now lay beside him on the seat of the buckboard. The owner of the store had given him a bitch and a pup. The bitch rode curled atop the load of supplies and Christmas toys. The pup had shivered so bad that Tisdale had wrapped it in his overcoat and placed it beside him on the seat. Tisdale could tell that the pup had been the runt of the litter, though he had not been told as much. That was all right. A runt could make a good pet for the children and would be an alert watchdog if not a fierce one.

Next to the pup was the shotgun. Next to the shotgun, the gift for his wife. Tisdale also wore a revolver in a shoulder holster under his jacket, but back in Buffalo it had occurred to him that it was going to be a cool drive to the ranch, with his jacket buttoned up, and the revolver would be difficult to reach if something happened. That was why he had bought the shotgun, for John Tisdale could taste something dreadful about to happen.

What did Chauncey Shanahan mean when he asked Ranger about Red Fork? He remembered Donaldson's words: " 'Bout time you got back to your wife and kids on Red Fork, ain't it, Tisdale?"

The trace chains sagged as the team made the turn into Haywood's Gulch, and Tisdale applied the brake down the grade. These gulches made him tremble. So many cutbanks to hide behind.

The look Dave Donaldson had given him at the general store: Pity? Hatred? Shame? Tisdale could think of nothing he had done that was so bad. Yes, he had taken up land on the CU range, but it was really public range. Chauncey Shanahan wasn't even a citizen of the United States! A man had a right to settle the public domain. Why did he feel so guilty? Was it wrong to have voted in that big meeting a while back in Buffalo? He had mavericked a few head, true. The traditions were old. You threw a loop on an unbranded calf and that was how you got ahead. Who were they to come here and make the traditions a crime?

The horses stepped into their collars and pulled for the south bank of the gulch. He shook the reins and clucked his tongue at them. He touched the puppy, reached for the gift he hoped his wife would like.

Something happened, and it hurt. A horse stumbled and blood spurted from its great arching neck. The shot was still echoing in the gulch. Quickly, John Tisdale gathered it in, his fear lifting in an odd moment of clear vision and thrill. The bullet had glanced off the grip of the revolver in his shoulder holster and had wounded the horse in the neck.

He grabbed the shotgun, his mind racing through a thousand calculations. He had figured about where the gunman was standing as he hooked a thumb over a hammer of the double-barrel. Yes, that look Dave Donaldson had given him was one of cowardly shame!

He began to draw the hammer back as he turned, trying to rein the team around, hoping the bitch would lie low. Something hit hard, and his thumb slipped off the hammer, which clicked against the firing pin, but not hard enough to make it fire. John Tisdale fell back among the toys he had bought for his children. The cur licked his face, sniffed the blood splattered across his chest.

SIXTY-SEVEN

HIRAM HAD LET years pass without visiting the cabin of Walker C. Kincheloe in the foothills. He remembered coming down that steep trail that led to Buffalo, so difficult to find even in the daylight. Now it was night, a quarter moon to light his way. He had chosen the same horse that had taken him down this path those several years ago—the one he had brought to Walker to get shod. The horse was getting on now, but had been spared of rough cow work over the years and used mostly as a pleasure-riding horse. He was sound. Moreover, he actually seemed to remember the path.

With his right hand holding the reins and his left glove in his teeth,

Hiram let his left hand brush against the tall pine he passed. He actually felt the blaze on the tree trunk. He had learned to trust a horse. It was important to come at night. He would make a poor target in this light. It was crucial to use the high trail to Buffalo. The assassins probably didn't even know it existed and would be watching the wagon road that led up the canyon.

He reached the summit and heard the waterfall splattering against the rocks. The horse quickened, going downhill now, remembering the destination.

When he was within a quarter mile, Hiram dismounted, loosened the cinch, removed the bridle, and tied his horse by the stake rope around his neck. He didn't want to go trotting into the open near the cabin, as murderers could be watching. On foot, he slipped along the tree line, proud that he had thought to wear dark clothing. When he saw the chimney smoke catching moonlight, he drew in a breath and whistled a blast of air past his teeth.

Walker C. Kincheloe rolled to the floor, his finger inside the trigger guard.

"What the hell?" said Hard Winter Holcomb as Walker rolled against his bunk.

"That was Hiram!"

"What was?"

"That whistle. I've heard him move cattle like that. Git up, fiddler, and get your gun."

Walker scrambled to the door, opened it, and stood concealed behind the wall. "Take cover, fiddler; a bullet could git you there." He returned the whistle that had come from the dark.

Caleb rolled from the bunk, grabbed a Winchester, and stood against the wall with Walker.

After several long seconds of silence, the sounds of footsteps emerged. One man was coming quick, and arrived at the cabin door at full sprint. "It's me—Hiram," he said, sliding out of breath across the floor as the door shut behind him.

"I know," Walker said. "Come to git your horse shod again?"

Hiram spent some time catching his wind on the edge of the bunk, his breath coming like the chug of a locomotive. "All hell has broken loose since you two left Buffalo. You know Elmer Freeman?"

"From the Cross H? Yeah, I know him."

"He rode into town a couple of days after you two left and said something had happened down on Haywood's Gulch. Said he had talked to

Charlie Basch, and Basch had seen a man with a rifle leading John Tisdale's wagon off the road, only he didn't see Tisdale. Sheriff Durham went to look and found Tisdale dead, sprawled out on the wagon, shot from ambush.''

"Oh, damn," Caleb said.

"That's not all. When he heard about Tisdale, Ranger Jones's brother, Johnny Jones, got worried because Ranger was late comin' home. We put a posse together and found Ranger dead on his buckboard near Muddy Creek. Shot in the back.''

"Son of a bitches," Walker growled, feeling his lust for revenge rise. "They want a war, goddamn it, I'll give 'em a war.''

"The day after we found Ranger, a friend of mine came to see me at the TW. I can't tell you who, because he made me promise. He said he was quitting the Cheyenne ring and going back east; that he couldn't have a part in murders. He said he overheard some talk about a so-called 'dead-list' in Cheyenne, so he snuck into the secretary's office and got a look at the list. Fifty to seventy-five names, he said. Ranger Jones and John Tisdale were on the list. So was Nate Champion, Jack Flagg, Walker C. Kincheloe, and Caleb Holcomb.''

"Why did this friend of yours come to tell you?" Caleb asked.

"Because my name is on the list, too. I'm surprised you two didn't get shot in the back on the way home like John and Ranger.''

"We left the buckboard in Buffalo," Walker said. "Bought three mules and packed our supplies in on the north trail to work the blazes over.''

"Wonder how Jack and Nate are?" Caleb said. It was spooky here in the dark hearing about the murders of friends he had played the fiddle for just days ago.

"Jack's fine. He's holed up in Buffalo. Nate went back out on the range somewhere.''

"Don't worry about Nate Champion," Walker said. "He don't light nowhere regular. He's hard to figger, and that makes him hard to waylay.''

"What are we gonna do?" Caleb asked.

"Go about our business," Walker said. "We've got to get the cows down from the high country and put 'em on winter range in the canyon.''

"But somebody's gonna be layin' for us," Caleb said.

"Hell, Hard Winter, you've had Mayhalls layin' for you for years. What's changed?''

Caleb absorbed the logic. In a way, it was a relief to know he was on the dead-list. Somebody was out there now, ready to find his back in their gun sights. Now he knew he had to stay alert, ride near the cover, keep his weapons handy. "How will we know when it's comin'?"

Walker was planning offensive maneuvers, as if a band of Comanche had stolen his horses and he was out to make amends. "Think like a bushwhacker, Hard Winter. If you was gonna back-shoot Walker C. Kincheloe, where would you lay?"

Caleb thought about that. What man would be fool enough? Walker had eyes that saw through stone; eyes that looked down the trail that hadn't even been trod yet. His confidence drifted back to him. If he was being hunted, there was no one he would rather ride with than the big Texan. If I were going to ambush Walker C. Kincheloe, he thought, where *would* I lay?

"Might as well lay in my own grave," he drawled in the dark. He heard Hi Baber chuckle and knew he had spoken well.

The wind in the high country made treetops roar. It tangled manes and stung men's faces. But with scarves tied around their necks, hats pulled low, and leather gloves on their hands, Hi Baber, Walker C. Kincheloe, and Hard Winter Holcomb bared only their faces to the wind. They made the gather in three days.

Caleb had begun the roundup with apprehension, seeing assassins in every shadow. But each day had dulled the edge Hiram had stropped with his arrival. He was beginning to feel safe here in the mountains. The killers had found their method of murder, and it was cowardly. They were picking off men perched on wagon seats, ambushing from gullies and bridges. They would not likely come here.

Pushing the herd up the last valley, the three men fanned out, Hi taking the valley floor, Caleb the northern slope, and Walker the southern. They would push the herd up to the head of this valley, over the divide, and into Walker's winter canyon. The rails had been let down on the fence, where the cattle could trail in. The older cows remembered the routine. There was tall grass in the winter valley. With any luck, the three- and four-year-olds would lead the younger stock right through the narrows to the high-walled canyon.

As he made his way around the thickets and through the parks, the fiddler could hear Walker whistling at some half-wild cattle across the valley, and he felt cheated that he had come across no strays himself.

Then things began to look up. Through a gap in the tall firs and spruces, he glimpsed a small bunch of cattle doubling back on Hiram. Whiplash saw it, too, and could scarcely contain himself. He was getting long in the tooth and had put thousands of miles of trail behind him, but most of those miles had been easy ones, as Caleb had spared him from many hard rides. A fiddler's horse fed well on the grub line. He was ready, and needed no prodding to lope.

Rounding a stand of timber, Caleb suddenly saw a large mountain park open up in front of him. At the head of the park was the divide, and the gateway to Walker's winter canyon. Hi was three hundred yards away, racing the cattle that were breaking right. Caleb was actually hoping the cattle would win, so he could have his own run after them. The gather had been eventful enough but was coming to a close and Whiplash had not enjoyed an all-out chase.

A blur of white drew Caleb's eye to the right, away from the running herd, and he saw a big cream-colored cow break for the trees with her half-grown calf. This was a stray that hadn't even been thrown into the herd yet, and she was spooked. Suddenly Hi's race meant nothing. Whiplash was already angling right at a gallop, reading his rider's mind, lunging headlong to cut off the cow and calf before they reached the cover of trees and low undergrowth.

It was going to be close, for that longhorn could run! The calf was nearly as fleet, lagging only two lengths behind. But Whiplash had the better grade, and the grass had been cropped by herds all summer—short enough to reveal the pitfalls. Caleb let the stallion have his head. They had taken many a ride together, and the rider knew every beat of his mount's gait.

The distance closed with marvelous ease as man and horse raced the cattle to the nearest point of cover. Whiplash bore down on the cow's near shoulder, and made her stop, stiff-legged, just one leap shy of the trees. Grudgingly, she doubled back to join the small bunch Hiram had managed to turn. And now Walker was coming around behind the herd, throwing his strays in, shaping up the whole bunch of two hundred.

Caleb felt the joy of picking up a couple of head to add to a friend's herd, the thrill of the pursuit winding down. It had brought a proper close to a three-day roundup. He had just settled into the seat when the cream-colored cow made a final bolt for freedom, the four-foot span of her horns pivoting in an instant. Whiplash sensed it first, and wheeled, causing his rider to reach for the horn.

Something warm splattered against Caleb's face, and he felt his mount stumble. A stream of red as big as his thumb arched from behind the Appaloosa's ear. The primal scream of pain mingled with the echo of the gunshot tossed fadingly across the canyon.

The only thing he knew to do was lay spurs to poor Whiplash's flanks, and the stallion responded with courage that made Caleb want to cry. Three great leaps brought the spotted stallion crashing into the underbrush, the rider leaping free as the horse collapsed. It was as if Whiplash knew he must rise one more time, for he had fallen on the off side, where Caleb booted the Winchester. Slinging the stream of blood as he roared and flailed his noble head, the horse floundered to his knees, then rolled onto his left side, stilled.

Caleb could see into the open park from this tree line, and he watched Hiram ride to safety as he drew his Winchester. He knew Walker would be coming soon. For now, he would hold off the assassins, wherever they were, and make his way toward Hiram.

Black hair exploded from the carcass of the horse and floated away on the wind. The sounds of the gunshots had come from so nearby that they had made Caleb flinch as if hit. The killers were in the timber with him! He hugged the earth and crawled, slithering against a huge fallen pine that showered him with bits of bark blasted loose by slugs. He hunkered into the hollow made where the tree's roots had been torn from the ground as it fell. The wind was such that gun smoke would be hard to find, and there wasn't much chance of spotting the enemy without making a target of his head.

Above him, the roots of the fallen ponderosa pine stood splayed like fingers on a huge hand that still held clods of dirt and rock between its digits. He took his hat off, hoping to gather courage enough to rise and peek between the roots for the men who had been sent to strike his name from the dead-list.

A rumble of hooves came from behind him, and Caleb whirled to see Walker coming at a gallop across the wide-open park. He glimpsed movement along the tree line and saw Hiram coming, too, riding more carefully along the fringes of cover. Coming to his aid—both of them. In the distance, the herd was scattering, and somehow this angered him above all else, to see three days' work close to wasted.

Shots erupted and bullets tossed dirt in Walker's path. Gritting his teeth, Caleb rose and looked between the roots that branched above his head. Instantly he saw the muzzle blast not more than twenty yards from where Whiplash lay. The shooter had a scarf tied across his face like a bandit, but the hat looked like the one he had seen Dave Donaldson wearing in Buffalo two weeks ago.

He swung the Winchester around a large pine root and worked a live round into the chamber. Donaldson caught the movement, and Caleb panicked, firing without aiming. At least he was drawing fire away from Walker. He pumped the lever, vowing to aim this time. He found Donaldson over the iron sights, saw the blast, felt the dirt pepper his face as the bullet slammed into the large ball of earth beside his head.

Caleb fell back, blinked the pain from his left eye. His right was clear, but blurring. Hearing the shots roar again, he stepped out from behind the roots and fired three blind rounds from the hip, leaping back for cover before Donaldson could draw a bead. Walker leapt from the saddle, into the trees, but there was a crossfire coming from somewhere now, and Hiram was nowhere in sight.

He couldn't risk jumping into plain view again. Donaldson might be ready. His right eye checked the deadfall behind which he was taking cover, his left eye still blinking at dirt. The trunk stretched a good hundred feet along the ground before the tangle of broken branches began. He could use the trunk for cover if he crawled, then he could rise in a different place every time he fired.

He hit the ground and tried to keep his rear end low as he slithered. Reaching the first obstructing branch, he stopped, took a couple of breaths to steady himself. He heard Walker and Donaldson trading shots, so he stuck his head above the tree trunk in relative security.

This was so perfect that it almost frightened him. Dave Donaldson with the scarf off his face now was reloading, looking Walker's way. A pair of broken pine branches on the other side of the deadfall framed him, like a window through which Caleb could fire undetected. Nervously, Donaldson was watching for the fiddler, but still had his eye trained on the roots of the dead tree where last he had seen Caleb rise.

Now gunfire came in a volley from Hiram's position along the trees, and Caleb knew without a doubt that Donaldson had partners. He drew the hammer back on the Winchester and slid it across the tree trunk for a steady rest. Donaldson had no chance, his eyes shielded by his hat as he reloaded. Three times, Caleb felt his heart swell as his finger felt the resistance of the trigger spring.

Should he shout? Give fair warning? Would Walker? Had Donaldson given such warning?

The eyes appeared under the hat brim, and the assassin brought his rifle to his shoulder. The look in Donaldson's eye and the sure way he wielded the carbine made Caleb know that the Cheyenne ring's stock inspector had found Walker in the woods.

The hard steel butt-plate of the Winchester kicked the fiddler's shoulder, and he saw Donaldson crumple in the brush. A crack in the woods drew his attention toward Hiram, and when he looked back, he saw Walker standing over the dead body of Dave Donaldson.

Caleb rolled over the deadfall and trotted to the man he had killed.

Walker kicked the corpse to make sure. Then the pall of hatred clouded his eyes and he kicked the body twice more, viciously.

"He's dead," Caleb said.

Walker picked up Donaldson's carbine, unbuckled the gun belt that held long cartridges for the rifle and shorter ones for the Colt. Gathering the captured weaponry and ammunition, he nodded his grim head toward the gunfire that had Hiram pinned down.

They ran almost at a sprint, closing the first hundred yards quickly, then they darted from tree to tree. The gunshots came louder, then the trees thinned, giving way to an old burn where charred and rotted stumps of evergreens stood like dark misshapen tombstones among the pale slender trunks of young aspens. The sun shone through a million golden leaves, all aflutter in the wind, making a kaleidoscope of Hiram's battleground.

Walker grabbed Caleb's shoulder and pointed to a cluster of boulders, fifty paces distant. Hiram was there, waving furiously, his horse nowhere in sight. The rocks seemed to encircle him like merlons. Whether he had chosen his ground well, or stumbled luckily upon it, the rocks had defended him.

Suddenly Walker was running toward the stronghold, and shots were firing. Caleb used the moment to locate a powder flash in the yellow glow, then he sprinted after Walker.

"Thank God," Hiram said. "I'm down to three rounds."

Walker lay the gun belt on the ground and peeked between the rocks. "You seen who you're up again'?"

Hi shook his head. "They shot my horse." His voice was steady, but the gun trembled in his hands. "Bullets glance around in these rocks. I can't tell where they are."

"I saw two of 'em," Caleb said. "One in the middle of the aspens and the other circlin' around along the edge of the park."

"I'm wadin' into the aspens, then. You two git that bastard in the park." Walker's corduroy shoulders hummed against two square boulders as he left between them.

Caleb knew he had better do as Walker said, so he led the escape from the battlement of boulders that had lain there eons, waiting to protect Hiram Baber from assassins. A bullet clipped an aspen twig that dropped before his eyes. He hit the ground. Hiram lit beside him. Their eyes met, and they sprang at once, dodging the trunks of aspen trees.

The brilliance of the sunlit park narrowed Caleb's eyes. He saw the man leading the horse: a slender man, moving uncertainly; young; nervous; familiar. That was Joe Mayhall, of Monument Park, Colorado!

From the stories he had heard—especially Buster's descriptions—

Caleb had formed an image of his father's death. He saw it play now in a whir, and Joe Mayhall was firing his shots. So was Terrence Mayhall, but Terrence was dead. So was Frank, and Walker was most probably stalking him through the aspens now.

The fiddler sprang like a cat leaping to kill something. His rifle swung up, and he jerked the trigger, firing at Joe Mayhall, cussing himself for rushing as he saw Joe fall—not hit, just hiding.

Shots rattled like popping corn from the aspen grove, and the voices of two men roared—bears in the woods.

"Joe!" It was the voice of Frank Mayhall. "Where are you, boy?"

Caleb knew Joe would rise, and he did, but swung under the neck of his horse and actually mounted on the off side, surprising the fiddler and Hiram Baber both. Joe used his spurs like a fighting cock, causing the mount to spring into the woods. In a moment he was hurtling among pines, leaping deadfalls, ducking branches.

Hiram and Caleb paced him with their rifle sights and pumped round after round through the trees, watching wood splinter over the smoking muzzles. Finally Joe broke into the aspen grove, and Caleb sensed a clean shot lining up. He tripped the trigger, but the hammer only snapped against the pin, wasting energy on an empty chamber.

"Come on!" he said, running back toward the aspens. Now he felt like Walker C. Kincheloe, anxious for blood. They had killed his father. Killed his horse! They had all but killed Buster that day in the ghost town. He was tired of being hunted, tired of thinking *Mayhall* every time he lay his head down to sleep.

He saw the blasts come from Walker's revolver, but the blasts came low. Walker was down, and must be hit hard.

"Get up!" Joe shouted. He was reaching down for his wounded brother's hand. Frank caught the hand, and Joe leaned far to the off side to lift Frank to his feet. Somehow he caught Frank's collar and pulled him higher; then caught his belt, lifting him still higher across the saddlebags, ignoring Walker's wild shots.

Caleb stopped and drew his revolver as Joe made off with his brother. He cocked and fired, cocked and fired, but the range was long for sidearms and the cover thickening with every lurching stride of the horse. Then a bullet got through. It made Joe's coat ride up at the shoulder and knocked him forward, almost out of the saddle. He rode off in a slump, still holding Frank's belt behind the cantle.

Hiram sprinted ahead to see about Walker, and Caleb followed. He thought of reloading, giving chase, and finishing the Mayhalls until he looked at Walker on the ground. Blood stained a wound on the big man's hip, and his left ear was almost torn from his head, the wound bleeding all down into his shirt.

"How bad are you shot?" Caleb asked.

"Not bad."

Hiram was checking the wounds. He looked up at Caleb, even paler now than in battle.

"I can't see straight," Walker said. "And I think my hip's busted."

"Looks like the bullet glanced clean off his head," Hiram said, sparing the bad news. "Damn Texans got heads like anvils." He knelt to look at the hip wound, but couldn't see much other than blood.

"Too bad about ol' Whiplash," Walker said, squinting against the pain. "That stud went to stock like a black-mouthed cur."

"Well, he sired a colt or two every spring down at the home ranch." Hard Winter looked at Hiram. "I'll get Walker's horse. We can make a travois and pull him to the cabin. I'll scout ahead to make sure the Mayhalls ain't layin' for us."

"They ain't," Walker said. "I hit Frank bad as he hit me. In the gut, I think. Maybe in a leg."

"Who lays down there?" Hiram asked, pointing toward the place where the carcass of Whiplash had fallen like a venerable old pine.

"Dave Donaldson," Caleb answered, rising. "And he'll lay there evermore."

They got Walker to his cabin and tried to make him comfortable. Hiram rode for a doctor, who arrived from Buffalo by the back trail at dawn the next day. While the sawbones was prodding poor Walker, setting his broken hip, Caleb looked around for Harriet, expecting to see her grazing somewhere nearby.

He borrowed one of Walker's horses and rode over the divide to find the old mule standing guard over the carcass of Whiplash. He knew it didn't mean anything. She was just a dumb brute conditioned by the years to follow the spotted stallion, and so she had followed him here. Still, it made him sad, and as there was nobody around, he sank down in the hollow made by roots pried from the ground. He hid there, watched the open park. He tried to sing, but only wept.

SIXTY-EIGHT

THE DREAM WOULD sleep as the dreamer woke and live as the dreamer slept. The dream was old now, as strong as the man. It was a struggle: night against day; dream against life. Now that the dreamer lay wounded, the dream awoke and felt strong. The man became the boy in the dream, hiding among the leaves and the drifted timbers. And the fog was lifting— the time-haze clearing—for nothing could shroud even a fragment of this memory in the dreamer's fevered mind.

The boy's horse-friend was looking back at him for help, standing knee-deep in the river. The Comanche warrior nearest the bank came into view over the long barrel of the Colt. The revolver roared and engulfed the boy inside a thunderhead of black smoke. A breeze made the blackness clear, and the Comanche splashed bloody into the water.

It was the way with this dream to make it hard, to terrify the dreamer. It was the way of the dreamer to torture himself with this dream. And so the hammer would not cock as the stolen horses lunged into deep water, and the boy felt nameless terrors, and horrors that surely had names.

The Indians whirled in confusion and searched the riverbank with their eyes as the boy tried to cock the gun but couldn't. Then the next warrior along the bank spied him, and desperately the boy used the heel of his hand to cock the pistol. The warrior grew wild-eyed and screamed the war yell that made the boy's skin writhe as if covered with snakes. Then the thundercloud erupted again, and the bullet ripped into the throat of the warrior, choking his yell in blood as he fell into the river.

Now the bearer of the lance prodded his mount from deep water, the warhorse lunging toward the shallows, toward the bank, toward the exposed hiding place of the boy. And the good old man's scalp, dangling from the haft beneath the bloody blade of honed steel, swept downward with the charge.

The boy cocked the hammer, cold as ice against his hand and hard as flint. He looked over the irons, down the length of the lance, and turned his finger back, snakelike, around the trigger. Blackness engulfed the warrior, but he burst out of the cloud, blood streaming down his bare chest. He squalled with a rattle in his throat and leaned forward with his lance. He used his weight as he fell, and the blade drove through the rotten wood and speared the earth between the boy's knees.

Fear fled from this boy in this horrible dream—fled like a startled deer.

The boy rose, feeling the hot stream of his own terror run down his pants leg. The old man's scalp was between his feet, crusted with dirt and chips of wood. And fear turned tail, for hatred exploded like a black thunderhead from the muzzle of the big revolver.

The brave was dying across the log, and the boy looked for the last Comanche in the river. The young warrior was riding alongside his dead tribesmen as they floated down the river, streams of red mingling with the swift brown current around them. He leaned far from his saddle and grabbed one by a braid, pulling him like a skiff toward the other. The young warrior floundered through deepening eddies, swimming his horse for the bank, pulling both his fallen comrades toward the shore.

Now the boy-turned-killer was running afoot downstream, merciless in his anger. He would kill them all. Kill them and avenge the good old man. Even this young warrior would die. Even this brave collecting his dead comrades from the field of battle. Even this Comanche barely older than the boy himself. Even this one who had shuddered and vomited as his friends tortured the good old man with grins on their faces. Yes he, too, would die. Red vermin. Red devil. Dead Indian.

The young brave was trying to pull a corpse across the withers of his mount when the boy cocked the pistol. And the young Comanche looked down the muzzle and panted, and a tear fell into the water, all brown and red. The dreamer remembered well the thoughts of the boy here. Let this brave take home the word of this defeat. Let him run scared back to his tepees with dead kinsmen across his lap.

But the eyes of the young brave, shining with tears—so wedged and rusted into the rotted memory of the dreamer—those eyes happened to wander down the body of the boy, and the boy knew that the brave noticed his wet britches where fear had fled in a stream, nevermore to return. He made the pistol buck in his grip and let three dead Comanche drift downstream. Now no one would ever know how frightened he had been.

The fog imploded again on the dreamer, as he stood full-grown. He waded, splashed the murky water all up his thighs. And the dreamer found himself here—a lonely man-child—every time he slept. He could no more wake himself than forget. He waded onto the banks and a shot blasted through the fog, startling him in this part of the dream usually so quiet and lonely.

Frank Mayhall was on the bank, shooting, and bullets tore the dreamer high and low. He fired back, and the younger Mayhall appeared, catching Frank as he fell, carrying him away. The man-child, the dreamer, lay in pain on the riverbank, staring up through the treetops of the Bighorn Mountains.

It was the way of the dream to double back on itself here, and the man-child heard the echo of that good old man's scream. And he would always hear it. A rattle and a trill. He would hear it again. And again and again. A shriek turned to a howl. There was the haze, the pain, and the old man's scream.

The dream was strong now. The dreamer was tired. The mind of this man-child was a battleground. The dream was winning the fight.

SIXTY-NINE

THE ROBE AND the blanket gave little warmth to Lizard as he plodded with the wind on his swaybacked nag. The snow was crusted and noisy, though muffled under an inch of new powder—still falling, chilling him.

Glancing west, he saw the sun halved by the horizon, reduced to a harmless glow by the flurries. The stalks of dead grass and weeds stuck up through the smooth snow, where once trillions of blades of tall dry grass had sustained the migrations of buffalo numbered in thousands of great herds.

Lizard remembered all this and felt empty. His horse was slow. If he did not see Quanah's tepee over the next rise, he would be too late. The ceremony always began at sundown.

So long had Lizard seen hopes dashed—even small ones—that it shocked him to find the trail of smoke in the next valley. The sun was gone, and he could just barely make out the forms of men and women walking in a circle around the tepee as Chief Quanah chanted. He urged his horse to trot, and the horse obeyed, as the grade went downhill now and other horses were in view.

Quanah came to him at the picket line where the mounts were tied. He signed: *You come to meet Father Peyote.* Quanah was handsome for a Comanche, whom Lizard had always considered ugly and ill formed, though suited to riding. Perhaps the blood of Quanah's mother had mixed well with his father's, the great war chief Peta Nocona. Quanah was no less a chief himself.

I come with no hope. This was Lizard's answer. He stood where he had dismounted, not knowing what to do.

Quanah took him to the tepee, put him in line with the others. They were Comanche, mostly, men and women.

I am the Road Man. I only show the way. Quanah made this known for

Lizard. The others had known Father Peyote before. *You are torn from the Earth, my brother. The Spirits no longer hear your words. Your heart is black with hatred for many men. You are alone. I am only the Road Man. I only show the way to Father Peyote. If you will speak with a straight tongue to Father Peyote, the creator will hear.*

Quanah entered the tepee and the others followed, Lizard ducking his head in turn to step through the flap. It was warm inside, and his shivering ceased almost at once. Quanah, the Road Man, went to the west side of the tepee, opposite the entrance, and sat on the bare ground of packed dirt. The others took their places, and Quanah motioned for Lizard to take a vacant space in the circle on the south side.

Drum Man sits here. Quanah motioned to an aged warrior to his right, who had a drum in front of him made of a three-legged iron pot. *Cedar Man sits next to Drum Man. He will offer cedar to the Spirits.*

Turning, Quanah indicated the woman on his left. *This is First Woman. Father Peyote will not take our prayers to the Creator without First Woman's blessing at dawn. Fire Man sits there, at the entrance to the sacred lodge.*

As Quanah slowly unwrapped a bundle of objects in a deerskin, Lizard took note of the fire. The wood had been lain in the shape that geese make in the sky when they go south in winter. But here, it was as if the flock flew west, toward the Road Man. It was at the point made by these logs that the small fire crackled, and the sound of it relaxed Lizard. Between the fire and Quanah stretched an altar made of packed wet sand. The altar took the shape of an old moon, thin and curved, the points spanning as far as a man could reach.

The Road Man was taking sacred objects from his bundle, blessing them as he lay them about. There was a fan made of eagle feathers; a rattle made from a gourd; tobacco, and cornhusks to roll it in; a staff; a whistle made from the hollow bone of an eagle.

Sage is sacred. The first growing thing the Great Spirit gave to Earth Mother. Quanah placed a few small branches of sage upon the crescent-moon altar. *My own button of peyote is sacred. I stalk it like a deer, south.* "Texas," Quanah said, using the Spanish pronunciation, knowing Lizard would understand this word. He then placed his peyote upon the sage. *It grows on the sacred cactus, humble against the Earth. This is Father Peyote. You look at him on our journey. He leads you the right way.*

Drum Man began to beat upon the taut skin with the base of a small deer antler wrapped in rawhide. He played rapidly, like a woodpecker tapping a rotten limb for food. There was water inside the drum, and it sloshed and made the tones sound like voices of lost souls.

Lizard heard the others humming, chanting, moaning. A song came to his own throat as well. It was a song of the Ghost Dance, but in Father Peyote's sacred lodge songs of all religions were welcome, for all religions were good. Lizard was the only Cheyenne in the lodge, anyway, and the others did not understand his hissing language, nor what it said:

> *My father*
> *My father*
> *His children*
> *His children*
> *In the greenish water*
> *In the greenish water*
> *He makes them swim*
> *He makes them swim*
> *We are all crying*
> *We are all crying*

The Road Man passed tobacco and cornhusks, and Lizard rolled his smoke. He followed the example of the others, praying as he exhaled the smoke, blowing it on his body and patting it against himself.

Quanah caught Lizard's eye: *The smoke goes up to the sky and takes your prayers to the Great Spirit.*

With a crooked stick, Fire Man raked some coals from the fire and made a pile of them inside the sheltering curve of the crescent altar. Cedar Man sprinkled slivers of the sacred wood on the coals, and a fragrant smoke trailed upward to the smoke hole. Lizard noticed some smokers placing the pinched ends of their cornhusks on the altar, and he got up to do the same. When all the smokers had finished, Fire Man brushed the burnt ends into his palm and took them away.

Quanah passed a branch of fresh sage, and Lizard did as the others before him, rubbing the leaves on his hands.

Now you meet Father Peyote.

A bowl passed in front of Lizard, and he took from it a slice cut from a peyote button. He ate it, fighting the urge to wince at its horribly bitter taste. He swallowed it quickly and wished for water, but none was offered.

The bowl went around, and Drum Man passed his instrument to Road Man. Drum Man played the gourd rattle awhile as Quanah played the drum. Then Quanah passed the drum to First Woman and took the gourd rattle. Drum Man took up the staff and pounded it on the ground in time.

So the instruments came around the circle until Lizard held the water drum. By now the rhythm and the chant was part of him, and he took it on with ease and played. It was then that his stomach twisted. He gagged in silence and saw a bead of his own sweat splash on the drum head. A woman across the tepee suddenly vomited in the dirt, and Fire Man came instantly before her, cleaning up the vomit with a scoop.

Lizard looked at Quanah, his insides seizing. The Road Man smiled with one side of his mouth and nodded. Lizard thrust the drum to his left and let his body push the old hatreds up his throat and onto the dirt floor. Fire Man came quickly to clean up the mess, then left. Road Man stood over Lizard and cooled him with blasts of the eagle-feather fan.

The bowl of peyote slices came around again, and Lizard swallowed another small piece, this time tossing it far back in his throat so he wouldn't have to taste it. He was playing the gourd rattle when suddenly the fire flared as if someone had thrown gunpowder into it. He gasped and looked across the tepee. His daughter Turtle-in-the-Water was sitting across the fire, smiling at him. The soldiers had murdered her at Sand Creek, many winters ago.

"I am well, Father," she said. "I bring your friends."

She spread her arms, and Lizard looked around the tepee. At his daughter's side sat his half-brother, Broken Feather, killed in battle on the Washita. Beside him was Lizard's sister, Porcupine, then his friends, Old Bear and Lame Man. They had all died of the white man's diseases and had not been spoken of since, for they had gone quite insane with the fever.

His eyes went around the tepee, and Lizard saw others he had known long gone. Grandfathers, uncles, friends. Comrades, rivals, wives, children. He tried to get up so he could embrace them, but he could not even raise his arms. He tried to speak, but only the bitterness came out, and was carried away by Fire Man, who flew before him now in the form of an owl.

Tears burned his cheeks, but still he saw the faces of the loved ones as plain as in the days when they had lived. His eyes swept the tepee, and with each round another lost face appeared in the place of one before. They smiled at him and raised their hands. Some spoke:

"My brother, my brother, all is well."

"Lizard, do you miss me? We will hunt again together."

"Lizard, the Spirits want to hear your prayers."

"My husband, my husband, the Great Spirit has a plan for you."

"Lizard, your path is with Father Peyote."

"Lizard, you take many scalps. Lizard, you need take no more."

"Lizard, the buffalo! Oh, the buffalo we will hunt!"

"My father, my father," said Turtle-in-the-Water, "the White Buffalo! The deer! Your horse wears the Medicine Hat! Your daughter waits!

Your wives wait! Your friends have made your arrows! My father, my father, the Spirits will listen. The Spirits hear all men. My father, my father, do not hate the white man. He learns the good way. He hunts the buffalo with my brother. The Great Spirit forgives the white man, and the white man weeps. My father, my father, there are many men. There is one Great Spirit!''

The tears were scalding Lizard, but he could not move. He wanted to speak, but his breath was gone. Then Old Bear rose, leapt into the smoke of the cedar shavings on the coals, and swirled up through the smoke hole. Broken Feather followed, laughing as he turned to smoke and floated away. Lame Man caught his heels and sped upward, and Porcupine followed. They all left, smiling down at Lizard as they joined the stars. He wanted to beg them to stay, but he could not speak, could not move, and his tears ran in many colors like the River of Tortoises whence his grandfathers had told him the Cheyenne had sprung.

And his friends rode the sacred and fragrant smoke of the cedar back to the world of Spirits, until Lizard was alone in the tepee, and sad. The fire burned and the cedar smoked on the altar. The drum played and the rattle sang, but Lizard was alone until he heard a man weeping. He looked toward the sound, expecting to see the Road Man there, but instead of Quanah he found Heap Killer, the horrible white man, and Heap Killer was weeping.

Heap Killer had blood on his hands, and he bled into a pool that grew around him as he wept. He could not walk, for his hip was shattered. A wound across his head bled into one eye. He was crying in great sobs of his horselike chest, and his power was almost gone. He appeared great, and fierce, and strong, but his strength was bleeding away. He did not look at Lizard, did not know he was there. He only wept and bled, and the pool around him grew until it touched Lizard's legs and burned him like boiling water.

''Paterson!''

The voice roared like a bull and hurt Lizard's ears. He began to sink into the scalding pool of Heap Killer's blood and tears. It was like quicksand, and it spread until it filled the whole tepee. It oozed into the fire and stank of burning hair, burning blood, burning human flesh.

''Paterson!''

Lizard was up to his chest in the pool of scalding blood and tears, and he couldn't move. He couldn't speak. He only sank deeper, and his fear began to consume him. His own tears made the pool grow deeper, and the air around him was too rank with the smoke of evil things to breathe.

''Pat . . . Pat . . . Pat . . .''

Lizard was lost in the scalding blackness, his lungs aching for air, when he heard the Road Man's voice:

"Mira al Padre Peyote!"

He opened his eyes and found Quanah sitting behind the altar of wet sand, fanning cedar smoke into the air with the eagle feathers. He repeated in Spanish, a tongue in which Lizard had some understanding and sometimes exchanged words with Quanah: *"Mira al Padre Peyote, amigo."*

Lizard looked at the sacred peyote button on the leaves of sage and felt a breath of cool air plunge down his windpipe. He was covered in sweat that cooled him now and gave him peace. As he stared at Father Peyote, he felt the fear and sorrow leave him. He was happy. The chanting and playing of drum and rattle made the lodge vibrate all around him. He found the staff in his hand, and he began to pound it upright on the dirt floor in time to the chant.

The bowl of peyote slices came around again, and Lizard spoke to the Road Man: *"No mas."* His voice felt like the hum of bees in the blossoms of a wild plum tree. The hues of the fire were like the feathers of red birds and blue birds and yellow birds—iridescent like the sun striking the splayed fan of a strutting turkey gobbler.

Fire Man brought water, and Lizard gulped. It was sweet as cold milk.

The night went on, and the peace lingered. Lizard began to pray. He kept his eyes on Father Peyote and prayed. He used neither language nor signs. He just prayed for this harmony, this serenity, this peace.

And he prayed until the Road Man welcomed the dawn with the whistle of a hollow eagle bone; until First Woman begged the Creator to hear the prayers of the night; until Fire Man raked the smoldering coals into the likeness of the Peyote Bird. And now Lizard knew Father Peyote, and believed.

SEVENTY

FRANK MAYHALL JERKED the half-hitch out of the leather saddle string and shifted the coils of his lariat in his right hand. He held the end of the rope in his left hand and looked up at the telegraph wire overhead.

He stood in the stirrups, favoring the leg that had taken Walker C. Kincheloe's bullet in the Bighorns. With a graceful sweep of his right hand, he tossed the bulk of the coiled rope over the telegraph line. His right shoulder hurt from the other wound Kincheloe had left him to ponder, but he didn't let it show. He had to set the example for Joe.

He had let up on his kid brother since that day in the high country. Joe had risked his hide to carry Frank out of the aspen grove. Once was the day that Frank had questioned his brother's courage. Now he knew the boy had guts.

What Joe lacked was the love of killing that which deserved no life. Joe didn't want enemies. He didn't understand that a man had to know battle, had to face death, had to kill to live the life of a true man. That was the way it was, the way it should be, the way it had always been, and the way it always would be among real Mayhall men. A fight to the death was glorious. Look at Valley Forge. Look at the Alamo. The Confederacy. The Indian Wars. Joe would learn to love killing his enemies sooner or later. Frank meant to see to that.

He caught the other end of the lasso as it swung past him. He ran the first end through the loop, tied it hard and fast to his saddle horn, and spurred his horse. The mount pulled against the telegraph wire above and lunged between the spurs. Chunks of sticky earth flew from the shod hooves and muddied patches of melting snow as the horse pulled against the wire. Finally the wire was stretched low enough for Joe to reach.

"Where's your nippers?" Frank demanded.

Joe Mayhall pinched the line in the jaws of the wire-cutting tool and pressed the handles together. The line parted and slacked.

Frank coiled his rope. "Let's ride, Joe. The train'll reach Casper tonight."

SEVENTY-ONE

NAVY COLT KINCHELOE threw the last sack of seed onto Red Hawk's buckboard and went into the store to pay the merchant. Seed was going cheap, for the owner of the store had ordered high last winter, gambling that the government would open the reservation in time for the new settlers to plow and plant. The gamble had cost him sorely, for it was too late now to break ground, and still the Department of the Interior had not set the date for the land rush. The only farmers who had bought seed this spring were Indians, or squaw men like N.C., who had taken allotments last fall and had had plenty of time to improve their claims.

"Mind if I leave my buckboard in front of your place while I do some business?"

The store owner frowned. "You see anybody else lined up behind you?"

N.C. paid in silver coin and shrugged. "Thought I'd ask."

"Who's all that seed for?"

"Me and my neighbors."

"You half-breed or what?"

"My wife's full-blood Cheyenne. My neighbors are Chief Red Hawk of the Arapaho and Chief Lizard of the Cheyenne. Lizard is also my father-in-law."

The store owner grunted. "I wouldn't brag on it. These boomers don't like it that you squaw men and your Injun pals got all the best allotments."

"It was their land in the first place. They ought to have got the best. Anyway, there's plenty more land. Good land, too." He left the store, oblivious to the sneer of the jaded merchant.

Crossing the street, N.C. stopped at the El Reno post office and asked for his mail. There was nothing but a letter from Buster Thompson. He sat on the bench in front of the post office, opened the letter, and read:

> . . . *Miss Amelia said to ask if the horses arrived in good shape. . . . She says if things don't work out there, your old job is waiting for you on Holcomb Ranch . . . As for me, I'm ready to come ride for Red Hawk in the land rush. Send me a telegram when the reservation opens up . . .*

N.C. smiled. It felt good to have friends to fall back on. He did miss Colorado, the Rampart Range looming like a huge wave in the west. But She-Rabbit's people were here, and so was his best chance of finding out whatever had become of his brother. He was very close to learning something.

It was on Christmas Day that Lizard had arrived unexpectedly at Red Hawk's house, where N.C. and Rabbit were staying. The old chief had just come back from the Comanche reservation to the south, where he had visited quite a lot lately with Chief Quanah Parker. He had called Rabbit and Eagle-on-the-Ground out to the front yard, for Lizard still refused to enter houses.

The chief had spoken to Rabbit, who kept her eyes respectfully on the ground.

"What's he sayin'?" N.C. had asked.

"He says he wants to make a bargain with you."

"What kind of bargain?"

Rabbit had asked, and listened, and her eyes had shone like moons.

"My father says that if your father will come and help him get more land in the land rush, then he will tell your father everything he knows about Paterson."

N.C.'s heart had throbbed a river of hope through his veins. "Tell him my father will come. Give him my word. He can tell me now what happened to Paterson. *Now,* Rabbit, in case something should go wrong."

Rabbit had pleaded as much as she dared with her father, but he refused to tell the tale to anyone other than Heap Killer. At least Lizard had looked N.C. in the eye as he spoke and offered his hand to seal the bargain.

"Why the hell wouldn't he just tell me?" N.C. had asked, after his father-in-law had ridden away.

"He said Father Peyote told him he must tell Heap Killer, and no one else."

N.C. had ridden to El Reno the next day to send a telegram to his father. The reply had come on New Year's Day and told of the ambush in the Bighorns and his father's severe hip wound. N.C. had wanted to ride north immediately, even in the dead of winter, but the telegram from Hard Winter Holcomb had expressly forbidden it. It was too dangerous and would accomplish nothing. Assassins were everywhere. So, he had waited.

Now, N.C. went to bed each night with a prayer that his father would recover and his father-in-law would enjoy good health long enough to keep his end of the bargain. Getting those two old enemies together to find Paterson was going to be the finest thing N.C. would ever accomplish. Even if it turned out that Paterson was long dead, that would be better than not knowing.

He put the envelope from Amelia in his coat pocket and rose from the bench when the postmaster burst from the front door.

"There you are! Here's another letter I just sorted, Mr. Kincheloe."

N.C. read the envelope and took the postmaster by the hand excitedly. "Thanks, partner. Thank you very much."

He tore open the envelope from Caleb. His hands almost trembled, for he hadn't received news in two months. He swallowed, and unfolded leaves to read:

Dear Navy,
Things is cold here, but all right. Your daddy is limpin'
around and cussin' like a whore. He rides some now, but it
still hurts him. Hiram and me is keepin' him mostly hid out
in Buffalo.
Me and Walker is ready to ride the land rush when it

*comes. Savannah is too, but her brother don't like it much,
but that don't make no difference to her.*

*No more killin' has happened, and we ain't heard nothin'
out of no Mayhalls. Don't know if Frank is dead or not. Ain't
no Cheyenne Club men around Buffalo no more, so we're
safe enough. The law caught one of the fellas that tried
killin' Nate Champion last fall, but let him go on bail. I
guess the Cheyenne Club knows all the judges.*

*Hiram has taken lead of the Northern Wyoming Farmers
and Stock Growers Association, and we have voted to hold a
roundup in April, with Nate Champion as foreman. You
know that is a month before the Cheyenne Club's roundup,
and Hiram says it is illegal for us to round up without say-so
from the Stock Growers Commission, but we aim to do it
anyhow. We aim to work this roundup, unless you telegram
us to come south and ride in the land rush.*

*The Cheyenne Club is callin' us rustlers again on account
of the illegal roundup we planned, and everybody is ready to
git shot at, but I don't think the Cheyenne Club can do
nothin' against so many of us here. Hiram says we aim to git
the laws changed around here, so the grangers and little men
can have fair chance at the range.*

*Your daddy says keep Lizard kickin' long enough for us to
git there.*

                              Adios, amigo.
                       Caleb "Hard Winter" Holcomb

N.C. beamed as he folded the letter and walked down the street. The
first saloon he came to had a sign hanging by the door that read No Indians, Half-breeds, or Squaw-men. It riled him some, but he kept going
to another saloon with no signs at all, not even one naming the establish-
ment. It was built of cottonwood logs on the bottom, with a canvas roof.

He entered, finding the place quite inviting with the midday sun making the canvas glow and the spring breeze flapping the loose edges at the
entrance. The bar was made of rawhide lumber, but built stout. Two men
were talking at the far end of the bar, one in overalls, the other wearing a
store-bought suit with frazzled holes at the knees and elbows. There were
no chairs or tables, so N.C. just leaned on the splintery bar.

"What can I pour you?" said the bartender, a weather-beaten man
about fifty years old.

"How much is a beer?"

"Two bits."

"I'll take a dollar's worth."

The bartender twisted the spigot on a keg and filled a glass. He picked up the silver dollar N.C. had left on the bar.

N.C. plunged his upper lip into the foam and sucked the beer, cool from last night's near frost, into his mouth. He sighed and looked out at the dirt street through the canvas flap. He was just taking another slurp when a gunshot outside made him flinch and slosh beer up his nostrils. A volley of six-guns followed, accompanied by a chorus of joyous wolf howls from the throats of hardened men. He looked at the bartender, and they both stepped to the door to investigate.

A boy, maybe thirteen or fourteen years old, came running down the street, waving a telegram. "It's openin' up!" he shouted, his voice cracking. "The reservation's set to open!"

"Let me see, boy!" said the bartender. He looked at the telegram the boy shoved in his face.

"Washington, D.C.," the barkeep muttered, squinting at the page he held at arm's length. "April nineteenth! Damn, that ain't but . . ."

"Eleven days!" N.C. blurted, figuring against today's date. His thoughts whirred. Could his father get here in time? Eleven days from Wyoming? Yes, of course! If he sent a telegram today, his father could start tomorrow, ride the rails, and be here with days to spare!

"Son of a bitch!" said the man in the overalls, crowding behind N.C. "It's about time."

N.C. looked at the smiles on the faces of the three men and yanked his revolver from his holster. He took a deep breath and let a whoop explode from his throat as he fired six rounds over the buildings across the street. The man in the threadbare suit pulled a pocket pistol from his coat and rattled it into the air. The bartender emerged with a twin-hammered shotgun and let both barrels go like an artillery salute.

N.C. ran to the telegraph office and stood in line for a minute or two. He printed a short message to his father: *Land rush set for April 19. Get here now!*

"You gonna wait for a reply?" the operator asked after he tapped the message.

"I'll be down at that saloon with the canvas roof. I still got six bits' worth of beer to drink."

"All right. I'll send a boy if anything comes back."

The telegraph needle began to click, and the operator grabbed a pencil. "Damn," he muttered, after scribbling awhile. "Line's down north of

Casper. They couldn't get your message through to Buffalo.''

"Well, how long will it take?''

"Usually don't take but a day or two to make repairs. Probably had a late blizzard or somethin' up there. Why don't you go on down and drink your six bits, and I'll see what I can find out for you.''

N.C. billowed his cheeks. "There's an extra dollar in it for you if you can get that telegram through today.''

"I can't splice it from here,'' the operator said.

N.C. left, feeling embarrassed and naive. He went back to the saloon, which had filled with celebrants, and drank his second beer. The conversation up and down the bar concerned the prospects of finding farms on the Cheyenne-Arapaho reservation.

He was on his third beer when a boy came from the telegraph office and told N.C. there was news from Wyoming. He trotted back with the boy.

"There's some kind of trouble up there, Mr. Kincheloe,'' said the operator. "The telegraph line's been cut for three days now.''

"What kind of trouble?''

"The operator in Cheyenne said an army of gunfighters left there by rail earlier this week.'' He looked at the notes he had scribbled. "They numbered about fifty men. They had three stock cars full of horses, and three brand new Studebaker wagons tied down on a flat car. There was also a baggage car, and a Pullman with the shades drawn. They left for Casper in the middle of the night.'' He looked up from his notes, over the round lenses of the wire-rim spectacles, and into N.C.'s eyes. "Rumor is they're going to Johnson County to execute rustlers.''

Eleven days. *Eleven days!* N.C. put his palms against his forehead and tried to make his head think. Walker C. Kincheloe had to be here in eleven days. He was beyond contact in Buffalo, Wyoming, with a party of gunfighters heading his way to execute him. Hard Winter Holcomb was in the same fix. So was Nate Champion, Jack Flagg, and even Hiram Baber now that he'd split ranks with the Cheyenne Club. They'd already killed Ranger Jones and John Tisdale. This was insane. How could a damn association of cattlemen convince a whole state government to allow a private war against its own citizens?

A steam whistle sang down at the depot, announcing the imminent departure of the daily northbound.

"Keep tryin' to git that telegram through,'' he ordered the operator. "I don't care if it takes ten days, keep tryin'! Give me your pencil and a sheet of paper.''

N.C. scribbled two notes and bolted outside. He looked around for mounted men. There were three in sight, and he judged them quickly by appearance. He chose the youngest, a clean-shaven youth of about twenty whose whole outfit told he was a cowboy of no mean pride. His leather was well soaped, his sougan rolled neatly and tied on the cantle, his guns oiled and slung ready.

"Hey, pardner!"

The cowboy recognized one of his own and reined toward N.C.

"You for hire?"

"Depends."

"I need a wagonload of seed freighted to my spread on the Washita. It's twelve hours by wagon. I'll pay ten dollars."

"I'm for hire. Where's the wagon?"

"Loaded and ready, right down yonder." He took two five-dollar pieces from his pocket and handed them to the cowboy. "My farm is next to Red Hawk's, chief of the Arapaho. Some of the seed is for him, too. Ask anybody where it is. If the army tries to stop you for a sooner, show 'em this note from me." He gave the youth one note, then handed the second up to him. "This note is for my wife."

The cowboy read the single word on the outside of the piece of paper folded in quarters. "Rabbit?"

"That's her name."

"All right. Where you goin'?"

N.C. glanced toward the depot. The couplings rattled as the engine began to chug up the tracks toward Kansas. "North."

SEVENTY-TWO

F RANK MAYHALL LAY still as a corpse at the top of the cutbank, hidden by brittle clumps of willow and box elder switches. Behind him, the middle fork of Powder River ran carelessly along, content that spring would soon make her rage.

The old-timer was coming from the cabin, past the stables, pulling a suspender over the left shoulder of his long handles, the water bucket rattling in his right hand. He looked almost like a ghost in the snowflake mist of early morning. Last night's frozen powder silently exploded with each dragging stride the old-timer took.

The gray-haired frontiersman passed right by Frank without seeing him, and Frank rose with the silence of a mountain lion. When the old man reached the edge of the river, Frank poked him in the back with the muzzle of a Smith and Wesson revolver.

"Don't holler, or you're dead."

The old man dropped the bucket with a clank and raised his hands. "I ain't hollerin', friend."

"Walk upstream."

The old man did as told, walking to the mouth of a draw that emptied into the river, where he met a dozen men wielding rifles and revolvers. Chauncey Shanahan stepped in front of the old man. A newspaper reporter from Chicago stood at Chauncey's side, taking notes.

"What is your name?" the Scot demanded.

"Ben Jones."

Chauncey frowned, for there was no Ben Jones on the dead-list he had committed to memory. "What are you doing at this cabin?"

"Me and my partner is out of work for the winter. Been trappin' some hides, till the spring cow work. Them two fellers in there just let us bunk."

"What is your partner's name?"

"Bill Walker."

Again, Chauncey pursed his lips downward. "And the two who let you stay?"

Old Ben Jones merely shivered.

Frank Mayhall pushed harder with the muzzle. "Answer the man."

"Nick Ray and Nate Champion," Jones muttered.

Shanahan smiled. He ordered the old man put under guard and sent Frank Mayhall limping back to the place where the trail from the cabin led to the river.

Frank considered himself crucial to the success of this operation. He had taken over many of Dave Donaldson's clandestine activities since Donaldson's death in the Bighorns. Kincheloe, Holcomb, and Baber had told Sheriff Brownie Durham of Johnson County what had happened in the mountains, but the Cheyenne Club had simply denied that Donaldson was on the payroll anymore, claiming he had only acted out of personal vengeance against Kincheloe, who had once beaten him with a pothook.

Frank and Joe Mayhall had been implicated by Holcomb and Kincheloe, who had recognized them, but Frank didn't worry about that. The Cheyenne Club had done a good job of painting the Johnson County men as lying rustlers. Besides, he and Joe were in Wyoming under assumed names now, and the Cheyenne Club had a virtual stranglehold on judges and prosecutors all over the state, if not on juries.

Frank had even gone to Paris, Texas, to hire gunmen for the Cheyenne Club invasion, succeeding in recruiting some two dozen regulators. Yesterday these same Texas gunmen had gotten cold feet and threatened to quit the invasion if not shown legal warrants for the rustlers they were supposed to execute. Frank had assured them that the warrants existed, though he knew they did not.

"You're gittin' five dollars a day, and fifty a scalp, ain't you?" he had railed, taunting the Texans. "What the hell's wrong with y'all? Are you gittin' scared now that the killin's fixin' to commence? What the hell did you come all this way for?"

He had succeeded in shaming the Texans into going ahead with the invasion. Yes, Frank Mayhall—alias Francis Hall—had become crucial to the success of this small-scale war. But, on a personal level, he would not consider it a success unless it led to the deaths of both Walker C. Kincheloe and Caleb "Hard Winter" Holcomb.

Now Frank watched the cabin of the KC Ranch from his concealed location behind the stable. It took half an hour for old Ben Jones's partner to come looking for him. Frank grabbed the man's collar as he rounded the corner, throwing the out-of-work cowboy to the ground and covering him quickly with the Smith and Wesson.

"Are you Bill Walker?" he said, poking the muzzle against the startled man's neck.

"Yeah. Who the hell are you?"

He pushed harder with the pistol. "Are you Ben Jones's partner?"

"We've been runnin' some traplines together, that's all."

"Who's in the cabin?"

"Champion and Ray."

Frank turned the prisoner over to Joe to guard and took a new position beside Shanahan at the top of the draw. They waited fifteen minutes. Nick Ray appeared at the door of the cabin, looking around for the two men who had gone out earlier.

"Wait," Shanahan whispered to Frank. "Perhaps they'll both come out."

Mayhall lay stonelike with his elbows on the ground, the stock of a Remington rolling-block rifle against his shoulder.

Seventy-five yards away, Nick Ray ventured a dozen steps from the door and balked. His eyes darted among the ranch buildings. He began slowly to turn back, his shoulders drawing up and his head pulling in as if he were a turtle.

"Take him!" Shanahan said out loud.

The Remington roared and Nick Ray staggered as if kicked in the chest, his blood bright against the new snow. Amazingly, he remained standing. Then the Winchesters erupted from the draw, from the stables, from the bluff, and Nick Ray hit the ground, his clothes alive with the impact of bullets. He began crawling back to the door of the cabin.

As Frank Mayhall calmly reloaded the single-shot Remington, he saw Nate Champion appear at the door and fire wildly at the stables with two handguns. Smoothly, Frank shouldered the Remington, but Champion ducked to catch Nick Ray by the collar, pulling him inside.

The cabin door slammed shut and the firing ceased.

"Damn the bloody thieves!" Shanahan blurted.

"Don't worry," said Frank Mayhall, as he eased the hammer down on the Remington. "That first one won't live an hour, and that other one ain't leavin' this ranch livin'."

Jack Flagg was enjoying the ride over the vast snow-covered reaches. His mind was free of worry. The Cheyenne Club hadn't tried anything in months, and Johnson County had become the stronghold of the little man. If there was going to be trouble, it would be in Douglas, where he was riding to attend the state Democratic convention. The Cheyenne Club would know he was a delegate and might well try to arrest or even murder him there.

But Douglas was two, maybe three days off, depending on how the weather held. Here, he was safe.

His seventeen-year-old stepson, Alonzo, drove a buckboard ahead of him, stripped down to the running gear. Jack Flagg liked this boy, his wife's son. Alonzo made a good traveling companion. It was well to share this snowy scenery with someone, even though they hadn't spoken in miles. Alonzo had pulled gradually ahead, his team a little more spry than Jack's saddle horse.

Flagg spotted the ranch buildings on the Middle Fork from his perch on the saddle. He remembered Alonzo's comment a few miles back: "I hope Nate's still at the KC." Jack smiled. Hell, any boy would admire the likes of Nate Champion: the bravest man in Johnson County, excepting maybe Walker C. Kincheloe.

Coming around a hump in the prairie, Flagg saw three men step out from behind the stable and speak to Alonzo. He squinted and leaned forward in the saddle as if it would help. "Must be ridin' the grub line," he said to himself. He spurred his mount and came up at a trot.

"Halt!" said a young man with a Winchester at the corner of the stable.

Jack Flagg took it for a joke, though he couldn't place the young man. That looked like a Texas crease in his hat. "Don't shoot us, boys. We're all right." Something was pulling his eye toward the cabin: a hint of something wrong in the gray and white of the wintry afternoon. He felt his smile drop when his eyes locked onto the blood-speckled snow, like the coat of a flea-bit gray.

"Jack Flagg! Jack Flagg!"

Jack recognized the voice: Charlie Ford, foreman of the TA, who had always bowed to his employer's association. His alarm surged so quick that it hurt, and he spurred his mount out of reflex as a rifle slug thumped the brim of his black felt hat. Alonzo was already running. Thank God that boy had brains. Flagg grabbed the horn of the saddle and hung shielded on the off side as guns crackled from the bluffs, the river. From everywhere! Snow puffed in his path where invisible hunks of lead met frozen earth.

Alonzo rumbled the buckboard over the bridge and Jack followed, sensing a safe haven from bullets when they made it over the south bank.

"Alonzo!" he shouted, catching up on his excited mount. "Give me the rifle!"

Alonzo drew rein, grabbed the rifle from the flooring in front of the spring seat, and tossed it to his stepfather.

"Hold up, boy. I'll cover you while you cut the wheel horse loose and mount him."

Alonzo leapt from the spring seat and began stripping harness from the horse.

Flagg levered a live round into the chamber of his Winchester and wheeled his mount to face the KC Ranch.

The snow-muffled rumble of hooves swelled on his back trail. "Hurry, Alonzo!"

A horseman appeared over the top of the riverbank. Then another, and another. They balked when they saw the wagon and Flagg let a round go in their direction, not sure who the hell he was shooting at.

Looking over his shoulder, he saw that Alonzo had the wheel horse free of rigging and was cutting the reins short with his knife. Wood splintered from the wagon seat, and Jack turned back toward the K.C., rifling two rounds among the horsemen.

"All right," Alonzo cried, grabbing mane and mounting the wheel horse bareback.

Jack Flagg spurred, wishing his back would shed bullets. He looked ahead with joy as Alonzo made it over the next rise. He marveled at his own luck when he made the same ground, unwounded, and wondered whose blood that was on the snow back there. His ears rang, and the frozen flakes kicked up by Alonzo's horse stung his eyes as he beat a fresh trail to Buffalo.

* * *

All at once, Joe Mayhall absorbed the utter shock of what his life had become. He wanted to cry out loud like a lunatic, but he just pulled another split pine rail from the corral fence and threw it onto the buckboard Jack Flagg had abandoned.

All day he had poured shots into the log wall of the cabin in which Nick Ray, who was probably dead by now, and Nate Champion remained trapped. He had aimed high all day, so that if one of his bullets happened to get between the logs, it wouldn't hit flesh. Not that it mattered. He was here, after all, riding with this gang of murderers, and that made Joe Mayhall guilty as the next man.

His head throbbed with unuttered protests of his own helpless voice.

The escape of Jack Flagg had thrown the invaders into hysteria. Nate Champion had to be finished, and the executioners had to be on their way to strike other sundry names from the dead-list before Flagg could gather his own army of defenders in Buffalo. A council of war had been called in the brushy draw, and the reporter from Chicago had scribbled furiously. The decision had been made to force Champion from the cabin with flames.

It all began to happen like a nightmare Joe could not force out of his mind. It was like the killing of Delton Little the day that building rolled down the weed-infested streets of Holcomb, Colorado; like the murder of poor old Ab Holcomb as he sat cleaning his gun in his own cabin; like the horrible death of Terrence flopping on the floor, and that drunken doctor in flames; like the senseless battle in the Bighorns last fall. Joe ran to the post he had been ordered to take on the bank of a ravine that reached like a finger toward the cabin. He watched it all happen: another horror to haunt his conscience.

The wagonload of straw and split pine posts crackled and flared high, sending black smoke into a sky almost as dark. Six men pushed it in a broad arch as forty others poured bullets into three sides of the cabin to keep Champion pinned down. The buckboard swung onto a course that allowed it to run slightly downhill, and it slammed against the cabin, showering the timbers with brands.

The roof caught fire. Smoke boiled, black as life in the deepest cavern. Flames roared like a thousand raging beasts. Joe wanted to cry for Nate Champion. He couldn't bear to watch another man dance the jig of a puppet jerked by bullets. Yet he could not tear his eyes from the inferno.

The roof cracked and roared like a billows, and still Nate Champion lay low. My God, he must be roasting alive! Joe remembered a rattlesnake he had once seen crawl into a brush pile. He had fired the brush and waited. The snake had withstood the agonies of the flames and died in that hell. Nate Champion was no snake.

A gust pushed down from the cold sky, like a palm pressing the hot smoke low against the ground between the ravine and the cabin. Black the cloud swirled, then lifted, and the specter of Nate Champion moved in and out of the cinders, coming headlong toward Joe Mayhall, a rifle held in both hands, legs pumping with ferocity, teeth bared in a defiant grimace. He strode long in stocking feet, with dreamlike grace, and made Joe Mayhall's guts rot with shame.

A shout, a roar of falling walls, a whine of some wasted bullet. Joe Mayhall felt three men scramble to his side as Nate Champion came nearer through the thinning veil of smoke. No, not here. God, not here! Don't run my way, Nate Champion!

With the eyes of a fleeing deer, Champion soared over the brink of the ravine and slid down the bank. He sprang to a fighting stance and wielded the cocked rifle, but the hired Texans at Joe's side were blazing away in a fearful fury. Champion fired high. A bullet shattered his arm and he dropped the Winchester. He reached for the revolver stuck under his belt, but the hailstorm bore him backward and slammed him against the ground.

Joe Mayhall returned from stunned oblivion when his brother clapped him on the shoulder. The others had been so intent on murder that they didn't even realize that Joe hadn't fired. Frank was congratulating him! Men were picking up Champion's weapons, rifling through his very pockets. Frank stepped past Joe and picked up a small notebook someone else had thrown aside on the snow. He thumbed through the blood-soaked pages, then handed the notebook to Joe.

Instinctively, Joe Mayhall turned to the last few pages written and found a scrawl that told as much as the words. He pushed aside the murmur of voices, the smell of smoke, the sight of blood, and read, sinking ever deeper into the mire of his ruined life:

> . . . *Nick is shot but not dead yet. He is awful sick. I must go and wait on him.*
>
> *It is now about two hours since the first shot. Nick is still alive.*
>
> *They are still shooting and are all around the house.*
> *Boys, there is bullets coming in like hail.*
>
> *Them fellows is in such shape I can't get at them. They are shooting from the stable and river and back of the house.*

*Nick is dead. He died about nine o'clock . . . I don't think
they intend to let me get away this time.*

*It is now about noon. There is someone at the stable yet. I
wish those ducks would go further out so I can get a shot at
them.*

*Boys, I don't know what they have done with them two
fellows that stayed here last night.*

*Boys, I feel pretty lonesome just now. I wish there was
someone here with me so we could watch all sides at once.
They may fool around until I get a good shot before they
leave.*

*It is about three o'clock now. There was a man in a
buckboard and one on horseback just passed. They fired on
them as they went by. I don't know if they killed them or not.
I seen lots of men come out on horses on the other side of the
river and take after them.*

*I shot at a man at the stable just now. Don't know if I got
him or not. I must go look out again. It don't look as if there
is much show of my getting away. I see twelve or fifteen men.
One looks like Chauncey Shanahan. I don't know whether it
is or not. I hope they did not catch them fellows that run over
the bridge.*

*They are shooting at the house now. If I had a pair of
glasses I believe I would know some of those men. They are
coming back. I've got to look out.*

*Well, they have just got through shelling the house again
like hail. I heard them splitting wood. I guess they are going
to fire the house tonight. I think I will make a break when
night comes, if alive.*

Shooting again. I think they will fire the house this time.

*It's not night yet. The house is all fired. Good-bye, boys, if
I never see you again.*

Nathan D. Champion

Joe read it over and over again, until Chauncey Shanahan grabbed the
notebook from his hands. Shanahan read the account, snatched the pencil
away from the newspaper reporter, and obliterated his own name with
scribbling.

"Here," Chauncey said, proudly handing the notebook to the newspaper reporter. "Let the world know what happens to cattle thieves in
Wyoming."

SEVENTY-THREE

N.C. HAD BORROWED the horse and saddle—stolen them, actually, though he intended to bring them back. The livery mount he had rented in Casper had played out before he ever hit the south fork of Powder River. He had arrived after dark, on foot, at the Two Bar Five—a homestead he knew well. The dogs had almost torn his pants legs off before he convinced them he was all right.

Strangely, no one was home. Not even womenfolk. The Democratic Convention was going on in Douglas, and he had tried to convince himself that Douglas was where everyone had gone. But there was an eeriness to the cold plains where patches of snow glowed in the quarter moon. Things weren't right in Johnson County. Rumors were flying like bullets all over Wyoming. He had checked at every depot on the trip north. The telegraph lines had been down for five days.

He had taken the best of the two horses in the Two Bar Five horse trap and the only good saddle he could find. He had ridden at a trot that had consumed mile after lonely mile. Crossing the bridge at the middle fork of Powder River, he had smelled smoke, seen the embers where the KC ranch house had once sprawled. There were tracks everywhere, as if an army had passed.

Crossing the North Fork at the headquarters of the Western Union Beef Company—a big Cheyenne Club outfit—N.C. had felt that unnerving quiet again. There wasn't even any smoke coming from the chimneys. He avoided the place and rode on in the dark.

Now the east was trying to shine, and Crazy Woman Creek was near. He knew these ranges, but they had never felt like this. Maybe it was fatigue. He had slept all he could on the long train ride north, but ninety miles in the saddle had to have some effect on a fellow's point of view. Damn, it seemed ghostly out here.

He smelled smoke again, spotted a campfire ahead. Another fire, and another. Hell, it looked like an army! That was the TA Ranch—another rich man's outfit. Was the army of Cheyenne Club gunfighters camped there? The rumors numbered them a hundred strong, with reinforcements coming from Montana. The rumors said they were lining up men on the "dead-list" and shooting them without a trial. Good Lord, look at the fires! There had to be hundreds of men there.

N.C. pulled rein and counted in time with the heaving blasts from the stolen mount's nostrils. Seventeen points of firelight twinkled at him from the valley of Crazy Woman Creek. Something began to sink in. The TA ranch buildings were dark down in the valley. Those fires were surrounding it. This was a siege.

The TA was a Cheyenne Club outfit. Had the little men risen up and chased the invaders into hiding there? Or had the so-called rustlers stormed the TA and captured it—perhaps lured in—only to be pinned down there by a superior force of so-called "whitecaps"?

N.C. didn't even know whence the term had sprung, but in Casper they were calling the Cheyenne Club invaders "whitecaps." He had heard so many rumors in Cheyenne, Douglas, Casper. Whole families of settlers and grangers were being put to death by the whitecaps . . . The entire population of Buffalo had taken up arms and slaughtered the invaders wholesale . . . He didn't know what to believe.

The horse was exhausted, and N.C. didn't want to be caught riding it, anyway. He dismounted with his guns, left saddle and bridle by the road, and turned the horse loose. He walked cautiously down the road toward the valley. Which side had which pinned down at the TA? He knew his father, Caleb Holcomb, and Hiram Baber were down there somewhere. Were they the besieged, or the besiegers?

He shivered with the cold that always seemed to precede the dawn in this country. If his father was trapped down there at the TA, N.C. was going to have to fight his way in.

He stopped on the road and looked. Men were beginning to stir around the fires. He could hear them. An unnatural hum of activity filled the valley that should have lain so quiet. For the life of him, he just didn't know what to do.

Then a particular strain cut clean and sharp through the general gnash of noise. It curled like a ribbon across the valley and made N.C.'s hair rise on the back of his neck. The familiar wail echoed across the bluffs, but N.C. located its source to the east. Only Hard Winter Holcomb could double-stop harmony that true and sweet on a fiddle. Relief billowed around him like the cloud of vapor his breath poured into the star-lit air. Navy Colt Kincheloe broke into a run.

Ten minutes later he was shaking his father's hand, having been escorted by a picket who had asked him at gunpoint: "You a whitecap or a rustler?" It seemed every man in the county had taken sides.

"My name's Kincheloe," he had replied.

"You look like wolf bait," Walker C. Kincheloe said when his son was brought to him.

N.C. was relieved to feel his father's strong grip and to see him standing straight as ever. "I rode like hell. Heard lots of rumors. What's goin' on?"

"The rich bastards and some hired guns from Texas—about fifty strong in all—murdered Nate Champion and Nick Ray at the KC," Walker said.

"Jack Flagg happened by, and they fired on him," said Caleb, cradling the fiddle in the crook of his arm. "He got away and rode hell-bent for election to Buffalo to spread the alarm."

"We've got four hundred men at last count," Hiram Baber said, "and more have been streaming in all night." He was standing there with his thumbs tucked into his vest pockets like a field general. "We've had them pinned down for two days, but the lunatics won't surrender."

"Probably scared to dance that strangulation jig," Walker said.

Hiram grabbed N.C. by the elbow and led him to a rocky point overlooking the TA. The light of dawn was bathing the valley in enough gray light for N.C. to see the whitecap defenses as Hiram pointed them out.

"They built a fort on that knoll west of the corrals. They dug trenches and used some lumber to build a bullet-proof wall with loopholes for shooting through. About a dozen men are positioned there."

Walker came to his son's side and pointed. "They're in the stables, too. And we've shot all the window lights out of the house, but they've got logs stacked behind the windows and doors. Only way to get a bullet in that house is to lob one down the chimney."

"North of the main house," Hiram said, "they have the icehouse boarded up with more men inside."

"What are we gonna do, then? Just wait?"

"Hell no," Caleb said, using his fiddle bow for a pointer. "You see that thing down yonder? That's our go-devil. We captured the whitecaps' wagon train two days ago and found two cases of dynamite, thousands of rifle rounds, handcuffs, and a copy of the dead-list. They come here to wipe us out, N.C., but it's all doubled back on 'em. We used their own wagon to make that go-devil."

"What the heck is a go-devil?" N.C. asked his father.

"We wired logs all over it six foot high so's they couldn't shoot through it, and we've been inchin' it closer to the ranch house so's we can throw their own dynamite in on 'em and blast 'em out. Takes about a dozen boys to push it, but it's almost close enough to start lightin' fuses."

N.C. shook his head. "Damn, this is like a war."

"*Like*, hell," Walker replied. "It *is* a war, and a long time comin'."

"Well, I hope we blast 'em out and finish 'em off today."

The three men standing around N.C. exchanged looks.

"Damn, you're bloodthirsty," Caleb remarked.

"It ain't that. The reservation's openin' up in six days."

The three men gawked in silence.

"Maybe you all should go ahead," Hiram said. "I know what's at stake for you all there."

Walker gritted his teeth. "We'll finish this today. I want to see those uppity bastards show the white feather. Besides, we've got to know whether or not them Mayhalls are in there. After that we'll ride like hell to Casper and catch the first train south."

"I wonder if there's a fresh horse left in the country," Caleb said.

Hiram jutted his thumb eastward. "I have some long-winded thoroughbreds you can use on the TW."

Walker shook his head. "I don't want to run good blood like that into the ground, Hi."

"You must. There's too much at stake. Let's finish this war on these self-appointed regulators and get you three started south today."

Hiram and Caleb nodded and walked back toward the campfire for breakfast.

Walker put his hand on N.C.'s shoulder. "I'm proud you came, son. You must've rode like hell. You tired?"

N.C. lied through his grin: "No, sir."

Joe Mayhall peeked between the timbers of the log stable. Wasn't this about what Nate Champion had been looking out at just four days ago? He was surrounded, pinned down by a hostile force many times the size of his own. That contraption the rustlers had built kept inching closer to the house. Joe Mayhall knew he was a fool, but he was not an idiot. Those men behind the log-armored wagon were going to set the house afire, or blast it to pieces with the dynamite they had captured. He had no idea what the rustlers would do to him, if he even survived the oncoming battle.

Rustlers. That was another thing. There had to be four hundred men surrounding the TA. Joe had never heard of so many rustlers in one place. Hell, they were farmers. He could see some of them wearing overalls, way off on the ridge, out of rifle range. They were merchants, small-time cattle raisers. Maybe a handful of them had occasionally shot some rich man's steer to get through the winter, or weaned some big outfit's calf early and branded it. Maybe they deserved to be fined or even jailed for it. But executed?

What the hell am I doing here? If I had possessed the guts to stand up to my brothers years ago, I could be like those men out there. Those men have families, farms, lives. All I have is nightmares.

He turned, squatted, leaned his back against the wall and let the Winchester lay across his lap. A shot cracked outside, and wood splinters needled the back of his neck. Joe dove forward into the horse manure as the fusillade pounded the stables. Something was about to happen. They hadn't mounted this kind of barrage the whole two days he had been pinned down here.

Joe crawled out of the stall and into the center of the stables for more protection. Two men took cover beside him. The first was his brother, Frank. The second was a young man called ''Idaho''—the only gunman recruited from that state for this disastrous expedition.

''What are we supposed to do now?'' Idaho shouted above the small-arms fire.

Frank shrugged. ''We didn't have time to get a signal from the main house. I guess we just lay low and get ready to fight. If it comes to us makin' a break for it, we're supposed to fight our way west, into the hills.''

''You sure we ain't supposed to surrender?'' Idaho said.

''So they can hang us?''

Joe covered his head with his arms, smelled the stale hay in his face. Chips of log walls and cedar shakes rained on his back, each one making him flinch. He wanted to cry. He wanted out. He didn't want to get shot again, like that day in the Bighorns when Caleb Holcomb's bullet made his shoulder look like it was full of sausage meat. He didn't want to hang. He just wanted to dig a hole and hide until it all went away. How long he lay there and how many rounds slammed against the stables he could not say.

Then the firing dwindled, like someone turning off a spigot. It fell off quickly, just a random shot or two lingering. For a few seconds, all was quiet. Then Joe heard the bugle far up on the hill. He scrambled to his feet and peered out through the crack between the logs. The U.S. Army guidons came over the hill, and the first wave of cavalry rose against the skyline as if they had sprung from the ground.

Now he understood the fusillade. The rustlers had seen the army coming and had only wanted one last crack at blasting the fortified invaders. Now it was over. Probably the telegraph wire had been repaired and the governor had called in troops from Fort McKinney to restore peace and save Wyoming from an all-out civil war.

''We're saved,'' he muttered. ''Idaho, we're saved!''

It seemed to take forever, but finally the army came down into the valley to parley with Shanahan and the expedition commanders. The citizens on the surrounding hills pulled back, and Joe began to embrace a hope that he would not be lynched today. Troops came toward the stables, and some Texas boys began gloomily taking the barricades down from the doors.

Joe was just going to help, to open the stables to the light of day, to turn over his weapons, give himself up, trust himself to the mercy of a jury. But a hand took him by the shoulder.

"There may be a way out of this," Frank said. Idaho was standing beside him.

Joe felt his mouth drop open. "Frank, it's over. The damn army's out there!"

"Come on," Frank said, and he climbed the pole ladder that led to the loft.

"Go ahead," Idaho urged.

Joe climbed the ladder between Frank and Idaho. Frank was kicking loose hay into a pile with his boots. Specks of daylight streamed into the loft through hundreds of bullet holes in the cedar shakes.

"Over here, Idaho."

Idaho lay down against the wall in a dark corner and Frank covered him with hay, stacking it high.

"Now you, Joe," he said pointing at the loft floor.

Joe could hear the Texans joking with the soldiers through the barricades they were removing. It was going to go on and on. Frank never surrendered.

"Hurry! We can't git Holcomb and Kincheloe from the stockade."

Joe felt besieged all over again. For a moment he thought he had no choice, then he spied a long steel tine curving down from a rafter.

He leapt for the pitchfork, grabbed it by the handle, and felt a splinter break his skin. The damn handle had three bullet holes in it! It was a wonder he hadn't been killed by now.

"*You* first, Frank," he hissed. "Come on, I'll cover you up with this." He physically pushed his brother down and covered Frank well. Then he threw a few more layers on Idaho. Quickly he used the fork to obliterate any trace of the maneuver.

He lay the pitchfork down as light streamed in from the opened stable doors. Joe started quietly down the ladder. "Shit!" he whispered loud enough for Frank to hear. "They seen me! You two lay still. I won't give you up."

"What are you doing up there?" a soldier shouted, as if on cue.

"Lookin' for a place to hide," Joe replied, surprised at his own gall.

"Well, there ain't no place to hide."

"I can see that on my own." He let the soldier frisk him, then walked

outside, falling in line with the other conquered invaders. Every step put
him farther away from Frank Mayhall. The freedom made his spirit soar
like a swan. Great God, the air was fresh out here!

Caleb trained the field glasses on the line of whitecaps walking up single
file from the TA. Suddenly the profile of Joe Mayhall filled his field of
view.

"There's Joe! Son of a bitch, bigger than hell!"

"What about Frank?" Walker demanded. "Do you see Frank?"

Caleb scanned the last of the line. "Frank ain't there. Just Joe. That's
all of 'em."

Walker squatted and rubbed the stubble of his chin. "Frank's dead.
He's got to be dead, boys, or else he'd be there with Joe." He slapped his
thigh. "By golly, I think we're finally shed of Mayhalls, boys!"

"Thank God," N.C. said. "Now let's go get in on that land rush.
We've got a lot of ground to cover in six days."

Caleb grunted. "That's funny," he said, still looking through the
glasses.

"What?" N.C. asked.

"Joe's smilin'."

"Smilin'?"

"Yeah, he's grinnin' like a shit-eatin' possum."

SEVENTY-FOUR

Now MAWL HAD grown old and wise, and he knew the ways of the
horse-men. When the horse-men appeared, he watched, and soon he
would know what they wanted by the way they behaved. If the horse-men
wanted him to join a herd, he joined. If they wanted him to lead the herd to
taller grass, he led. He knew the ways of horse-men and did not fear them.
But they were his master, and Mawl knew his place among them.

Now a horse-man appeared on the rise and ran hard toward Mawl.
Mawl thought the horse-man wanted him to run away, so he turned and
trotted, his head high and his great bulk rippling with muscle upon every
step. But the horse-man got in front of him and made him run another way,
then another. Now Mawl was confused, and confusion made him fear, and
fear made him hate this horse-man who did not know the ways Mawl had
learned.

The horse-man came very near, and Mawl felt pain from a thing that whistled through the air before it struck him. He turned on the horse-man and huffed a great warning through his nostrils. He raked the earth with his hooves and felt his hide crawl over the muscles of his great shoulders.

The air sang again with the thing that struck Mawl and stung him, and Mawl moaned and wielded his long horns as a warning. The horse-man made a noise Mawl did not like and struck him again, and Mawl was confused, and afraid, and furious. He lowered his head and ran with all his strength at the belly of the horse-man who did not know his place.

Then the old sound he feared came loud and suddenly—the sound of man's thunder. It hurt his ears, and made pain swarm so terribly through his whole head that Mawl felt the earth slam against him and smelled its moist sweetness. Then, very soon, Mawl felt nothing at all.

Milo Gibbs holstered his smoking revolver and coiled the rope he had used to flog the bull. "One shot," he said to himself. "Right betwixt the eyes." He was rehearsing the story he would tell the boys later. "Son of a bitch come at me, so I kilt him." He swung down from the saddle and stood over the fallen beast.

He chuckled a little, thinking of someone eating this tough old bull. Hell, nobody would know the difference. Slow elk was slow elk. The boys would be along soon with the wagon, and they would throw the back strap and hindquarters on top of all the others and haul them to the smokehouses hidden in the foothills.

Wasn't much cause to hide out anymore. The owners of the big outfits were all on their way to the Fort McKinney stockades. This damned old motley-faced longhorn bull was wearing Chauncey Shanahan's brand, and nobody gave a damn for Shanahan in this county anymore. Milo had seen Shanahan's mansion burning from several miles away. There were some rough ol' boys ridin' these ranges since the army ended the seige at the TA, but Milo Gibbs reckoned himself about as tough as any of them.

He took the knife from the scabbard on his gun belt and stropped it once or twice across the top of his boot that stood tall outside his trouser legs. The end of the red sash he wore around his waist dangled almost into the top of his right boot. They were calling themselves the "Red Sash Gang." Had a ring to it. Nate Champion had worn a red sash. Maybe that's where the idea had come from. Nate was a hell of a man, but not too bright, getting pinned down at the KC like that.

Milo Gibbs swelled about the chest, thinking of how he was still alive and Nate was all shot up and buried. They had killed Nate for rustling, and

Nate didn't know a damn thing about what rustling was. Milo Gibbs knew. He had done it every which way, and yet the damn Cheyenne Club had never applied his name to a dead-list. Milo had checked. Milo was slick.

He had killed cows, hauled their calves far away over his saddle, bottle-raised them, and marked them with his own unregistered brand. Why register a brand? Hell, most people never cared enough to check whether or not it was registered. Oh, once in a while some stock detective would think to run down that brand and maybe confiscate a half dozen head at some shipping point—a half dozen out of the hundreds Milo rustled every year.

He had changed other men's brands, too. You had to be creative to think of what else that brand could become. This was no line of work for the thickheaded.

Milo Gibbs had split the tongues of big calves so they couldn't get milk. He'd brand them then, knowing they'd go to grazing. Who was going to know which cow that calf came from, unless they saw the calf sucking? The open range was tailor-made for rustlers.

Hell, Nate Champion was a disgrace to rustlers. A brave man, but not a rustler at all. Nate Champion had only meant to make a point, leading men in plain sight of the roundup, roping out calves and branding them. That wasn't rustling. That was political commentary. Nate Champion was a fool.

Milo Gibbs was too slick for all that. He had made his living off the free range for years. He had ridden the grub line. He had never been black-balled. He had rarely been chased. He had never been caught. Milo Gibbs lived as free as any man ever born.

And now . . . Hell, half the citizens of Buffalo would probably give him a medal if they could see him out here, fixin' to skin Chauncey Shanahan's damned old motley-faced bull.

Once was the day when Milo Gibbs had skinned buffalo for a living. He knew how to make quick work of this. No need to gut the critter. Just skin down the back to get the back strap, hack off the hindquarters, and go on to the next head of CU stock he might find. Or any other big outfit's stock, for that matter. He and the boys would be selling smoke-cured slow elk from here to Denver. They knew all the buyers who asked no questions.

Milo grabbed a handful of slack hide and made a quick slash, crossways to the spine. The mottled hide jerked tight across the massive hump and pulled from his grasp, surging upward into the rustler's face. The bull rose under his elbows. Milo's lifeblood ran with electric fear, and he jabbed the hide with his knife, instantly realizing the folly of it.

Milo dropped the knife and tried to draw his revolver, but the beast wheeled with such speed and power that it seemed to coil around him like a rattlesnake. He was cocking the pistol when the base of the horn busted half his ribs and launched him through the air like a stick thrown for a hunting dog to fetch.

Creased him, he thought, as he flew through the air, seeing the whites of that bull's eye every time it came around in the circle of whirling earth and sky. The bullet had just glanced off that bull's thick skull. He hit and felt the broken ribs cut him up inside. The ground was rumbling under him.

Somehow Milo sat up with his revolver in his hand. He cocked and pointed it as the huge face, mottled and bloody, came into focus a mere instant, lunging like a monster's. He fired, felt an excruciating explosion of wind up his throat, and flew silently through the air again.

Mawl's anger burst from him in a scream as the power of the man's thunder struck him deep in the chest. His knees touched the ground, but he refused to fall. Mawl had felt the bones of the man crack against his great head and knew he might yet master this man who did not know his place.

His own blood blinded one eye, but Mawl forced himself to rise, and he turned until the other eye caught sight of the man stretched low on the ground, twitching like the meat-eaters Mawl had torn open and crushed in days passed. The bad power of the thunder moved yet in his chest, and Mawl felt the strength of all his many victories pouring out of him.

He moved toward the man, but it was not easy to move, and something tried to make him fall, first to one side, then to the other. Mawl smelled horrible things, felt pain he had never suffered, watched the man twitch on the ground. At last he was upon the man, and he lowered his head. He fell to his knees, goring the man with the tip of one horn. But his neck was weak and he felt the enemy give under him, heard the rattle of death from the man who did not know his place.

And Mawl rested on his side, his neck twisted on account of his great horns. He blinked. All he could see was sky. His strength left him. He could not make his chest draw in the cool air, and he grew very warm. He could not smell. At last, he could not feel pain. But Mawl knew the pride of this victory. He was master of his own kind, and even master of this man upon whom he lay. He looked at the sky. It grew darker, and darker, and Mawl knew peace in the darkness.

SEVENTY-FIVE

BUSTER PULLED THE watch from his vest pocket, looked at it, and frowned. "They ain't gonna make it," he said. "Somethin's gone wrong, else they'd be here by now." He tightened the cinch around the sleek paint horse Red Hawk had provided him with to start the run.

Piggin' String McCoy tried to blink his hangover away. He had been celebrating this little holiday away from Tess by backsliding into some of his former ways, but he was damned if he was going to miss the land rush on account of a hangover. "Why don't you stop worryin' about them and just look out for yourself for once't," he said to Buster.

Dan Brooks laughed down at Piggin' String from the saddle. "You're a fine one to talk. I found you lookin' out for yourself in the ditch behind the whorehouse this mornin'!"

Javier burst into laughter and slapped the shoulder of Angelo, who was mounted beside him. Angelo's mount sprang forward, almost over the furrow scratched far across the plains as a starting line for the land rush. Angelo grew wide-eyed as he yanked back on the reins, stopping the horse before it crossed. Angelo had been told that the army would shoot "sooners"—anyone trying to get a head start on the rush. Four soldiers stood about a hundred yards away. Their rifles were stacked, but Angelo wasn't willing to test their marksmanship.

A young Arapaho, Tommy White Fox, held three Appaloosas from Holcomb Ranch, and a paint from Red Hawk's stables. They had been saddled for Caleb, N.C., Walker, and Savannah, who were supposed to be on their way here now. For months, these chosen mounts had been grain-fed, exercised, and made ready for the land rush.

Buster checked his watch again. It looked as though the four horses Tommy White Fox held were not going to run today. What had happened to Caleb and his friends? They had sent a telegram from Casper three days ago. Seems they had had trouble finding horseflesh to ride out of Johnson County, to the railroads. They had borrowed some thoroughbreds from Hiram Baber, but these mounts had played out on the plains, and the party had walked into Casper. Still, it would seem they could have made it here by now. Buster hoped they hadn't gotten caught up in more of that trouble up there.

Piggin' String McCoy poured half the contents of his canteen onto his forehead and replaced his hat. "Thing I like about a hangover," he said, "is when it's gone, you always feel so damn good by comparison."

"Makes you want to go out git stinkin' drunk all over again, don't it?" Dan Brooks said.

"I ain't there, yet."

"Makes you want to swill a whole big ol' bottle of rotgut whiskey, don't it?"

"Goddamn, Dan, don't speak its name out loud." String climbed laboriously into the saddle.

"Chase it with castor oil."

"Go to hell."

Javier doubled over his saddle horn with laughter.

"Pay attention," Buster said. "One minute to go."

All along the single furrow, hopeful immigrants formed their ranks, sensing the nearness of the moment. A few horsemen pranced on spirited mounts. Most rode poor animals—all they could afford. Buggies and buckboards inched forward, hitched to teams of mismatched horses, mules, even lumbering oxen. Then there were men on foot, women with babies on their hips. Every man carried a wooden stake to claim the home he hoped to win.

Buster had asked some army officials: as near as anyone could guess, about twenty-five or thirty thousand homesteaders were spread out over the miles, ready to run. He would have to ride hard to beat the others to Red Hawk's allotment and help him add to his holdings.

The gun sounded, and horses leapt all down the furrow, thousands of hooves beating the earth in the biggest horse race Buster had ever seen the likes of. The air instantly became saturated with a common yell, spontaneously howling up the throats of men, women, and children, in a thousand different tones, harmonious and dissonant. The four riderless mounts reared and pulled against their reins, longing to run with the others, but Tommy White Fox handled them well, showing no fear of the sixteen hooves powered by thousands of pounds of muscle.

Buster tugged on his hat brim as the breeze hit him. It was a shirtsleeve day in Indian Territory, perfect for a race. Grass was coming up green, and wildflowers speckled the plains, bunched here and there in colorful little communities. He looked left and saw Piggin' String McCoy listing fearfully in the saddle.

He wished he could enjoy this spectacle that made the whole earth tremble and clouded the sky with her dust. But Caleb was on his mind. Why wasn't he here yet? It had ruined the whole thing.

The fine paint gelding ran like a warhorse into battle, but Buster could only look back—back at Tommy White Fox holding the mounts intended for Caleb and his friends. He thundered ahead until Tommy and the horses disappeared behind a roll in the prairie.

Suddenly Buster yanked back on the reins.

"*¿Qué pasa?*" Javier asked, slowing his horse.

"Go ahead," Buster replied. "I thought I seen 'em." He turned back, rode again over the low ridge.

Far off to the northeast, three riders rose and fell like pistons out of time. They vanished into a swell, sprang to view again. Three? Maybe it wasn't them. Or maybe it was them, and the girl had decided she didn't want any part of any land rush. Maybe they were too late, even if it was them.

Buster loped back to Tommy White Fox, who had spotted the riders by now. The furrow, where thousands had stood waiting, now felt abandoned and silent, tracks and manure all that was left of the horde gathered there just minutes before. Buster spurred northeastward and drew rein to get a close look. By golly, that big man had to be Walker C. Kincheloe!

They came nearer, and Buster's heart warmed as he recognized Caleb's pose in the saddle—a slouch born of decades on the trail. The horses were tired, for the legs of the riders beat their flanks mercilessly with spurs.

Something flashed over Caleb's shoulder like a flag of surrender, and Buster realized that Savannah was riding double behind him, her arms wrapped around his waist. He smiled wide, turned back to Tommy White Fox, and waved for the fresh horses.

The tired horses came alongside the new mounts in stiff-legged jolts, and Savannah slipped off Caleb's cantle and into the saddle of an Appaloosa. Without saying a word to anyone, and without even looking at Buster or Tommy, she took off on the Appaloosa, doubling the speed at which she had arrived.

"What took y'all so long?" Buster asked.

"A freight train jumped the tracks ahead of us in Nebraska," Caleb replied, jumping down.

"How far behind are we?" Walker demanded, looking as serious as Buster had ever seen him.

He pulled the watch from his pocket. "About eight minutes is all."

"Thanks, Tommy," N.C. said as the young brave handed a rein up to him in the saddle.

Walker spurred the largest paint, bending low to catch the dangling right rein. The four men galloped in the dust trail Savannah had left for them to follow. Buster noticed that she was angling too far north, but she would catch on if he knew Savannah Baber. That little temptress was bright as she was pretty.

They crossed the furrowed starting line, almost ten minutes behind, and Caleb let a joyful yelp escape his throat, soon joined by the voices of the others. Even Walker hollered, for there was still a chance—a chance to catch up, win a few more acres for Lizard, and put his mind at ease about Paterson. His mending hip was sore and his hope just hanging on, but Walker C. Kincheloe knew how to make the most of an outside chance.

They passed the settlers plodding ahead on foot, pitying them in their desperation. Savannah noticed the direction the men were taking and angled to join them. They overtook lumbering wagons pulled by oxen, tired mules, and horses too small to pass for draft animals. Sweat began to gather on the saddle horses in lines of foam, but they were willing, and sensed that they had been left behind. Soon, Red Hawk's riders were passing the stragglers on gaunt horses, and a mile ahead they could see clear blue sky through the long ribbon of dust the rush had raised.

"This way!" N.C. yelled, taking a rough trail down into a dry wash that others had avoided. He had ridden this route several times and knew where all the relays had been stationed. He could see the tracks left by Javier, Angelo, Piggin' String, and Dan Brooks before them and knew they had to be among the leaders by now.

Five Arapaho boys waited under a cluster of willows, holding the first relay of fresh horses. The riders moved from one saddle to the next, never touching boot leather to the ground.

"Is this legal?" Savannah asked.

"Sure," N.C. replied. "This is Tommy White Fox's allotment. Red Hawk had him choose it just so we'd have a place to stake the first relay of mounts. The best horses are yet to come where Red Hawk's lodge wife lives. We'll finish the rush on them, so there's still a chance we'll beat everybody to the best parcels."

"Better ride like liquored Injuns," Walker said. "No offense," he added, glancing at the Arapaho boy who had held the second big paint as he jumped off the first.

They thundered up out of the ravine, quickly using the fresh mounts to make up for the time they had spent switching horses. Soon they began to ride among a better grade of racers, most of them loping now as Red Hawk's riders passed them at a gallop. The field diminished. The thickest part of the dust cloud fell behind, and blue sky became streaked with only the dust of the fastest riders.

Buster was ordinarily a mule man, for he liked their surefootedness in the foothills of home. It had been a long time since he had ridden such a fleet horse, and the way the ground rushed under him—furlong upon furlong, mile upon mile—made him cringe with fear and grin with joy all at once.

The timber along the Washita came into view, and N.C. recognized the tall cottonwoods where Red Hawk's lodge stood dappled by the shade of new leaves. A few settlers had staked their claims here and there, hoping to reach well water with windmills, but most rode on, determined to get beyond the Indian allotments and win farms right on the banks of the river. The surveyed squares just upstream of Red Hawk's farm were the first and best unclaimed parcels. The race would end there for Buster, Walker, N.C., Caleb, Javier, Angelo, String, Dan, and Savannah.

More young Arapaho braves held the best of the mounts across the Washita from Red Hawk's tepee. There were three Appaloosas and two paints. Savannah got there first and picked the smallest mount. Walker came next and singled out the largest. Buster, Caleb, and N.C. took the first horses they found.

Pounding through the litter of last fall's leaves on the trail, they galloped onto the sunny flats, feeling the increase in speed from these, the best mounts. In their desperation to catch up, the five riders had devoured miles and now were in view of the leaders: Javier, Dan, String, and Angelo. But first they overtook two strangers who had started the rush on good mounts, now almost exhausted.

When Savannah passed them, the two men just stared at her, as if she were an angel on a winged steed. Buster and Walker closed quickly on them next, and the two men saw the party coming at a gallop when all they could get out of their tired horses was a long lope. They were lean, weather-toughened men who knew how to sit a saddle. Their mounts slung flecks of froth and lolled tongues beyond their bits.

"Hey!" one of them shouted as Buster and Walker passed him. "Where'd you get them fresh horses?"

"Injuns give 'em to us!" Walker answered.

"You liar. You're goddamn sooners!" He clawed at his saddlebag and at length produced a rusty six-shooter.

But Walker was already pacing the man in his pistol sights. "Throw that down, mister, or you've rode your last race!"

The man looked at the muzzle of the big Colt, and at the stubbled jaw and the grim visage of the big Texan beyond it. He let the rusty revolver fall from his grasp.

"Those are our boys comin' up behind you, so don't try nothin' else."

Caleb and N.C. caught up, and the four men rode abreast, taking turns watching for trouble from the two strangers.

"Howdy, String!" Caleb shouted, catching up to the lagging cowboy. "Damn, you look like hell."

"The sight of you don't help none," String answered. "But that little lady there perks me up."

Savannah looked back at String and smiled, her loose hair floating like a bird's wings above the rises and falls of the galloping horse.

Buster was listening to all of this from behind and aside, out of the dust, when he saw Walker use his quirt. The big man was hellbent on winning this race, and Buster figured the least he could do was to make a contest of it, so he leaned low to cut the wind and gave the horse its head. He spoke, and even though he and this mount had never met, they understood each other, for Buster could talk horse.

Suddenly, Buster and Walker were streaking past String, Caleb, and Savannah, each getting the most from his mount in his own way.

Caleb used the long ends of his reins to lash his mount. "Not much, Mary Ann!" he shouted, and tickled the Appaloosa's flanks with spurs. "Angelo!" he cried, when he felt the dirt of his son's ride in his face.

The boy looked over his shoulder. "Papa!" He reached wide with his right hand and let Caleb come up to grab his wrist, and they rode stride for stride grinning at each other. "You made it!"

"We ain't made it yet, son."

The leaders now were Buster, Walker, and Savannah. Caleb, Javier, Angelo, N.C., and Dan ran close behind, while Piggin' String McCoy lagged. Looking north and south, the leaders could see that they had won control of the race. The relay of mounts had worked even better than planned, and they all drew abreast of each other in one line of riders across the plains, even allowing Piggin' String to catch up.

"How much farther?" Walker asked.

N.C. pointed. "Around that bend." He smiled. Red Hawk was waiting there. So were Lizard, She-Rabbit, and L.W. There were enough riders here to add almost fifteen hundred acres to the spread Red Hawk and Lizard had already started together. Best of all, Walker was about to keep his end of the bargain with his old enemy, Chief Lizard. This would be the day that N.C. found out what had become of Paterson, the brother he had never known.

SEVENTY-SIX

WALKER GLANCED BACK, and it seemed the world's largest posse was on his tail. He could see hundreds of riders dotting the plains all the way to the eastern horizon and knew thousands more rode out of sight, hazing the air in their desperate quests for land and livelihood.

Then he looked ahead, and Lizard's tepee appeared around the bend in the river. He gave his mount another lash with the quirt and felt his heart pound. The hip had been bothering him a great deal when the rush had started, but suddenly he realized that he hardly felt it anymore. Red Hawk's house came into view across the river, surrounded by rail fences.

He was inside a mile when he noticed the five riders off to his right. "Who the hell is that?" he shouted, pointing.

They were coming fast from the open plains to the northwest, and it looked as though they might arrive first at the open parcels above Red Hawk's spread.

"Damn!" N.C. shouted. "They've got to be sooners. They must have hid out on the prairie overnight!"

There was nothing to do but urge more speed from the horses and hope the sooners could be pushed farther upstream. Red Hawk's riders thundered into the valley of the Washita and formed ranks behind the two leaders they had been ordered to follow. N.C. led Javier, Angelo, Dan, and Piggin' String splashing across to the south bank, while Caleb led Buster, Walker, and Savannah up the north bank. They had all been instructed on which parcels to stake.

Red Hawk was mounted in his front yard and directed the south bank party to their proper claims. Lizard was on his warhorse, guarding his allotment. It was still unimproved, but his tepee stood among the timbers along the bank.

Walker glanced at the sooners, still coming fast. He rode between the stakes that marked the corners of Lizard's allotment. His job was to stake the next parcel upstream, while Savannah, Caleb, and Buster would take the three beyond, claiming homesteads that they would soon deed to Red Hawk and Lizard.

The wind was making his shirtsleeves pop as he rumbled across Lizard's allotment. He glanced at the chief, who was holding a Springfield rifle across his thighs. It was his hunting rifle, for it had a feather dangling by a string from the barrel to help the hunter judge wind direction. Walker passed very near the Cheyenne chief, and their eyes met. Lizard's face never changed, but his hand rose, the fingers standing upright like four comrades.

Walker knew now that Lizard was going to keep his word. It was as good as done. He passed his reins to his right hand and pointed at Lizard with his left index finger, smiling. Quickly, though, thinking maybe a pointing finger might be interpreted as offensive, he opened his rough palm and waved briefly, turning his attention back to the sooners coming from his right.

Perfect! It seemed the sooners had mistaken Lizard's allotment for the first available claim, the ribbons tied to his corner stakes having faded in the winter sun. They would try to stake it first, Lizard would run them off, and they would move upstream, but too late. Buster, Caleb, and Savannah already had the lead on that trail.

Walker took no chances. As soon as he crossed the invisible line that ran between the survey stakes, he tightened his reins, gripped the saddle horn, and swung down, favoring his mending hip. He sank to his left knee as he drew the wooden stake from the belt where he had tucked it. His arm rose high and he stabbed the earth, ending his day's ride in glory. His eyes pulled south, and he saw his son and the others swarming along the south bank, Angelo dropping from the ranks to sink a stake in the parcel of land for which he had been made responsible.

My God, what a day! Twenty-five thousand, and he had beaten them all! What a ride! He was winning land for Indians, and it felt good. He stood to remount and walk the horse some around the homestead he would soon relinquish to an old enemy. The hip still wasn't bothering him, and Walker knew for the first time since the shoot-out in the Bighorns that it would heal entirely. He was strong again. He settled into the saddle and reined back east, toward Lizard's allotment.

The old Cheyenne warrior was waving his hunting rifle in the air; not as a threat, only as a proclamation. The muzzle pointed straight up. He was trying to tell the sooners to move on, that this parcel had been claimed by allotment. But they didn't understand, or didn't want to. The first of the riders in the land rush loped by on an exhausted horse, and the sooners grew impatient with Lizard. Walker began to trot, figuring he'd better explain to the sooners before they lost the chance they had cheated for and got mad about it.

A sooner got down from his horse, waved Lizard away with a stake. He bent to stick it in the ground, but Lizard moved in on the man, bumping him aside with the shoulder of the warhorse. The chief waved his rifle again, the tassels on his blackened buckskin shirt shaking like the feather on the end of his rifle barrel.

"Hey!" Walker shouted.

The sooner who had been butted aside tripped over his own feet, fell on his face. As he rolled onto his back, he drew a revolver from a holster.

"No!" Walker shouted, angling his spurs in as his eyes grew wide.

The shot tore up through Lizard's ribs, and he lowered the muzzle of the Springfield, drilling the man on the ground with a single bullet in the chest. Guns rattled among the other four sooners, and muzzles spit puffs of smoke as their fresh horses fanned out. Impact jerked Lizard backward on his Cheyenne saddle, but he held on with his heels and prodded the warhorse forward. He grabbed the forestock of the Springfield overhand and wielded it like a battle-ax, catching the nearest sooner on the bridge of the nose, taking a second bullet almost point blank. The sooner fell away, hitting the ground unconscious.

"No!" Walker shouted again. He drew a Colt and fired over the heads of the sooners.

Lizard's horse fell from a shot, and the old chief himself caught a third bullet, rolling backward across the hips of the warhorse as it fell. He tried to rise, but the sooners kept firing.

Walker was there, charging along the front lines of the sooners, growling bearlike as he knocked another man from his horse with the sharp edges of the Colt. The gunfire ceased, and Walker dropped from his saddle, shielding the wounded chief. "Lizard!" he yelled, pressing his hand over a chest wound, as if it would stop the blood.

The chief said something Walker had no way of understanding.

The big man shook his head. "Somebody!" he screamed back toward Red Hawk's house. He saw the Arapaho chief coming.

"He run at Bob!" one of the sooners said, lifting a half-conscious friend from the ground.

"Shut up!" Walker shouted, his eyes still darting over Lizard's riddled body.

The chief looked the big man in the eye, made some gesticulations with his hands. Walker mistook them for convulsions and tried to still the chief, but Lizard twisted his arms free and grabbed Walker's shirt, leaving a bloody handprint. He shook the white man, released him, paused, made the signs again with his hands.

"What?" Walker shrugged. "I don't know that talk."

Lizard made the signs again, paused. Made them again. Again, and again. Walker began to think beyond the panic and saw the pattern in the graceful motions. He heard Red Hawk splash into the river, but Lizard was quickly growing weak. He held his hands before him as if in irons, collected his wits, and nodded at the chief. "Show me. Show me again."

Lizard's hands trembled as he raised them to the sky. He held both palms open, facing each other as far apart as his body was wide. The hands went down toward his hips, then scooped inward and upward, as if gathering a dozen arrow shafts together. Then his left hand fell away like an actor making an exit, and his right hand alone made the final sign: the index finger raised in front of his face, the back toward Walker.

Walker tried to mimic the signs, but Lizard grimaced and shook his head. He made the scooping gesture again, blood running down his wrist. The index finger punctuated the message.

Walker watched every twist and detail this time. He repeated the sign exactly as he had seen Lizard make it.

The old Indian smiled, closed his eyes. He reached out and grabbed the index finger Walker was holding in front of his face. The grip was strong for a moment, but quickly loosened, and Walker lowered his hand to Lizard's chest so the bloody hand would not slip away but remain wrapped around his. He felt the handhold slack, heard the last breath.

"Let's git the hell out of here," said one of the sooners, helping to drape his dead partner across a saddle. "There's lots of Indians across the river."

Red Hawk arrived as the sooners left, and the Arapaho chief lit silently at Lizard's side, opposite Walker. He spoke, but it came out in Arapaho, and Walker couldn't understand.

The big man slipped his hand out from under Lizard's. "He taught me this sign." He repeated it carefully, fearful that he had already forgotten some nuance. "Do you know what it means?"

Red Hawk nodded, and spoke again in Arapaho.

"Don't you talk American?" Walker said.

Red Hawk saw the terror in Walker's eyes: reflections of horrors seen long ago, floating in the wide and shining orbs; reflections that lived unending dream lives, unable to escape that troubled soul.

"Yes, I speak your tongue, Heap Killer. That sign means Plenty Man. It is a name."

"A name? Whose name?"

"I would assume it is the name of the man to whom Lizard sold your son Paterson."

The hip suddenly began to hurt, and Walker rolled sideways onto the seat of his pants. "But what tribe? Who the hell is Plenty Man?"

Red Hawk reached for Walker's shoulder. "Don't worry. I'll help you find him. I remember Plenty Man, but it has been a long time since I even thought of him. He was a trader. He moved among the tribes. If he is still alive, we will find him.''

A pang shot through Walker's lower body and seemed to join all his old wounds together in a web of misery. He groaned and lay back on the ground. "Plenty Man," he said to himself, as if he might forget. "Plenty Man.'' He realized, with his eyes closed, that he was making the signs Lizard had taught him.

SEVENTY-SEVEN

'' 'JESUSITO EN CHIHUAHUA,' '' Javier said, before Buster could announce another tune.

"Oh, that's a good one," Caleb said. Standing in the doorway between the hallway and the parlor he caught the eye of Buster, who stood in the doorway between the hallway and the kitchen. "In A, one, two, three . . .''

Seventeen days had passed since the land rush. The Appaloosas had recuperated and were ready for the trip back to Holcomb Ranch. The deeds won by Caleb, Walker, N.C., Dan, String, Buster, Javier, Angelo, and Savannah had all been duly transferred to Red Hawk. Tents and shacks had been thrown up all along the Washita and out on the plains by new settlers. Some had already struck groundwater and built homemade windmills. Most had plowed garden patches, though it was awfully late to plant.

Lizard had been laid to rest on a scaffold of poles far out on the prairie to the west, out of sight of the new farms and shacks. The sooners who had killed him had turned themselves in at Fort Reno, knowing they would beat any charges brought. At least they had failed to claim land in the rush.

As Red Hawk's house was the finest in the area, he had invited all his new neighbors to a farewell feast and dance for the friends who had helped him build his spread. The furniture from the parlor, one bedroom, and the kitchen had been stacked on the front porch. The rugs had been rolled back and the floors made slick with paraffin shavings to facilitate dancing.

Now Caleb was standing in one doorway and Buster in another in order to spread the driving wail of the fiddles through as much of the house as possible. There was a guitarist for each room—N.C. in the front bedroom, Javier in the parlor, and Angelo in the kitchen.

The three rooms shook with dancers and reeked with smoke. Women squealed as their men whirled them to the old Mexican polka. Men laughed as whiskey made all their trials worthwhile. Red Hawk and Walker C. Kincheloe merely sat on the back steps at the end of the hallway, talking and looking at the stars, the noisy crowd behind them. Red Hawk smoked while Walker drank.

"*Jesusito en Chihuahua*" made Caleb grin, for his favorite part was coming. Gripping his bow with three fingers and anchoring his thumb on the corner of the fingerboard, he plucked the strings with the free index finger of his bow hand, rendering a series of notes that sounded like birds warbling. Oh, it was a joy to play this one with Javier, for here the vaquero always muted his guitar with the heel of his hand to let the softer string plucks of the fiddle come through.

The effect was such that the dancers in the parlor looked to see how the sound was made, and just then Caleb snatched the bow back between his thumb and forefinger and bowed the melody once more, Javier loosing a *grito* as he strummed all out on the guitar again. Caleb nodded at Buster, who took the lead for the dancers in the kitchen, and the drifter turned his ear to his own fiddle strings, for he was just bouncing the bow now, chording rhythm to back up Buster in the other doorway.

Savannah broke away from her partner in the parlor, leaving him stunned and disappointed, a farm boy barely over twenty. She waltzed by Caleb, skewering him with her tempting eyes as she stroked a hand across his shirt, just above his belt buckle. She moved into a shadow, then whirled in the light from the kitchen as her eyes flared for Caleb again. Her full skirt touched the walls on either side as she spun to the back door and threw herself over Walker's shoulder. It took her only a moment to persuade the big man to dance.

When she led Walker past Buster and into the kitchen, Walker smiled at Caleb and shrugged a sign of surrender. Hard Winter Holcomb turned back to the parlor. The windows were open and fires were burning outside, for the crowd had swollen beyond the capacity of the house. Dancers had staked wagon sheets to the ground and were making them hiss with boot leather.

Among the couples outside, a man moved alone. He caught Caleb's eye through the open window as he stepped awkwardly up onto the front porch. Was he drunk? No, just limping. His hat was pulled low, and he wore a woollen poncho. Is it that cool tonight, he wondered, or is the fiddling just keeping me warm?

The man passed out of sight behind the wall, and Caleb glanced at the other celebrants outside. No one wore so much as a jacket. Some even had sleeves rolled up.

When the man appeared in the doorway, the fiddler studied the beard ranging out from under the dusty black hat. One step, a limp. The eyes glinted, and Caleb looked away, his stomach suddenly turning to cold rock as surely as if he had just spotted a snake.

Buster was plucking the strings to *"Jesusito en Chihuahua"* and Caleb suddenly jumped into a double shuffle, rocking the bow rigidly across the E and A strings.

No one other than the musicians noticed, but Buster scowled over his shoulder at the blatant attempt to upstage his finger plucks. Then, quickly, he interpreted the expression of alarm and followed the toss of Caleb's head.

Hard Winter turned back to the parlor. The man in the poncho had worked his way to the opposite corner. Caleb wore no sidearm. Nor did Javier or Buster. Only Walker was armed, and he with his usual brace.

The brim of the dusty hat rose, and Frank Mayhall's eyes locked on to Caleb's. They stared, Caleb still sawing on the instrument. Javier had sensed something wrong and noticed the man in the poncho. Twisting into the kitchen, he continued to play and joined Buster in trying to catch Walker's eye, but Walker was fascinated by his nimble little partner.

Frank had his hands under the poncho, but Caleb stood firm. He hit a sour note but fiddled on, the whole house shaking in time to *"Jesusito en Chihuahua."* Frank could whip out his weapons now, but Frank knew Caleb could duck behind the dancers. Caleb could run, but Caleb knew that all hell would break loose. Still, Walker did not know what was up.

The dancers were getting tired, but the song began another round. N.C. looked from the bedroom with a twisted upper lip and saw Caleb's face before the fiddler moved from the doorway of the hall, taking two steps and standing now in the doorway to the kitchen. Frank Mayhall moved two steps with him, determined not to let the fiddler make a break for the back door.

Hard Winter risked a glance into the kitchen and caught Savannah's eye. She read his face, glanced at Javier and Buster, and knew trouble was near. She would alert Walker. Too late? When he looked back into the parlor, Caleb saw Frank Mayhall weaving among dancers, coming at him across the floor.

Escape was useless now, for a bullet would catch him in the back before he could cut through the crowded kitchen, and anybody might get shot. A sodbuster complained, bumped aside by an elbow under the poncho. The fiddle croaked horribly, and dancers began to feel danger, making way for Frank Mayhall to do his killing.

Caleb took the left-handed fiddle down from his right shoulder, passing it by second nature to the crook of his left arm, cradling it there like a babe, as the bow remained between the fingers of his left hand, making his right hand free. Guitars died, boots stomped out of time, and Hard Winter Holcomb looked desperately into the kitchen. He found the butt of a revolver waving, grabbed it, and felt Walker Colt Kincheloe fill the doorway beside him.

The poncho rose like a tent flap billowed by the wind, high enough to momentarily blind Frank Mayhall, revealing the two Smith and Wessons. Caleb found himself running head on as the dark holes in the muzzles came together to pierce him like snake eyes. He was six feet away by the time his thumb found the hammer, four feet when he pulled the trigger.

He felt himself spinning and didn't understand what had whirled him so. He dropped his fiddle and fell against Walker, listening to the screams of terror and the stomping feet. He looked up at Walker's face, but the big man's eyes were locked beyond him. He craned his neck and saw Frank Mayhall on his back, heaving, the poncho covering his face. The two Smith and Wessons were lying beside Frank's knees, beyond reach.

Pain struck like bee stings, and Caleb knew he had been hit in the left shoulder and through the left ribs. His stomach tightened and he tried to hand the borrowed revolver back to Walker.

Buster grabbed him, lowered him to the floor, and dragged him to a sitting position against the wall. The strong hands guided a knife up the side of Caleb's shirttail.

"Busted ribs. You ain't bleedin' bad, Caleb. You'll be all right, now, you hear?"

"What about my bow arm?" he asked, looking at the fiddle he had dropped.

Buster slit the sleeve. He lined up the bullet holes, moved Caleb's arm like a wing. "Missed the bone. You'll be playin' again in no time."

"Is Frank dead?"

"Dyin'," Walker said, pulling the poncho from Frank's face.

Caleb grabbed Buster's shoulder and pulled himself to one knee. Javier lifted him from the other side, and they helped him stand over Frank. Caleb was shocked to see consciousness in the dying man's eyes.

"You stood your ground, fiddler. You kilt me, you son of a bitch."

Caleb sank to his knees beside Mayhall. "You'd a-killed me."

"Goddamn right." He breathed in shallow gasps and his blood began to ooze down the cracks between the flooring. "It ain't over."

"It's over for you," Walker said.

Mayhall ignored him. "Joe's comin'. He's gonna git you, Holcomb."

"Joe's in the stockade at Fort McKinney, Wyoming."

"Won't be there forever. Sooner or later, he's comin' to git you, fiddler. I wouldn't light on one roost too long if I was you."

Caleb felt sick. "Where's Angelo?" he said. He felt his son put a hand on his shoulder. "Is everybody all right?"

"Yes, sir. Papa, everybody is fine."

"Take me outside, boys. I want to go outside."

SEVENTY-EIGHT

THE MIST OF long ago, the haze of lost time, the fog of far-gone days: it was the earth upon which the dreamer crouched, the air he breathed all sticky and cold, the source of all that moved and spoke and lived in this unending nightmare.

The boy heard the old man scream again, very near now. A turkey gobbler in the pecan bottoms answered the scream as though it were a challenge from a rival. The boy had slipped from his horse, tied his reins to a mesquite switch, and slipped among the branches that materialized from the fog ahead. He heard laughter and fell to his stomach, crawling under the bright green leaves of a spring sumac.

This was the worst part of the dream, for here all the fear of the dreamer passed into the boy, so small, so young, so full of his own fears. He lay paralyzed under the sumac. Knowing, yet not knowing, what would happen next. He could not breathe. He could not move. He could not scream or cry or wake himself from this horror.

The good old man emerged from a swirl of fog, his arms all trussed up behind him. His gait was awkward, and every step made his whole body writhe with pain. He stopped. A lance came from the mist and poked the old man in the back, making him scream aloud in anguish. The Comanche warrior who followed the lance from the haze laughed and made the poor old man stumble forward.

"Now holler!" the warrior said. "Holler boy come!"

The old man grimaced and looked at the ground. Slowly, dreamlike, he began to shake his head. "Hell, no."

The spear pierced him again, and the old man stumbled to his knees as his scream rattled from his throat in a blast of dark smoke. A second warrior rode over him, leaned from the saddle, and lifted him by the hair to his feet. Then a third warrior appeared. And a fourth—a very young warrior who pitied the old man and wept for him.

"Walk!" the brave with the lance ordered. He stabbed the old man again, and the scream made the young warrior flinch and cover his ears as tears of pity fell from his eyes. The three older braves noticed and laughed at the younger one, ridiculing him.

They all came nearer now, and the dreamer trembled with such terror that the sumac shook around him and he feared they would see him.

"Holler boy come!"

The old man stopped and whirled. He gathered his strength and spat a mouthful of blood onto the warrior with the lance. "Run, boy!" he screamed. "Run away home, boy!"

The young brave covered his ears as the lance rose high and came swiftly down. And the dreamer—who had lain here evermore—fought violently inside the body of the boy, yearning to be free of this nightmare. He was the prisoner of this memory locked in haze, a slave to the eyes of the boy who watched in horror as the good old man was killed and torn apart piece by piece in a rain of blood. And he kicked and squirmed and grunted his muffled screams to be free until a hand reached through the sumac and pulled him away.

SEVENTY-NINE

KATE LLEWELLYN FOUGHT off the flailing fists of Walker C. Kincheloe as he woke.

"Walker! It's Kate! It's just me, don't fight!"

Walker drew in a huge gasp of air and felt his clothes sticking cold to him as he glanced around the dim cabin. She had heard him, he gathered, and come across the cabin to wake him; to save him. His heart hurt from beating so, and his shame consumed him. Yet she was warm and strong, and he was glad she had woken him.

"It's that dream, ain't it? What is it, Walker? What haunts you so in your sleep?"

He grabbed her upper arm, so firm and strong above his pallet on the floor. "Are you all right? I didn't mean to hit you, Kate. You shouldn't wake me like that."

"You were screamin', Walker. I can't listen to you suffer like that. What is it? What is that dream?"

He let the tension go and fell back on his blankets. "It was a long time ago, Kate. It don't matter no more. I can't change it."

"Can't change what? I never asked you much, Walker. You know that. But you've got to tell me what haunts you so. You can't just suffer it alone."

He shook his head. "I was just a boy. I was just ten years old."

"In Texas?"

"Yes."

She took his broad jaw between her hands. "What happened?"

"Indians."

"Comanches?"

He nodded and knew she understood, for her hands were stroking his waves of hair back from his sweaty face. "I used to hunt cows with this old man up the Blanco. About six miles up the river from our place." He stopped. He shouldn't tell her. Kate had her own nightmares to live with. But the fingers of one hand were pulling through his hair while those of the other rested upon his barreled chest. He wanted so badly to tell her.

"And? Tell me, Walker."

"He was gonna take me cow huntin' one day. He was a good old man. He'd always cut me in on the take from the hides we got off of 'em. They were just wild cattle then. No market for the meat. We'd just kill 'em for hides and tallow."

She waited, then asked: "What was his name?"

"His name was Blaylock. Everybody called him Uncle Bob. Anyway . . ." He thought he would dread this, but it wasn't like the dream. He could breathe here, keep his wits about him. He could move, and speak, and control his fear.

"Some Comanches had raided around San Antone with the light of the moon and was on their way back north. Four of 'em come acrost Uncle Bob. He was on his horse, waitin' for me to meet him down in the pecan bottoms. He made a run for the cabin, and I heard him shootin'. I looked, and I seen 'em chouse him a piece down the trail, then they all rode behind the trees.

"I was just ten years old. I didn't know what to do. I didn't have no gun. I tore down off the bluff, into the bottoms, scared as hell, but thinkin' I might do somethin'. Maybe help the old man swim the Blanco and git away." He put his hands over his ears and closed his eyes. Only Kate's palms pressing against him kept him from busting out in boyish tears.

"What?" she said. "What did you hear?"

He felt his jaw trembling as he moved it to speak. "I heard poor old Uncle Bob scream bloody murder. The damnedest thing, I'll never forget. The turkeys was struttin', and when the old man screamed, one of 'em gobbled at him. And every time he'd scream, that old gobbler would answer.''

"That was God sharin' his pain," Kate said. "Go on. Tell me what you did, just a little boy and all.''

"I got close and jumped off my horse. I crawled up closer. Don't know what I thought I'd do. I wished I'd never gone. I wished I'd run for home.'' He held his breath long enough to push aside the boyish emotions. "They had cut the bottoms of his feet off, Kate. Peeled all the hide and meat off down to the bones, and they was makin' him walk. If he didn't walk, they'd stab a lance into him.''

Kate sighed and held the big man's hands tight in hers. "You couldn't do nothin'. You had to lay low, else they'd see you.''

"One of 'em spoke a little American. He told Uncle Bob to holler for me. I guess they'd seen us ridin' together before and figured I was around. But Uncle Bob wouldn't do it, and they kept makin' him walk till finally he yelled for me to run and then spit on the brave with the lance.

"I seen 'em kill Uncle Bob. But before he was dead, they was cuttin' him to pieces. Then they rode off with his scalp.''

"He must have loved you, Walker.''

"I did a bad thing that day.''

"No you didn't, Walker. You was just a boy.''

"No, it was after. See, one of the braves wasn't much older than me. On his first raid, I reckon. All the time the others were torturin' Uncle Bob, this young brave was cryin'. He even begged 'em to stop once't, but they made fun of him.

"Now, after they kilt Uncle Bob Blaylock, I got mad. Uncle Bob kept an old Walker Colt pistol hid out in the shed. I fetched it. It had rained the night before, and the river was up. There was only one place to ford without swimmin', and that's where I headed, hopin' I'd catch them Indians. They'd taken all of Uncle Bob's horses from the corrals, and I rode my pony hard, way around 'em to git to the ford. I was layin' for 'em when they got there.

"I kilt 'em all, Kate. I had six shots, and I made 'em all tell. That old Walker never missed fire. The last one left livin' was the young one. I didn't have no call to kill him. He didn't even have a weapon. It was meanness.''

Kate shushed him. "You ain't mean at heart, Walker. The Good Lord judges you by your heart, not your actions taken in anger.''

He lay still, but there was more. "Kate.''

"What, honey?''

"Sometimes the dream changes things up. Sometimes it ain't the old man they're torturin'. Sometimes it's me, full growed. I mean, I'm layin' up under the sumac, a ten-year-old boy, and I'm watchin' 'em poke me, full growed, with that spear, and I just wish they'd go ahead and kill me." Walker C. Kincheloe bit his lower lip so hard that it hurt. "And sometimes," he said, trying to swallow a sob, "sometimes it ain't me or the old man."

"Who is it, Walker?"

"It's Paterson." He burst into sobs and tried to turn away, but Kate pulled him back and pressed her face against his. "It's Paterson, and I can't help him." He felt her warmth across his chest as it heaved and shuddered. He put his arms around her and held her.

At long last, he patted her back, feeling awkward now. "The Lord's punishin' me, Kate. Once 't was the day I thought Indians didn't have no god. Now, Red Hawk, this Arapaho—he says white men and Indians have got the same god. Well, I believe he's right. And you know what else? I believe the Lord favors the red man."

She rested an elbow on his chest. "The Lord don't favor no race of man above any other," she said, almost scolding. "Anyhow, what about this Plenty Man you told me about? You should take hope."

"I ran dry on hope years ago."

"Let me ask you somethin'," she said. "Did you ever once think in that thick head of yours that maybe you ain't the only one lookin'?"

"What do you mean?"

"Well, what about Paterson? Don't you think he's wonderin' about you? Worryin'? Don't you think he'd rather know you're hopeful, instead of givin' up? Don't you think he's lookin' for you, too?"

"You mean, over the divide?"

"Maybe. Maybe right here on God's green earth."

They lay in silence as the night sounds chirped and fluttered outside. The cabin smelled good—like coffee, wood smoke, and coal oil. And Kate smelled like lilac. They lay in silence a long, long time.

Kate kissed him on the cheek and snuggled closer to his side, her skin warm through her nightgown. His hide tingled, and he turned his face toward her, slowly, as though he was afraid he'd frighten her off. His hand fell upon her waist, and when she moved he felt the lean curve of her hip.

"Do you always sleep in your clothes?" she asked.

Her breath was warm on his face. "Kate," he said. His hands were shaking, and warmth began to charge his flesh in a bracing wave.

"Hush."

She pressed her lips on his, more tenderly than any touch he had ever known.

"Don't you know how long I've waited?" she said. "Don't you know how much I've wanted you all these years?"

"But you always said no man—"

"You ain't just any man, Walker. You're God's own gift to me."

He closed his eyes and let her strength empower him. Somewhere a haze cleared, a fog lifted, a cloud exploded silently in a flash of new hope. Somewhere, a boy ran laughing.

EIGHTY

C ALEB HELD A personal tradition that had become something of a legend in Monument Park. And now that Holcomb Ranch entertained guests from abroad, the legend had reached even beyond the park—far beyond.

Caleb's brother Pete was buried on a hill at the foot of the Rampart Range, overlooking the ranch from the west. Every spring, as he returned from his wanderings, it was Caleb's tradition to appear on the hill by the grave of his brother. He would camp there, his fire like a lighthouse, seen by every settler in Monument Park and every dude on Holcomb Ranch.

"Anyway, I'm healed up all right," he told Pete the night he returned from Indian Territory. "Don't know why Frank pulled both shots to his right, unless my bullet twisted him a little. The other boys brought the horses back from Red Hawk's place while I laid up there another couple of weeks. N.C. and Rabbit decided to sell out their claims to Red Hawk and come on back here with us."

He stirred the fire with a stick, then threw the stick into the new flames. "Walker drifted on back north. Said he wanted to visit Kate Llewellyn. Shame you never met her, Pete. She's a hell of a fine woman. Walker figured he'd meet Red Hawk in the Sioux country and ask around about Plenty Man. He was known among them, and the Northern Cheyenne and Arapaho, and the Crows. They said he traded all over with the tribes. I never heard of him." Slipping a harmonica from his pocket, he blew a few notes of nothing in particular.

"Had me a talk with Savannah before she left east. She wanted to come out here for the spring, but said she's in trouble with her folks. Come to find out, when Hiram quit the Wyoming Stock Growers Association, the

Cheyenne Club started spreadin' scandals about Savannah in the society columns back east. Well, they was mostly true, but it read like scandal. She said my name even got printed in Boston and Philadelphia!'' He laughed, thrusting his chin proudly at his brother's grave marker.

"I told her when she left that before she came back she had to tell me whether or not she was gonna marry me. Hell, I asked her seven months ago, and she's been stallin' me. Her family cut her off on account of the scandal, but I told her I didn't care if she was dirt poor. I'll sure marry her, if she'll say yes.''

He lay back on his bedroll and looked at the stars. "I got somethin' on my mind, Pete. Say Savannah don't want to marry me. I almost hope she don't. I know this may not be right, seein' as how Amelia was yours, first . . . I think I'm in love with her, Pete. I hope you don't hate my guts. I never would've let it happen if I could stop it. To tell you the truth, I think I fell for her the first time I seen her. You remember? I was seventeen when Matthew brought her home. I never told nobody and never even admitted it to myself, but it like to have kilt me when you two got married.''

He recited a line that had come to him somewhere out there: " 'We've seen the gals we love all up an marry other fellers; and we're damn fine story-tellers, but we haven't got no wives. So we've rolled up all the rugs, and we've tuned up that old fiddle; and we've waltzed into the middle of the dance floor and our lives.' ''

He sat in silence some time, thinking about that.

"I hope you don't hate me, Pete. I ain't even gonna ask you if I can marry her, because I know you can't answer. If Savannah don't come through, I'll have a mind to ask her.'' He listened to a coyote howl miles away.

"Hell, it probably don't matter, anyhow. Think she'd have me?'' He sat in silence a long time. "My God, what if Savannah says yes? Then I'll never know whether Amelia would have had me or not.'' He laughed. "I don't guess either one of 'em'll take me, if they know what's good for 'em!''

Caleb stood and stretched, realizing that he was talking more to himself than Pete now. He could see the lights on in the inn Buster had moved to the ranch. It had been hailed as an engineering marvel, Buster moving a building that large. He had used the running gears of six freight wagons bolted together with timbers, and ten teams of mules. It had taken two days to move the three miles from the sagging ruins of Holcomb, Colorado.

He could hear Buster's fiddle down there now, playing for the dudes from back east. Caleb smiled. He knew they were looking up at him from the gallery, talking about the sweet strange sadness of a drifter who would camp by the grave of his brother every year. He liked being a dude wrangler. He pretended not to like it, but they treated him with such awe.

He turned back to Pete. "Did you ever think it would turn out like this?" he said.

A form rose from behind the gravestone. Hat, face, shoulders. Gun metal! "Can't say that I did."

Caleb backpedaled a few steps in alarm. He had left his Winchester in the saddle scabbard and his gun belt draped across the saddle. "I'm unarmed, Joe."

"I know you are. I've been waitin' to catch you unarmed. I knew you'd camp up here when you came back home. You always do. That's a good way to get killed, Caleb, bein' predictable like that."

The fiddler's hands were in the air. "Frank didn't give me no choice in the territory. I had to defend myself."

"I know. Settle down, Caleb. I didn't come here to kill you."

Caleb's heart pounded so hard it hurt the wound Frank Mayhall had made through his ribs. "I thought you were in jail in Wyoming."

"You should have kept a closer eye on that mess. They up and let us all out. Those rich men have lots of pull."

"They didn't hold you for murderin' my father? What about that land inspector, and that doctor down in Old Town?"

Joe scoffed. "I wasn't usin' my real name. In Wyoming I went by Joe Hall. They didn't know I was wanted anywhere else." He came around the gravestone and got between Caleb and his guns.

"What do you want, if you didn't come here to kill me?"

"I want you to shut up and listen, or I might change my mind and kill you anyway."

Caleb felt a chill waft down from the high country. "I'm listenin'."

"I never killed nobody in my life, except for that doctor in Old Town, and he was fixin' to shoot me. In them scrapes you and me had, I always shot wide, or high, or low. I know I'm just as guilty as Frank and Terrence and Edgar because I went along with 'em, but I never tried to kill nobody. I've seen three brothers die on account of a quarter section of land your old man stole from us, and I ain't about to join 'em if you're willin' to make a deal."

Caleb heard Buster strike up "Dry and Dusty" down in the inn. He thought about arguing whether his father had indeed stolen that quarter section, but decided against it. "What kind of deal?"

"One that keeps you and me from ever seein' each other's face again."

"How's that?"

"I'm movin' west of the Great Divide. I aim to die west of it and never cast my shadow this side of the Rockies again. Long as you stay east of the Great Divide, we'll be shed of each other.''

Caleb thought of all the places he wanted to see across the divide. Then he thought of this burden of death lifting. "What about your kin in Georgia? How do I know they won't come after me?''

Joe stood a long time, then shook his head. "I'm the last one, Caleb. My brothers' wives have moved back to Georgia and married into other families. My nephews have taken names of their stepfathers to protect theirselves. All the Mayhall men are dead. The war and feudin' has killed 'em all. I'm the only one left.''

A peal of laughter rang from the guest ranch below.

Caleb knew his place was down there. "I'll stay east of the divide.''

"If I was to see you over there, I'd have to assume you was comin' to kill me.''

"I'll stay this side of the divide, Joe. Let's put it to rest.''

Joe holstered his revolver. "Shake,'' he said.

He stepped forward, met Caleb halfway. Their hands clasped firmly and shook. Their eyes met. They did not blink.

Joe stepped back and looked down on the lights dotting Monument Park. "I used to live down there,'' he said, pointing. "Never did like it here all that much.'' He backed away and disappeared in the dark.

Caleb waited a few seconds, then spoke in a clear, strong voice, as if addressing a roomful of dudes: "Good luck, Joe.''

EIGHTY-ONE

ALL AT ONCE, everybody wanted to fiddle.

Javier, having gone almost broke in New Mexico, had sold what was left of his Penasco River spread and moved to Holcomb Ranch with Marisol and her children by Caleb, Marta and Elena. Angelo, of course, was already residing there. Now that they had become dude wranglers with Caleb, Javier and Angelo both wanted to fiddle.

N.C. had also grown tired of having his guitar upstaged and wanted to fiddle.

Piggin' String McCoy didn't give a damn for fiddling, but his wife, Tess, figured she could learn some, and sing, as well, when she wasn't cooking or doing laundry or cleaning the big inn.

Now Dan Brooks was sawing on a fiddle, too, though he was so shy about it that he would only practice about two miles away from the ranch house.

Caleb had bought a three-quarter-sized fiddle from the headmaster of a traveling singing school and had given it to his nephew, Pete, whom he declared was going to be the best fiddler in Colorado one day.

Buster had started a school for fiddlers.

"Play that part up close to the frog," he'd tell his star pupil, Tess McCoy, as she practiced "Devil's Dream."

"What's the frog?"

"The part of the bow right next to the nut."

"What's the nut?"

"The part you got aholt of, girl!"

"Well, I don't know what you call it!"

Little Pete Holcomb and Dan Brooks took lessons together, and Buster would make them hold the bow at the wrong end to practice.

"What in blazes for?" Dan would ask.

"Because that nut is heavy out there on the end, and it will help you stroke just right. Then, when you turn it around after a while, your bow will feel so light you'd swear you could outfiddle Caleb."

When Javier practiced "Leather Britches," Buster would stop him and say, "Now, when you fiddle these-here breakdowns, try puttin' your thumb on the bottom of the nut, Javier. Gives you more range of motion."

And when Angelo would rush through "The Nightingale," Buster would caution him: "Here, now, boy, slow down. Take longer strokes on your waltzes. You play your waltzes like a breakdown."

"I don't like waltzes," Angelo would complain.

"Well, girls likes 'em. Don't you like girls?"

When Dan Brooks developed the bad habit of resting the fiddle neck on the heel of his hand, limiting his reach with his fingers, Buster glued a sharp tack to the bottom of the neck, so it would poke Dan's hand if he didn't correct the habit.

He made Little Pete watch himself in the mirror, to make sure his bow was tracking straight across the strings.

When Tess wanted to improve her double shuffle for "Gray Eagle," Buster borrowed tobacco and rolling papers from Dan Brooks and pulled the shades in the parlor of his house. Gloria came in from Amelia's mansion about that time.

"Fiddlin' in the dark!" she yelled.

"Oh hush, woman!" Buster ordered. "Set yourself down and watch. You might learn somethin'. Tess, go on and roll yourself a cigarette."

"I don't smoke!" she said. She was plenty scared of Gloria.

"I don't want you to smoke it. Just roll it."

With the cigarette lit, Buster made Tess stand in front of the mirror with the smoke between the fingers of her bow hand. "Now, go on and double shuffle. Rock that bow acrost them strings. When you see that coal make a curve like a letter C, you know you're rockin' the bow just right."

"I don't want you in the dark with that white gal no more," Gloria said after Tess left.

"Woman, I'm just givin' fiddle lessons."

"You don't give Dan Brooks no lessons in the dark."

"Dan Brooks can't double shuffle."

"That's what I mean!" she said, making no sense at all to Buster.

One day he found Caleb stacking sacks of feed in the barn. "I need you to teach my fiddle lesson for me today so I can go to Colorado Springs, pick up a new seed drill."

"Hell, Buster, you've forgot more than I know about fiddlin'." His shoulder wound from the gunfight with Frank Mayhall had healed well and hadn't affected his playing, but he couldn't see himself teaching.

Buster grabbed a sack from the buckboard and carried it into the feed room. "Shoot, you're the best fiddler on the ranch. Best fiddler in the state, more than likely."

Caleb stopped and stared. There had been a time, years ago, when he had thought he would never play as well as Buster. His mind was still locked into that way of thinking, yet here Buster was calling him the best, and Buster did not engage in false flattery. "Who do you want me to teach?"

"I've put Angelo and Little Pete together. They done left Dan Brooks behind."

"What'll I teach 'em?"

" 'Don't Let the Deal Go Down.' "

A few days later, Buster—giving Tess her lessons on the front porch of the Cincinnati house now—hollered at Caleb as he rode out with N.C. to bring some horses up. "Tess wants you to show her how to get vibrato out of an open string."

Caleb trotted up to the fence in front of the house. "Why don't you show her?"

"I ain't figured out how you do it."

Caleb climbed through the fence and pulled his gloves off. "Well, my left-handed fiddle's in the house, but . . . There's two ways."

"All right," Tess said, eager to learn.

"One way is to sharp that open string. Stretch it just the other side of the fiddle nut while you're bowin' it."

Tess tried, and rendered a meager vibrato. "Won't that stretch the string out of tune?" she asked.

He looked at Buster and smiled. "A fiddle's built to go out of tune, anyway. That's what Buster always said. It can't help itself."

Buster laughed. "There's half a chance you'll stretch it *in* tune!"

"What's the other way?" Tess asked.

"Bow the open A string. Now, finger an octave above on the E string and wobble that finger, but don't bow the E string."

Tess tried, heard the vibrato somehow coming from the open string. "How does that work?"

"It throws its voice," he said. "Them strings are close together. It's like when you git close to somebody who knows how to play; pretty soon you know how to play, too, even if you can't explain how you learned."

Recitals were held before the dudes in the dining room of the inn. As a dude ranch, the Holcomb spread operated all spring, summer, and fall now, and many of the dudes were return customers. Little Pete was their favorite at the fiddle recitals, owing to his youth, but Tess was obviously the best fiddler among the students. Javier, Angelo, and N.C., with their musical backgrounds in guitar, made steady progress. Dan Brooks was far too bashful to play in any recital.

It was late June when Walker C. Kincheloe and Kate Llewellyn arrived to stay at the ranch for a spell. The surprise arrival called for a huge celebration. There was something different about them. They would walk arm in arm at night and were together almost all the time. N.C. grinned every time he saw them, and Amelia would clasp her hands and sigh.

One afternoon Caleb was putting new strings on a mandolin, sitting on the front porch of his father's cabin, where he stayed now. He saw Walker go from the inn to the barn, saddle a horse, and ride to the old log cabin.

"Fiddler, I wanted you to be the first to know, after N.C." He lowered himself from the saddle and spread a smile across his face. "Me and Kate is gonna drive through the rest of life in double harness."

Caleb tried to act surprised. "When are you gonna call the preacher?"

The laughter bounced off the far mountain slopes. "Hell, we already did, up in Denver. This here's our honeymoon!"

Caleb turned a tuning key and stretched the new string. "You two wasn't foolin' nobody, gettin' rooms next door in the inn like that. Where are you plannin' to live?''

"We're gonna sell Kate's place so we can buy my canyon under the Bighorns.''

"Well, it's high time you settled down.''

"You and me both, fiddler.'' He got up, mounted his horse. "Careful you don't stay too long at the dance.''

Caleb didn't finish stringing the mandolin just then. He sat and watched Walker ride back to the barn, unsaddle his horse, and meet Kate on the steps of the inn. Caleb went into the cabin, found a pencil, scrounged a scrap of paper from a fiddle case, and wrote across the top of it in big letters:

TOO LONG AT THE DANCE.

That night he carried his instruments to the inn and tuned up with the rest of the players. By previous arrangement, this was to be Dan Brooks's night to get over his stage fright, though Dan didn't know it.

It started when the dudes came in for the show, and Amelia seated Dan at the edge of the crowd. There were twenty-some-odd guests from back east, in addition to all the regular residents of Holcomb Ranch and several young members of Monument Park homestead families who had come to hear some music and do some dancing. Among the Easterners was Albert Farnham, the hotelier, a major investor in the Holcomb Guest Ranch venture.

The show started, as always, with a fiddle duel between Caleb and Buster, as they traded verses to "Give the Fiddler a Dram" and "The Unfortunate Pup." Tess McCoy kept time on a washtub bass she had built, and played to perfection. Javier added the strum of a guitar and N.C. chorded a mandolin, rather tentatively, for he was still learning it.

Buster could hold his own with the fiddle, of course, but it was Caleb who fascinated the audience as he came down from the stage, stood on chairs, fiddled all around the room. He particularly liked to get between Albert and Amelia, for the former tended to follow the latter around like a puppy.

The pace changed as Caleb sang "I'd Like To Be in Texas for the Roundup in the Spring'':

I've seen 'em stampede o'er the hills till you'd think they'd never stop
I've seen 'em run for miles and miles until their leaders dropped

I was the foreman of a cow ranch, the calling of a king
Oh, I'd like to be in Texas for the roundup in the spring

Dan was given another drink as Tess stepped forward next, to sing a tune her mother had taught her called the "The Tee-Roo Song," in which the devil stole a farmer's wife but brought her back after she "swept out hell and burned up the broom."

Then it was on to Caleb's rendition of "The Zebra Dun," and more fiddling with "Dusty Miller," which Caleb would play with the fiddle on his hip and the bow behind his back.

Finally Caleb nodded at Walker and Piggin' String to take their positions. He cleared his throat when he saw Albert Farnham whispering something in Amelia's ear. "Folks," the fiddler announced, "we're fixin' to hear a tune from a guest fiddle player."

Tess Wiley stepped onto the stage with her fiddle and winked at her husband, who was poised behind Dan Brooks.

"This-here fiddler has been practicin' a tune for you called 'Soldier's Joy,' and his name is Dan Brooks!"

Walker and String grabbed Dan one to each arm and dragged him halfway to the stage before he knew what was going on. They escorted him into place, Tess jammed the fiddle under his chin, and Caleb started the song. As String and Walker were guarding Dan on each side against escape, he had no recourse but to play. It was less embarrassing than standing there like an idiot, and he was just drunk enough and just surprised enough to be immune from his usual nervous rigors.

His fingers fumbled at first, but Caleb had started the tune with an agreeable cadence and was playing along with Dan to lead him. The longer he played, the more naturally his digits seemed to fall to their places. He *had* practiced this tune. Caleb backed away, let his fiddle fade, and Dan Brooks played the last round himself, his toe tapping unconsciously, his neck craned and eyes locked on the fingerboard, apart from the realities that existed outside of "Soldier's Joy."

He did not want to get off the stage then, and Caleb had to call Walker and String back up to escort Dan away. The applause made Dan beam; men reached for his hand and ladies shouted "Bravo!"

"Well, folks," Caleb said, sweeping his hat and fanning the fiddle Dan had played. "I know y'all want to dance some." He paused to let the guests applaud. "We're gonna pull the chairs back and let y'all scoot a little boot leather after one more little ol' song."

Caleb turned to the musicians behind him as he put his fiddle on a table and lifted his hat to pass the guitar strap over his head. He looked at Tess, one foot poised on her washtub bass; N.C. with an ear turned, the mandolin cradled, anxious to hear the name of the next number; Javier, resting his arms on top of his stout little Mexican guitar; and good old Buster, smiling, wrinkles fanning out from the corners of his eyes.

"Boys," he said, trusting Tess would feel obliged to include herself, "y'all ain't heard this one. Listen to a verse once through and jump in when I h'ist my boot heel at you. It's got five chords in it."

"What key?" N.C. asked.

"D." He turned quickly back to the audience. "The title for this song is 'Too Long at the Dance,' which was the idea of Walker C. Kincheloe, who sits out yonder now with the new Mrs. Walker C. Kincheloe—here on their honeymoon."

Walker stood, worked the crowd. Kate blushed.

Caleb began strumming the instrument as the applause rose and fell for Mr. and Mrs. Kincheloe. He waited, letting the eyes come back around to him. Amelia was the first to gaze his way, and she smiled. He smiled back. Little Pete was in front of her, and it made Caleb's heart leap when Albert Farnham put a hand on Little Pete's shoulder and Little Pete brushed it promptly away.

He waited. The cadence in the single D chord was growing monotonous, but Walker was still shaking some dude's hand. He waited. Finally, he had them. Walker hugged Kate around the shoulders and nodded to Hard Winter Holcomb, smiling. The hush he longed for in a room fell all about him; the look of expectation filled the eyes. And he began.

EIGHTY-TWO

We rode the ranges way back when
the ranges had no fences
So we took leave of our senses,
and we strung 'em all around
Where once we used to parley
with the Indians in their lodges
Now the farmer's milch cow dodges
as his harrow turns the ground
We kilt off all the buffalo

and elk and deer and pronghorns
And we stocked so many longhorns
now the tall grass no more stirs
But we're too proud to think about
our saddles growin' dusty
And our rowels a-growin' rusty,
should we hang up our old spurs

We've been too long in the saddle
Too long with the rattle
of the long horns on the cattle
And we've squandered our last chance
We came to shake a leg,
but now it's time to pay the fiddler
The boys have stayed too long at the dance

Tess McCoy sensed the coming of the second verse. She saw Caleb signal with the heel of his boot and walked the washtub bass up from the A chord to the D, pouring a platform for N.C. to build on with the sharp, muted brushes of his thumbnail across the mandolin strings. Javier put a Mexican flare on the same guitar chords Caleb played, finding his higher on the neck, making the overall tone richer, broader.

Buster was biding his time.

Well, we never had much schoolin',
but we learned the things we should've
And we learned some we could've
done without knowin' at all
Now we don't draw no time
a-workin' jobs we hadn't rather
We're all waitin' for the gather,
gittin' scarcer now each fall
But I guess we've had some fun,
prob'ly more than other fellers,
And I know we've heard the bellers
of the cows, some in our sleep
And I guess we've seen some sights,
and I swear we've had some chuckles
And we've busted saddle buckles
shippin' cows too poor to keep

Here, Buster made his entrance in the second chorus, but with such respect for the vocalist that never a note slipped out from under his bow to step on a lyric. And when the song said "time to pay the fiddler," he made the instrument under his chin laugh so quick that Caleb thought it had taken on a life of its own.

> *We've been too long in the saddle*
> *Too long with the rattle*
> *of the long horns on the cattle*
> *And we've squandered our last chance*
> *We came to shake a leg,*
> *but now it's time to pay the fiddler*
> *The boys have stayed too long at the dance*

And after the chorus, Caleb bowed to Buster, and Buster played a lead, just half a verse long, and made it pour so pure and flawless from the cat-gut that the other musicians might well have faded beyond the reach of a spotlight.

And then the lead faded, and the cadence hung for an extra measure or two, as if Caleb wanted the tones of the fiddle to echo away before he sang the last verse. Buster was discreetly bouncing the bow in a meter that opposed yet complemented every other instrument onstage, and Caleb suddenly got the idea that he should just quit playing and let his friends carry him; let them lay a path of sweet harmony and rhythm down which he might sing ever clearer, freer, ever stronger upon their shoulders.

He spread his arms and circled his wrist as if whirling a lariat to let the musicians know they should maintain the beat, and when he felt the path was lain, he sang:

> *Well, we've seen the gals we love*
> *all up and marry other fellers*
> *And we're damn fine story-tellers,*
> *but we haven't got no wives*
> *So we've rolled up all the rugs,*
> *and we've tuned up that old fiddle*
> *And we've waltzed into the middle*
> *of the dance floor and our lives*
> *But we've had our finer hours,*
> *and you can see it in our faces*
> *And we've all earned our places*
> *through the blizzard and stampede*

And we cannot mend our ways,
'cause we're all too damn bull-headed
But there's common ground we've treaded
and on one thing we're agreed:

We've been too long in the saddle
Too long with the rattle
of the long horns on the cattle
And we've squandered our last chance
We came to shake a leg,
but now it's time to pay the fiddler
The boys have stayed too long at the dance

Now the song started a mill, like a herd of swimming cattle, doubling back with such suddenness that it surprised even the musicians. Walker C. Kincheloe had picked up the words and was standing among the dudes, belting the chorus back toward the stage with all the gravel and grit of his hard years grinding in his throat.

So Caleb used his hands like a conductor to rouse the rest of the audience into song, and it grew. A church-trained lady or two and a vocally skilled tenderfoot found harmony lines. Caleb felt the flesh crawl behind his ears, down his neck and shoulders, and into his gracefully sweeping fingers. He turned his palms backward and muted the musicians by degree—lower, slighter, softer—until only voices rang in the room.

And they blended into one singer of many notes and timbres. Some closed their eyes without thinking to do so, letting the ocean of human music carry them away. The words became meaningless, nonsensical. Arms were clasping about shoulders out there, and cowpunchers swayed with bookkeepers.

Caleb Hard Winter Holcomb felt his power—a vast benevolent reign over loved ones and strangers. It was dangerous, seductive. He had felt twinges of it before, in parlors and camps, bunkhouses and road ranches. But never like this. Here he wielded a spell, wove a snare. But he had grown wise, and knew it was well to release his subjects before they knew he had charmed them so. He wasn't even singing anymore. Just listening.

Another turn about the chorus, and he held up three fingers . . .

The boys have stayed too long at the dance.

Then two fingers . . .

The boys have stayed too long at the dance.

Now one, and he slowed the gait . . .

The boys have stayed too long at the dance . . .

EIGHTY-THREE

He nudged the door aside with his boot and shuffled in with his three instruments. It was dark, but he knew the layout in the cabin. Since he was a boy, it had always been spacious and sparsely furnished. Not much to run into or trip over.

He might just as easily have gone to bed, but tunes yet rang in his head. It was not easy to put an instrument aside after a night such as this, when the audience hung on every note and the dancers begged for more.

He struck a match, touched flame to the wick, and turned to hang the lantern on the peg. His lungs sucked in a gasp, and he made out the form of a man sitting on the fireplace hearth.

"I didn't mean to startle you," the man said. He was old, small, dressed in fine trousers and matching vest with a starched shirt and a boiled collar. His bowler perched on his knee.

"Sir, are you lost?" Caleb drawled. "This here is my house." He didn't like getting spooked in his own cabin.

It wasn't the face of an ordinary dude that smiled. It was creased deep and darkened, perhaps by sun, or perhaps by bloodline. "Not lost, but gone before."

"Sir?"

"I came to thank you for the music this evening."

Caleb shifted his eyes. "Were you in the crowd? I don't remember you."

"It's my way to blend in."

He nodded. "Well, thanks for stoppin' by. I was just fixin' to turn in."

"The one song you sang, 'Too Long at the Dance.' Did you compose that one?"

Caleb snorted. "No, sir. I just made it up, is all. I wouldn't know how to compose somethin'." He noticed the man's suit coat draped over some object on the hearth.

The little man stood. He was trim, but slightly stooped. Good Lord, how old was he? Seventy? Eighty? His eyes were tiny, but so bright. He turned. His hair was long! Bound up tight and tucked into his collar! Stopping in the middle of the floor, the old man turned, an actor. He spread his hands beseechingly.

"If I might impose, son. Your composition reminds me of one of my own. Mine possesses no melody, as yours does. My tunes are frozen up in the horn. No, it's just a poem. Just a little poem. Would you like to hear it?"

Out of the corner of his eye, Caleb thought he saw something move, but it turned out to be nothing. "Well, sure, I guess I'd just as soon hear it." He moved to the old table made of thick-milled pine slabs and sat on the bench that ran along that side.

The old man looked around the room for a few seconds, then began to recite:

I was younger then
I am wiser now
It seemed larger then, somehow

I heard the calling of the wilderness,
I ventured out into her tracklessness
I led my legions over desert, glade, and sward,
I planted flags; the year was of our lord
I staked a road across a sea of grass
I placed a mile post at the mountain pass
She covered up my tracks before I could return
She swallowed every trail and trace and burn

She healed herself at first, my iron and embers
*   never even left a scar*
But it's hard now to think back that far

I was younger then
I am wiser now
It seemed larger then, somehow

I hollowed hills beneath the great divide
I tunneled deep into the mountainside
I funneled blizzards to a single spout of rain
And I bled the rivers like an open vein
From the ice above, to the brine below

My big guns slaughtered all the buffalo
Like a fading peal of thunder from the past
Hell, I tried to be the man to kill the last

And the bones bleached before the guns were limbered
* and silence shook the plain*
And looking back now, I wish I could explain

I was younger then
I am wiser now
It seemed larger then, somehow

I conjured lines to mark with rail and stile
I parceled ranges on the quarter mile
I drove my harrow where the narrow grass did stir
And I skinned her of her turf like it was fur
The virgin woods were in their verdant prime
They didn't seem important at the time
I held a dollar when I felled another tree
And I rode them down, I rode them to the sea

And I swear to God, I never knew the timber
* would ever fall so fast*
I promise, children, I thought that it would last

I was younger then
I am wiser now
It seemed larger then, somehow

I had my cause to curse the wild red man
You were not there, you wouldn't understand
But oh, to hate a man who lives like that is hard
Who'd rather make the charge than stand the guard
Who loves the dirt, and calls it brother, too
Who finds his gods in fire and wind and dew
But he was savage, oh, and I was savage, too
While I was many, he was but a few

And he fell back one day in cold December
* but not without a fight*
And looking back now, I see where he was right

I was younger then
I am wiser now
It seemed larger then, somehow

And now it's all become as I had wished
It's platted, mapped, it's tamed: impoverished
I look upon it from the dark unknown
I hop across it like a skipping stone
I raise my monuments to me and mine
And spoil the view to those of God's design
It's small as daylight now, where once it measured moons
It's told in tales and long-forgotten tunes

But the dawn breaks on no man who remembers
   the splendors gone of yore
And looking back now, I should have known before

I was younger then
Am I wiser now?
It seemed larger then, somehow

Caleb sat, awestruck. The old man had paced and gestured, railed and whispered. He had made a mockery of every doggerel carol Caleb had ever sung.

"Who *are* you?" the fiddler said.

The old man clasped his hands and laughed. "Like you, I am known by many names."

"Like me?"

"Yes. You are Caleb. You are Crazy Cal, the Colorado Kid. Catgut Caleb Holcomb. You are brother, son, father, friend. You are White Wolf, Fiddler, Hard Winter, Bitter Creek."

He shifted nervously. "And you are?"

"I am nothing. I am everything. I am a taker of life, and a giver of freedom. I am a thief, and a priest, and a fugitive."

Caleb only sat on the bench with his mouth open. "How do you know me?"

"I have heard you play. I rode with Cheyenne Dutch and would listen from the hills as the black man taught you."

"I never saw you with Cheyenne Dutch."

"You looked right at me. I saw you among the Comanches that winter. I tried to buy you from the Snake Woman and take you home, but she wouldn't sell. I was in Black Hawk the night you first got drunk. Do you remember? You dropped your fiddle!''

Caleb nodded, grinned to one side.

"Bull Bannon's Extravaganza of the Western Wilds. I was in the tent when you played 'The Shortgrass Song.' You didn't notice me, did you? It's my way to blend in. Long Fingers was my friend. He asked me to look after you.''

"He never mentioned you to me.''

"An Indian won't tell you anything unless he has need for you to know it. Besides, I was taboo among the old ones. They never spoke of me. I have medicine.''

"What kind of medicine?''

"The same as you.'' He walked to his suit coat on the hearth. "I keep it here.'' Throwing the coat back, he revealed an oblong case of fine deerskin, fringed and beaded, colored with fine quillwork. "My song is almost sung and passed. I would like for you to have this.''

Caleb stood as the old man put the bundle on the table and drew from one of its ends an old lacquered violin case. He pushed it in front of the fiddler and bid him to trip the latches. "I smuggled it from the Old World,'' he said. "It's a Stradivarius.''

Caleb opened the case and looked at the instrument, imbedded in velvet. "A what?''

The old man smiled. "A pretty good violin. Someday you'll know. May I?''

"Hell, it's your fiddle. Go ahead.''

He threw a patch of golden suede over his right shoulder and rested the violin upon it. "It was made left-handed, for those of us with that manner of medicine. Very rare.'' He plucked the strings. "Just a few bars, White Wolf, and quietly. I wouldn't want to rouse attention.''

When the single note came, Caleb had to twist his neck, for he had never heard such a tone ring from a fiddle. It began low, then wavered, picking up a second tone. They slid together into a higher plane of melody. The gnarled fingers caressing the neck did things Caleb could not fathom, and the strain tripped up an octave, then another, trilling like the voice of some bird turned angel. But it was brief, and the old man seemed tired.

"Call me Plenty Man,'' he said.

The name struck like a hammer in the fiddler's stomach. "You didn't come here to play me no music, did you?''

"You know why I have come. The one you called Lizard asked me to help.''

"You know about Paterson?''

He lay the violin and bow back in the case. "His name now is Henri Gabriel Saint-Amant—the name of his adoptive father in Canada."

"Canada?" Caleb's heart was beating fiercely and he longed to run for Walker, but did not intend to let Plenty Man out of his sight.

"He was sold to a Canadian farmer by the Miniconjou, several years after his capture."

"Sold by the what?"

"The Miniconjou Sioux."

"How'd they get aholt of him?"

"I gave him to them."

"Where'd you git him?"

"I bought him from Lizard. He cost me five good Nez Percé horses. He was not treated well among the Cheyenne, and I thought it better that he live with the Miniconjou."

"Why didn't you take him back to Walker?" Caleb demanded.

"You mean Heap Killer? I promised Lizard I would not do that. I am a thief and a murderer, White Wolf, but I am not a liar."

Stunned, Caleb reached out and touched the old man on the shoulder. He shook him gently, not knowing why he had been compelled to do so. "Well, where is he now?"

"Who?"

"Paterson! Or Henri, or whatever his name is!"

Plenty Man smiled, put on his coat, covered his head with his bowler. "Come with me," he said.

Caleb followed him through the cabin door, down off the steps, and into the night. The lights were still up in the inn, for some of the dudes had stayed after the dance to drink and converse. In the light streaming through the panes, Caleb saw a man standing on the ground in front of the inn, tall and spare. Plenty Man led him far enough along the path that he could see around the corner of the inn and onto the front gallery.

Walker stood there, big and lantern-lit, looking down at the man on the ground. Caleb took a few more steps, then stopped. He watched Walker step down from the gallery. The two men shook hands. They were the same height, but Walker was broader. He took the younger man by the shoulders. Words were passed, and Walker's head bowed. He drew the young man to him and smothered him in his arms.

"Is that him?" Caleb said. He turned. Plenty Man was gone. He heard Walker's voice calling for N.C. Caleb ran back to his cabin. The violin rested in the open case. Beside it lay the sheath of fine buckskin, speckled with quills and beads, tasseled with soft fringe.

He noticed the corner of a leaf of paper sticking out of the case and pulled it out. It was the poem the old man had recited, written with an old quill pen. At the top were three words, and Caleb spoke them out loud: "Plenty Man's Lament."

EIGHTY-FOUR

CALEB PROPPED HIS boot heels on the porch rail of Buster's old Cincinnati house and lay back on the floor, using a chunk of stove wood for a pillow. He looked down toward Monument Creek. One of Buster's Durham bulls was grazing, switching his tail with content. Buster was sitting on the porch with the *Rocky Mountain News* spread across his lap, wearing his spectacles and talking politics. Politics, of all things! But it was Amelia and Marisol, picking dewberries down by the irrigation canal, who held Caleb's attention.

Women made about as much sense to Caleb Holcomb as politics did to a Durham bull. He had spent several winters with Marisol down in Penascosa, New Mexico, and had fathered three children by her. No, he had never married her—Javier had beat him to that—but he had treated her all right.

Now, his children by Marisol—Angelo, Marta, and Elena—still treated Caleb like a daddy. Marisol, on the other hand, acted as if he were some distant cousin she barely remembered. She wasn't discourteous, just aloof.

Then there was Amelia. The whole time Caleb had been wintering with Marisol down south, Amelia had made constant sport of the relationship, making sundry references, thinly veiled, to that Mexican harlot, that trollop, that little Latin slattern.

Now look at them! Giggling like school girls down in the dewberry patch! Suddenly they looked up toward Buster's house and burst into fits of laughter. Telling stories on me now! he thought.

"The old trail was market-driven," Buster was saying. "Now that rail fare is droppin' off, there ain't no reason for no National Cattle Trail." He tapped the newspaper column. "These-here idiots want to spend taxpayers' money to prop up some trail-drive industry that's done served its purpose and is almost dead anyway!"

Caleb picked his teeth with a splinter and sighed. He noticed a few clouds building in the mountains. "You reckon it's gonna rain today?"

Buster shook his head and turned the page. "The almanac don't give much chance for rain this year at all."

"If you'd git your nose out of your damn almanacs and newspapers, you'd know what's goin' on around you. Ain't you seen them clouds in the mountains?''

''I seen 'em before you did.''

''Like hell.''

''I know what's goin' on around me. I even know what we're havin' for dessert tonight after supper.''

''What?''

''Dewberry cobbler.''

Caleb frowned, but couldn't help chuckling. ''All right.'' He rubbed his thumb across the calluses on his fingertips.

Gloria stepped out on the porch and threw a pan of water over Caleb's head. She scowled at him just for good measure and went back inside.

Caleb saw the mail hack coming from the south, which was what he had been waiting here for. Since the town of Holcomb had died, Holcomb Ranch had gotten its mail by hack out of Colorado Springs. He sat up and looked down across the ditch. Amelia was looking back, smiling. She waved, then covered her mouth to giggle. He knew Marisol was telling off on him. He shook his head and looked away.

Amelia was the hardest one of all to figure out. What did she want? She wanted him here, but why? To look after Little Pete? That was what she always said. Why hadn't she remarried? She had been a widow going on eight years now. Who was she waiting for? Waiting for him to ask her?

''Hey, Buster.''

''Yeah?''

''You want to come down to the cabin and do a little fiddlin' this evenin'?''

Buster folded the paper and got up with Caleb to meet the mail hack. ''You bet.''

''Telegram for you, Caleb,'' the hack driver said as he turned the vehicle around. He handed the Western Union envelope to the fiddler.

Caleb smirked at Buster and opened the envelope. It was from Savannah Baber:

CALEB,

COMING TO HOLCOMB RANCH FOR OUR HONEYMOON NINE

OCLOCK TRAIN TONIGHT

SAVANNAH

His chest roared with a fire that he had forgotten even burned there. Women made about as much sense to Caleb Holcomb as politics to a Durham bull.

* * *

By the time he got to the depot, rain had carved trenches in the roads. He had borrowed Amelia's three-spring buggy with the lamps on the front and the glass windshield and canvas canopy. He stepped onto the depot landing almost without getting wet at all. Not that it would matter to Savannah, anyway.

He was so nervous he could not stand still, and paced up and down the depot for twenty minutes. The train was running late from Denver, which caused him to pace another fifteen minutes until the whistle finally blew. It was over now. No more drifting. No more trails and troubles. No more waking up alone. More children. Think of the beauties he was going to sire by Savannah. Caleb liked kids on his knee. He wondered if her family had cut her out of the Baber fortune. Hell, that didn't matter to him. He wasn't even going to ask her.

The boiler blew steam and raindrops, the brakes caught and squealed like pinched pups, couplings rammed together all the way to the caboose. A conductor set a stepping stool down, and Caleb pulled his mustaches into shape. He hadn't even had time to shave his chin or change his clothes. Not that it would matter to Savannah. She liked him all cowboyed up. He bunched the wildflowers he had plucked alongside the road before the thunderstorm hit.

A new sheet of rain pelted the depot roof as Savannah appeared at the door. He licked his lips. She stamped her little feet and squealed, jumping all the way over the stepping stool the conductor had set out for her. Damn, she was excited, he thought. He had expected something a little more dramatic. Hell, but she was glad to see him!

He walked toward her, reached for her waist with his free hand. Her lips went by like kestrels and she clamped her arms rigidly around his neck. Damn, it almost hurt meeting your betrothed at the depot.

He looked past the mounds of hair pinned up on her head and saw passengers stepping off the train. One dashing young gentleman in particular had stopped to smile at the dude wrangler meeting his society belle. He stood there in a silk hat, rocking on his heels with his hands in his pockets.

"We didn't expect you to meet us personally!" she said, virtually pushing herself away from him. "I assumed you would send Buster."

His brow lowered and something shifted in his innards. The man in the silk hat was sauntering his way. "We?" he said.

She took the gentleman by the arm as he came near. "Caleb. This is my husband, James Bigelow."

"Jim," the gent said, extending his hand.

Caleb was conditioned to reciprocate with his own hand. The palm of
Jim Bigelow felt cold and soft, with the grip of a dead fish.

"Caleb is such a dear friend, Jim. You have no idea what kind of ad-
ventures . . . He let me shoot his gun!"

"I've heard some tall yarns about you," Jim Bigelow declared. "How
are the gunshot wounds mending?"

Caleb reached for his ribs. "Fine," he said.

She took the flowers and smelled them. "You thought of everything,
Caleb. Are you all right?"

No, he was not all right. "Your telegram said . . ." He didn't know if
she was cruel or just unbelievably inconsiderate, but it felt like hell either
way. "Well, the thing is . . ." He chuckled in spite of himself and grabbed
the back of his neck.

"What's wrong?"

"Is there a problem?" Mr. Bigelow insisted.

"All aboard!" The conductor was bent on making up the lost time.

"Yeah, the thing is," he said, "there ain't no room on the ranch. I wish
you'd have wired sooner. We're just full up with dudes. Even the bunkhouse. Never seen the likes of it. Even the barn's full of grub-line riders."

Savannah pouted. "You don't mean."

He jutted his chin. She was not going to shame him on his own ranch.
He had never turned a soul away from a roof or a meal, but he wasn't sure
Savannah had a soul, anyway. "I'm afraid so. You all had better git back
on the train."

The nine o'clock began to move.

Savannah donned her most whimsical smile and turned her palms up in
front of her. "We can stay at the Broadmoor until the ranch has a vacancy."

"No room at the Broadmoor," he said, thinking quickly now. "I
checked. You two had better get back on. Santa Fe's a hell of a place to
honeymoon."

"How can the Broadmoor be full? It's huge!"

"I don't know," he said. He took one newlywed in each arm and led
them alongside the open door of the Pullman car.

"You folks gettin' on?" the conductor demanded.

"Yes, sir, they are," the dude wrangler insisted. He literally lifted
Savannah and passed her to the conductor. The end of the platform was
coming, and the whistle blew loudly. A wall of rain was waiting beyond
the covered platform.

"Shame we couldn't stay," Bigelow said.

"Yeah, sure is," he replied. He did not want them coming back. "The truth is, Bigelow, your wife made a fool out of me, and she's not welcome on my ranch. Ever. Do we understand each other?''

Bigelow stepped into the moving doorway and looked back at Caleb. His words were lost in a blast of the whistle, but he nodded.

The rain hit Caleb as the door closed on Bigelow's stunned face. That should take care of them. They wouldn't be back. Cold water played his brim like an Indian drum. Damn, it hurt to be a fool.

EIGHTY-FIVE

THE DRIVE BACK to the ranch seemed to take no time at all. The team knew the way, and Caleb didn't care if the carriage slid into Monument Creek and floated him out to sea. Walker had warned him about Savannah Baber. She had twisted out from under him like a three-year-old filly. The funny thing was, his heart didn't feel broken. It was just the foolishness of it all that made him feel so bad. He never should have asked her to marry him. It had spoiled even the good memories he had of her. She had made a fool of him, and he had made it easy.

But there was something worse. Caleb had shrugged Amelia aside for Savannah. Amelia was the woman he had always wanted, always needed. He had been distracted by Savannah's flashing shock of hair, her energy, her willingness. He thought of Amelia alone in the big house. So beautiful. She didn't try to catch every man's eye in every room, like Savannah, but she was just as attractive. Amelia's beauty was more substantial, more honest.

Anyway, this wasn't about looks. When Savannah walked into a room, Caleb had always stood taller, stroked his mustache straight. She made him nervous, self-conscious.

Amelia made him like who he was and what he did, even though she often criticized both. He was comfortable around her. He cared what she thought about him, but not to the point of posturing. All these years he had been denying the truth about Amelia. She made his heart pound. He would find himself thinking of her when he drifted off to sleep. This he had ignored, first because of Pete, then because of Savannah. Now he may well have ruined it all.

He wanted to redeem himself. Now. He could hardly remember what Savannah looked like at this moment. Amelia's features came to him in a thousand images: glances across the room, smiles in the sunlight, waltzes to music he played. Words she had said came to him.

There was a light on in the mansion when he arrived at the ranch, and

Caleb saw it as a glimmer of hope. He turned the horses into the barn and left them standing, though he knew Buster would have given him hell for not rubbing them down and feeding them right away. He ran to the mansion through the rain and looked into the kitchen door. She was there, taking a teapot from the stove, her hair falling loose around her shoulders.

And his heart pounded, as it almost always did when he caught sight of her. He looked for a few seconds, then tapped on the glass. She turned, and her white nightgown floated across the floor.

"Caleb," she said, letting him in, reading his face. "What happened? What's wrong?"

"Nothin's wrong. It's all turned out right."

"Where is Savannah?"

"I sent her on south. I wouldn't let her come."

She reached for the collar of his wet coat and helped him get it off. "What do you mean?"

"She's not the woman for me, Amelia. I ain't marryin' her."

Amelia's eyes grew wide and fetching. "And so you just sent her away? Just like that? In the middle of the night?"

He thought about concealing the facts, but she would find out the truth soon enough. "It wasn't me she wanted to honeymoon with on the ranch. She showed up at the train station with her new husband."

Amelia put her hands over her cheeks, then reached for Caleb and led him to the kitchen table. "But the way the telegram was worded. You don't think she deliberately misled you?"

"I don't know. Don't care. It would have been the mistake of my life marryin' her, anyway. And I've made some big ones in my time, Amelia."

"You're right." She smiled sympathetically. "It would have been an awful mistake." She was sitting across the corner of the table from him, and she took his hand in hers. "You're freezing. Let me make some hot tea for you."

She got up, and he missed the warmth of her hands on his. "Amelia," he said. "This time I'm really done with it."

"With what?"

"Driftin'. Ridin' the grub line. I know I've told you that before, but things have changed. They've changed out there. Too many fences. Folks don't leave the latchstring on the outside of the door for you no more. But things have changed here, too. This dude wranglin' is all right. It's like driftin' because there's a new bunch of folks to play for every week. But it's better. I can stay home, and the folks come to me. They pay for it! I can't git over it."

She came to the table, smiling, carrying the tea service. "I knew you'd like it. And I'll tell you something else. It wouldn't work without you. You don't realize how much you entertain the guests. When you're gone, this place just doesn't have the energy. We have guests who wire and ask whether or not you're going to be here before they make their reservations.''

Caleb wrinkled his brow where his hat had pressed a shock of hair flat. He just couldn't gather folks making such a fuss over him. ''Well, now you can tell 'em I'm always here. This driftin' can kill a feller, Amelia. And now Angelo and Marta and Elena are here. Little Pete's learnin' to fiddle. I'm tired of missin' out on life at the home ranch.''

''I hope you do stay.'' Her voice carried her sincerity, but couldn't mask the doubt.

He tried to gird himself up. This moment had been a long time coming. He poured so much cream into his teacup that it ran over. ''There's one way I can prove it to you,'' he said.

''How?'' she said, almost coyly.

''I can marry you.'' He was kicking himself already. Why couldn't he have said it better? Why couldn't he have rehearsed it and played it for her like a song?

''I beg your pardon,'' she said, as if she thought he were joking.

Caleb saw his second chance, a rare one. The rain had chilled him, but now he was about to sweat. He reached across the table, took her hand, and tried to think quickly. ''When I was gittin' shot at a thousand miles away this winter, I just kept thinkin'—what if I don't see Amelia no more? I'm tired of feelin' like that. I want us to be together. Always.'' *There!* That was good. He squeezed her hand and smiled, more at himself than at her.

Quickly she yanked her hand away. ''How dare you!'' she blurted.

''Huh?''

''How dare you exercise your cowboy charm on me!''

''Charm?''

''I may have been on your mind a thousand miles away, but who was in your bed?''

He tried to keep up with her thinking. ''Well, Walker was. I had to sleep on a pallet, because he was wounded and couldn't be shook around.''

''Oh!'' She sprang from the table. ''How dare you come in here straight from your failed rendezvous with that little trollop and treat me like your consolation prize!''

''My what?''

She stomped her bare foot on the hardwood floor. ''I will not be any man's second choice.''

"You've always been my first choice. Since the first day we met. It was *me* that was *your* second choice, behind Pete!"

"How do you know? You were never here!"

He rose across the table, his voice climbing to match hers. "That wasn't my fault!"

"Nothing ever is!"

"What's that mean?" He flapped his arms like a bird learning to fly.

"It's bad enough that I have to listen to Tess McCoy talk about how you rescued her from that brothel in Texas."

"She wasn't supposed to tell that!" he shouted, as if that were a damn good argument.

"Well, she said it was a boardinghouse, but I always suspected it was a brothel. Now I know."

"You don't know. You wasn't there."

"No, but I have to hear about it. And on top of that, I have to watch your children by that Mexican woman play with my own son."

"I thought you liked Marisol."

"I adore her. It's you I don't hold much favor for!"

He felt as cold as the weak tea in the cup before him. He turned away, grabbed his coat on the hook by the door. He was expecting her to stop him, for those were mean things she had said. But her silence stabbed him like a knife in the back as he put the wet coat on. "I have horses to look after," he said.

"Oh, you know how to take care of horses. You treat women the same way. Ride one till she's tired, then hop on another."

He opened the door.

"Caleb!"

He stood, but did not turn.

"You stayed too long at the dance."

He stepped outside, slammed the door behind him. He took several paces, then stopped. The rain had ended, but he could feel the cold water seeping through the seams of his boots. The lantern light went down behind him, and he was left under the clouded sky of a lonely night. He started to stomp toward the barn, but something held him. He listened.

Good Lord, she was crying. Caleb Holcomb felt as rotten as any dead tree.

EIGHTY-SIX

BUSTER KNEW THE aroma of wood smoke from a stove and the odor of grass smoke from the dry plains. He had scented smoke from the iron forge, the cook fire, the hearth. This was different. He drew deeply through his nostrils as his dreams scrambled to make sense of the smell. He heard the distant crackle, somewhere outside.

Opening his eyes, Buster saw the flicker of orange on the wall—four squares of wavering firelight patterned by the windowpane. Gloria's neck was on his arm, but he yanked himself free without waking her and wheeled to see the source of the light.

Flames poured from the windows and doors of the old Holcomb cabin in ribbons of wicked light. The walls were afire, the roof letting tongues of flame escape. "Caleb," Buster said, the voice deep with waking dread. Then he saw him and blinked hard to clear his eyes.

Caleb Holcomb wielded a pick-ax overhead, backlit by the burning cabin Buster had helped to build years ago. He was in the family burial plot, the tall spire of marble marking the grave of Colonel Ab Holcomb, the small markers poised over the resting places of brother Matthew, and Ella, Caleb's mother. Behind him the fire roared and leapt as a broad patch of cedar shakes fell in. Caleb stopped for a moment to watch, then removed his coat. He commenced digging in the family plot again, the fire glinting on the faceted marble around him.

Buster pulled his clothes on, stomped boots onto his feet, and trotted out into the light drizzle. He felt the heat as he came nearer, but Caleb remained in the graveyard, standing now with his boot heels locked over a spade.

"Caleb! What the hell you doin'?"

The fiddler's face was grim. "Burnin' the ridge log." He shoveled a glob of damp earth aside.

"The what?"

"The ridge log!" He pointed at the crest of the cabin roof as the shakes and rafters fell away to reveal the log, as if White Wolf had medicine enough to have made it happen.

It had been a long time since Buster had thought about the ridge log—about the day it rolled off and killed Caleb's mother. He realized now that he had made a mistake by burying Ella and hoisting that same damn log up to the ridge to finish the cabin. It had been notched and fitted. Seemed logical. But that log had hung over Caleb's head for thirty years. He had always thought it was his fault. His mother had rushed to throw him clear when the ridge log hit her.

Buster used his forearm to shield the heat from his face. "Did you git the Stradivarius out?"

The light found Caleb's smirk, though his hat was perched sideways on his head to block the heat. "I'm crazy enough to burn my own house, Buster, but I ain't crazy enough to burn a left-handed Stradivarius."

Buster found the heat hard to bear, so he took Caleb by the arm and led him a good fifty paces away. "Whose hole you diggin'?" he said, eyeing the spade Caleb still held in his hand.

"Pete's."

"You gonna dig him up on the hill?"

"Well, I ain't gonna tunnel under the creek to him! Of course I'm gonna dig him up!"

"How come?"

"Papa never should have buried him alone up there on the hill. He ought to be down here with Mama, and Papa, and Matthew."

Buster heard the timber begin to crack and turned his head to see the orange ridge log fall into the inferno. He stood for long wordless minutes with Caleb, watching the walls crumble inward and spray brands like sea waves.

"I'm gonna need a new house," Caleb said.

"I'll help you move one from town."

"I don't want a house that's been used for a store or a café. I want me a house, Buster. I want to build one from the blocks up, just like I want it."

Buster smiled, even as his brow gathered wrinkles. "I'll help you do that, too."

"I want to tear down the depot you and me built, and use that lumber."

Buster nodded. "That'll make a fine house." He looked over his shoulder, but didn't see anybody else coming. That didn't really surprise him. Buster had a theory that certain phases of the moon made people sleep sounder. Except for Gloria. She always slept like a hibernating grizzly, and woke up with the temperament of one. "That'll sure make a fine house, but first we better finish diggin' that grave."

Amelia trudged up the hill at dawn, almost crazed for want of explanation. "Caleb!" she shouted, hoisting her skirt out of the mud. "Buster!"

They had a team of horses, and a wagon, with all manner of tools and rope hanging over the tailgate. They were swinging picks like rail builders, having dug a trench knee-deep around her dead husband's grave.

"Answer me!" she pleaded. She knew the significance of the burned cabin. The fresh hole in the ground and the exhumation in progress made sense as well. But why now? They had been working all night long! What did it mean? Was Caleb leaving? Was this his parting deed?

Caleb threw his pick aside as she approached and he reached for a shovel. He glanced at her. "I'll deal with you later, Amelia," he said. "Right now I've got work to do."

She flailed her arms and slapped her palms against her thighs. "I said some things I shouldn't have last night."

He stabbed the wet ground with his shovel. "You were right in everything you said. But I don't have time to talk about it right now. Go home. I'll call on you this evenin'."

She tried to protest, but Buster was shaking his head at her, warning her away with his frown. She turned, and slipped on down the hill.

She looked out later and saw that Buster and Caleb had boxed in the crumbling grave with boards and were winching it carefully into the wagon. The sun had come out and burned a dry crust upon the ground.

At noon, she saw them packing dirt around the new grave, and watched as they drove back up the hill to get the polished stone marker. It was two o'clock in the afternoon when they took off their hats and bowed their heads to the newly positioned tombstone. They seemed to pray a long time.

Then they trudged on back to Buster's house, and Amelia turned away from her window. She figured she'd better get ready for Caleb's call.

EIGHTY-SEVEN

C ALEB RODE THE snowflake bay stud horse called Drifter. For Amelia he had saddled the prettiest mare in the stable—a stunning white with black mane, black tail, and a wealth of round black Appaloosa spots on her rump that bunched and became solid black hind legs. Her name was Katie Hill, after the fiddle tune.

When he got to the mansion, he didn't even have to dismount. She came to the front door, wearing her riding clothes. She sure looked good to him. Amelia was his own age, but much better kept. Maybe a weathered hide looked fine on a cowboy, but Amelia's skin was still fair and smooth. All the work she had done in her life was by choice. She had never really had to lift a finger, coming from a rich back-east family and marrying Pete after he had made a fortune in cattle.

She was just a fine-looking woman, and always had been. He remembered the day he first laid eyes on her, how her beauty had seized him like some kind of paralysis. She had been a flirtatious little society belle back in those days. My, how people could change. Here she was a rancher, recognized all up and down the Front Range for the quality and beauty of the Appaloosa horses she raised.

"Where are you taking me?" she asked.

"Just mount up," he said. "Try to let me do the talkin', and if I dig a hole for myself, give me a chance to claw out of it."

She smirked, and tripped gracefully down the steps, taking the reins he handed to her. "You have some explaining to do."

"I know that. Come with me up the Arapaho Trail."

He didn't say anything until they got to the hill where Pete had been buried until today. "When I was a kid, I used to play on this hill," he began.

The wildflowers were standing tall, turning last night's rain into bright petals. The pines swallowed the riders up, and they continued on, the horses familiar with the ancient path that wended its way over hills everchanging.

He told her things she knew well, things she had never considered, and things she could never imagine. The ridge log, the gunfight between Matthew and Cheyenne Dutch. Matthew had been protecting Caleb. It was all over a prostitute—Caleb's first. She blushed at some of the things he told her, speaking only to ask for explanation.

He talked about the first time he saw her, how bashful he was. How he had felt when Pete married her.

How the argument with his father had begun. Life out there. Saloon fights. Sleeping on the wet ground one night, on a feather bed the next. Women—whores, farm girls, more whores. About drunken miners who didn't give a damn for a song. Trail-worn punchers who would weep to the tune of "Annie Laurie."

The rain had charged the evergreens with fragrance, and the good horses handled the trail well, even the slippery spots. A jay flashed across their path. A deer bounded. They had been riding an hour, and Caleb was talking about his years with Marisol—explaining, but making no excuses.

It was warmer down there. He was lonely. She was motherless. Had never known her father. She was skinny back then, and, well, she had taught him Spanish, and then some. Then he'd drift, return to Marisol in the winter, visit the home ranch in the spring. He held no grudge against Marisol for marrying Javier. He loved the children.

When Pete died—oh, but that had changed things. He had found himself unable to celebrate, unable to grieve. He'd drift, play, drink, whore, work. Didn't mean a thing.

"You were here," he told her. He looked at her as they ducked a low branch together. "But I couldn't measure up to Pete. Me, a scoundrel and outcast of the family. I'd think of you when I was out there. But what did you want with me? You said you wanted me around to bring up Little Pete, but you never said you wanted *me.*"

He rambled then. The chronology got muddled, and he just spilled whatever thought came to him. His skin tingled when he brought the old fights to mind. He had never gone looking for any of them. But the Comanche had gutted Elam Joiner on the buffalo ranges, and he had ridden for revenge. Angus Mackland, Shorty, and Kicking Dog had kidnapped Tess, done unspeakable things to her. It was usually quiet out there, that's why folks liked the music. But every now and then the quiet would give way to hell and bullets, blood and screams of dying men.

Those moments stuck with a man. Some men went crazy, did crazy things, wound up dead.

"What kept you sane?" she asked, forcing her voice through her own astonishment, speaking for the first time in two miles.

He felt the shapes of words in his mouth, and settled on just one: "Music."

They were high now, and stopped on a crest to look down at the plains pushing into the endless haze to the east. Everything he said kept coming back to Amelia. In some way, she had become a reason for everything that had happened to him since he first saw her face.

He swung down from the saddle and tied Drifter's reins up around his neck so he could graze. "We're almost high enough, now," he said.

"For what?"

"For the columbines."

Amelia felt her feet touch the ground and gave Katie Hill the freedom to graze with Drifter. "I've never seen one."

"Never seen a columbine?"

"I don't have time to ride up this high," she said. "I don't even know what they look like." She glanced around her, thinking she might see one.

"Well," he said, holding his rough hand up, palm facing Amelia, slightly cupped, "it starts with five purple petals, pointed like a star. But it's more like a shootin' star, because on the back each petal has a tail, straight like the spurs on a fightin' rooster." He used the back of his hand to show where the purple tails would extend.

"That sounds pretty."

"Oh, that ain't the half of it." He took her by the wrist and placed the back of her hand against his cupped palm. "It has five more petals—white, rounded, a little smaller—in front of the purple ones. Like your hand is smaller, compared to mine. And they're just off-center to the purple ones. Like this . . ." He made his fingers move in between hers, softly, without clenching her hand.

"Oh," she said.

"Then," he continued, touching the middle of her cupped palm with the trigger finger of his free hand, "right in the middle, there's a center of pure gold." He let his finger make a small circle in the middle of her soft hand.

She looked up at him, her eyes misted. "You must find one for me," she said.

"They grow on this trail."

"How do you know?"

"You know I always drift back home by this trail," he said, "even if I have to ride out of my way to meet up with it."

She began walking with him, slightly uphill. "I know."

"You know why?"

"Yes. You always came this way because you wanted to camp up there and talk to Pete. And I always suspected that you just liked making a dramatic approach to the ranch, loping down off the hill like that."

He pointed to a stand of aspens up the trail and began to stroll that way, offering Amelia his arm. "Guilty on both counts," he said. "But there was another reason, too."

"What?"

"You'll see."

He led her into the shade of the aspens. The breeze was light, but even a touch of wind could make the green leaves quake, and they sounded like breath above the heads of the strollers.

"Oh, look!" Amelia cried, for she had spotted the first of the columbines Caleb had just described so well: shooting stars, hands cupped together, hearts of gold. She plucked the flower by the stem and smelled the golden center.

"They like to grow up here among the aspens," he said, "where it's damp and cool. You know what's good about an aspen tree?"

"What?" She was admiring the beauty of the columbine, turning it on its stem.

"Not much. Don't burn worth a nickel. Can't build nothin' with 'em but rail fences, and they don't last long. Now, they're awful purty. Trunks like ivory, leaves green and flutterin' like that. And t'wards fall, them yeller leaves can sure make a cowboy pine for a ride in the high country with his gal.''

She laughed, and her laughter rose to join the breath of rustling leaves overhead.

''But you know the best thing about an aspen tree? You can carve on it. That white bark is so soft that a sharp knife will cut through it like a hot iron through lard. And the tree don't mind, either. I've got an idea that if you carve somethin' on an aspen tree, it makes that tree want to live longer. Gives it somethin' to believe in.''

''What would you carve?'' she said.

He put his hand over the trunk of an aspen tree at his left shoulder. ''I already did. When I rode back from Indian Territory a few weeks ago. I rode out of my way to take this trail home, like I always do, and I stopped to carve on this tree right here beside the trail.''

Amelia's mouth turned up in a smile, and she felt as if she had been on a treasure hunt all day, and here was the treasure. Beneath his hand she saw two lines come together in an angle. Above his thumb, she saw a curve; another over his fingers. ''Let me see,'' she said, grabbing his arm and pulling.

He was stronger, and teased her for a minute, as if he would not reveal the thing to her—the thing he had brought her here to see—the thing he had carved in the soft white bark of the tree. Then he let the cool mountain air sting his nostrils and hoped, then prayed, that his last chance would not go squandered.

The heart was well formed, its lines made of thin strips of white bark taken from the trunk. The greenish layer underneath betrayed the freshness of the mark. But the characters within made Amelia's eyes glisten with wonder. Under one curve of the heart was the letter C. Under the other was an A. And under them, in the point at the bottom of the new-carved valentine, the numbers 9 and 2 told the year.

He watched, his hope mounting, as her hand covered a cheek and her eyes remained locked. ''Oh, Caleb,'' she said. ''I don't know if you'll believe me.''

''I'll believe anything you tell me here.''

''Your brother Pete was a good man. You know that. But I married him for just one reason. I knew I couldn't have you.'' She pulled her eyes away from the carving on the tree. ''No woman could have tamed you back then. It wasn't your fault, it was just your lot. You were meant to drift all those years. I believe that. I believe you have touched so many souls out there, and made so many people dance.'' She took his hand in hers.

"Please believe me. I always thought of you first. You were never second best."

"Even now?" he said, growing bolder.

"Yes, even now, but . . ."

"What?"

"Caleb, I know you wouldn't lie to me, but how do I know you could stand to settle after all those free years?"

"All those free years, I had you on my mind."

"*This* year you had me on your mind." She touched the number 92 on the carved heart. "How can I be certain it will last?"

He took his hat off and set it farther back on his head. Slowly, he began to smile. "You've always been on my mind," he said. "You can be sure because it's carved all down the years, and all up the trail." He stepped aside and swept his hand westward, up the old Indian trail.

She looked, at first seeing nothing. Then a line, a curve, a shape caught her eye. By no means as fresh as the one beside her. This one was a scar, a year old, the letters in their places, the numbers telling 91.

She gasped and laughed at once, then clutched to her breast the columbine she had found. She looked at Caleb, but he only rolled his fingers in the air, like a magician directing attention. Then he made magic.

Another carving wrapped around the ivory curve of the next tree up the trail.

Caleb loves Amelia. 90.

There were others, climbing the slope and falling back among the lost seasons. They became black and mottled scars, some pierced by arrows, some marred by unknown events. The one numbered 88 had even been clawed by a bear marking his domain. They grew older, craggier. But somehow they were most beautiful in their cracked agedness.

She moved like a dancer from one to the next, touching each, trying to remember that year, trying to know Caleb then as she had failed to see him. Her eyes blurred, but she defied emotion to keep her from her discoveries.

How long could this go on? 79, 78 . . . She was laughing when a sob of joy escaped. So many years. The aspens chided her. Hadn't she seen before?

"That's why I always took this trail home," Caleb said, his voice coming now from far down the path.

73, 72, 71 . . . It could not go farther. That was the year Caleb left to drift. Yet it went farther still. Caleb Loves Amelia. 1870. The year they met. And each of twenty-two years since.

"Can you believe the likes of it?" His baritone, just a shade gravelly, spoke like a song from twenty-two trees down the winding path. "Grown man like me, a-carvin' hearts on trees for the gal he loves?"

She brushed the hair back from her face and pulled a sleeve across her eyes. She wanted to see this clearly, remember it well. "Ask me now," she cried.

He took his hat off and raked his hair back. From this far off her eyes shone like stars, and her shape traced perfect curves among the straight trunks of the aspens. She was seventeen years old up there where she stood, and that was the way he had always looked at her. "Amelia Dubois," he sang. "Would you take my name?"

She covered her cheeks with her hands and came down the slope, gliding effortlessly through a past that had changed for her in a moment—a lifetime bettered by a glimpse into lost days long gone. He was waiting, his arms ready to catch her.

She fell against him, and he whirled her with a motion that must have looked practiced to the aspens who had waited so long. She looked into his eyes as she caught her breath.

"Yes," she said in a whisper, then added her voice: "I'll marry you, Caleb Holcomb. I'll do whatever it takes to make up for all that lost time."

He tossed the old hat aside and waited for the avalanche that had been poised so long to slide. He tasted the tears on her lips and felt his arms wrap around his fondest dream given life, stronger now against his pounding chest than in his countless musings.

There had been times, thinking of her out there on the trail, when he would suddenly flinch in the saddle and wonder where the hell he was, which way he wandered, and how long he could go on. Now he was lost to everything but the taste and the fragrance and the caress of Amelia.

The light danced and the aspen leaves gossiped. The grass whispered to the columbines. The mountainside warmed, and the ever-changing slopes changed once again and were made finer and higher and great.

Caleb Holcomb felt every song he had ever known play at once, and the old familiar trail finally led him home.